Cult & Run

Cut & Run

Cult & Run

Kelly MacPherson

TRASHY ECLAIR PUBLISHING

Copyright © 2023 by Kelly Buddenhagen

This book is a work of fiction. Names, characters, places, and incidents are the product of the author's imagination or are used fictitiously. Any resemblance to actual events is unintended and entirely coincidental.

Trashy Eclair Publishing
Breinigsville, Pennsylvania
trashyeclairpublishing.com

All rights reserved. No part of this book may be reproduced in any manner whatsoever without written permission except in the case of brief quotations or embodied in critical articles and reviews.

Designed by Kelly MacPherson

First Edition, 2023.
Printed in the United States of America.
ISBN 978-1-68564-080-4

For my husband Ed.

Delco is my favorite cult.

(Go Birds)

"Jim takes me down, he's a fire eater
Before the dawn or the valley shines
Jim takes me down to the river
All the way, past the mines

Girls in nightgowns hold their hands forever
Girls with pink lips cultivate the sound
They watch, we kiss on a bed of roses
As he lays me down."

Lana Del Rey, "Cult Leader"

CULT & RUN PODCAST TRANSCRIPT
SEASON 2, EPISODE 1

ALEX PARKER: From Carbon Fiber Studios, this is Cult & Run and I'm Alex Parker.

SHEENA FAVROSIAN: And I'm Sheena Favrosian, Alex Parker's more intelligent co-host.

ALEX PARKER: Alex Parker does not disagree with that.

SHEENA FAVROSIAN: Today officially kicks off season two of the pod, which dives into a group a whole lot hairier than The Society of Extraterrestrial Equestrians from season one.

ALEX PARKER: Unicorn-riding aliens with an eco-communist agenda involved a lot of glitter, Sheena. Don't forget that.

SHEENA FAVROSIAN: Don't worry, Alex. I never could. Today on the pod, we have Zosia Short, author of the Vox article "An Offer She Should've Refused", her story of dating a member of the Eastern Pennsylvania cult known as The Committee. Alex, what do you know about The Committee?

ALEX PARKER: It's Pam, Phyllis, and Angela, right?

SHEENA FAVROSIAN: That's "The Office", and no. Or maybe. There seems to be a Pam in every cult.

ALEX PARKER: The Committee is known for the self-help teachings of its leader, Walker Wilkes, a former high school English teacher turned soothsayer turned poor man's Tony Robbins.

KELLY MACPHERSON

SHEENA FAVROSIAN: I'm searching for a way to make a joke about that, but it's no funny.

ALEX PARKER: Proving once again that you are my more intelligent co-host.

1

Sucker Punch

Compound words are supposed to make sense.

Usually, they do.

Railroad. Moonwalk. Sportscar.

However, the world was changing. Metaverse and meet-cute were on course to make their way from new editions of the Oxford English Dictionary and onto third graders' school spelling lists. But so long as my preschool students weren't discoursing about catfishing each other on their parents' iPads, all was well.

Except in the instance of one word:

Athleisure.

It's little more than a marketing term designed to trick the brain into believing that overpaying for a pair of high-waisted leggings equates to the same endorphin rush as twenty minutes on a Peloton. Athleisure also sells the sham promise that showing up to your

3

annual Pap smear head-to-toe in Nike sweats are two sides of the same self-care coin.

"I'm having a comfy day," I've heard people say. No one has a comfy day. Comfy is an illusion. I wouldn't call myself a cynic, but nothing fleece-lined or built for medium-impact could lower my stress level after a day in which I've left work early to have my cervix scraped only to drive off with my travel mug forgotten atop the roof of my car.

Not one to dissect the English language in my free time, this line of semantic contemplation was sparked by something much more flagrant than a four-year-old telling me he has drip. And no less peculiar.

A man.

More specifically, a man enjoying "a comfy day" one Friday afternoon in late September outside the front doors of the learning center where I taught. He'd positioned himself before the side of the doors used for exiting, leaning against a trashcan filled with to-go coffee cups after that afternoon's pick-up. It'd finally reached Friday after a long week of teaching three- and four-year-old children to recite the alphabet and cough into their elbows, and I was having less than comfy thoughts at being forced to use the wrong door because some guy with a Dick's Sporting Goods rewards card needed a place to pretend to have a cool-down.

I sized up the loiterer from within the lobby. He wasn't the parent of a student. I knew all the parents of the students since the learning center served only infancy through age five. It was also smaller and more exclusive than a typical preschool thanks to a Waldorf-esque program. I waited for a quad stretch to reveal the guy as some run-for-fun flexer, but the only moves he made were looking up at the sky and down at a cell phone. Gray joggers and a zip-up hoodie didn't scream child abductor, but I knew enough not to judge anyone on looks.

Level of self-awareness? I definitely judged that.

I gave the guy one hell of a hard look as I made my way out to the parking lot.

Nike boy noticed.

"Hey, do you know where I can find Walker Wilkes?" I heard him ask as I passed.

I staggered a bit, the chunky heel of my left clog going sideways. It wasn't every day someone asked me that question. "Excuse me?"

"It used to be on the corner of Tenth and Maple," he continued.

"What are you talking about?" I asked back, my stomach teetering at my ankles.

"Starbucks." The guy's eyebrows rose up his head, two dark elevators. "I was taking a walk and wanted a latte."

"You wanted a latte?"

"Vanilla oat milk," he answered.

"I'm sorry. I thought you said something else."

The stranger laughed. He pushed his hands into his pockets, the strings of his hoodie swinging a bit with the movement. He must've noticed me noticing. "I usually jog," he said. "But I sprained my ankle a couple weeks ago and have been taking it easy. Getting my steps in, though. Every morning."

"It's the afternoon."

"I slept in."

I sized him up, conspicuously, since it was within my right to get the measure of the man who'd rubbed some of the shine off my TGIF. Dark brown hair cropped close. Brown eyes. The lingering summer tan of someone who probably did spend a decent amount of time outdoors. Handsome, sure. Enough at least. But not my type. The guy looked like an over-grown child about to enter a dodgeball game.

5

"Must've been a busy day at the office, I suppose," I replied, continuing toward my car in the lot.

He followed me. "You could say that."

My key fob was in my fingers, but this Walking Nike Swoosh spoke before I could get home to a pot of tea and episode three of a Teal Swan documentary before Aashri dragged me out to happy hour.

"How long have you worked at that preschool?" the man asked. "I'm Kyle, by the way."

"Well, I'm busy, Kyle By the Way. And six years." I took another step toward the parking lot. We stood atop the sidewalk that separated it from the learning center. For someone looking for a coffee shop, this stranger seemed overly interested in a private preschool program.

I turned to face him, wearing my features like an indictment. "Are you some kind of pervert?"

"Am I *what*?"

"Don't pretend you didn't hear me."

Kyle laughed. "No," he said. "I'm not a pervert. You could ask any of my exes. They'd say I was a workaholic, but, as far as I know, that's not a kink. I do gaze longingly at my stash of Cool Ranch Doritos whenever I open my desk drawer, but that's less an arousal thing than an MSG addiction."

"Anything can be a kink."

The sparkle in the guy's eyes was a red flag blown up ten times its usual size. "Tell me more."

"I'll tell you goodbye," I said with a quick twist back towards my waiting vehicle.

"I heard this place used to have a life-sized Barbie in the window."

I closed my eyes. My temples throbbed. Ten off-key voices had

Cult & Run

given me their best rendition of "The Days of the Week" song that morning, sung to the tune of "The Addams Family", but a headache hadn't arrived until that moment. Kyle By the Way wasn't searching for the nearest place to waste his disposable income after all those snack chips and athletic wear.

He was here because of The Committee.

The learning center entertained its fair share of gawkers, people who'd heard about Cormoran and The Little Cult That Could. The Committee had no temple, church, or formal building of worship. It existed as a group of families dedicated to becoming their highest selves, meeting in homes since true intimacy is marred by institutionalization. And taxes. And zoning laws. And making yourself a target for public scrutiny. Although, as it turned out, one didn't need a headquarters to do that.

"Look," I said, turning back. "There was never a Barbie. Those creepy life-sized ones are only life-sized if you're a three-year-old. We had mannequins."

"What do you mean 'mannequins'?" Kyle asked.

"Mannequins," I said. "Like in a department store."

"Do you mean the people, the fake people who—" Kyle positioned his hands at an awkward angle, as if prepared to simultaneously demonstrate both The Robot and rigor mortis.

The polite thing would've been to smile at this attempt at humor. But I was not polite. "I wouldn't say these 'fake people' are modeling clothes since modeling is a verb and mannequins are, as you said, fake people. But yes. Plastic figures wearing clothes. In stores. Those are mannequins."

"What do mannequins have to do with your—" Kyle checked himself in time. "Organization?"

"Nothing," I replied, knowing that he knew an awful lot more about The Committee than he'd led on.

7

"But you said—"

"I said nothing. You asked if my place of employment — a children's school — once had a life-sized child's toy in the window. I told you that, no, it was in fact a bunch of mannequins. You also mentioned Walker Wilkes and then gaslit me into believing you'd asked about a Starbucks that had never been at Tenth and Maple, which I am quite certain of because Cormoran is mid-sized at best, and I've lived in this town all my life."

"I did say that." Kyle's tone held none of the remorse I would've liked. His hands were out of his pockets, fingers playing with the strings of his hoodie. It was cocky. I was not a fan.

"If you're some true crime bro who wants the inside scoop on Walker Wilkes, hit up The Committee's subreddit. There's loads on it."

"Is any of it true?" Kyle asked, still arrogant, still fiddling with those strings.

I feigned innocence. "Why wouldn't it be? How could an organization that dresses up old Bloomingdale's mannequins bought off eBay be anything but forthcoming with the public?"

"What were they dressed as?"

"Freud, Jung, and Gotti."

Kyle dropped the strings. "I've never heard of Gotti," he said.

"Oh, yes, you have," I said back. "Two of these things are not like the other. He was the mobster."

Kyle nodded once. "Right."

I waited to see if he'd say anything else. He did.

"Why were they in the daycare?"

"Learning center."

"Why were they in the learning center?"

"The building was storage before it became a learning center. I'm assuming that since you've heard of Walker Wilkes, then you'd know about The Barbara Gala. If not, that particular subreddit has some great tips on preventing split ends."

Kyle's face had really begun to irritate me.

"They were party decorations," I added. "This isn't some weird sex doll cult if that's what you're thinking."

Kyle smiled, but not because he was polite. Because he'd gotten me.

I'd said it.

Cult.

As I've established, I am not polite, so returning his grin wasn't going to happen, especially considering I'd already said more than I'd planned. Being interrogated by a stranger in joggers and three-hundred-dollar mid-tops may have been an interesting diversion to some, but I wasn't looking for interesting. I was looking for quiet.

"Cult," I said again. "You're asking about The Committee because you think we're a cult."

"I don't think you're a cult," Kyle answered. "I think whatever you're mixed up in is, yes."

"What I'm mixed up in is an association of independently operating self-help contractors."

"Who are a cult." Kyle fingered something in the pocket of his hoodie. I wished he'd keep his hands still. I wished he'd realize that he'd left his oven on or his dog outside or his stash of Cool Ranch Doritos exposed.

I pointed to where his fingers rummaged around within gray cotton. "What do you have in there?"

Kyle met my eyes. His gaze was playful, which meant that whatever came out of his mouth next had already annoyed me. "Maybe I'm just happy to see you?"

"Have a nice rest of your day," I replied, halfway to my car before this ingenue of friendly conversation made it clear that he hadn't attended a quality preschool himself. A major theme of my classroom was Personal Space, which someone clearly hadn't mastered.

"Miss Scissors, hold up."

Kyle swung around in front of me, blocking my car from view. It was a BMW, an M4. Kyle's neck cracked as he did a double take at the kidney grill behind him.

"Can I help you with anything else?" I asked.

"Is this your car?"

"It's not proper to answer a question with a question," I said. Another value I imparted to my young students.

Kyle leaned back against the hood and smiled. The seat of his gray joggers perched on the lip of my Beamer as if he owned it.

"Get off my car," I said, my teeth clenched tighter than last month's budget.

"This thing?" Kyle turned to take it all in. "I can't imagine how a daycare teacher affords a $100,000 vehicle. Do you even get dental?"

"I don't pay retail," I told him. "Get off."

"Is that a perk of being in The Committee? Visualizing your way toward impeccable German craftsmanship? I hear the price of parts is a killer."

"Well, you'd know since you've killed my peaceful afternoon. It's been a horrible displeasure making your acquaintance." I stamped past Kyle, who stood there with a smile fixed to his face like butter on a roast turkey, and slid into the driver's seat of my BMW. Kyle lingered a few moments at the front, his body reclining further back along the hood. I pressed my horn loud enough to result in a slow head turn and wink in my direction.

A middle finger was my salute.

Kyle's hand lifted in farewell and his lips in a grin as I peeled out of the learning center parking lot and onto Center Street. It wasn't until I'd parallel parked before my walk-up townhome apartment, less deftly than usual, that I noticed he'd followed me all the way home.

But not in the way that'd earn Kyle a knock-off Kate Spade purse to the head.

After shutting off the ignition and taking one, two, three deep breaths, I'd reached into the backseat to grab a box of fundraising packets. The Committee's annual Barbara Gala would be held in a month, and I didn't need the drudgery of behind-the-scenes work to become a last-minute nuisance. Kyle's business card was lying on the back seat beside the cardboard FedEx Office Print and Ship box. I must've seemed idiotic for holding my key fob between us like a sword. My car hadn't been locked at all. Its providence also had not been a surprise. Neither, as I was slowly realizing, was I.

I stuck the business card in my purse.

Apparently Detective Kyle Alaric had decided to get on my case.

2

Highlighter Story

In the fifth grade, I ate a highlighter for lunch.

Yes, a highlighter. The perennial office supply choice of college students and salespeople and teachers alike. My future self would invest in fancy pastel ones off Amazon, erasable as I preferred all my writing utensils to be. However, as a child, I had foregone the horror of confessing my secret crush in a game of Truth or Dare and, instead, been challenged to consume a highlighter.

It'd been neon yellow.

And had tasted like I imagined nail polish remover smelled.

"You've never had painted nails, Dal. You wouldn't know what that smelled like." Helpful was what my best friend Aashri had attempted to be. It wasn't that she was trying to activate the inferiority complex budding in the fertile soil of my hyper-sensitive young heart. She'd shown up to our first day of fourth grade with plum

12

purple nails shellacked with glitter. Her college-age older sister had done it, and I'd never been so jealous.

"It's not so bad," I had told both Aashri and the group of my peers who'd gathered to watch me balk at my felt-tipped entree. Not that it truly was an entree. A highlighter is a snack at best.

The worst part about the whole ordeal was brushing my teeth before bed that night. Bits of the tip were stuck in my molars, and I'd cut my tongue on the plastic cap. I hadn't swallowed anything but the felt part, neon dye marking all the important parts of my esophagus.

Unknown to me was how much a simple office supply would impact my life.

It was the peer pressure, my mother had said, that'd caused me to ingest fluorescein and triphenylmethane. The year was 2001 and Dr. Google had not yet gotten their medical degree. My mother's high-level knowledge of chemical compounds had come from our neighbor. My family's last name was Scissors; our neighbors' was Shears. Despite the oldest son of the Shears bunch shouting "Edward Scissorhands" whenever he spied me on my bicycle, they weren't all bad. Until the highlighter incident.

Mrs. Shears let my mother know that eating a highlighter wasn't just the result of maladaptive social skills and a toxic public school environment but was toxic in its own right. I could be facing down death or a burgeoning autoimmune disease. I could puke up neon orange stomach acid. When I'd pointed out that the ones at school were all bright yellow, Mrs. Shears helped my mother usher me into the backseat of our Toyota minivan and over to Walker Wilkes' house.

I knew Walker Wilkes but had never seen his house, let alone visited it for what felt like an awful lot like an appointment that a physician should've supervised. Walker Wilkes was no doctor.

13

According to my mother, he was a spiritualist.

I thought she'd said spitballist, and so I was partially disappointed and more than a little bit scared when he'd told ten-year-old me to open up so he could "exorcise the demon of my ego". I'd asked if that was some sort of sinus infection and my mother had left the room in tears. Walker Wilkes was only thirty-something back then, with a quiet wife, one son. And yet, for all his forgettable ordinariness, the man had been poised to become a large fixture in my life, like an armpit boil that nixes sleeveless tops from your wardrobe. I hadn't known it then, just as I hadn't known I'd abhor showing off my triceps anyway. As a child, I hadn't known a lot of things.

Like that I was growing up in a cult.

After drinking Walker Wilkes' homemade tonic, ironically the color of the highlighter that'd sent me to him in the first place, he'd prescribed an immediate withdrawal from the Cormoran Public School System and the beginning of exclusive homeschooling by The Committee.

I'd heard the name before, even played with the kids of my parents' friends, including the younger of the Shears children, during the book clubs hosted in my home. I'd assumed that the dozen or so adults squeezing themselves into my parents' living room had given their group that moniker — *The Committee* — of their own accord. These weren't the brightest stars in the sky, let alone the juiciest highlighters in the box. Many years later a *Philadelphia Inquirer* article would refer to them as The Totalitarian Regime of Idiot Soothsayers with A Sunday Gravy Complex.

Walker Wilkes, of course, had been their leader. Until he'd diagnosed me with "attention-seeking syndrome", known to anyone else as *being a child*, I'd assumed the man was simply a Tony Soprano fanboy with a publishing deal. I'd later come to find out that, for all his mentions of "The Bing and Christopher Getting What He

Deserved", Walker Wilkes detested sexuality, violence, and mispronouncing the names of Italian dishes. I'd heard him once correct my mother's pronunciation of arrabbiata, following it up with a graphic walk-through of "Long Term Parking", the name of what I would later learn was episode twelve of season five of "The Sopranos".

"Does that guy only talk about TV?" I'd asked my mother the day after I'd tested the nutritional value of ink.

"He's a prophet," my mother had said. She hadn't elaborated, and so I'd assumed that a prophet was an unemployed mafia wannabe in a two-tone dress shirt.

As an adult, looking backward, I no longer possessed the innocence of a child who saw only a misguided, slightly haphazard mother and her misguided, very haphazard acquaintance. A foolish man, a silly one. Walker Wilkes had been those things to me once, but, at thirty-one, I could not deny that my life was headed in one direction before that fateful trip to Wilkes' house and shoved onto a very unfortunate detour afterward.

My youth was categorized by the chaos of terrible Italian cooking, phony healing, and an FBI sting operation whose name would become one of the top trending hashtags on Twitter when HBO produced a documentary on a failed investigation ten years later.

Long live #Focacciacolypse.

I'd have gone with something less carb-heavy, but whatever catches on.

Unfortunately for my mother, her arrabbiata never really did.

"It was an article about the seafood trade, and I'll be damned if I ever eat a spicy tuna roll again." Aashri slipped from kitchen to bedroom, a complicated drying turban twisted on her head. Her apartment was the size of a spring roll, so she was back as quickly as she'd left.

"The Way of Tuna," I said, continuing a conversation that Aashri was already sick of.

"That was the name of his speech?" Aashri removed the turban and ran her hands through her dark cropped hair. She smoothed a few pieces down, running her fingertips over the complicated design razored just above her neck. Aashri didn't go to a salon. She visited a barber. His name was Hondo, and she had a crush on him. She also had a crush on a bartender at the spot she was dragging me to in half an hour. Aashri was only exclusive about her gym, so these two men, and about a dozen others, had no bearing on her emotional health.

But, judging by the look on her face, this tangent of mine did.

"Moonies, John Frum, Devotees of the Golden Arch," she said.

"That last one is McDonald's."

"My point is—," continued Aashri, shoving her feet into a pair of black Timberland boots which she never untied, "—that you can't just talk about cults all the time. Especially since you're in one."

"I'm not 'in' one," I said back. "I grew up in one. There's a difference."

Aashri added a baseball cap to her head. "You work for a

preschool built by its funds."

"And what about Catholic schools? Quaker schools?" I pushed myself deeper into her poofy couch as if it'd somehow swallow up my budding unease, leaving only the assured, stoic version of myself that I preferred. The persona was a lie, but I was fine with that. No, not a lie exactly. More a self-improvement goal. Thinking in those terms — self-refinement — reminded me of Walker Wilkes, and I shoved my body further into Aashri's ridiculously expensive yet insanely comfortable sofa. "Not to mention Ivy League universities," I continued. "Talk about a scam *and* a cult."

Aashri faced me with her hands on her hips. She'd shoved her wallet in the back pocket of her jeans and adjusted the watch on her hand. Aashri gave people her attention. She wouldn't go to happy hour just to sit on her phone. She didn't even like to check it for the time, which is why she wore a watch, in addition to monitoring her vitals and her steps and her astrological transits or whatever else tech could do. But I didn't need a gadget to tell me I'd far exceeded Aashri's generous patience, knowing that our cult talk annoyed her even more than what she hated most: overpriced shoe drops.

Aashri was ready to head out, and so I stood, filled with an uncomfortable urge to make one final point. "You know, Heaven's Gate wore Nike Decades when they—"

"Are you trying to drive me to the bottle, Cruella?" Aashri pulled open her front door and gestured toward the hallway with a smile. "After you."

"You know I don't like when you call me that," I said, grabbing my purse and stepping onto the luxury vinyl of the corridor. The neighbor in the apartment across the way had moved out the week before and Aashri had stuck a prank flyer onto the door for the incoming tenant. Observing its presence still hanging beneath the peephole, someone new had yet to arrive.

17

"I know you don't like it, Cruella, but I need a wing woman. Not a bestie going on and on about messiahs in flying saucers."

"So tonight's the night you ask Tom out?" I gave her a fake punch on the arm. "Get 'em, tiger!"

"You are so weird." Aashri brushed away my humor with a bit of a blush. She was a lovely thing with a terribly intimidating way about her. Until you got to know her, of course. Tom would be a lucky guy if he returned her affections. I hoped he would. If not, we'd switch bars so she could go after another of her many love interests, and I really liked the bathrooms in Tom's.

I followed Aashri down the hall, leaving my cult talk back in her apartment. The prank sign on the door of her someday-neighbor flapped in the breeze of our motion. I didn't give a second thought to the newcomer who'd eventually happen upon it, no doubt perplexed by a Lost and Found poster for a bearded dragon named Martha Washington last seen wearing a rhinestone collar and sometimes answering to the nickname Smooth Mama M.

Between the two of us, Aashri was the creative one.

3

Walker Wilkes

Is Dead

"I think my appendix ruptured. My side hurts."

Aashri let the door hit me in the foot as she stepped ahead of me into Wilma's. Wilma's was the bar where her cute bartender Tom worked, and had, as far as I suspected, once been a deli, because the inside smelled like Black Forest ham. Aashri never seemed to notice, nor had the few patrons I'd asked regarding the aromatics of the place.

"I may need surgical intervention," I added.

"You for sure need an intervention," Aashri answered. "First thing in the morning I'm taking your laptop. No more Googling Illuminati shit."

"I don't use Google," I said. "Its search algorithm is gender biased."

Aashri took a seat at the end of the bar. I looked around for a commercial meat slicer.

"Did this building happen to be a slaughterhouse once upon a time?" I asked Tom as he sauntered over with that ridiculous mustache. It hung past his lips like someone had smacked him in the face with a sandy blonde worm.

"Actually, yes," he said.

I turned toward Aashri with an exaggerated grin. "Told ya!" To Tom, I said, "Where's the old meat locker?"

His light eyebrows pinched. "No meat locker. And you're sitting on the dance floor."

Aashri laughed.

"I thought you said this was a slaughterhouse?" I asked.

"It was *The* Slaughterhouse." Tom's mustache wiggled up into a smile. "Best dance scene in Bywood County."

Aashri bumped my arm with a fist. "Hey, Macarena, get a drink and take the edge off."

I ordered a gin and tonic because craft beer was a cult. Aashri was having some sort of mosaic, no doubt brainwashed by brand loyalty. When Tom placed the highball glass down before me, I felt that pain in my side once again. It wasn't a lie when I'd told Aashri that my internal organs were crying out. This happened sometimes. My mother would call it anxiety and tell me to stop buying vitamins on the Internet. I didn't believe in Walker Wilkes' healing tonics, but I did believe in adaptogens, oil of oregano, and homemade elderberry syrup. Aashri believed in something called The Doctor, but I couldn't bring myself to consult a fallible human being about my health. Relying on two-day shipping and four-and-half-star ratings seemed safer.

"Maybe I'm going to have stress diarrhea," I blurted.

"Whoa, whoa, whoa!" Aashri held her hands before her like I was a vampire. Tom had moved down the other end of the bar, pouring drinks and making small talk. "Did something happen today to make you want to be shunned from society?"

Something had happened.

But I didn't want to tell Aashri about it.

I did anyway.

"A cop," I said. "He was waiting for me when I left work. Made up some lame excuse about looking for a Starbucks."

"In Cormoran?"

"Yes."

Aashri laughed into her beer.

"Like I said, he was waiting for me, made up some dumb story, and then asked me a bunch of questions about The Committee." I swirled the extra-large cube of ice inside my drink. How did Tom make these things? It looked like a little kid's Duplo.

Aashri grew quiet. "What did you do when he started asking?" she said.

"Talked about the mannequins. Not much else."

"Dalmatia, oh my God. He probably heard you'd planned to take Wilma's restroom hostage with your bowel movements."

"You're only increasing my anxiety, so count yourself an accomplice," I replied.

"You need to relax." Aashri raised a hand toward Tom. She wanted another beer. She wanted his attention back. I was useless there, a ticking time bomb of organic fiber pills and cortisol.

"What do you think he wanted?" I didn't want to mention the part that upset me the most. *Federal Bureau of Investigation*. I pushed the gin and tonic away. It tasted like someone who'd be up all night worrying into her pillow while listening to a Daniel Kahneman audiobook on her AirPods.

"The same thing they all want," Aashri continued. "An indictment. He's not just a cop, is he?"

I shook my head. Aashri was right about more than Kyle Alaric's true providence. The Feds had been after Walker Wilkes for years. Foccaciacolypse was more than a cute term coined by the media. It was a 2012 investigation into Walker Wilkes' tax returns. He'd written off thousands of dollars dining at Italian ristorantes as a business expense, which gave the IRS a moment's pause considering his occupation as self-employed author. Aside from all the chicken parmigiana, Wilkes also claimed several burial plots as a work deduction. Foccaciacolypse had been The Committee's biggest press coverage to date, but it remained just that. No charges had ever been filed against Wilkes for his heavy use of marinara and nuance.

Likewise, the child abuse allegations swirling around Walker Wilkes had never stood up. Most parents affiliated with The Committee took their children for regular check-ups at regular physicians and employed run-of-the-mill antibiotics when their families were sick. But they also used something *extra*, like Walker Wilkes' healing remedies. How was it any different than buying supplements at Whole Foods? Or making kale smoothies? To members of The Committee, maintaining physical health was an investment in mental health, and mental health was critical for attaining spiritual enlightenment.

Classic cult talk.

But there's more.

Walker Wilkes wasn't just some faith healing, apple cider vinegar drinking, cuckoo guru who organized self-help book clubs around works he'd published himself on Amazon. He'd founded The Barbara Gala.

"I wonder if your FBI guy knows about all those wigs," Aashri

Cult & Run

said with a shudder.

"What wigs?" Tom asked, leaning both elbows on the bar. The hint of a tattoo slid out from beneath his shirtsleeve, a woman's legs rendered in shades of gray.

Aashri pulled his arm closer. "This new?"

Tom pushed the fabric away from the design. "My grandmother," he answered, a beautiful pin-up on display atop his bicep. "A month old." Tom smiled. "The ink, not her."

"She's absolutely gorgeous," Aashri replied. She was still holding onto Tom's wrist, and he wasn't making a move to draw it back.

"She made me my first old-fashioned, believe it or not," Tom said. "Trudie McCairn. She brewed moonshine during Prohibition and ran a speakeasy in her cattle barn."

"My kind of girl," Aashri said. She exchanged her grip on Tom's body for her bottle of beer. Tom watched a little too intensely as she put it to her lips. Aashri winked at him. He laughed.

"You remind me of her," he said.

"It's the legs, huh?"

Tom reddened properly this time. A patron called from the opposite end of the bar, and he gave Aashri a mock flex with his skinny arm and a big grin before taking off. I wondered if Trudie McCairn minded being immortalized as a pickup line.

"Maybe he's saving that other bicep for you," I told Aashri once Tom was out of earshot.

She cracked her neck. "I was thinking of my face somewhere else."

"Okay, that's enough." I sipped the gin and tonic. It'd gone watery. "Make me feel better about this cop thing. I'm almost out of Ashwagandha."

"For someone who hated growing up on The Committee's bullshit, I'm perplexed as to why you take all this weird stuff."

23

I had no answer for her.

"It's complicated," I said.

"Your 2009 Facebook relationship status is complicated," Aashri answered. "This is something else. Maybe you should—"

I knew what she was going to say.

Therapy. Anti-anxiety medication. Relocation. A lobotomy.

Aashri regularly suggested the first two, but they'd be moot until I stepped away from The Committee entirely. Being as I worked at the organization's child learning center, that would be hard. Not that teaching preschool was exclusive to the town of Cormoran or the group in which I had been raised. I stayed in Cormoran and taught at the learning center because I knew who I was in both, and it was easier to be cynical about a predictable world than make the mistake of trusting too much in one less certain.

That's what I would've said to Aashri had I been therapized enough to be in touch with my feelings.

But I wasn't, and I didn't.

"What's that look for?" Aashri set her empty bottle on the bar. Tom had turned her way, but she paid him no attention. "Dal?"

I'd stuck a hand up to silence her, the motion involuntary. My cell phone was clenched in my other hand. It'd buzzed from within my purse, set to vibrate as usual. Technological melodies made me want to hurl. Aashri grabbed my hand and gently laced her fingers with mine. "What's wrong?" she asked.

I found my mind as blank as my reply to the text I'd just received from my mother. I squeezed Aashri's hand. "Walker Wilkes is dead."

She squeezed mine back.

4

Bed, Bath, and The Beyond

Aashri and I left Wilma's with both our dignity and wallets intact. I wasn't the best of company after Walker Wilkes' Death Text from my mother, and Aashri was too compassionate to force me to listen to her and Tom's conversation about a mysterious fifteen-foot-tall pile of plates located in a forest somewhere along the Eastern Seaboard. Tom also comped all our drinks send us off with two orders of pizza rolls to go.

I spent the night searching online for news of Walker Wilkes' passing. Nothing. I contemplated giving my mother a call but pumping her for answers past eight P.M. never resulted in anything but questions about my ability to make friends and promising to email

25

me an article about dating in your forties. I was thirty-one.

It didn't matter. In the end she called me. My mother was, as she told me three times in as many seconds, experiencing a life-altering loss. This proclamation made it hard to ask questions, such as how the guy bit the dust. We made plans to meet the following day. I could ask then. Little did I know during our brief phone call how life-altering the demise of Walker Wilkes would prove to be.

Two lattes and plenty of meaningless conversation later — lattes mine, evasion my mother's — I sat across from her at the coffee shop on Main Street, the one named simply "Coffee Shop", and decided it was time to press for answers. My insistence would've been in poor taste had my mother been a grieving widow or a mourning child, but she was nothing of the sort. She was a groupie, a roadie, a number one customer.

"You really don't know how he died?" I asked. My second caramel latte sat between us. My mother glanced toward it with derision. She despised caffeine almost as much as she abhorred Ragu.

"I'll know when I know," she answered.

"You'll know when you know?"

"I'll know when I know, Dalmatia."

"So, you don't know?" I asked her.

"If I knew, don't you think I'd tell you?" my mother replied. Her eyes flicked toward where my fingers closed around my latte, and she grimaced as I lifted it to my lips.

"I'm not sure," I told her after an exaggerated swig. "You asked me here to talk about what happened to Walker, and you've said more about Dad's attempt to change the air filter in your RAV4 than the death of a man you've known for almost thirty years."

"Thirty-three," she said in a small voice.

My mother wanted company. She wanted an audience. She didn't want to share with me. I'm not sure why I'd thought my presence here, with her, would be anything but a mirror.

"Tell me again about how Tony accidentally blew up the microwave at his auto shop," I said back.

My mother launched into the story behind my dad's newfound zeal for car repair, adding exciting new details to a tale I was sure to hear many times again.

As I paid for my lattes and my mother's untouched Earl Grey, my knowledge about the death of Walker Wilkes remained relegated to the previous evening's text, a clipped phone call in response, and a couple soundbites about the unfairness of it all. The man hadn't even hit seventy. He should've been dishing out kitchen sink wellness concoctions and philosophical mumbo jumbo for another couple decades.

I walked my mother to where her Toyota SUV was parked a few spots behind my BMW at a meter along the street before the coffee shop. She popped her trunk and handed me a box of ceramic knickknacks she'd meant to paint but hadn't gotten around to. Most were Christmas elves and reindeer, but among the menagerie was a chalky-white Santa missing a boot.

"It broke off," my mother said. "I thought you could still make it work."

I regarded Kris Kringle's misfortune. "Is there an elixir for this?"

My mother sighed. "It'll give you something to do, Dalmatia. Maybe bring them to your class and have the kids take a go."

My students were four and five years old. Having them "take a go" meant a bathroom break.

"Dalmatia, that place is so *loud* and smells so rancid that I didn't have a chance inside to let you know, but I'm having a small reception after Walker's service. Just family."

"Mom, he's not our family."

My mother's face did that thing it normally did when I

27

contradicted her, which meant her eyes widened to hold back tears and her mouth flipped down to let me know about them. "Dalmatia, Walker Wilkes cared for you as a second father would."

We'd been here before, my mother and me. This conversation. It was okay that I wanted to get in my car and leave.

Better than strangulation.

"Is it a typical Committee funeral?" I asked.

"Yes. I promised Walker I'd adhere to the standards he's always upheld for others."

That was strange. Why had they discussed his funeral prior to him kicking the bucket?

"Just promise me you'll have him in a casket," I told her.

It was The Committee's firm belief that a person could not ascend to The Realm while locked inside a box. Is a corpse supposed to have the tricep strength to push the lid off a coffin beneath six feet's worth of topsoil? Walker Wilkes knew this and buried the group's deceased accordingly: no casket. It was a hush-hush situation, and one that Wilkes kept on the down low by holding burials on his sprawling ten-acre parcel of land at the edge of Cormoran.

"The casket, Mom. Please use a casket," I reiterated. I found the whole process of a Committee burial incredibly unseemly, not to mention criminal in the commonwealth of Pennsylvania.

"You're always so dramatic," my mother replied. Besides painting her emotions all over her face, she also pulled her skinny limbs in toward her body, raising palms to the sky as if questioning how on earth she ended up with a daughter like me. It was also a spot-on impression of a T-Rex. I'd heard they ate their young. I believed it. "I'm giving him a beautiful send-off into The Realm, Dalmatia. Now, are you open to being an usher or—"

"What do you mean *you're* giving him a send-off?" I asked.

My mother blinked once, long and slow. "I'm his next of kin,"

28

she answered.

My heart began to race. "Mom, you are not Walker's next of kin."

Her tiny laugh was a dead giveaway that more was coming, and I would not like it. "Dalmatia, you're so ridiculous."

I clamped my tongue between my teeth to keep from choking on my heart. "Mom, what are you trying to say right now?"

"It's funny," she said with a girlish smile. "How you can know someone for so long and yet never realize just how special they are to you."

"Mom, no!"

My mother was gazing at the sky now, the wonder on her face so like a cartoon lion cub's that I was pretty sure an ulcer animated in my gut where there hadn't been one before.

"Mom, tell me what you've done."

"We're married, Dalmatia. Walker and I."

I resisted the urge to shake her. My mother was a wisp of a thing, a turkey wishbone without the hope of good fortune. "He's dead, Mom. You're not married."

"Dalmatia, you know how this works," my mother continued. "We're united for eternity. Once I complete my time on earth, I'll join my husband in The Realm."

"Your husband is Dad, and I'm pretty sure he mentioned mowing the lawn yesterday *at the house you both live in together*."

"You're not wrong," she replied. "But you're not right either, Dalmatia. There are things you've never been able to…understand. To accept. The Committee's views on marriage, for one."

She was correct in that respect. The Committee upheld strange ideas about marriage, namely that whomever a member is legally wed to in the "earthly portion" of their life does not necessarily have to be their partner in The Realm. The Realm was reserved for the most enlightened beings, and The Committee prided itself on an eighty-nine percent entrance rate. In the event of finding yourself married to someone with little hope of up-leveling in the afterlife, members of The Committee partook in a ridiculous mock ceremony in which they wed another Realm-bound member of the group. They'd reunite in whatever version of The Realm appeared to them upon arrival, the most popular of which resembled a posh senior community on the Florida coast. My mother's recent bent toward tropical prints began to make sense.

"Does Dad know about this?" I asked.

My mother played with the Boscov's watch on her wrist. She wore my father's ring, so there was a very good chance he had no idea. "Of course, he does," she said. "He understands completely."

"Understands why his wife secret-married her cult leader? I doubt it."

I'd done it again, referred to The Committee as a cult the second time in as many days.

"If you don't want to be a part of it, then don't be, Dalmatia. But don't you ever use that word around me again!" She took off, running to the driver's side of her car and jumping behind the wheel. I could hear the wails, and I could hear the snot blowing from her nose, and I could also hear my mother chanting Walker Wilkes' name like a prayer.

That's what upset me the most.

Not that my mother had never seen him for what he was, but that she'd thought that *what Walker Wilkes was* had been what'd made him special.

Driving home from the coffee shop, I almost stopped at a local park and dumped my mother's box of regifted ceramics into a trashcan. But it was Saturday, too early in the weekend for such an immature response. If I ever decided to leave the learning center, I had — along with the pink hammer in my pink tool case — the beginnings of a rage room operation.

Thinking of my place of employment forced me to remember its origins, which did zip to diffuse my bad mood. I reminded myself that I may have worked at The Committee's learning center, but I was not an active member of the organization. The Committee was unlike other groups in that it didn't banish former members or dissidents from their families and communities, which proved both part of its appeal as well as its power. Empathy, even the shallow kind, is often mistaken for trustworthiness.

They are not the same thing.

I may have had empathy for my mother and her off-the-wall grief, but I couldn't think good thoughts about this new turn of events in her relationship with Wilkes. Our relationship had never been good in a happy-to-make-holiday-plans-with-you way, but it'd descended to a new level of the Underworld six years ago after a failed attempt at Reconditioning in which my mother and Mrs. Shears from next door turned a Galentine's Day pedicure into one of the many reasons Aashri encouraged me to seek counseling. I'm not keen on feet to begin with, but I'd much rather endure having my cuticles pushed back than forced to drink a cold chai latte in the backroom of a Weis supermarket while Mrs. Shears and three other women from their study group subjected me to a character assassination. "Recommit to The Committee," they'd said — to which I had pointed out the redundancy of such a statement — or I would allegedly end up reincarnated as a hermit crab until I finally accept the truth and attained Enlightenment.

The hermit crab part was facetious, of course.

And yet it was all I could think about — this episode in which I did not get a pedicure I'd never wanted in the first place but instead received such a traumatic tongue-lashing that I could no longer watch Bravo! reunions without crumpling into a ball of PTSD.

It was my lack of tools to deal with life that worried Aashri. After I'd been yanked from Cormoran Public and sentenced to the tutelage of Mrs. Shears, Aashri and I had managed to stay in touch through a stealthy system in which I'd do "quiet studying" at the Cormoran Library but instead ride my bike to her house and hang out until after dinner. For all my parents knew, I was the studious kid who gave up Pizza Friday in favor of perfecting a PowerPoint presentation entitled "Johnny Appleseed: American Folk Hero or Audubon Vigilante?"

I'd actually been stuffing myself with paneer and broccoli masala whipped up by Aashri's mom and heading home with increasing anxiety over the disparity between my life and my best friend's. Aashri had told me a thousand times that it was perfectly normal for a kid not to share their family's enthusiasm for religion. She wasn't as devoted to Hinduism as her parents, but it seemed to me that Hinduism had a lot going for it.

For one, attaining reincarnation and Enlightenment weren't relegated to white middle-class suburban folks. And secondly, Walker

Cult & Run

Wilkes wasn't in charge of the whole shebang.

After deciding to head home and call Aashri, I moved my mother's craft box to the trunk of my car and waved hello/goodbye to a bewildered passer-by who watched me curse an unpainted ceramic penguin that'd tumbled out toward its dusty death on the parking lot. I peeled out of there as quickly as I could, finally understanding why my mother had wanted to have a quick cup of coffee at the little shop in town she claimed to detest. Talking openly about her posthumous love affair with Walker Wilkes in front of my father would have gone over about as well as taking her to Wilma's for a pint instead.

When I pulled my Beamer into the designated spot before my walk-up apartment, calling Aashri with a scandalous update about my mother slid to second place in my conversational agenda. First up: complaining about the man sitting on the second step of my walk-up.

Kyle smiled as I exited my car.

I pressed the fob to lock it. *Dramatically*. However, if my little display bothered him, he didn't show it. I pointed toward the to-go carrier balanced on his knee, cradling two cups of coffee nestled inside. "So, you found the Starbucks, huh?"

Kyle stood. He wore jeans this time. A gray Henley, too. He didn't look like an FBI agent, but what did I know about how an FBI agent looked? My knowledge of law enforcement was relegated to "Law and Order: SVU".

"I thought we could talk," Kyle said.

"About how there's no Starbucks in Cormoran? Are those from the Exxon station?"

"A quaint little coffee shop," Kyle said. "I think you know it."

The tell-tale logo on the side of the paper cups hit me like a stone the chest. "So we have a coffee shop in common," I answered. "I'm

33

assuming you saw me with my mother."

"Could we go inside?" Kyle raised the to-go holder an inch higher, positioning it in one hand like a waiter or a suiter or an asshole. The guy had another thing coming if he thought I'd be tricked into spilling Committee secrets for something I could brew well enough in my own kitchen. Mr. Coffee had indeed proven himself the most gentlemanly man in my life.

"Why don't you tell me what you're after, and then I'll tell you no with a clearer conscience," I said. "I wouldn't want to find out you're chasing down a lost dog."

Kyle nodded toward my Beamer and laughed. The sound was clipped, a belt being snapped. I didn't like it. "You know, Miss Scissors, you shouldn't leave your car unlocked. Glad to see you not making that mistake twice."

"And you, Officer Friendly, should learn to read the room." I answered, before remembering where I was. "Or the sidewalk."

It took him a beat, but Kyle's shoulders relaxed. He brought the coffees before his stomach, a look of contrition on his face. "I'll be straight with you, Miss Scissors. I want to talk to you about Walker Wilkes." He cocked his head to the side, the slightest hint of a dimple visible on his left cheek. "By the way, is that German? Scissors?"

"English."

"Interesting."

I wanted to tell him that, no, it really wasn't. But the thought of prolonging this torture *was* torture.

"You may be familiar with the allegations that Walker Wilkes was financially abusing members of a group called The Committee," Kyle said. "You may not be aware he'd received threats of murder."

That had my attention. I remained quiet, letting him continue.

"It was Mr. Wilkes who'd contacted the authorities," Kyle went on. "I'm not here to investigate you or anyone else for illegal activity." He meant my mother, of course. This man before me, hopefully burning his hands on too-hot Arabica, knew a lot more than he'd first let on. "I'm trying to figure out who threatened Mr. Wilkes' life."

Kyle was conducting, what, a murder investigation?

I knew nothing about how Wilkes had perished, but if I invited Kyle up to my apartment it was sure to come up in conversation. First, I'd have to rush in there and push a drying rack of damp bras into the shadows. I also couldn't be sure whether a half-eaten cauliflower frozen pizza was currently ruining the ambiance of my coffee table. I'd put in a good two hours at HomeGoods picking out decor after moving into my place six years ago. I hadn't updated it much since, but positioning a microwaveable dinner beside the sandalwood candles and creamy-white shells didn't give off the stylish, untouchable impression.

But murder? I had to know more.

"You can come in," I said. "But I don't have much time."

5

Walker Stalker

Asking a man into my apartment typically did not happen unless he possessed the Amazon access code to deliver packages to my vestibule. My monthly Subscribe & Save order of SPF moisturizer was worth even a fifteen-minute conversation with Kevin, the UPS guy who liked to regale me with tales of his good old days at FedEx. I reasoned that I could handle a quarter of an hour with Kyle so long as our discussion of Walker Wilkes' death didn't give way to glory stories about his FBI training.

Kyle stepped aside for me to ascend the eight stone steps up to my apartment. I fixed my eyes on the freshly painted double doors before me, forest green, not touching the wrought iron railings or catching sight of the graying summer foliage hanging limp from the first-floor apartment's window boxes. Once inside the small vestibule, I considered knocking on the door of Mr. Hakema, my lower-

36

Cult & Run

level neighbor, and escaping while he kept Kyle captive with stories of his own about the late Mrs. Hakema's variety of Guinness World Records. Kyle guided the front door gently shut behind us, and I decided to leave Mr. Hakema to his memories.

I took the carpeted stairs up to my place and shoved my key into the temperamental lock. When it finally acquiesced, I shot into the living room, pushing the drying rack of undergarments from its spot in front of my radiator and into a less conspicuous position in the center of my small kitchen. My place was open-plan — nothing more than a great room split into a living room/dining nook with a tiny corner kitchen made visible past a breakfast counter. My bedroom was out of sight, out of mind, and it'd stay that way.

Kyle eyed me as I adjusted the rack of worn Victoria's Secret push-ups behind the sink. It took up most of the space in my kitchen, but who cared? Kyle would not be receiving a tour.

"So, what about this Walker Stalker?" I asked, gesturing to the couch. The coffee table was free of last night's dinner, which made me want to smile. Instead, I perched on the end of a chaise lounge at a right angle from Kyle and kept my mouth in a flat line. No need for anyone to get too comfortable.

"Walker Stalker?" He pulled two woven coasters — a clearance find — into the center of the coffee table and placed a to-go cup atop each. "One's regular and the other is decaf. You can choose."

"Thank you," I said. I should take the decaf. I took the caffeinated instead. If Kyle was anything like the cops I'd watched on TV and drank coffee by the gallon, then maybe he'd come down with a caffeine withdrawal headache. Tête-à-tête over. I sipped the coffee he'd brought me. "This is…"

"Caramel," Kyle replied. "You had it earlier today in your latte, so I figured you liked it."

If the guy wanted a reaction, he could keep waiting.

"How long have you been an officer of the law?" I asked, leaning back into a backless chair.

Kyle followed me with his eyes as I brushed away my gaff as a back itch. "Two years," he said. "I've been working the Wilkes case for the last six months."

"Is that when he was first threatened?" I crossed my legs. I uncrossed my legs. I crossed them again.

"Are you nervous, Miss Scissors?"

"I'm tired, Detective Alaric." Kyle met my eyes. "Yes, I found your card in my car. And yes, I would like to report a break-in."

"Noted," Kyle answered with a lopsided grin. "I'd be happy to take on your case."

A sudden sigh made me wonder if my mother had entered the room. But it was just me.

"Mr. Wilkes received an anonymous letter six months ago. I have a copy on my phone if you'd like to take a look." Kyle shifted, pulling a cell from the pocket of his jeans. A bit of his abdomen, the waistband of his boxers, flashed with the motion. He tapped the screen a couple times and handed the phone to me.

The first thing I noticed was how low his battery power was. Fifteen percent at half-past noon didn't present as particularly smart on his part, especially since Kyle was FBI. He must've had a portable charger somewhere in his car. I wondered what he'd been doing to waste so much power — streaming videos, listening to music. Was there a battery-hungry FBI app that'd helped him tail me? Maybe he'd planted a listening device. I flipped the cell over. It looked like a regular phone. An older model of my own.

"What do you think?" Kyle asked. He wasn't inquiring about my thoughts on his phone case, which was boring black with a Run DMC pop socket.

I tapped the screen to keep it active and studied the photo Kyle

Cult & Run

had pulled up.

He wasn't lying; it was a letter. A few simple sentences typed in, of all things, Comic Sans font. It was hard to take a death threat seriously when delivered in the same aesthetic as a child's birthday party e-vite. But threaten death, it did. According to its author, Walker Wilkes was "being watched" and "would pay for his crimes with his life". It was signed "Realm-Breaker".

"I prefer Walker Stalker," I told Kyle, handing him back his phone.

"Agreed. Realm-Breaker sounds like a video game avatar."

I met his eyes once more. Please, God, don't let this man be a gamer.

"I have a son," Kyle said, sudden as a popped bubble. "He's seven, and all he wants to do is play Roblox. I'm kind of a helicopter parent and have gone down a thousand rabbit holes about gaming just to make sure I don't let him get into something unhealthy when he's older."

I wasn't expecting Kyle to be a father.

"I don't have any children," I said, wondering why I'd felt the need to assert personal information.

"I ran a background check, so I knew that."

"On me?"

"On you." Kyle stuck his phone back in his pocket. I kept my eyes averted this time. "Anyone could do it, you know," he continued. "It costs twenty-five bucks. For a civilian, that is. If you're on any dating apps, you may want to run a check. People are creeps out there." He took a sip of his own coffee. "Are you on any?"

"Any what?" I asked.

"Dating apps?"

"*Dating apps?*" I shook my head. "If you ran a background check on me, then you know I'm the last person to threaten Wilkes' life."

39

"Well, I don't know that," Kyle replied. "But I do think you're probably at the bottom of the list of people who wanted him dead."

I looked at him then. Really looked at him. "How old are you?" I asked.

"Thirty-five," Kyle answered back.

"And how's your relationship with your mother?"

"Complicated."

"Then we have that in common." I said, still unsure whether I wanted to have this conversation. *Any* conversation. "Look, I'm guessing you're here because you've talked to members of The Committee about this Walker Stalker situation, and no one has given you anything. They won't. That's how The Committee operates. Tight lips, tight fists, tight everything. They're notoriously secretive, except toward Walker Wilkes."

"What do you mean by that?" Kyle asked.

"I mean that Walker controlled everyone. He knew their secrets. Upon pledging fidelity to the group, Walker became personal counsel for each member of The Committee. It's part of the initiation process. You know, conditioning by a charismatic leader."

"I've been looking into cults," Kyle said. "A bit."

I laughed. Loudly and without a lick of composure about it. "*A bit*? Detective Alaric, if you plan on nailing whoever threatened Walker Wilkes, you're going to need a crash course in high-control organizations."

"That's why I'm here," Kyle said. I could see it in his eyes. He'd been building to this all along.

A request.

"I know you work at the learning center, but I also know from those I've spoken to that you are no longer a member of The Committee. You don't practice its principles. You're not bound by them."

"This is true."

Cult & Run

"So, I'd like you to teach me," Kyle said. "About cults, about The Committee. I need your help finding out who threatened to kill Walker Wilkes."

He had to be kidding. Kyle took a sip of coffee, his face revealing not one iota of humor. I moved my eyes over to the large bank of windows running along the length of the far wall of my living room. It'd been what had drawn me to choose this apartment in the first place. The Cormoran skyline materialized through the day-brightened glass, a few church steeples and an old-fashioned theatre marquee breaking up what were mostly rows of redbrick townhomes in this section of town.

Cormoran had been my home for as long as I'd been alive. First, my parents' house with its tiny front windows, blinking out toward the quiet street and furiously wiped clean by my mother and her homemade Windex solution. Afterward, while earning my early childhood education degree from the community college, I had lived in an apartment on the other side of town. It'd been larger than my current abode, but I'd shared with three other girls, which made it claustrophobic. I still had Marnie's pizza stone in a cabinet of my kitchen. She'd left it behind when moving into her boyfriend's place, but I kept forgetting to return it. I also kept forgetting to keep in touch with her. She hadn't been so bad. My pizza-making skills, however, much to the chagrin of my mother's passion for Italian cooking, were abhorrent.

When I turned back to Kyle, I saw that his gaze had roamed as he awaited my response.

His eyes wandered over my apartment, taking in the random objects I'd hung on walls and set on surfaces. I didn't own a lot of stuff, but what I did I made sure to enjoy. Unfortunately, adult decor tended to involve more cloches and faux succulents than my eyes could handle, so I'd gone a bit more eclectic.

41

A set of toile plates hung beside my front door, fast food items — hamburgers, French fries — set in a pastoral scene instead of the usual couples and animals. I'd found them for a quarter each at a thrift shop down the Jersey shore last summer. A wicker basket of magazines, all various issues of *The New Yorker*, was positioned beneath my coffee table. The table itself was a piece I'd picked up at a garage sale a couple streets over from my parents' house and painted robin's egg blue. Apart from the magazines, most of my decor had once been other people's things, but I liked each and every one. It all made me feel as if I wasn't alone.

"Not trying to case the joint, right?" I said to Kyle.

"I like what you did with the plates," he answered. "My son used to be really into those pottery painting places and made a few things I could hang like that."

"That's actually really cool." I felt a softening between my shoulder blades. The second I'd seen Kyle waiting for me outside, I had gone rigid without realizing it. "I bet he'd like if you displayed his artwork."

Kyle smiled. "*Artwork*," he said. "You're definitely a teacher, calling it that."

I smiled back. It was involuntary. "What else would you call it?"

"His mom says it's clutter." Kyle's grin drooped a bit, but he scooped it back up before I had a chance to see how far he'd let it go. "But she's used to everything having a place. Just how her brain works. She loves him a lot."

"Of course, she does. She's his mother."

Kyle nodded, more with his eyes than his head. He took a sip of coffee before pulling out his phone once more. The quiet settling between us after what I feared had been too vulnerable an exchange wasn't unpleasant. "Would you mind if I get in touch sometime?" he asked. "Or I could wait for you to give me a call if you need to think about helping me out? I know you have my number because some thief left it in your very fast car."

"If you're insinuating that I drive over the speed limit, Detective, I can assure you that I do not." There was a sting of disappointment behind my light teasing. I couldn't be sure if it was because I knew that Kyle was wrapping up our time together or because I'd begun to let my guard down in front of a cop.

"Not at all," Kyle said. "And you can call me Kyle."

"Then I'll be Dalmatia," I answered. "Can I ask you a question?" Kyle looked up.

"How did Walker Wilkes die?"

"Oh," he said, obviously surprised I didn't already know. "In his sleep. Heart attack." Kyle read the confusion on my face. "He wasn't killed by this Walker Stalker," he added. "But I can't let whoever sent those letters off the hook. At the very least I have a harassment case on my hands."

Again, my body did something involuntary.

I looked at his hands.

No wedding ring.

"It makes sense then why my mother wasn't launching a full-scale investigation." I wasn't sure why I was suddenly warm. I also wasn't sure why I now wanted Kyle out of my apartment as fast as I could make him leave. "I actually have to meet up with a friend soon, so..."

"Oh, right, sure." Kyle stood. He pointed toward the coffees on the table. "Can I toss these for you?"

"Don't worry about it," I said. I walked him to the door and held it open. The staircase and vestibule below it smelled like shrimp Pad Thai and nail polish remover. It reminded me of my past with a high-lighter. It reminded me of many things. "I need you to know that I may not be a part of The Committee anymore and it was never my

43

choice to be part of a cult, but those people…some of them weren't so terrible. They were just misguided. Walker Wilkes did that, you know. He confused people, got them tangled up."

Kyle studied me. What he was looking for, I had zero idea.

"People get all tangled up in a lot of ways," he said back. "You teach me about cults, and I promise never to judge someone for what they couldn't control."

"It's good to have an open mind," I said.

"I'll talk to you soon, Dalmatia."

"One more thing," I added quickly before he could step out the door. "What was the postmark on the envelopes? Of the letters?"

Kyle shook his head. "None," he replied. "They'd been stuck in Wilkes' mailbox in plain, unmarked envelopes. His home health aide had been the first to find one."

"The diabetes," I said. "That's right. Walker had someone coming in to help him. My mother thought she'd been sneaking bites from the lasagnas she'd been bringing over."

Kyle lingered a moment, and I wondered if I should say more. But what was there to say? I was being asked to reopen a wound I'd waited for most of my twenties to grow closed, and now, at age thirty-one, it'd need to bleed out so the government could prosecute some random individual for a non-injurious crime against a man who had committed so many.

Kyle left, taking the stairs down. I shut the door to my apartment as he hit the final one.

Thirty seconds later I was sinking into my chaise, putting through a DoorDash order.

Boba, Pad Thai, and an add-on from CVS for some pink quick-dry nail polish.

CULT & RUN PODCAST TRANSCRIPT
SEASON 2, EPISODE 2

ALEX PARKER: Let's talk about the wig thing.

SHEENA FAVROSIAN: Ooh, the wig thing.

ALEX PARKER: Yes, the wig thing.

SHEENA FAVROSIAN: I think we've established that.

ALEX PARKER: As legend goes—

SHEENA FAVROSIAN: As our research informs us.

ALEX PARKER: As our research into legend informs us, Walker Wilkes, founder and leader of The Committee, stumbled onto a link between physical wellness and mental health when his cousin Barbara sadly began to lose her hair.

SHEENA FAVROSIAN: The way Walker always talked about it was highly denigrating to the many people struggling with medical-related hair loss. Truth be told, Babs Wilkes spent a little too long in the stylist's chair getting a perm back in 1994 — do you remember perms, Alex?

ALEX PARKER: Don't make me relive that era.

SHEENA FAVROSIAN: It was painful for all. Barbara, mostly. Within the first twenty-four hours after the treatment, her blonde cork-screw curls began to slough off her scalp like skin from a Microderm abrasion treatment.

KELLY MACPHERSON

ALEX PARKER: Ouch.

SHEENA FAVROSIAN: Fried hair or exfoliation?

ALEX PARKER: I'm not sure…both?

SHEENA FAVROSIAN: Well, Walker Wilkes was inspired. He created The Barbara Gala to draw attention to the plight of women's low self-esteem, which he felt led them to seek societal validation through dangerous beauty treatments.

ALEX PARKER: It sounds like Barbara Wilkes just should've switched hair salons.

SHEENA FAVROSIAN: Spoken like a man who's never had a bad pair of bangs.

6

I Heart My Grand Dog

"Do blondes really have more fun?" Kyle asked.

"I wouldn't know," I told him. "Why don't you put this on and see?" I shook a short blonde pixie cut wig in his face before slipping it over a Styrofoam head.

We were at my mother's house unpacking one of the many packages I'd spent the past few weeks collecting from the P.O. Box she kept at the Cormoran post office. Janice, the octogenarian postmaster, asked if I'd invested in Stitch-Fix. I could tell from the way she'd been eyeing my outfits that Janice was a sympathetic confidante of my mother. If she started matchmaking me with Derrick the postal carrier, I'd need to contemplate finally changing zip codes. Derrick

47

was nice, but I didn't want to date anyone who knew I had a *double* subscription to *The New Yorker* in the event I spilled coffee on the cover of one. I loved the covers, and the coffee disaster had occurred twice prior to my brilliant idea. I'd subscribed a second time in the name of an ex-roomie's deceased cat — R.I.P. Timothée Cat-alamet. I was not an animal person. Timothée, in his own right, was not a Dalmatia cat. We'd been quite the pair.

Kyle and I were not a pair, although he proved pleasant enough to work with and definitely put those strong arms to use. It wasn't that I needed him to push his sleeves up and reorganize my mother's work room, but he ended up doing so anyway. It'd please my mother that her bins of supplies for The Barbara Gala were stacked alphabetically along the wall instead of eating up the center of the room she'd designated for it all.

"Your parents have a nice space for this gala stuff," Kyle said. He'd begun unboxing wigs, as well, carefully separating them from their tissue paper wrapping.

"It was our dining room," I replied. "Before my mother became co-chair of this ridiculous thing."

"You think it's ridiculous?"

I set the wig I'd been unboxing back into its cardboard packaging and faced Kyle square. "Listen, the most important lesson to learn about cults is that they are damaging to everyone involved, whether it seems that way or not. The happiest members probably end up the most devastated."

We worked a few moments in silence until Kyle lifted a black bob with platinum blonde money pieces from the box he was working on.

"Oh wow," I said. "That one's totally you."

"You're into it?"

I looked away, hating that, as a woman, I'd been conditioned to blush when a man was possibly flirting with me. As I chanced a glance back his way, Kyle held a wig up in the air, a bald cap with a hot pink mohawk running down the center. "I put through some of the orders," I told him. "Just to help my mother. Like I said, being in a cult is disappointing."

Kyle motioned toward a Styrofoam head along a windowsill.

"I'll keep that one for later," I said, grabbing the wig from his hand. He passed it my way with a grin. "Unless you need it for some sort of undercover operation?" I added. "Wait a second!" I feigned shock and awe. "Was that you in the leather vest and mullet at the coffee shop yesterday?! Is that how you escaped my notice?" I squinted sharply at his face. "Is there a fake septum piercing in your pocket?"

Kyle's grin stretched wider across his face. He'd worn a plain white T-shirt to my parents' house along with the gray joggers I was now wondering if he maintained as an off-hours uniform. He'd worn a baseball cap, too, flipped backwards once we got to work. Neither of my parents had been home to receive us, not that "receiving us" was something my mother would do. It's why I hadn't informed her I'd have help. No use in allowing her to build up an unhealthy level of excitement over what she'd consider a potential son-in-law. Kyle wasn't even a friend, and marriage, an institutionalized legal contract with heavy societal expectations, was not my thing.

Kyle began removing packages of place cards and other fancy signage from a box. He cut an incongruous shape through my parents' canary yellow former-dining-room-turned-psychopathic-party-headquarters. The man dressed like a teenager but behaved like a seventy-five-year-old who hadn't gotten the notification that chivalry had passed.

And then Kyle opened his mouth.

"Why don't you have a boyfriend?" he asked. I almost choked

on my tongue. I almost choked *him*. "Or a girlfriend. I'm not saying one's better than the other."

"Wow, you really make it your business."

Kyle studied a shrink-wrapped bundle of auction labels. "What do you mean?"

I pulled the thick stack from his hands, ignoring that he held onto it a bit tighter than was polite. "Let's get back to Cult 101 and leave my personal life off the syllabus, okay? I agreed to help you. That's enough."

"What if I told you something about *my* personal life?" Kyle answered instead.

I was pretty sure he was trying to shock me into a heart attack. I'd meet my end surrounded by Styrofoam packing peanuts and synthetic side parts.

"Go for it," I told Kyle. "But it doesn't mean I'm going to reciprocate."

"I was only asking about relationships because of what I already know about The Committee. The marriage thing," he said. "They like you to keep it within the group."

It was true. The Committee recruited new members for one reason: Walker Wilkes' bank account. Encouraging marriage between fellow members was a financial tactic, like locking in a good mortgage rate. Nothing at all to do with romance.

"That's how it usually works, yes." I paused in my work to lean backward. My spine gave a purposeful pop. Kyle looked squeamish. I got back to unpacking. "Okay, lesson two about The Committee and cults in general: it's easier to keep members when they're emotionally invested in *other* members. The cult leader's job isn't to develop a personal relationship with each person in the group; it's to facilitate one between the others. For example, it's really hard for a wife to leave a cult when her husband is still a willing participant.

And a cult without members means a leader without power."

"What about kids?" Kyle asked.

I'd almost forgotten he was a father.

A shard of something rough and dirty sliced through me. I didn't like talking about my childhood growing up in The Committee, and I knew where this conversation was headed. Kyle would want to know why I continued to work at the learning center if I wasn't a practicing member. He wouldn't understand.

"It's not fair," I said, hoping he didn't pick up on the emotion in my voice. "Kids don't get to choose their parents, let alone what kind of psychological trauma those parents put them through."

Kyle was quiet for a moment. "I'm sorry. I didn't mean to push."

"You're not." The pain in my chest hadn't been a fresh wound. It'd been opened many, many times over the years, but, thankfully, closed back up as quickly as it'd been re-split. "Kids aren't under Wilkes' thumb as much as I'm maybe making it seem. Not when they're young. Parents can choose to send their children to public schools, any schools really, but they're sometimes removed from those environments when factors like peer pressure or bullying become an issue."

"And then what happens?"

Kyle had stopped working to listen to me. I'd stopped working, too. "They're homeschooled. From fifth grade on. Another Committee member homeschooled a bunch of us kids like a one-room schoolhouse in hell situation."

The expression covering Kyle's face almost made me laugh.

"Not really," I continued, wanting to put him at ease. "When I was a student, my version of hell was assembling different types of ancient Roman columns from marshmallows and toothpicks."

Kyle looked perplexed. "Is that even possible?"

"No." I dropped my eyes toward a box still sealed-up with

packing tape. I laughed the small, harsh bark of someone attempting to cover up hurt with humor. "But I didn't like it. I missed my best friend Aashri during the day, and my homeschool teacher wasn't the brightest bulb in the...bulb store." I shrugged. I had nothing else.

"Who was it?" he asked. "That homeschooled you?"

"My family's neighbor, Mrs. Shears."

It was Kyle's turn to smile now. "Scissors and Shears lived next door to each other?"

"Wow," I said, making my eyes wide. "You're so original."

"What are the other Committee members named...Paring Knife? Hacksaw?"

I opened my mouth to tell him where he could stick these sharp pointy instruments, but Kyle waved his hands before his body like a kid on a one-track train of thought. I wondered if his son did the same thing. It was—

"Ginsu and X-Acto are cousins!"

—not cute.

We finished the job and cleaned up all the wrapping, supplies, and the two coffees I'd brewed us in my parents' old Mr. Coffee. There'd been a new Nespresso machine on the Formica countertop in the kitchen, but it felt like a violation to use it. It also felt as if I'd be consenting to something I didn't actually want to be involved in, as if piercing open and brewing one of those little flying saucer-shaped dark roast pods would collect my auto-signature for a friendship contract I did not want.

Kyle and I left, pulling off my parents' street together since I'd driven us over from my apartment. The last thing I needed was someone copying down his "strange" license plate. Mrs. Shears, the lone blade left in the scabbard, had moved off the block a few years ago for mission work in Rhode Island. I wasn't sure what new allegiances she'd been dredging up, because Cormoran certainly didn't appear awash with a slew of new, financially fit eligible soulmates. The learning center had broken construction on a gymnasium a few months ago, so maybe she was a better evangelist than I'd guessed.

I chatted with Kyle for a few minutes beside his Jeep, not at all liking that he had a bumper sticker for the local football team. Two stickers, in fact. The second read I HEART MY GRAND-DOG.

"Are you sure you're an FBI agent?" I asked, making a show of peeking at the rear of his vehicle. "You seem pretty good at keeping secrets and using retinol, considering you're some Lhasa Apso's Pop-Pop."

"Cindy is a beabull. Her mother Amy was a Beagle."

"Okay, hold up. Cindy is not a dog name. Neither is Amy. What's the dad…Terrence?"

Kyle's eyes went wide. "How do you know him?"

"Dad humor and Grandpa humor. You're getting better to work with by the minute." I didn't like the twinkle in Kyle's eye or the way he smiled at me.

"I adopted Amy from a puppy mill rescue when she was a senior dog," he said. "She'd been mistreated for a long, long time. She was the best girl. The very best."

Kyle looked as if he would cry. I got nervous, unsure what to do with a grown man in a backwards ball cap about to openly weep beside a Jeep that I realized also wore a bumper sticker announcing he'd run a 5K. This was not good.

"Amy was my first baby," Kyle continued. "When she passed, I was devastated. The humane society where I'd adopted her was so kind. They'd sent flowers—"

He liked flowers?

"—and added her name to a brick on part of the dog walking loop on their property. The first time I was able to go see it in person after Amy died, I ended up deciding to sign up as a volunteer. That's when I met Cindy, Amy's daughter."

"Wait, what? Her daughter?"

"Her daughter! Can you believe it?" Kyle's eyes were gleaming, and he was animated now, talking with his hands. I was no better, leaning into every word. "Turns out the mill where Amy had been living was shut down, and Cindy was surrendered by a family who couldn't keep her. They'd had twins and she'd become too much. I fell in love with her instantly. She was chewing on a shoe, which the volunteer said was the only way she'd calm down enough to sleep in her kennel without howling all night. The rescue told me she'd be a tougher adjustment because of the shoe thing—"

Kyle definitely liked his shoes.

"—but I didn't care. She was the one for me."

We stood there together, both of us slightly out of breath. Kyle, from relating Cindy's origin story with such enthusiasm, and me, from apparently being an adoption stories stan.

"When did you find out Cindy was Amy's daughter?" I asked.

"When Marissa was helping me with the adoption papers, she mentioned that the Cindy had been surrendered in a town in Ohio. I knew that'd been the location where Amy had been rescued from, and, I mean, the *names*." Kyle smiled. I hadn't noticed the faint dimple in his cheek. "Like you said, who names their dogs Cindy and Amy?"

"Someone who loves them very much," I said. It was so unlike me I wanted to vomit.

Kyle looked a bit surprised but regrouped. "Actually," he replied, "they came with the names."

Size eight-and-a-half brown leather clog, meet my mouth.

"Marissa had suggested I keep the names, since the dogs had been through enough trauma already. It'd give them a sense of stability. She'd been the volunteer adoption assistant both times." Kyle pushed his hands into the pockets of his jeans. He wanted to get going, and I was keeping him. I waited for a key fob to emerge, but it never did.

"Are you and Marissa still in touch?" I asked. What was I doing?

"Marissa is my ex-wife."

And there it was.

My exit.

"Oh crap, my phone's buzzing. My mother probably got home and noticed I'd put those mugs back in the wrong spot. I'm pretty sure she has the place under surveillance." I hadn't told Kyle about my mother's new ties to Walker Wilkes — those of the woo-woo marital variety — and I'd washed and put away the mugs we'd used that morning so I wouldn't have to confess anything to my mother, as well.

"It was good helping you," Kyle said, as I turned to go. "And thanks for helping me."

"I've barely told you anything about cults," I replied. "Maybe you could come up with a list of questions and email me."

"How about I take you out to dinner instead?"

It was way he said it. Take me out *to* dinner, not have dinner or buy dinner. Kyle no longer looked so much like a cop. Not that he ever had. The mention of his ex-wife had lit a fire under me to get my behind into my apartment ASAP, and now I couldn't decide if his offer further spurred my avoidance or made me linger right where I was. I considered the boyish expression on Kyle's face and the way he wore that hat. The hands pushed into his pockets, anxiously, not to make a quick getaway but to muster up the courage to remain. I liked it. I liked *him*.

It felt horrible.

"Dinner?" I asked, stalling. "Will Marissa mind?"

"Marissa and I were married for two years. We've been divorced

KELLY MACPHERSON

five. Luke, my son, is the best thing we ever did together. We co-parent, which isn't always the easiest thing, but we make it work."

"Okay."

I had zero idea what I was okaying.

"I'd adopted Cindy after we split, and Marissa helped because she'd already volunteered at the shelter. It's what I initially fell in love with. Her heart."

"Okay."

"I'm saying too much." Kyle laughed.

"Okay."

"Is that an okay to having dinner with me or an okay that I'm a lunatic?"

"Both. Dinner!" I blinked hard as if that'd banish my awkwardness. "I'll have dinner. With you. Dinner with you is okay."

"I'll let you get going and handle your mom," Kyle answered with a smile that made my stomach hurt. "I think she's going to have some questions for you...didn't we finish your parents' half and half?"

Kyle continued to grin.

And I questioned my sanity.

"I'll text you later, and we'll make plans," he added. I moved toward the stairs leading up to my apartment, and Kyle unlocked the door of his Jeep. I wasn't sure if I said goodbye, but I'd gone inside after doing a wave that looked as if I'd tried to give Kyle the middle finger but with both hands. I'd done a two-handed wave. And badly.

Once inside, I let my purse slump to the floor.

I was going to dinner with an FBI agent who may or may not show up in sportswear.

Aashri was going to love this.

56

7

Maybe Bleeding

Since my youth, I'd shed several unwanted things: acne, capri pants, and a home address listed as my parents' house.

However, one attribute persisted.

Despite my last name being Scissors, I was so clumsy enough around anything sharp that reloading a stapler could send me to the ER. Not that I'd go. I would rather spend the rest of my days recanting the sad tale of why my left hand was permanently affixed to my forehead rather than be squeezed to death by a blood pressure cuff.

After cleaning my apartment and arguing with Aashri over the culty properties of dating apps — in my opinion, Tinder was a charismatic leader I would do well to avoid — a series of events began, which led to my fatal flaw rearing its wildly klutzy head. Not first thing, of course. When Aashri first appeared at my apartment, I was still too full of anxiety over learning that Kyle had an ex-wife *who loved animals* and that he wanted to take me out. I did not love animals, and I did not love that I wanted to go to dinner with this guy.

"It'll be good for you," Aashri said as I dumped a half-bag of frozen strawberries into my little-used blender. "And be careful with that thing."

"I know how to use a blender," I answered. "And going out with some cop isn't an exercise in self-improvement."

Aashri had her feet up on my coffee table. She was the only one who could get away with it, not that many people graced my space. "One word. No, two words. Garbage disposal. You thought you knew how to work that, too. And a third word...you'll have fun and get outside your head for at least two hours unless you let the dude spend the night, which I can't imagine. But maybe you will, and I'll become Aunt A to a cute little FBI baby with itty bitty Air Maxes and an anxiety disorder."

"I cannot even begin to explain to you how that is way more than three words," I replied.

Aashri recrossed her legs the opposite way, sunshine yellow Vans hitting my eyes like the real thing. "I dropped a Word, capital W. That's what that was."

I hit the power button on the blender and watched it go.

Aashri's fears proved unfounded. Two full glasses of strawberry, kale, and whole milk vanilla yogurt were shared between us in my living room without incident. We toasted my ten fingers and relaxed into everyday conversation. Aashri worked as a pharmacist at a CVS with the best candy section I'd ever seen. I never filled prescriptions since I never visited doctors, but I made it a point to drive over to Aashri's store for the largest Haribo gummy selection this side of the Atlantic.

"Where do you think Tom is in this picture?" Aashri asked.

She passed her cell phone my way. I took it, coming face to face with Tom the Bartender wearing a terrible Hawaiian shirt. "It looks like he's posing in an atrium. A very poorly themed wedding? Where'd you get this pic?"

Aashri licked a fleck of green off her lip. "LinkedIn."

I stopped mid-sip. "LinkedIn?"

"It's social media."

I looked at the photo again. Tom, in an ultra-bright, hibiscus-patterned button-down, also wore a gray fedora and held something in one hand, for sure intending for it to make the frame of the photo. "Is that—"

"Pig in a blanket," Aashri finished, motioning to have her phone back. "On a toothpick."

I handed it her way. "Wedding," I said. "I was right."

"Actually," Aashri continued, "I think it's his work ID."

I did not want to know how she came about this information.

Nor did I not want to know why Tom dressed for work like a rum-drunk ukulele player.

But then it occurred to me. "Why does he have identification for the bar?"

"Because he also works somewhere else," Aashri said. "His LinkedIn profile lists him as a media director for Carbon Fiber studios. He's in podcasting." Aashri set her smoothie on a woven coaster and stretched her triceps. I knew she had a gym session later with her weightlifting trainer, Pandie. What Aashri knew was that I loathed podcasts, and so my estimation of Tom had just fallen six feet under.

"Don't even say it, Dal."

"He's dead to me."

"Dalmatia!" Aashri squealed as if I'd insulted the width of her quads.

"You know I don't like pods." I set my glass down, too. I should've swapped out the kale. "I like articles and books. I read."

59

Aashri squinted her eyes, aware that my haughty intellectualism was as false as my enjoyment of smoothies with kale. "You listen to that gossip one, so don't pretend with me, my dear, long-time friend. Remember the mix tapes?"

Yes, I remembered the mixtapes.

They were not, as one would assume, compiled of songs.

"Remember the one where you'd pieced together the funniest parts of that *Maury Povich* episode with the extreme makeovers...the mom whose kid said she dressed like a truck driver? Even back then, I liked her style. You mashed it up with Dr. Phil and Oprah talking about living with authenticity. And then another *Maury* ep with a paternity test? Or was it bad kid boot camp?"

I cringed. "It was paternity."

"My point is that you don't hate podcasts. You'd basically made one back before online media was a whole big thing. You hate podcasts about The Committee, about cults, because of how you grew up. There's no shame in that, Dalmatia. Not in how you were raised and definitely not in wanting to avoid reliving it through someone else's eyes."

Aashri wasn't wrong, and we'd been through this before.

"Does it say what podcast Tom the Mystery-Meat-Loving Don Ho works for?" I asked.

"It does not," Aashri said. She tapped around on her phone screen. "Carbon Fiber Studios is thirty minutes from here and has three employees. That's not S-Town."

"I loved S-Town."

"I know."

I rubbed my eyes. Flakes of mascara came off on my palms along with at least one eyebrow. I used a cheap pencil. "I sometimes like podcasts," I admitted.

"You don't say," Aashri replied. She rolled her neck and

shoulders, preparing to make the four-foot trek from couch to door. I didn't want her to go, but I knew she couldn't stay. I just didn't want to be alone. Aashri pushed her phone into her pocket and stood, bending forward into an arms-dangling pose she called Rag Doll. It looked like she was ready to receive the Heimlich from a ghost. "I'm gonna get going," she said. "Are you okay?"

It was my face. Always my face. Aashri may contort her body into a variety of Yogi positions, but I worked my eyes and mouth with the same flexibility but far less peace. "I'm good. Ahh! Hold on! I have something for you!" I wasn't stalling. I truly did.

I ran into my bedroom, tangling my feet in a ridiculous faux fur throw rug I'd bought because Aashri said it'd reminded her of the last field trip we'd spent together in the fifth grade, a visit to a working colonial farm. She'd fastened a souvenir rabbit pelt to the back of her collar and ran circles around Ms. Willis, calling herself Super French Lop. Aashri had known a lot about animals, but less about etiquette.

"I don't want whatever unused booty bands or three-pound weights you bought with very misguided intentions!" she called after me. I righted myself and the rug, sped into my bedroom, and whipped the item I'd been saving for Aashri off the end of my bed. A highlighter had been resting atop it. The neon purple cylinder rolled onto the ground. It hadn't been fully capped, and the inky tip smooshed felt-first into my carpet. My cream-colored, unstained carpet.

An omen.

I grabbed Aashri's parcel just before the rug was pulled out from under me. Not literally, but also not quite metaphorically. I screamed and stumbled into my full-length mirror as Aashri grabbed me from behind.

"What happened?!" she cried.

I whacked Aashri over and over with what'd attacked me. It hadn't been the rug.

"*The New Yorker?*" she asked, taking the object I'd meant to give her from my hand.

"I can't open my eye!" My left eye was useless, impossible to open, and my mouth was as equally restrained by sympathy pains.

Aashri tossed the issue onto the couch. "Calm down!" she ordered.

"Don't ruin it!" I cried. "I haven't even peeled the address label off yet!"

"You have a backup!"

"That *is* my backup!"

Aashri led me to the living room and away from the latest edition of *The New Yorker*, which featured a humorous piece about burpees I'd wanted to show her. Aashri helped lower me onto the couch. "Two things, Dalmatia. First, I am never going to read anything you give me. Second, stop cutting yourself! I trusted you with that blender, and now you've given yourself a possible corneal abrasion with a sheet of groundwork gloss text!"

I couldn't be sure if my eye was tearing up or bleeding out before my best friend and a disapproving HomeGoods candle. "Do you think that's what I did?!"

Aashri sighed. "I don't know. I'll take you to Urgent Care."

"But you have a workout scheduled!"

"Well, then whatever bodybuilding satire you were trying to get me to read is just going to have to include best form for bench-pressing a few triage nurses."

"I don't want to go to the doctor," I said in a voice so small it couldn't have belonged to a thirty-one-year-old woman. I was in the beginning of the fifth grade all over again, in that oblivious period before Walker Wilkes. Prior to the highlighter incident, I'd never minded as much as a vaccination. TB test? Flu shot? No big deal. Now I avoided them all.

"I'm not leaving you here to bleed all over a couch I've come to love as well as my own," Aashri replied.

I pulled her toward me with the strength of a stay-at-home mom lifting a Subaru off a half-used Starbucks gift card on the first day of fall. "I don't want to be bleeding!"

"Get a grip! You're not bleeding, Dalmatia! We're going!"

And off we went to the Urgent Care with Aashri behind the wheel of her Chevy Silverado and me crying — maybe bleeding — all the way.

8

The Return of Jenna Shears

One town over from Cormoran was a hospital, a shiny, sparkly high-rise structure backlit by sunsets fond of dipping beneath the Blue Mountains of Pennsylvania. It'd won regional awards in both oncology and emergency medicine.

And so I found it unsettling when Aashri pulled up to a Sheetz gas station.

"Get out. I'll park and come meet you," she said.

"Is this about a breakfast quesadilla?" The pain in my eye had dulled to a pinch, but my nerves were stung to hell. Aashri unlocked the passenger door, signaling for me to go. She must've thought I'd flee the second I saw a diesel pump. I considered it.

Standing atop the pavement before the gas station, my good eye caught sight of the building connected to the big red roof with its oversized SHEETZ logo. Large white letters spelled out URGENT CARE, similar enough to the gas station's signage that I wondered if I'd arrived at some synergistic franchise. A place called SMILES DENTAL bookended the other side. Fill up on flu shots, fluoride, and fuel without losing your parking space.

Aashri pulled around the side of the building.

"This is bull-Sheetz" I whispered to myself as I watched her go.

The interior of the Urgent Care was pretty close to what I assumed a proper emergency room would look like if a proper emergency room could be squeezed between a dentist and a gas station. I took one of a dozen hard-backed chairs in a waiting area, covering my eye with one hand, while Aashri checked me in at the counter. She'd taken the insurance card from my purse, barely used and just a formality, and was also privy to my non-existent medical history. The policy wasn't great, but the learning center used it to court childcare professionals with four-year degrees.

The man behind the desk didn't bat an eye at any of our nonsense. Over a cute pair of purple glasses, he looked my way and then raised an eyebrow at Aashri. "You've got a live one there," he said. She agreed.

After being ushered to an exam room, waiting wasn't so bad. Aashri attempted to show me funny articles she'd saved, since my phone got poor reception and my right eye vision was at a twenty and my left was Jack Sparrow. "25 Times People Looked Like Guinea Pigs," Aashri read aloud. She chuckled to herself. "You need to look at the screen for that one. It'd be easier to describe 30 Times Celebrities Looked Like Stoplights. Want that?"

"I'll pass," I answered. Being at Urgent Care made me wonder about more than the conjunction of fashion sense and traffic law.

"My mother never told me how Walker Wilkes died…or when his funeral is. Don't you think that's odd?"

"Do I think your mother is odd?" Aashri smirked. "Yes, about everything, but especially Double-Dub."

"Isn't that the fictitious bearded dragon who's gone MIA in your building?"

"That's Smooth Mama M, and I'm pushing the story she's haunting the elevator."

Aashri scrolled on her phone while the doctor took their good old time, and my eye pain began to fade into the humiliating worry that I hadn't needed medical attention after all. "Did anyone ever move in?" I pinched my injured eye shut even tighter, hoping to feel it ache anew. "To the apartment across the hall?"

Aashri shuddered. "Yeah, someone with a Peloton."

I thought of Kyle. Was he truly athletic? He'd moved my mother's junk easily enough, the lean muscles of his back working through his T-shirt. I thought about it and decided that I much preferred whatever form of physical fitness Kyle practiced rather than some early morning cycling fanatic who'd become Aashri's neighbor. I was sure I'd lay an eye on him soon enough.

"Miss Scissors, what brings you in today?" asked a new voice, a physician assistant voice, a woman's voice.

A *familiar* voice.

"She cut her eye on a magazine, which is why everything should go digital."

The physician assistant smiled. Her veneers were like the tiny white tips of candy corn, and I wondered who'd made them so small and why. "Hi, Dalmatia. Long time."

This woman was no doctor.

She was Jenna Shears. As in Jenna Shears, my childhood neighbor. As far as I'd been aware, the former Campbell Road resident had

Cult & Run

gone to college elsewhere along the East Coast. I'd assumed she had then settled in Rhode Island with the rest of her mission-minded family. Why was Jenna in Cormoran? It wasn't a large town by any means, and this was the first I'd seen her back.

"It has been a long time," I replied, forgetting why I was face to face with a girl — a *woman* — I'd hoped to never see again.

Jenna and I had been homeschooled together along with several other Committee members' children, and it wasn't that she'd been a star student who'd shown me up or even teacher's pet, considering her mom had been our instructor. Jenna Shears had been a nuisance. She'd been in trouble almost constantly, writing lines on the chalkboard for forcing me to talk to her during lessons or visiting Walker Wilkes for special ego-healing tonics long after my one and only foray to his place due to the highlighter incident. Jenna Shears had made my childhood hell not because she'd rejected me but because, despite needing constant attention from everyone around her, adults included, she'd never let me reject her.

So, when Jenna Shears spoke her next words, it wasn't only my presence in a medical establishment that was out of place that day.

"I was such a little shit as a kid, wasn't I?" she said, beginning to wrap a blood pressure cuff around my arm. "I'm sorry about all that."

"I don't really remember," I answered.

Jenna Shears, P.A., smiled. Those tiny teeth were disconcerting in such a large grin. Her hair was the same light brown it'd been when we were kids. Cut the same, too, although the fringy bangs and medium-length straight style became her an adult. I looked closer at her mouth as she stuck a clip on my index finger and shined a light in my good eye. Her teeth really weren't so bad or so small, I thought. Definitely veneers, though. Interesting.

"Can you open it at all?" she asked. "I'm assuming a corneal abrasion, but I should check closer to be sure."

KELLY MACPHERSON

Aashri high-fived herself from a chair.

"I'm trying," I said. I managed to pop open my eye for a milli-second, and Jenna hit me with her spotlight. I stifled a scream.

"You really should get checked out by an optometrist for good measure," she said, sticking the device back into the pocket of her white coat. "I don't see much more than redness, but that could be from squeezing it shut so tightly."

"Or from slicing it open on paper."

Jenna laughed at me as if anything corneal or abrasive was a light matter. Her bedside manner left much to be desired. "I don't think you sliced anything," she continued. "But I'm going to prescribe you some antibiotic drops just in case. See an optometrist within the next few days."

As if that was going to happen. I realized then why Aashri had brought me to the Urgent Care — quicker service than the ER and a lot less invasion. I was perplexed, however, as to why Jenna, having been raised with the same strange health programming as me and even more of the Walker Wilkes line of witchy brews, had become a physician assistant.

"A nurse should be in shortly with your discharge papers. You can check-out with Tyler at the front desk. It was good seeing you again, Dalmatia." Jenna turned to go, the blunt ends of her hair swishing in farewell.

Before she had a chance to pull open the exam room door, I called to her. "Can I ask you a question?"

Jenna was slow to turn around, but she answered without missing a beat. "Sure."

Aashri watched, brows furrowed into question marks.

"Why are you in medicine?" I asked. "After all we went through as kids? And why are you back here? In Cormoran?"

Jenna approached me, lips pressed tightly together. Her eyes did

68

not look the slightest bit amiable. I scooted back on the exam table. "Walker Wilkes does not get to have control over how I live my life," she said in a low voice. "He did not then, and he does not now. And he's dead."

"So, you know about that?" I asked.

It was then that Jenna smiled, full and big and almost drunkenly pleased. "Yes," she answered. "I very much do."

I very much knew something then, too.

Or at least had begun to heavily suspect it.

The threats to Walker Wilkes' life were not as innocuous as a heart attack in his sleep may have alleged.

Jenna Shears, P.A., possessed both an intimate knowledge of the human body and more than one reason to want a certain lunatic dead.

CULT & RUN PODCAST TRANSCRIPT
SEASON 2, EPISODE 3

ALEX PARKER: At Carbon Fiber Studios, we are nothing if not lushes, so, Sheena Favrosian, what'll be your bev of choice this Thirsty Thursday?

SHEENA FAVROSIAN: Well, Alex, it's not Walker Wilkes' Lymphatic Drainage Tonic for Trauma Recovery.

ALEX PARKER: Maybe it's Walker Wilkes' Testosterone Balancing Milkshake Powder?

SHEENA FAVROSIAN: It'd be the Estrogen Promoting Herbal Tea for me. But no.

ALEX PARKER: In case we're worrying our listeners, Sheena and I have absolutely zero interest in doing anything with Walker Wilkes' line of body and mind supplements aside from wondering if they'd somehow contributed to his demise.

SHEENA FAVROSIAN: That's still a mystery, isn't it?

ALEX PARKER: It is. We've done our research here at Cult & Run — over an artful gin and tonic if I do say so myself—

SHEENA FAVROSIAN: Which you do.

ALEX PARKER: And the death of Walker Wilkes hasn't become public knowledge. But our inside source assures us that the man is, in fact, deceased.

SHEENA FAVROSIAN: Funeral arrangements?

ALEX PARKER: As unclear as the cause of death…or exactly why his Testosterone Balancing Powder was banana flavored.

9

Maybe, Baby

The last date I'd gone on had been seventeen months ago, and I'd spent most of it helping the guy pick out clothes for another date later in the week. With someone else. Thanks to Reddit, I learned this circumstance was not wholly uncommon. In a way, I was disappointed we didn't work out. The guy'd read all of Dostoyevsky and had a nice head of hair. On the other hand, I was inspired to splurge on a new pair of shoes.

Before Kyle met me outside my apartment at seven PM, the Monday evening after I'd had my corneal abrasion diagnosed by a former fellow Committee kid who I now suspected of, at the very least, potential manslaughter, I checked various dating subreddits for the frequency in which daters showed up sporting an eye patch. My students had loved it earlier in the day. I'd gone with an adjustable padded number from Walgreens, black as was piratical tradition, to

Cult & Run

please them.

Once again, I was surprised. According to Reddit, the eye patch was a look that ranked just below dressing in anything fancier than sweatpants while dining at Burger King.

Although an eye patch was a far cry from showing up in a wedding dress for a first date, an event with an entire subreddit of its own, I kept my face toward the door of my apartment building as I pulled it shut behind me. Going out with a cop could be a wrong move. For many reasons. The least of which may be his skill with a pair of handcuffs. Some women would call that a perk. I called it a pipe dream. Bondage did little for me unless it involved mending split ends.

What did I even know about *Kyle* to begin with? I was helping an FBI agent puzzle out who'd threatened the life of my former cult leader, whose death I'd begun to assign to a particular suspect. A suspect who spelled my last name wrong on my prescription, which I couldn't help but think had been on purpose.

If I happened to fall down my front staircase, I wondered if Kyle would mind me skipping our date. But I'd never do such a thing, not that night of all nights. Walker Wilkes was being laid to rest with my mother in attendance and me, conveniently sick at home, not.

"I like your shoes," Kyle said. I brushed some hair over my eye while taking the steps slowly, and, all the while, wishing for a nice pair of side bangs to distract from the small patch of black fabric obscuring my face. I had good eyelashes, too. It was all very unfair. "Whoa! What happened to you?"

Kyle helped me down the bottom two steps, holding onto my arm like I was a child. I knew, because I held onto the arms of children all day long. He didn't have to baby me. "I'm fine," I told him. "Small set-back in an otherwise illustrious career as a champion *Where's Waldo?* finder."

73

Kyle's mouth did a little downed-turn thing. I liked it. I hated it. "It doesn't look like nothing," he said.

"I was attacked by my most intimate companion," I told him. His face froze up in a look of shock turned anger. "*The New Yorker*! The magazine!"

Kyle's jaw unclenched a bit, but he didn't smile. "You have a funny way of saying things, Dalmatia."

"It's my accent, isn't it?"

I got a grin this time.

"I thought we'd walk over to the vegan place on Hill Street. It's not that steep." Kyle glanced down at the chunky-heeled suede mules I'd paired with a navy-blue dress. "And the tofu is crisp."

"I'm not sure—"

"Oh!" Kyle reached into the pocket of his jeans — no joggers — and pulled out a wallet and keys. "Would you mind holding all this? I get a bit winded climbing in these shoes."

I stared at him a moment, a Botox-sticky look of shock, before dropping my eyes to his feet.

"Jordan Fives," Kyle said. "The soles aren't as thick as they look."

It'd take less than three seconds for me to turn myself around, slam the door in the face of this chauvinistic weirdo, and eat the weight of my disgust in freezer foods.

Kyle began to laugh. "I'm kidding!" He stepped closer and gently grasped my shoulder. "Dalmatia, it's a joke. A very bad joke because I'm nervous as hell, but I'd never take you to a vegan restaurant or make you hike in those...what kind of shoes are they? They're nice."

Kyle's light touch was almost as distracting as realizing I'd been played by a man with a gummy bear key chain. "Mules. My shoes are mules. And so long as you never mention tofu again, I guess we're good," I said, not sure if I liked Kyle's easy way of teasing me.

"I'm glad you're not mad," he answered. The hand on my shoulder fell back to his side. "I really was — *am* — kind of nervous."

He'd said as much, hadn't he? Nervous. To take me out. An FBI agent at that.

"I was thinking of Benny's downtown," Kyle suggested.

"I love that place."

Whatever bits of awkwardness had clung to either of us fell away. Kyle nodded with a smile bigger than my high jump back up the stairs would've been. He held open the passenger door of his Jeep, and I slid inside. It was clean. And ocean scented.

The ten-minute drive to Benny's was filled with amiable conversation about exactly how I'd become a victim of Condé Nast. A familiar green-and-white striped awning came into view before I had a chance to mention Jenna Shears or Walker Wilkes' funeral, which was going on at that moment.

Sitting tight as Kyle parallel parked in the perfect spot right outside the little French place, I wondered how smart it'd be of me to tell him about either. Not only was Kyle investigating the death threats made to Wilkes, but he'd been asking a lot more questions than actually sharing what he knew. I'd inquired whether the FBI had any leads and was met with a joke about escargot. I had a funny feeling in my stomach, and it was not entirely due to how unexpectedly attractive I found this version of Kyle, all cleaned up and nervous. Why did the investigation need a preschool teacher's help anyway?

I knew the reason, of course. I'd been brought up in The Committee. I had slight access to its current goings-on thanks to my mother and a wealth of background knowledge thanks to my past. What I didn't have were crime fighting credentials or costuming — capes were a faux pas — and Kyle didn't truly know me well enough to believe anything I told him.

We moved out of the waning daylight and into the dimly lit, mahogany-rich, cheese-and-bread scented interior of Benny's. It made me feel a little drunk. The fragrance of it all, the candlelight, Kyle's hand on the small of my back, lingering.

I'd keep the bit about Jenna to myself for the time being, but I'd attempt to suss out any connections to the former neighbor who had reentered my life with most ironic timing.

All while eating my weight in fresh-buttered baguette, of course.

10

Ranch

It's easy to want a date to go well. It's harder to want it to go bad.

And so it seemed I was pushing a boulder up a hill.

I didn't want to loathe my time spent with Kyle. I truly did not. Benny's was beautiful, and I ordered a dish that looked as if it'd been painted onto the plate. Too pretty to eat, too aromatic not. It was a roast chicken type situation. I did drip a bit of savory grease onto the front of my dress, but the eye patch was a distraction and so it was fine.

The conversation was pleasant. Kyle told me more about his son, Luke, and how they were building an entire kingdom for Luke's pet hamsters, Bug and Face.

"Bug and Face?" I asked.

"Not their original names." Kyle wiped his mouth with a napkin. I liked how he did it, leaning back in his chair afterward, sitting taller, settling in to tell me a story. He had a lot of stories, this guy. And that was good. I wouldn't have to tell so many of my own. "Luke started with one hamster." Kyle held a finger before him. "Bug Face."

"Definitely the only kid in class with that name," I replied.

Kyle nodded. "Exactly. None of that Bug Face A., Bug Face G., Bug Face Z. business."

"I was Dalmatia S. for years. I get it."

Kyle paused, surprised.

I smiled. A more socially confident woman would've winked, having made a man stumble over a joke, but I was not a socially confident woman. And I was cosplaying Cap'n Crunch.

"Touché, Miss Scissors."

"You speak French now!"

Kyle gestured to the space around us. "When in France…"

I lifted my glass in acknowledgement and sipped my Perrier with lime. "I believe we were talking about the commonality of the name Bug Face in the rodent educational system."

"I hear it's brutal. Like being stuck on a hamster wheel."

"Touché yourself."

Kyle sipped his own drink, a red wine I would not share. I liked Kyle, and I did sort of trust him, but I wasn't going to get too comfy with a man who'd broken into my car and career-splained his way out of it.

"Bug Face was Luke's first hamster, and then his mom bought him a second for her house. Turns out Marissa is allergic to the stuff they put in the cages. The shredded-up egg cartons. Her animal sanctuary doesn't work with small mammals, so she couldn't have known."

"Uh-huh."

"That's how both Luke's hamsters ended up living at my house. He'd named the second Krispy Kreme, but 'she' turned out to be a 'he', and so that name was nixed." Kyle pulled a finger across his neck.

"Yikes," I answered, making the sign of the cross.

Kyle's jaw dropped a bit, the fate of Krispy Kreme's name forgotten. "You know how to do that?"

"The sign of the cross?" I asked.

"Yes, I just…where'd you learn it?" Kyle waved a hand before himself. "I'm sorry. That's rude of me."

I could've told him the truth: I'd researched Catholicism after turning eighteen, having known The Committee wasn't for me. Buddhist retreat centers, birth chart readings, Daoism. I could've told him how I'd tried it all. I didn't want to get too close, and yet I unable to lie my way through his question. "Books," I told Kyle. "Documentaries, too."

"About cults?" he asked, seeming genuinely curious.

"Not exactly." The bubbles in my glass continued to pop. It really was a very high-quality seltzer. "I do read and watch a lot of things about cults. Puzzling out what made The Committee tick, not just Walker Wilkes but all of us involved — why families joined up, why they stayed, how it affected them — is part of it. But it's more than that." I watched the ice bobbing within my drink. "I always wonder if I would've been the same no matter how I was raised. No matter where. Or in what."

Kyle was quiet. I was afraid I'd said too much, exposing my own unintelligence, stunted by the environment I'd grown up in. I was scared he'd see me as someone hiding under a rock, clinging to a past she claimed to hate. And hate it I did. It was a strange thing then that a part of me wanted to protect it.

Kyle looked into my eyes, and I braced myself for the disappointment that'd follow what he really thought of me. "Dal," he said. "I'm sorry. I'm sorry you grew up with people who didn't know how amazing you are."

"Um, thank you," I replied. Not what I'd expected. Kyle's response was even more surprising than discovering that the name Krispy Kreme wasn't gender neutral.

Kyle cleared his throat. "I wish…"

"It's okay," I said, waving him off. "I was fine. I *am* fine. I know how to work an air fryer and occasionally pay my taxes on time." I laughed. Kyle did not. "Joking, of course. Do you have ties to the IRS?"

"I'm sorry I wasn't here to get you out of the Committee."

I laughed again, trying to peer pressure his face into mirth, lightness, anything but the look of guilt it wore now. His eyes were two big saucers full of soupy gravy. I did not like mashed potatoes, and I did not like being called on to react to emotions I had absolutely no idea how to hold.

"Face," I said instead. "What's up with the Face part?"

Kyle gathered himself back into something quite close to a look of composure. "It became the name of the second hamster," he answered.

I wanted to shake the darkness from his eyes, like sending back an over-peppered carbonara. But we weren't in an Italian restaurant, so bad analogy; it was a French one, and a very stuffy French one at that. I looked around us, noticing that the tapered candles, carved wooden chairs, tapestries and textiles were a heavy weighted blanket over what should be an easygoing night. First dates weren't meant to be roundtable discussions on childhood trauma.

"Where does Luke like to eat?" I asked.

Kyle hadn't expected that. If I'd wanted to flip a switch on his mood, I'd run my hand along the right wall.

"McDonald's," he said.

I glanced down at half a chicken that looked as if it'd been working with a Thighmaster and realized I really was very angry about that grease drip after all. "I left a cauliflower pizza on my coffee table for two days. Maybe three."

"Okay…"

"So, I'd like to stay true to my preservative-rich, sodium-laden diet. Let's get McDoubles."

"McDoubles?"

"Or nuggets. You can have nuggets if you want. I'm not a fan of the smell of barbecue sauce, but maybe you'll go with zesty buffalo to be a gentleman."

Kyle laid some bills on the table. A man who carried cash. Not the norm. He stood and gestured for me to join him. "I actually prefer ranch."

"Then ranch it is," I answered with a smile and my hand.

And ranch it was.

Better conversation, too. We discussed other pets Luke planned to have, namely a dragon named Fort Knox, for reasons Kyle explained quite sensibly. He spoke a bit about Marissa. They'd met when he'd lived out of state, and she'd been a transcendental meditation teacher while volunteering at the humane society. Family money, Kyle said. She'd come with that, and it'd been that which had come between them. Kyle didn't want a bankrolled life because a bankrolled life meant trying to please the one writing the checks. Marissa hadn't seen it that way. What else had she ever known? But to Kyle, the money was a cage, and he couldn't exist within its bars.

"Just so you know, I have pickle breath," I told him as we waited at the foot of the stairs up to my apartment. The McDonald's portion of our date had given way to an easiness that almost made me wonder what'd been in that Perrier. Kyle and I stood in the coolness of the night under a covering of stars that sparkled like pieces of shattered glass. A streetlamp not more than a few feet away had blown out.

81

Kyle was close enough that, even with one eye covered in itchy black polyester, I could see that he wanted to kiss me.

I wouldn't have objected, so I had no idea why I'd made the pickle comment to distract him.

Kyle glanced toward the front door of my walk-up and then back at me. "I've never smelled a pickle," he said.

"Well, if you get any closer, you will."

Again, it was lost on me why I was saying these things.

"Dal, are you maybe…"

I stepped closer. Instead of looking at me, Kyle's eyes flicked to the street-facing windows of my place on the second floor.

"Maybe what?" I asked. His hands found my waist, and I relaxed into Kyle's touch.

"…having company?"

"Wait, huh?" I spun to face the top floor of the building. My apartment was lit up. "Someone's in there!"

"Wait here," Kyle said.

I did. I waited for him to get his FBI-issued weapon from the Jeep, call in the SWAT team, toss a Batman grappling hook up toward my windowsill to get there quicker. Instead, Kyle asked for my keys. I handed them over, and he moved me further toward the burnt-out streetlamp. Neither a mask nor a theme song made an appearance.

And yet something did appear.

A person.

A shape moved past my windows, the row that provided the lovely view of Cormoran I'd come to appreciate so much. I counted the seconds as Kyle entered the building, leaving the door to the street ajar in his wake. It was silent where I stood on the sidewalk, headlights and taillights just missing where I remained in the shadows. The silhouette of Kyle's body moved into view within the

82

window closest to my front door. A small table stood before it, and I could see the spiny leaves of my snake plant pointing up his way.

"Dal?"

The sound of a gait I recognized, along with a voice I did, too, closed in from behind. I turned in time to see Aashri approaching with a puzzled look. It began to rain. The weather report had called for nothing but a few passing clouds.

"This weather's attitude problem is worse than Pandie's today." Aashri lifted her gym bag over her head like an umbrella. "The gym lot was packed, so I had to park at the garage at the end of your street. Are you okay?" Aashri looked from my feet to my face, doing the same from the front door of my apartment building up to the windows I called mine. "What are you doing?" she asked.

Aashri. Kyle. The intruder in my apartment. It was all too much. Too confusing. Too many directions to move my eyes. "I'm...Kyle's...there was someone..."

"Dal? What's going on?" Aashri had taken my hand, and I realized then that she was shaking. No, not her. Me. I was shaking.

"There's someone in my apartment," I said.

We both looked up toward my home.

A second later, it went dark.

83

11

Now Booking

Retirement Parties

"Benny the Bull is in your window."

Aashri said those words like they made sense. I stared at her. "Excuse me?"

She pointed toward my top floor apartment, and my eyes followed. "There. Benny the Bull."

My window was now completely dark. I was more concerned about Kyle and the sudden lack of lighting. "Benny the Bull is a 'Dora the Explorer' character. Kind of rude, too."

"No," Aashri answered, gaze still stuck to windows as dark as the evening around us. "The Bulls mascot."

"Chicago?"

Aashri stabbed her finger up into the night. "Right there!"

I saw it, too. A flickering deep within my apartment as if a candle had been lit or an oil diffuser was on the fritz. Had I left my curling wand plugged in? No, of course not. I smoothed down my limp hair, searching for what I'd seen a moment before: two curvy white horns above a flash of red and black. Sure, it could've been an NBA mascot, which I knew could be booked for private events. But I wasn't throwing a lame retirement party in my tiny apartment, so I doubted it.

"I'm going in," I said.

Aashri grabbed the back of my arm as I took the first step. "Wait for Hot Cop to come out. Let him do his thing."

"Don't call him Hot Cop," I told her. Aashri looked as if she'd seen a ghost. The ghost of Chicago's Jordan-helmed early-nineties three-peat. "Are you okay?"

"I'm okay," she said. "Just be smart and wait here."

I would've argued, but Kyle emerged a second later from the front door of my building. "You ladies will want to see this," he said to the two of us. If Aashri's presence was a surprise, Kyle was too focused on the job at hand to register it.

Aashri turned my way. "That's Hot Cop?" she asked with absolutely zero chill.

Apparently, you could suffer a sunburn at night, or at least that's how it felt with Aashri's claws in my arm and her question a hundred decibels too loud.

"You're calling me Hot Cop?" Kyle asked as I ran up the stairs and barreled past him into the vestibule. I ignored the lopsided smirk, which I found completely unprofessional in a situation like this. "It's empty," Kyle said, FBI tone melting some of my unease. "But be careful where you step."

I hoped I wouldn't find a horse held in the doorway. My

apartment was wall-to-wall carpeting circa Y2K. Not even a crime scene would get my landlord to replace it.

When I walked inside, it wasn't "The Godfather" that came to mind.

Aashri entered behind me. "I'm gonna pass out," she said, fanning her face as Kyle stepped past her. "This is worse than you burning ten of those soy candles at a time."

"They're $7.99 each. I can afford it."

Comeback aside, I lacked the ability to speak about what waited before me. It wasn't a Francis Ford Coppola film that I'd walked into. It was *The Secret Garden* if the children's classic had become a horror movie. Flowers overflowed from atop my coffee table. Three dozen, no, four dozen, five. A shit ton of flowers. The whole surface was covered, my carefully curated aesthetic drowning in a homecoming float's worth of botanicals.

"What else was there?" I asked Kyle, knowing instantly what this was. His gaze was as sober as mine.

"It's like a damn wedding!" Aashri cried.

"No," I said. "It's like a funeral."

Although considered a symbol of purity, *Lilium Longiflorum* is rooted in the misogyny of Western mythology. Zeus, king of the gods, sired his famed son Hercules with a human woman and desired his wife

Hera to play wet nurse to the babe. Only the very best for his bundle of joy. Hera refused and, being that he was a total creep, Zeus laid Hercules at her breast as she slept. These days it's blocking dick pics, and in Ancient Rome it was closed eyelids, but the silence of a woman minding her own business will always cause a man to try harder.

Hera shoved Hercules away from her body.

Breastmilk dripped to the earth.

The first lilies rose, ambrosia-white, from the spot.

For a long time, I'd hated that story. It's not like Mrs. Shears' homeschool group had been educated with any sort of worldview other than Walker Wilkes', but the little mythology to which I'd been exposed had made me angry. Women born from men, women fighting over men, men dragging their phalluses over the earth like a harvester's scythe. No, thank you. I wanted none of it. Instead, I focused on facts: historical documents, verified sources, eyewitness accounts. At times even science seemed suspect. My vantage point was surface-level, and I did not regret it one bit.

And so I knew the scientific names of things and the histories of others. Names, dates, patents, aliases, former S-corp affiliations. As Aashri knew, I read a lot. From best-sellers to Reddit threads, I parsed my knowledge into separate categories while pushing toward a single end: truth. I'd been denied it as a child, but never would be again.

Aashri's voice found me in the present. "Dal, what is this?"

From the other side of the coffee table, standing tall before tall flowers, Kyle watched us.

Benny the Bull was somewhere else, not here, most likely in the form of a college kid slipping on his costume in the bathroom of a Ramada Inn with thirty minutes till game time. I didn't know enough about the NBA to be sure how mascot life worked, but a human in a bull costume was not in my apartment. White lilies, petals fastened tight, yet to bloom, rose tall enough to be visible from my windows. What I'd erroneously believed to be horns were really two fresh stems topped with milky-white buds of *Liliaceae*. The neon glow of the Cormoran Theater marquee reflected off my windows, red and black in the night.

"I'd tripped on the cord of your lamp coming in," Kyle said. "I plugged it back in." His face wore a disjointed expression that my heart read before my brain. "I didn't see him," Kyle continued.

"But he left this with the flowers. I wouldn't have read it if I'd known, but I thought…"

"What did it say?" I asked, holding more tightly to Aashri's hand. My good eye watched Kyle, while the other teared up behind cold polyester.

Kyle looked as if he was debating asking me to sit down. The guy didn't know me very well, but he knew enough not to do something as patronizing as that. He also didn't ask if I wanted to read the letter myself. I knew what it was and who it was from.

I felt a thousand things at once. All of them bad.

And then I felt another.

"It's not anything like—" As quickly as the idea formed, the words I'd given it tangled on my tongue.

"No," Kyle answered. Aashri let me go and crossed to my kitchen. The tap ran a second later, and I knew what she was up to. Comfort coffee, decaf. "It's not like the threats made to Wilkes."

The *beep, beep, beep* of my coffee maker cut through my thoughts, and my adrenaline drained into a wet puddle in my shoes. Aashri opened and shut cabinets, and I sank into my couch. Kyle stood, contemplating where to go. He took a seat in a chair but was obscured by the ridiculous number of floral arrangements dwarfing my coffee table. I moved aside, and he joined me on the sofa. The letter from James was a boundary between us, set atop the crack

Cult & Run

between two cushions.

Promises and willpower usually ended up giving way to habit. I read the letter.

"He was in your house," Kyle said. "But no one broke in. At least, not that I could tell." His eyes asked a question I didn't want to answer.

"He wouldn't need to break in." I kept my eyes on the letter, a few scribbled lines on the back of some advertisement James had probably grabbed from wherever he'd been staying while in Cormoran for his father's funeral. These were Walker's flowers, ones my mother would've arranged for the occasion of his burial. "He had a key," I told Kyle. "He was…my…"

"He was a pain in her ass for three years." Aashri lifted the largest two arrangements from the center of the table and laid a wooden serving board in their place. "All I could find," she said. Some Babybel cheeses, a handful of pepperonis, and an opened bag of Pepperidge Farm cookies formed the saddest charcuterie board in the world. I loved Aashri for trying to make me feel better. "And that's me speaking kindly," Aashri continued.

She removed the rest of the flowers, setting them on the floor behind the coffee table. In addition to the lilies, I now owned a small garden's worth of roses, zinnias, tulips, that white nonsense they stuff into bridal bouquets, and a few other varieties of blooms that James left in my apartment with the key he'd never returned.

Kyle waited for more of an explanation, but I didn't know where to start.

Instead, he read the letter aloud, voice gentle but firm. "Dalmatia, it's been a long time. Maybe too long. I don't know anymore. I'm back, and I'd like to see you. Don't let anyone tell you these are from my father's service — wink emoji, hand-drawn. Signed James." Kyle set the letter on the newly cleared table. "He's Wilkes' son."

89

"We were on and off," I said. "For three years. That's what Aashri meant."

She popped a slice of pepperoni in her mouth. "I meant he was an asshole, but that, too."

"He wants to see you again." Kyle had turned his knees my way, body facing me like a cop even though his voice sounded like a boyfriend. He wasn't a boyfriend. He was barely a date. James had been barely a boyfriend but usually a date. I hated everything.

"He said he does. But I don't know. It ended bad."

Aashri disappeared back into the kitchen. My coffee maker gurgled.

Kyle hesitated. "Dalmatia, I think I should go."

His proclamation was a gut-punch. Aashri re-entered the living room with a mug in each hand, steam wafting above an ordinary blue one from my alma mater and another shaped like a porcupine. "Pork You" was etched across its belly.

"Yeah, okay," I said, rising. Kyle stood, too. We looked at each other, both wanting to say something or hear something but neither quite sure what that should be. "Thanks for tonight."

Kyle's shoulders sagged. He stepped toward me but kept his hands to himself. I'd wanted his touch again, but I also suddenly wanted a quiet, empty apartment, as well. "Dal, I had a good time tonight. I'm not leaving because of you. It's work." He looked over at the jungle spread out across my rug. "This has become work."

"Let me know if I can help," I said in a voice much quieter than I would've liked.

"Why don't you get some rest," Kyle replied.

I waited for an "I'll call you" or a second attempt at a kiss goodnight. Not likely with Aashri the Nosey Barista right behind us. Kyle could've chosen to end our date as a man instead of an FBI agent, but he didn't. Because that's what he was destined to be to me: a cop. A cop who was now suspicious of my involvement with The Committee. I'd claimed to have been over it, hated it, moved on from it but had just acknowledged that I'd dated the eldest son of Walker Wilkes for a third of a decade. It'd also become government knowledge that James Wilkes was comfortable entering my apartment when I wasn't home and leaving five hundred dollars' worth of flowers in his wake.

Good thing I hadn't mentioned Jenna Shears.

After Kyle let himself out, I took a mug from Aashri, my thumb sliding over the porcupine's ceramic quills. "You know what we need to do, right?" I asked her.

"Try Tinder?"

"Solve the Walker Wilkes' death threat case for ourselves."

Aashri flapped a hand in the air. "Oh, that." She smiled. "Good thing you hadn't mentioned Jenna," she said, knowing all too well my thoughts about her possible involvement. "And good thing Hot Cop didn't see this."

Aashri waggled a grimy old photo of James and I in my face. I'd forgotten it even existed, probably fallen beneath my fridge years ago only to be unearthed with quite serendipitous timing by the last person whose opinion I needed to hear right now.

"I know I'm the last person on earth whose opinion you need to hear right now," Aashri said, "but maybe you should think about putting the trash out tonight, hmm?"

I ripped the picture from her fingers and tore it in half right through James' face.

Too bad his stupid grin had long ago been committed to memory.

12

Click, Click, Boom

After the chaos of the night before, I had a more than a few questions. Not to mention shock, no awe, and plenty of disappointment.

How long had James been back in Cormoran?

And how the hell had it coincided with Jenna's homecoming?

Had either attended Wilkes' funeral?

Should I have my locks changed?

Of course, I should have my locks changed. I did that the following day after work. Kyle hadn't called or texted. Not that I'd expected him to, but I had kept my phone close during the school day like the sucker I was. James hadn't contacted me either. He also hadn't left a number with his note unless he happened to be squatting at DeLongo's Pool and Spa.

I may not have been able to count on Kyle for the answers I needed, but that was fine.

Cult & Run

I had another option.

"James Wilkes? He wasn't at his father's service," my mother said. She ran a dust cloth over a framed photo of Walker that'd been hung beside the front door in the foyer of my parents' home. After the locksmith left my place, overpriced service completed, I headed to my parents' house.

"Wasn't my college graduation picture in that frame? And in this spot?" I asked, scratching at the place where the eye patch had been. The antibiotic Jenna prescribed had done the trick.

My mother continued to shine Walker's graven image. "Was it?"

"Mom, I need to know if you've seen James. He left me flowers. *A lot* of flowers."

That got her attention. "Dalmatia!" My mother's eyes brightened. She didn't know he'd stolen them nor from where. "Do you think this means what I think it means?"

"What you hope it means? No, I do not. I think he's a bastard who wants attention. As usual." My father ran a weed-whacker out back. I heard it catch on one of my mother's many ceramic forest creatures. "Dad decapitated the beaver," I said.

My mother shuddered. "You're so gruesome!"

Rich words for a woman who worshipped a dead guy.

"Have you seen James? At all?"

"No," she answered, turning her attention back to Walker. "But if you see him, tell him I say hello and it'd be lovely to have him to the house."

"And what you think he'll say when he sees the shrine you've made to his father?"

The glass in the frame was shiny enough to catch my mother's eyes roll in her reflection. "It's a single photo of a man I dearly love, Dalmatia. Stop making everything something that it's not."

Sure, it was *me* getting this all wrong. I marched away from my mother, through the house, past all the dust she wouldn't bother tending to because none of it obscured the visage of Walker Wilkes. Instead, I went out into the backyard, where my father was shutting the shed door on his yard care gear. "Hey Dad," I said. "Mom's gone insane."

My father smiled and shook his head. He looked a little sad. He looked a little older. "Your mother's a goose," he replied. "Always has been."

"You know about her and Walker, right? What she did?"

He pushed the padlock shut on the shed door. "She's grieving."

"She's bound herself to a dead man while married to a living one. No offense."

Wiping his hands on the front of his jeans, my father shrugged. "It's religion."

"Religion is giving up swearing for Lent. It's not tossing a forty-year marriage out the window in the hope that your afterlife includes a community gym and Mahjong club." I followed him back into the house, passing the ceramic beaver whose head was indeed missing an ear.

"Your mother didn't toss anything out, Dallie," my father said.

"So, you're okay with this? There must've been a ceremony, Dad. I know Mom. She's over the top. She makes scrapbooks for everything. Right now, in this house is a napkin bearing Walker Wilkes' spit sandwiched between sheets of vellum paper." I fiddled with my hands and ignored my need to push more horrid thoughts into my father's brain. He had to understand the gravity of what my mother had done.

My dad and I stood together in my parents' kitchen, where I had sat at our little round dining table, eating the Lucky Charms cereal my father had snuck me on my thirteenth birthday because my mother had purged all sugar from our house. We'd sat in the faint glow of a gathering dawn, picking colorful marshmallows from between bland bits of cereal, loading our spoons with the good stuff. My mother had woken a few minutes after we'd started on our third bowls, speed-walking through the kitchen to grab a pre-made Walker Wilkes smoothie from the fridge before a Committee book club meeting that morning. No happy birthday. No notice of the rest of her family giving into the gluttony of simple carbohydrates while she prepared to prostitute her mind before a charlatan who claimed to have discovered turmeric.

Turmeric had been around for over four thousand years.

And it originated in India, not Bywood County, Pennsylvania.

"Dad, are you really okay with all this?" I asked, leaning against the counter. A few feet away, my father pulled open the fridge and took a swig of something dark brown and grainy. The glass jug had been washed upwards of a hundred times and yet nothing could remove the discoloration from the variety of elixirs it'd been filled with over the years. Tonics designed to calm the colon, boost the mood, lower the cortisol, and clean out the bank account. "Dad?" I asked again.

When my father looked at me, holding the half-full jug in front of his belly, I could've sworn he was a stranger. "Would you mind running some of your mother's things for The Barbara Gala over to the Wilkes' house?" he asked. If his expression was blank, it would've been better. The man I knew, the one who'd covertly fed me sugar on my birthday, stared with apathy. "She's mourning right now, so it'd be a kindly help."

"A kindly help?"

"A kindly help."

If it meant figuring out what the hell was happening to everybody, I'd play the game. I wanted to call Kyle and tell him where I was headed. He'd like checking out the Wilkes house. I wasn't sure how being an FBI agent worked and if he had access to the place or not. It would've been smart to have asked him. "Do you have a key?" I asked my dad instead.

He pulled it from a hidden spot beneath a butter dish shaped like a cow. I absorbed his instructions about what boxes to remove from my mother's storage room and began loading up my car. Kyle and I had been in that space not so many days ago, and it felt odd now to be in it once again alone. I pulled my cell into my hand, fingers tapping out a text to Kyle only to delete it.

I called Aashri instead.

"Hey," I said into her messages. Aashri didn't allow calls to go straight to voicemail, except while at work or the gym. She was there when I called. "Get back to me when you have a chance. I'm headed to Wilkes' house and torn between burning it down and selling his medicine cabinet on eBay."

I ended the call and turned to wave at my father, but he wasn't watching from his usual spot in the bay window at the front of the house. It was fine. I was fine. I'd drop off the boxes for him. For my misguided, brainwashed mother, too.

And I would continue hating Walker Wilkes' the entire way.

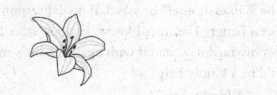

The Wilkes house wasn't a house as much as a headquarters. The outside was bare, never decorated for holidays or seasons. Immaculately

landscaped and well-maintained but with zero personality. My parents' home was a riot of decorations and garden shrubs, including a few ornamental varieties that shouldn't have survived outside of Southeastern Asia. Wilkes' place, on the other hand, looked as if someone had sterilized it.

I pulled into the rainbow driveway, an eccentric characteristic of a property so plain, and parked before the front walkway. A carport beside the house covered a white Land Rover. I paused. What sort of car had Wilkes drove? He'd had a steady stream of chauffeurs, including, but not limited to, athletes from the local high school whose parents were members of The Committee. Not everyone homeschooled their children. Only the lucky ones. The fortunate ones. The *devoted* ones.

I put my BMW in park, wishing I hadn't brought it. My dad's old truck would've been a smarter choice. He'd probably call me to make a second trip anyway, and I'd have to go back. At least then my dad would be speaking to me. I wasn't sure what I'd done wrong, but it felt like he'd backed away from an invisible boundary we'd drawn together against the nonsense of The Committee.

"Thought is action in rehearsal," I said to myself, popping the trunk. Walker Wilkes self-published a whole book based on the famous quote by Sigmund Freud. His own spin involved eight core principles of manifesting. "Health is wealth, and your body is your temple," I continued.

Creativity wasn't Wilkes' wheelhouse.

"I should've dumped these behind K-Mart," I told no one as I leaned over the short stack of stairs before Wilkes' former home and pushed the heavy Rubbermaid bins onto the porch.

"I think that's an IHOP now," said a disembodied voice at my back. Two arms, not my own, pulled the final bin from inside my trunk. I slammed it shut, narrowly missing the lip of the lid and the knuckles of hands whose flesh I had sworn never to touch again.

The devil be damned.

James Wilkes grinned my way.

If the container he held hadn't been filled with forty pounds of synthetic hair, I would've smacked it to the ground. "Did you like the flowers?" he asked.

What's the appropriate answer to give to an on-again-off-again ex who'd ghosted you for three years? I was surprised James even recognized me. The only face he'd ever cared about had been his own.

"Fuck you, James," I said, stalking up the porch steps.

James followed. "All it takes is flowers? No dinner? You've lowered your standards, Dalmatia, but sure."

As I readied Wilkes' spare key to enter the house, I wondered how quickly I could open the door and slam it in James' face. It didn't matter. The front door of the Wilkes place was ajar. "Where'd you come from?" I asked James, stepping inside. The foyer was as sparse as I remembered, deer heads lining the staircase to the second story and little else.

"Tinseltown."

"From in the house, I mean." Something was off. I moved my eyes over the space, trying to figure out what it could be. "Is it usually unlocked?"

James didn't answer. The front door slid shut at my back, and the hairs on my arms screamed toward the ceiling. I flicked a light switch up and down, but the house remained cloaked in afternoon shadow. Was it that? The utilities had been turned off? The place felt like a tomb, but a tomb in the middle of a raid. Could the something-wrong within the Wilkes house simply be my presence?

A clicking noise further down the hall stole a bit of my focus but not enough keep me distracted. I decided to help myself out in that department, looking anywhere but at James. Wilkes' home wasn't entirely untraditional except for Walker Wilkes' refusal to furnish it with anything homey or comfortable. It would've been a fine family property if described in an MLS listing. I moved down the hallway past the dead eyes of unfortunate deer. The kitchen opened up, gleaming and empty. The fridge hummed, so the electricity hadn't been cut.

"Were you in here when I pulled up?" I asked James.

"No," he replied, coming into view at my side. He looked much the same as he had three years ago. Handsome, which I hated. Floppy hair, falling perfectly around his face. And tall. I'd once found his height intoxicating but now gauged how quickly I could run away if I had to. Three years in a relationship; three years out. I didn't know why the math mattered. It shouldn't. He shouldn't. He *didn't*.

"Where were you?" I asked again, stepping into the family room. A *click, click, click* sounded from the half-bath on the other side of the wall with the flat-screen TV. I noticed it'd been unplugged. So had the floor lamp beside it. "Don't say Tinseltown again."

"I wasn't going to." James' face cinched tight.

I followed the sound to the bathroom, James gently attempting to push me aside and enter first. He'd forfeited the right to ensure my welfare back when he cut communication. I bumped the door open with my hip and got in front, tripping over the fluffy rug covering the center of the itty-bitty space. Walker may have been shit at making a home feel like a home, but he'd apparently treated this bathroom like a penthouse suite. Seasonal candles, long since burned down. Lotions with coordinating antibacterial soaps. Faux flowers, dusty with inattention. The whole thing mauve and taupe. The color of disillusionment.

James shouldered past me and lifted the toilet seat, fuzzy brown-pink-beige lid cover and all.

"Let me give you some privacy," I said to him, making sure the guy couldn't miss the sarcasm.

He set the lid down and raised the top of the water tank instead. I quickly grabbed a vase of faux mums before they landed in the trashcan.

"What are you doing?" I asked.

"The noise," James answered. "It's coming from in here."

"I know," I said, acknowledging to myself that the clicking had grown louder. It was rhythmic, and it was timed. "But I don't think someone hid a Rolex in the can."

James opened the cabinet above the toilet and pushed rolls of Cottonelle here and there, finding nothing. I backed out of the bathroom and examined the unplugged television set. Several more lamps and a wireless router were similarly untethered. Walker Wilkes' gigantic aquarium was empty of all water and sea life, its fluorescent lighting gone dark.

"Dal, get out! Now!" James shoved me across the living room. I made eye contact with the Bambi at the end of the line as he ripped me down the hallway, a button on my shirt coming away in his hands. "Go!" The front porch met my knees as James sent me flying out the front door, pulling it shut as the sound of a combusting car engine rocked my head.

"My baby!" I cried, fixing my eyes on my M4. But it was as pristine as if just driven off the lot.

James scooped me into him, and we booked it to the driver's side of my car as if I could've ever used my most beloved possession as a shield. James commanded me to stay where I was and ran back inside. Every cell in my body yelled for me to hightail it out of there, but I couldn't. Running off was James' Wilkes thing, and I needed to know what was going on.

When James appeared on the porch a moment later, empty fire extinguisher in hand and a look of relief on his face, I was glad I'd

Cult & Run

stayed. Not only because I knew this situation had to be somehow connected to the death of his father but because James' beloved hair had been singed in the process.

"A fire," he said, voice a bit shaky. There was static in his eyes, like he couldn't believe it himself, and I felt it in my stomach — the need to bind him up.

"Where?" I asked. James came down the stairs toward me, and I met him beside the passenger door of my car. It felt a lot like the last time I'd seen him. Funny how I would've given anything back then to set his selfish ass ablaze, and now here he was, James Wilkes, standing before me looking like someone had finally crisped his bacon.

"In the refrigerator," James said. "We have to call 9-1-1."

"What do you mean in the refrigerator? We were just in the house!"

"This was behind a roll of toilet paper in the bathroom." James handed me a small black device.

"It's a doorbell cam." I met his eyes. "And it's wet."

"I dropped it in the toilet tank. By accident." James pushed his fingers through his hair. A few crinkly strands broke off in his hand.

"Okay," I said. He looked genuinely frightened. "I'll make the call. You just…" I winced at James' hairline before swiveling my eyes over toward the untouched Rubbermaids lined up on the porch. The ones filled with—

Oh, right.

James stalked to the Land Rover parked under the carport, unlocking it with his key fob as he went. "Fuck you, Dalmatia."

I smiled. Someone else's standards had dropped, too.

101

13

Ring Camaraderie

After James had gone, chaste mouth in tow, I made an executive decision.

I brought in the professionals.

Well, one.

I called Kyle.

Twenty minutes later a red Jeep pulled up behind my BMW. James took it as a cue to emerge from within his Land Rover. There must've been something in his glovebox to fix his hair, because James no longer looked like such an air-fried jerk. Later there'd be time to unpack my feelings about seeing him again, and I'd be lying if I didn't say almost being blown up didn't provide a semi-welcome distraction.

Kyle listened as I told him what'd happened at the Wilkes' house, and James waited a few feet behind, nodding in the wrong places and letting me do all the talking. For a guy who'd always liked to get the last word, his silence wasn't as satisfying as it would've been

102

Cult & Run

three years ago. He wasn't really listening to me anyway. He was sizing up Kyle.

Pulling in a deep breath, I finished my account, failing to seem as circumspect as I'd have liked. A refrigerator going up in flames twenty feet from where I stood on a highly flammable wooden surface was destabilizing enough. But having words with my ex and introducing him to a man I'd gone on a maybe-date with both took the cake.

If that cake was frosted with hot coals and baked in hell.

"Could I see the cam?" Kyle asked me.

"Hold on a second," James said. He'd been quiet long enough. Time for some personality.

Kyle extended a hand in James' direction. "Detective Kyle Alaric."

James shook it too hard. He was well-practiced at politeness, just not very good at it.

I held my breath, not yet ready for whatever may spill out between the three of us. I didn't know why I'd thought this was a good idea. Calling 9-1-1 would have been a *good* idea. Furthermore, if Kyle was investigating the death threats sent to Wilkes, then how come he hadn't already tracked down James? Obviously, they had not spoken.

"Last time we spoke, you didn't mention coming to Cormoran," James added.

I made a mental note to have my intuition tuned up.

"My investigation brought me this way, Mr. Wilkes." Kyle pulled a cell phone from the pocket of his jacket. He checked it quickly, tapped a few buttons on the screen, and slid it back in.

"Another case?" I asked.

Kyle stared straight at James. "Always," he answered.

James didn't blink. "What are you doing here, Detective?" James slipped between me and Kyle, transforming us into a triangle. It

103

wouldn't due for him to be left out. "Dalmatia, why didn't you call 9-1-1 like I told you to?"

"First of all," I said, whipping my finger his way. "You didn't tell me anything, Jimbo. You hid in your car until I called Kyle."

Anger was a beet-red hue on James' face. "Do not call me that."

I pressed a hand to my neck, fingers clutching invisible pearls. "What...Jimbo?"

James ignored me and ushered Kyle toward the porch steps. "Detective, would you like to see the house?"

"Yes, I would." Kyle moved his gaze slowly up James' forehead toward a crispy bit of hair.

I knew James' eyes well. Especially when filled with anger.

He hung back, letting Kyle enter the house first, and then turned before going inside himself, making sure I received the ire that Kyle had not.

I turned a wide smile toward James Wilkes' furious expression, hoping my sweetness was sickly enough to make him hurt. "Want me to come along?" I asked.

James slammed the door in my face.

I guessed not.

According to the Internet, doorbell camera security systems were more likely to turn users into neighborhood narcs than prevent randos from snatching deliveries off porches. Online message boards were filled with stories about homeowners using doorbell cams to spy on the families next door, power walkers, landscapers, their own teenage children. In some communities, HOAs have put a ban on the cams.

Others found new uses for this technology. In Arkansas, a group of thirteen-year-olds terrorized an elderly neighbor by hacking her doorbell camera to project inward, shouting obscenities into her Precious Moments' filled foyer. Unluckily for the youth, Mildred Anders' granddaughter was married to a tech-savvy woman who worked for Apple. A few days later, octogenarians everywhere had the last laugh when the teen hooligans attempted to buy soft pretzels for a bunch of girls at the junior high football game only to find that tapping Apple Pay turned their screens into a photo of Mildred in the buff. Legend had it she'd freshly manicured her middle finger.

The doorbell cam in Walker's house may not have been involved in anything quite so salacious, but, having been hidden in the half-bath of his home, which was obviously the case, made me wonder. There'd been no sign of the device installed beside the front door. James insisted he didn't have access to his father's accounts, which, if the cam had been Walker's, would've included cloud storage of its recordings.

Kyle, James, and I perched on the sterile white furniture in the Wilkes' living room, with Kyle on the couch, James on a Lay-Z Boy, and me on a rocking chair. The floor was beige tile. The walls were beige skim-coating. The lighting was daylight glow LED. I may as well have been stuck in the world's dullest chick incubator.

"Someone purposely started a fire," Kyle explained. "It was controlled, intentional."

"How is a fire controllable?" James asked, his measured voice at odds with the scowl worn from brow to bottom lip.

"All the electronics were unplugged except the fridge," I added.

Kyle leaned forward, elbows on knees. My stomach fluttered, seeing him deep in criminal investigation mode. I shifted backward in the rocking chair, trying to stifle the nuisance of unwanted physical attraction. The chair *thunked* into the wall, and I bit my tongue.

Kyle looked up. "Unplugging everything would make it seem like an accident."

"How can you tell?" James asked as I felt inside my mouth with a fingertip. "Dal, do you need to go wash your hands?"

I wanted so badly to pull a Mildred Anders. I was losing it.

"The entire house is unplugged, and every circuit breaker but the one connected to the refrigerator area of the kitchen is switched off," Kyle said. "That makes me think someone wanted to burn down the house and make it look like an accident."

I ricocheted forward in the rocking chair, smacking into the drywall once again. "Wait, burn down the house? What house, *this house?*"

"No, *that* house," James snapped. He stood and began to pace before the sliding glass doors that opened to the backyard. They'd been smeared with foam from the fire extinguisher as if James had wildly aimed it everywhere within sight of the refrigerator, which was now a blackened husk.

I ignored him. "How could someone burn down an entire house using the refrigerator?"

"The circuit breaker was taped," Kyle said. He watched James. James watched mourning doves settle on the concrete patio beyond. "Someone used duct tape to keep it in the ON position and then overloaded the fridge."

"How?"

"I'm guessing whoever taped the breaker compromised the refrigerator compressor. That'd cause the fuse to trip, but, since the breaker box had been tampered with, a fire could start at the electrical outlet."

"Which is what happened," I added.

"Exactly what happened," Kyle said.

James sighed. Loudly, dramatically. "My father should've replaced that thing a decade ago. And he'd been the one to tape the breaker, not some *arsonist.*" He looked right at Kyle as the word sliced from his mouth. "It was always tripping. Ask your mom, Dalmatia. I'm sure he complained to her about it."

"I'm not sure." I shrugged my shoulders at Kyle. "I can ask her, but—"

"He was cheap," James continued. He turned from the birds and the backyard and laid one hand against a pinewood bookcase filled with his father's work. "Dad had wanted everything unplugged after his death. He'd left instructions about the house, and that was one of the first things he'd asked for. 'Unplug everything. Cancel the newspaper. Rehome the koi fish.'"

I scrunched my face. "There are koi fish?"

James went on. "I left the fridge plugged in because I'm only human. I need to *eat.* I never thought I'd almost light myself on fire because my father couldn't upgrade his appliances more than once in a half-century."

I locked eyes with Kyle. I couldn't tell if he believed James' insistence about his father's neglect or thought something more nefarious had gone down. After all, this was the property of a cult leader. Not a family-friendly sitcom house.

But there was one variable I couldn't seem to place.

"What about the ring cam?" I asked. Either of the men in the room could've answered. Instead, they both looked at each other, and, for the second time in as many minutes, I couldn't read Kyle's face. "The ring cam in the bathroom. I have it." I pulled it from the

107

pocket of my skirt. "It'd fallen in the toilet."

Kyle's eyes widened.

"Not *that* part of the toilet. The tank. Have I ever given you the impression that I'm *not* a closet germaphobe?"

"You ate a fry off the table without a napkin, so I can't really say," Kyle answered. A small grin played at the corner of his mouth.

James frowned. "What fry?"

"The longest one in McDonald's history, and I'd abided by the One Minute Rule. It wasn't like I ate it off a public restroom toilet seat."

Kyle winced, but his eyes were bright. "Too much toilet talk."

"If you guys want to go hang out with the Charmin Giant, we can be done here." James stood and cracked his knuckles above his head.

"It's a bear. You're thinking of peas."

Kyle laughed. I did the same. It wasn't every day I delivered a clever pun.

James bent his arms behind his head and sighed again. I'd greatly appreciated those triceps once upon a time, but I'd never appreciated the way he could deflate me with a rumble of his vocal cords or the set of his face.

"Are you going to investigate?" I asked, handing Kyle the ring cam.

"I'll look into it." Kyle's eyes roamed the last known address of Walker Wilkes, absent of family photos, mementos, or any decor not previously breathing. Framed somethings had once hung on the wall behind the couch. Had they been moved years ago by Walker? Or had someone truly tried to set fire to this home, taking a few precious items with them before doing so? Only a couple people cared enough about Walker Wilkes to do something like that.

One had resumed pacing.

The other was my mother.

"The important thing is that no one was hurt," Kyle said, looking at me.

James' gaze toggled between the two of us. "It was good I was here then," he said. "With Dalmatia."

I certainly wasn't glad he'd been there. All I'd wanted to do was drop off a ton of hair and get home. I'd tossed James' flowers in the dumpster behind my building that morning, but the place still reeked of unwanted horticulture. I thought ahead to a long night of reading with the windows open and the added fragrance of burnt popcorn, hopefully a successful game plan to rid both my apartment and my psyche of his return.

"Wait," I said, pressing pause on my rush to away from James. "Why was the cam clicking?"

Kyle turned it over in his fingers. "The back-up batteries were still running. I'm guessing it was hidden in the bathroom for a reason. It's also covered in some crusty green stuff." Kyle scraped away a fleck that looked a lot like my bad attempt to blend kale. "I don't think it's too far out to assume that whoever started the fire wanted this to burn, as well as the house."

"According to who?" James asked. "You're not a fireman. You're not a CSI. You're disgracing the memory of a dead man by issuing that someone tried to burn his house down. You're going to publicly embarrass my father for being frugal!"

"I think you mean 'insinuating'," I said.

Kyle raised his eyebrows. "I'm eager to hear more about your take, James. And your father."

I stood up, no longer able to sit in a soup of contentious energy. "What do you think, Professor? Was it the revolver in the den or the candlestick in the ballroom?"

"Why don't you show me some identification, Detective?" James had his hands in his pockets, posed in that smug way I'd seen many times before. He'd stood the same on the night he'd told me he loved me. Much like my earlier bout of intuition, I had read him all wrong back then. "I don't think you've shown me your badge."

"Not a problem," Kyle said, rising from the couch.

James lifted a finger toward Kyle as if tying him up on a leash. "Let me get my phone first." He stomped past us, out of the house, and down the porch stairs, knocking into a Rubbermaid bin full of Rachels my mother had scored at a major discount.

"He's like this with everyone," I told Kyle as James' swearing faded away.

Kyle didn't appear perturbed, but that changed the longer we waited for James. "Is he with you?" he asked.

"With me?"

"Does he *act* like this with you, I mean. You two obviously have or were...*are* something."

"You know we dated for three years. And we've been completely over for three years. No contact." I supplied the information as if James was a bit of medical history I couldn't avoid offering but would refuse to be ashamed about. An errant wart.

"Not amicable?" Kyle asked, moving closer. The Wilkes' house seemed to stretch away from us, its impersonal, forgettable color palette slinking into the shadows.

"Nothing about James Wilkes is amicable."

Kyle nodded. "I'm glad you called me," he said. "And your friend out there's an asshole, but I'm glad he was here, too. Even if I want to waste him for the way he's treating you."

A plug released somewhere deep in my core, allowing my tension to drain away. It was replaced with something lighter and much, much better. "I used to call him Johns Wilkes Booth," I told Kyle. "When we were young."

Cult & Run

"You're still young, Dalmatia," he said.

I met Kyle's eyes. "It doesn't always feel like it."

James' footsteps sounded against the front porch of his father's place.

Kyle touched my arm. "Listen, what are you doing later today?"

"I've got to go," James announced. He was pink-faced and slightly winded. He was also standing as if he'd left one foot out in the driveway.

"What'd you do in those thirty seconds, a Couch to 5K?" I asked.

Kyle dropped his hand from my arm. "I look forward to speaking with you later," he told James.

James offered him a mock salute. "Sure thing, Captain."

And he was gone.

Kyle and I looked at one another.

"Do you need help bringing those bins in?" he asked.

"Sure." I answered.

"And then get lunch?"

I considered it a moment.

"Actually," I replied. "I have a better idea."

111

14

The Poms

Cormoran wasn't known for much more than the lot at Ninth and Bishop being the only free Amtrak parking between Philly and New York. The town was like a flowerbed well-planted but wrecked by early frost. Back when industry meant factories and old money, Bywood County grew up tall around Cormoran, pushing dirt over everything but the newly laid rail tracks. It was the tracks that I took Kyle to now. I'd done some dirt-moving myself.

"The nurse," I told him. "Or home health aide. Whatever she's called."

"What about her?" Kyle asked, standing before an old town-home built sometime in the late 1800s. The commuter rail line ran not twenty feet from its front door. I wasn't sure that was legal.

"She was taking care of Walker Wilkes before he died. She'll know if anything strange was going on before he passed."

More specifically, things involving *James*. Or Jenna.

Kyle and I had stopped for McFlurries, left my car at the back of the lot, and driven over in his Jeep. On the way, Kyle said he'd file an official report on the fire and call in a team to investigate. He'd done a bunch of tapping on his phone in the drive-thru but more listening than talking as he drove. I chattered non-stop. It was nerves.

Now, as Kyle and I stood before a house dolled up with several strings of holiday lights weeping from its front porch roof, the look on his face was a let-down.

"What?" I asked.

"How did you figure this out?"

I was beginning to remember why I hadn't liked Kyle in the first place. "The same way everyone gets their information these days. The Internet."

"Dalmatia, I want you to stop doing this," Kyle said.

"So sorry, Detective. Next time I'll run it by my superior before using the phone I paid for and the data plan *I also pay for*."

"That's not what I mean," he said, softening. "You can't just show up at places unannounced."

"Isn't that how fast-food works?"

Kyle blinked long and slow. This side of him wasn't new. I'd seen it outside the learning center. Cockiness. I was a means to an end, for his investigation or otherwise. It was atrocious that I'd gone on a date with this man. Strike three for intuition. "You're going to get yourself in trouble," Kyle continued.

"I'm starting to think I already have."

I hoped he could read my face as easily as I could read his.

Kyle sighed. "We may as well do what we came here to do," he said, looking at the house. A breeze sent a macrame Santa Claus tapping against the weathered front door.

"Her name is Malorie Hathaway-Kurtz," I told Kyle. We walked side-by-side to the front porch. It sat low enough to the cracked sidewalk not to need a staircase. Kyle and I ascended it at the same time, but he ended up at the front door first. I wedged between the edge of the porch and a wicker chair I couldn't be sure wasn't actually a very large bird nest. "She was Wilkes' in-home health aide, like I said. She also works nights stocking shelves at Pick'N Buy Mart."

"You got all this from, what, her LinkedIn profile?" Kyle asked.

"Facebook."

He rapped twice on the door. Old Saint Nick twerked in response. "Dalmatia, you need a hobby."

"I *have* a hobby," I answered. "It's vigilante justice."

"Hang on!" a woman called from inside the house. She sounded ninety. She sounded twelve.

When the door opened, she was neither.

"Malorie?" I asked.

Kyle gave me a look I could only describe as withering. "Is Malorie home?" he asked the person at the door.

"She's at work," the gatekeeper said. "Are you from that podcast?"

"Yes," Kyle said before I could ask what the heck was going on.

"Come on in," the man at the door said, stepping aside. "Watch the mess. The dogs own the place. I'm just their housekeeper."

"How much do they pay you?" I asked him. It wasn't as much a joke as evidence of my unraveling nerves. I hadn't expected a not-Malorie. I hadn't expected Kyle's shift in attitude. I hadn't expected a near miss with amateur arson.

"They pay me shit," not-Malorie answered. "Literally."

Kyle and I were led into a deceptively large living room full of patio furniture.

Not-Malorie tossed some throw blankets off a plastic lounge chair. A couple of shredded tennis balls dropped through a gap at the back. I hoped not to make his employers' acquaintance. "Sit wherever," he said. "Sorry for the mess. The Rascals don't leave me much time to tidy up."

I picked my way to an iron bistro chair. "Animals are time-consuming."

"The Rascals are the neighbors," Knock-Off Cesar Milan said. "I babysit them."

"Dogs *and* kids?"

I couldn't hide my bewilderment, but the guy wasn't fazed. "Got to keep the Poms in turkey jerky."

Rascals, Poms, Walker Wilkes. The connection between the people and things of this world was truly bizarre.

"So, the podcast." Kyle had pulled his phone from the pocket of his jacket. "Would you mind if I recorded our conversation? We can connect with Malorie later, but it'd be great to have another voice on the air."

"I'd be on the radio?" the guy asked.

Kyle and I looked at each other. Someone in the room didn't know what a podcast was.

"Yes," Kyle replied. "I can send you a link if you'd want to share it with anyone."

Wheels turned in the guy's mind. "Yes," he said, tapping his chin with a finger. "That'd really make Nancy jealous. Let's do it!"

Kyle started the voice recorder on his phone, and we settled in for an officially not-official interview for a fake podcast. "Could you state your name and age?" Kyle asked.

"Norman Hathaway, fifty-two years young."

I gave myself credit. Middle of both my guesses.

Kyle continued on. "What's your relation to Malorie Hathaway-Kurtz?"

"I'm her older brother," he said. "And landlord."

115

"Are the Poms hers or yours?" I interrupted. Kyle's fingers clenched around his cell.

"The Poms are mine." Norman adjusted his collar and smoothed back his hair. It was the color of weak coffee. I was pretty sure he thought he was being filmed. "And they're at daycare. You can stop by again if you'd want to meet them."

Kyle laid his phone on his leg. "That's not—"

"Yes!" I buzzed with delight. I did not want to meet these dogs, but I did want to a reason to return in case we didn't get all we needed from this visit. "I'll make sure to bring turkey jerky," I added.

"Human grade," Norman said. "You won't want to face their wrath if it's the cheap stuff."

"Are you familiar with any of Malorie's home clientele?" Kyle asked, steering the interview away from canines and toward whatever angle he'd decided to work. I was as curious as Norman but tried not to show it.

"Yes," I added. "The, um, sick folk?"

Kyle's displeasure was palpable.

"That's right," Norman said. "You're here about the kook."

He meant Wilkes. Of course, he meant Wilkes. My heart had been locked in a vice grip since we'd left Walker's house, leaving James, the fire, and the strangeness of it all behind. Sitting on the rusted patio chair, I realized that I wasn't scared of what we'd find out about Wilkes. I was frightened of what it'd expose about *me*. I was terrified of how Kyle's estimation of me would change upon learning more about Walker Wilkes. I'd grown up under his influence. So what was I?

I was the kook.

In many respects, it wasn't something I had outgrown.

"I wouldn't call him that," Kyle replied. I felt his eyes on my face and knew what they'd be filled with. Pity. He agreed with Norman.

Wilkes may have been a dead lunatic, but a living one currently perched in an old bistro chair atop wall-to-wall urine-stained carpeting. "Walker Wilkes was his own kind of animal."

If he'd said it to me, I wouldn't have known. My face was angled toward the door.

"Animal, right." Norman laughed. It was so like a dog's bark that I half-believed one of the Poms had Uber'd home early. "He was an asshole. The way he treated Mal? Terrible. Unheard-of. He'd make her bathe him in these, these—" Norman drew shapes in the air with his hands, chaotic puppetry designed to communicate Wilkes' absurdity. It served to make Norman appear equally as crazed. "Oils," he finished. "He had all these oils. And bath bombs!"

"Yes, the bath bombs," Kyle said, nodding. "Tell us about those."

Norman's eyes grew wide. "They were made from all sorts of things. Chalky stuff that dissolves, but also crystals and herbs and owl pellets! Do you know what an owl pellet it?"

"Yes," Kyle said.

"Oh gosh," I joined.

"They were supposed to help cure regrets and constipation. No, regrets and seasonal depression. And thyroid issues." Norman watched out the front window as an Amazon delivery van driver left a package on the front porch. "Not every kibble is unhealthy," he said, staring at me. "The Poms' diet is sensitive. I get the single-protein stuff."

"Totally," I replied.

"Anyway, Wilkes died a couple hours after Mal's shift ended. We'd been next door for Tommy Rascal's birthday party — they had to invite us because I babysit them after they get off the school bus — and Mal got the call. Her supervisor let her know she didn't have to make her morning shift with Wilkes, because he was dead."

"Did they tell her how he died?" Kyle asked. He was sitting on the edge of the couch, phone jangling as his knee bounced. I wasn't any calmer.

"Yeah," Norman said. He smiled, revealing both a missing a bicuspid and that he had eaten something with spinach before we'd arrived. "It was weird, because he'd had her mix up this big jug of lemon water and salt the day before. Supposed to banish thoughts of revenge, he'd told her. We both thought that was weird, but, seeing as his son had come into town, it made sense. Me and Mal have had our own share of family drama. Mom won the lotto five years back and ran off to Costa Rica with her foot surgeon."

The delivery van lingered at the curb before Norman's house. Its engine rumbled, and a face in the corner of the window caught my attention. The driver popped his head back in and away. Had he been staring at us?

"Did he drink the concoction?" Kyle asked. "The lemon and salt?"

"No," Norman answered. "That's what was so odd. The last time Malorie saw Wilkes, she said he just sat there looking out the window, waiting for his son to come back from getting his flu shot. I thought it was odd, his son getting a flu shot right after coming back into town to visit his dad, but maybe it was the responsible thing to do. Keep that sick old kook from catching something. Malorie never said exactly what was wrong with Wilkes, why he needed home healthcare, but he had all sorts of problems that made me think it was diabetes."

Kyle glanced toward the front window, too. The van slowly pulled away. "Why did you think that?" he asked Norman.

"The no sugar thing." Norman's eyes flicked to a clock on the wall. "I've got to get the kids off the bus in about fifteen minutes," he said. "You two are welcome to wait if you have more questions.

Mal should be home at about seven."

"I think that's all we need. Thanks," Kyle said. "We really appreciate you taking the time to talk with us." He stood and shook a seated Norman's hand. Norman rose and piled the throw blankets back onto the lounge chair.

"The Poms like comfort, huh?" I asked.

"Do they ever," he replied.

Norman walked us to the door. I turned back to ask one final question as Kyle stepped onto the porch. "Did Malorie ever dispense Walker's medication?"

"I don't think she's qualified," Norman said. "Mal's not a nurse. Home aide is different. You'd think she'd get paid more for having to wipe shit all day, but the money's as bad as the hours."

I smiled, thanked Norman, and followed Kyle onto the porch. He had the Amazon package in his arms and laid it inside the door of Norman's house. It was pretty big. Dog food, for sure.

"We'll be in touch with Malorie," Kyle was saying as he stepped onto the sidewalk and around to the driver's side of his Jeep.

"Like I said," Norman replied. "Come on back any time."

Something misty shone in his eyes. It could've been seasonal allergies or the sun. It could've been denial about being allergic to dogs. I thought, though, that it looked a whole lot like what I saw in my own reflection each night when I wiped my makeup away in the bathroom mirror. "I'll be back," I told him. "I always deliver on my turkey jerky promises."

Norman grinned. "Only the best for the Poms," he said.

I smiled right back. "Only the best."

Kyle opened the passenger door of his Jeep, and I got in. I turned to wave at Norman as Kyle pulled away from the curb, but Norman had already gone inside.

"You know," I said to Kyle as we crossed the tracks at the end of

KELLY MACPHERSON

the street, "I noticed something missing on that front porch."

"I took the package in," he said. "What are you talking about?"

"There was a spot on the frame of the door."

Kyle's foot jerked off the accelerator. I kept my eyes straight ahead and a small smile on my lips. The FBI agent had been bested by the kook.

Norman's house was missing a doorbell cam.

120

CULT & RUN PODCAST TRANSCRIPT
SEASON 2, EPISODE 4

ALEX PARKER: I have it on good authority that Walker Wilkes was last seen smoking an Arturo Fuento Opus X in his driveway on the evening he was found dead by a member of his...

SHEENA FAVROSIAN: Congregation?

ALEX PARKER: Is coven not the right word?

SHEENA FAVROSIAN: Leave witches out of this. Modern medicine owes them everything.

ALEX PARKER: My apologies, Sheena, listeners. Sincerely. Should we go with the simplest term for Wilkes' group of followers? Cult.

SHEENA FAVROSIAN: A charismatic leader, systems of influence, coercion and conditioning...yes, cult fits.

ALEX PARKER: Sheena, you keep this little podcast a classy operation, you know.

SHEENA FAVROSIAN: I do know, Alex. Now what's this about Walker Wilkes having a cigar fetish?

ALEX PARKER: Right! You'd think the only things entering his mouth would be a bunch of falsely efficacious herbal remedies with jacked-up prices and zero evidence of their effectiveness.

SHEENA FAVROSIAN: And maybe a Wawa hoagie.

121

ALEX PARKER: Everyone likes Wawa. Even Wilkes wouldn't have been able to resist a meatball shortie.

SHEENA FAVROSIAN: Has his cause of death been released? I'm assuming it wasn't deli meat.

ALEX PARKER: We couldn't get that lucky.

15

Three Years

It's one thing to be on the edge of my seat while scrolling never-ending subreddit threads like r/MegLoMania and r/fivedollarcoachpurse, the former my favorite source for multi-level marketing scams and the latter a collection of hilarious first-person accounts of being swindled.

But less than an hour after confirming with Norman that his and Malorie's doorbell cam had indeed been purloined two weeks before, I found myself sitting in the passenger seat of Kyle's Jeep, bent forward like a misshapen paper airplane to avoid the stench of the garbage filling the back seat. Not the sort of edge of my seat experience I was accustomed to. I'd also assumed that stealing a dead man's trash with an FBI agent would pan out a bit classier.

"Are you allowed to take this?" I asked for the hundred-and-fiftieth time.

"It's evidence," Kyle answered, eyes straight ahead on the road.

"Yeah, but isn't there protocol? A procedure to follow? I don't

123

want my fingerprints getting me in trouble."

"No one's going to pin Wilkes' death threats on you," Kyle said. "You weren't even around him when he died."

No, I wasn't. But Kyle had never asked where I *had* been.

As an FBI agent, shouldn't Kyle Alaric have asked me, a woman who could very well be helping him under the false pretense of self-preservation, where I'd been the day Walker was killed?

I ran a finger along the interior of the car door. No dust. No grime. Very clean. "It's interesting," I said.

"Hmm?"

"I was just thinking how weird it is that you don't have a partner."

Kyle cocked his head to the left, checking the side mirror. He switched lanes. "You're my partner," he replied.

"Don't be cute," I said back. "That's not what I meant."

He smiled. "You think I'm cute?"

A complicated knot cinched tighter in my stomach. "Why didn't you show James your identification earlier?"

The Jeep swerved away from downtown Cormoran and out toward the rest of Bywood County. The entrance to the freeway loomed in the distance. A two-story Target, recently remodeled, winked into view above an overpass.

"He'd asked to see it, and you didn't show him," I continued.

"James went to his car," Kyle answered. He didn't sound angry. He didn't sound worried. He didn't sound anything at all except like a man driving a car in a direction he shouldn't be going. I, on the other hand, was now wholly concerned.

"I know, but it's...weird."

"Would you like to see my ID?" Kyle asked.

I did.

"No," I replied. "I don't need to."

I didn't need to, but I wanted to. Just as I'd wanted to see the footage of what'd transpired the night the doorbell camera had been stolen but was left hanging. Whoever had hijacked the device off the door frame had been shrouded in black. Besides, Norman didn't have the password, and Malorie was working. Kyle said he'd circle back later.

Forcing Kyle to pull out his FBI card or badge or whatever he carried — I had no idea — wouldn't get me any closer to proving that Jenna Shears killed Walker Wilkes or at least assisted in his death. She'd remained a secret as Kyle and I had stolen Wilkes' trash, ensuring that James' Land Rover was absent during the mission. Whoever had been tasked with wrapping up the loose ends of Walker's life certainly had not been my mother, because the garbage can remained in the garage, obviously not put out for collection since before he'd died.

Jenna was my past and my problem, so she'd stay my own secret person of interest. The more I pondered all I knew, the more certain I was that James couldn't have had a part to play in the whole thing. He was too dumb and self-involved to be back in town for anything but some of his father's money. I'd need to clue Kyle in on Jenna eventually, but I had to see what else we'd uncover first. It wouldn't do for Kyle to go digging around in Jenna's past, since most of it was also my past. Not until I had evidence of a solid connection between Jenna and Walker Wilkes' demise.

I looked over at Kyle. No, I didn't want anything from him. Certainly not. Encountering James after three long-short years had worked my guts into barbed wire. If I forced Kyle to soothe pain he hadn't inflicted — by showing me his FBI Star of the Month certificate or otherwise — where would it end? I'd ended up stapled to every single movement he made from body language to physical distance. I relied on myself. I sometimes relied on Aashri. I did not need to undermine my self-sufficiency with an authority figure. I'd learned that lesson long ago.

"You know," Kyle said. "This cap's real FBI-issue."

"I'm sure wearing it backwards like that is a secret indicator of your clearance level."

Kyle's eyes widened in surprise. "Who've you been talking to?"

I pinched his bicep. He laughed.

Target was a pencil eraser in the rearview mirror.

"There's a spot in Weymouth Heights where we can go through this stuff," Kyle said, meaning the landfill of Hefty bags filling the backseat and trunk of the Jeep. "No one will ask questions."

"Isn't that what the local precinct is for?" I asked. "Why don't we take it there?"

"This is better." Kyle took the freeway at a quick clip, unworried enough to begin easing any doubts I had as to the veracity of his FBI credentials. This situation was too odd to be anything but what he claimed. "I've got a long-time informant up this way who works days at a spot we can use."

"Do you have official evidence collection equipment?" I asked. "Baggies or gloves and all that. Magnifying glasses?"

"Magnifying glasses?"

"Microscopes?"

"I don't know what you think we're looking for, Dalmatia, but I'm pretty sure our eyes will do the trick. You didn't find anything else out of place at Wilkes' house when you were in there?" Kyle asked.

"No," I answered. "It'd been a long time since I'd been inside anyway. The last time was right before James left."

"Three years ago, right?"

I should've been further away from the hurt. But I was still there, in the last place James had seemed like the James I'd known. Or at least thought I had. Kyle pulled off an exit, the pockmarked freeway becoming a smooth road of traffic lights and big box store signs.

"Right," I answered. "Three years."

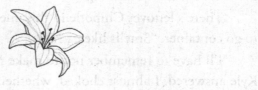

What we knew could've fit on a postage stamp:

Someone tried to set Walker Wilkes' house on fire.

A doorbell cam, most likely from Malorie Hathaway-Kurtz's house, had been found in the bathroom.

Malorie Hathaway-Kurtz, home health aide, had been the last to see Walker Wilkes alive.

James had returned and apparently been back for the past few weeks.

Kyle and I had stolen thirty pounds of Wilkes' garbage.

And now I sat beside Kyle at the foot of a lumpy full-sized bed atop a scratchy duvet in a Motel 12, going through said trash with only cheap plastic gloves to protect my skin. I gave him a mini TED Talk on the delusions of David Koresh in exchange for a pit stop at Walmart. Skin is the largest organ of the body and an important component of the immune system.

"Are you sure these gloves are medically safe?" I asked Kyle as he rifled through a black trash bag at my side. I turned my hands over, my skin glowing yellow through the milky latex. "Or do they just prevent pregnancy?"

Kyle ignored me, pulling and pushing trash around inside the bag. I watched, horrified, as something I hoped was yogurt came away on the exposed skin of his forearm. He'd rolled up his sleeves, causing my body to warm a bit as we'd prepared for our pungent reconnaissance mission. But admiration gave way to abomination the more I watched him dig.

"There's leftover Chipotle in this one." I tapped the foil lid of a to-go container. "Smells like carnitas."

"I'll have to remember not to make Mexican our second date," Kyle answered. I almost choked, whether on his unexpected words or the smell emanating from a half-empty bottle of PowerGreenz, a super expensive organic smoothie brand that'd been shoved below the discarded Chipotle. "Assuming you have the stomach to tackle refried beans after this."

"A second date?"

Kyle stopped searching. He sat up straight, elbows on his knees and gloved hands, messy and rank, dangling between his legs. "We didn't really get to finish our first one."

"No," I said. "We didn't. I don't know what I thought, but it wasn't that you'd want to go out again."

"Well, I did. And I do," said Kyle. "But after a shower."

I smiled at him smiling at me. The awkwardness of the drive over began to dissipate, but the whirlpool of emotion at seeing James again wouldn't recede so easily. If only I was a calmer woman, one with no regrets. I could at least pretend. "No Mexican," I told Kyle. "Ever. I have a thing about tortilla chips."

"Who has a thing about tortilla chips?" he asked. He resumed digging. I did the same.

"Someone who once sliced her lip open on one, that's who."

It was apparent Kyle wanted to laugh but was too nice. "What's with you and edges?"

I shrugged. My fingers ran over a second bottle of PowerGreenz, which'd been completely emptied and rinsed out. "Somewhere along the line I pissed off geometry," I said. "Now anything's a razor's edge."

"I shouldn't have asked you to help me," Kyle replied. "What if there's an envelope in here?"

"Or a hard piece of crust?"

"A potato chip could be lethal. I can't let you take the chance."

I nodded. "Lay's brand has had it out for me for years." Kyle's eyes glowed soft and warm. I wanted to lay my fingers on his forehead and check him for a fever. I didn't know what I'd do with him after I had, but I wanted to all the same. I turned his way and knocked into the trash bag as I did. My knee connected with something sharp poking through the plastic.

"Oh shit," I said. "Shit shit shit."

Kyle pulled the bag out of my way. "Did you get hurt?"

"No," I said. "Maybe. No, I'm okay." I examined my knee. All was intact, but the Hefty bag had a point pressing through its flexible plastic. "What the heck?"

Kyle pulled a gallon sized Ziplock bag from inside. A Ziplock bag containing a single syringe.

"Walker was diabetic, right?" he asked.

"Right," I replied.

"So, this makes sense?" Kyle didn't sound so certain.

Was it commonplace to toss needles in the trash along with last night's leftovers and paper towel rolls that should've been recycled?

Kyle held the bag by two fingers. I was glad we'd worn gloves. No contamination.

"Your lab can test that," I said. "Because maybe it wasn't used for insulin after all."

Kyle's eyes traced the shape of the syringe as if it had a story to tell. I was sure it did. "Yeah," he replied. "You could be right."

"Of course, I'm right. It's used, after all. Get it checked out. DNA, toxicology, whatever."

"If I didn't know any better, I'd think you were a closet 'Criminal Minds' fan."

"I limit my TV viewing to Food Network," I told him.

"Really?"

"Want to know how to keep fondant from drying out?"

Kyle's smile hadn't dimmed. "Yes, I do," he said, laying the Ziplock bag on the desk across from where we sat. He'd covered the particle board top with a newspaper from the lobby in case we came across something worth investigating further. I'd say we had. "I'll pay Malorie another visit to get a better idea of Walker's healthcare needs. Would anyone else know the extent of how he cared for his diabetes?"

The next part of the conversation was inevitable.

"My mother was close with him," I confessed to Kyle. "She entered into a little, um, arrangement with Wilkes before his death. I guess once he started getting those letters, he made her an offer…that she couldn't refuse." I tried to laugh. It came out like croup.

"What kind of offer?"

"Just your regular run-of-the-mill cult leader marriage proposal. Together in the afterlife and all that. Not legally official, just part of Walker's harem. Like the Playboy Mansion but without the pool parties." I waved my hand casually, sending the scent of cumin and wilted vegetables into the air.

"Your mother married Wilkes?" Kyle asked. "But she lives with your dad."

"I know," I said. "I don't understand it either. She sees it as a duty and a privilege. I thought my dad would be less enthusiastic, but he seems unbothered. I sort of think he's mad at me for caring."

"I wouldn't be mad at you for caring." Kyle pulled off his gloves and dropped them into the trash bag. I waited for him to put new ones on before tying it up, but he didn't. Not everything about a person could be a green light. He did wear a backwards baseball cap, after all.

"Well, you don't know my parents," I answered.

"Maybe I should change that." Kyle noticed the scrum on his arm and wiped it off on his jeans. I cringed a bit inside, but it was his next words that made my blood run colder than if he'd used *my* clothing as a napkin. "Let's pay your mom and dad a visit."

16

Be Careful

"Dalmatia Louise! What on earth are you doing involved in a fire? You didn't buy any of those off-brand Yankee candles, did you? I told you about Debra's hair stylist!"

The autumnal glory of the maple at the edge of my parents' property was dusty pale as a washed-out complexion compared to the red sheen of anxiety covering my mother's face. She was out of the house and over to my BMW before I could shift into reverse.

"I'm fine," I told her.

My mother wrung her hands. "And the wigs?"

"The wigs are fine, too."

She gave a little nod before nocking her ire toward her next target. "How could you let the hard work of so many almost go up in flames?" she cried into Kyle's face.

I gave him credit. Kyle barely raised an eyebrow.

Cult & Run

"That's a funny way of saying it takes a village," he answered.

"Excuse me?" my mother asked, face going topsy-turvy.

"To raise a child."

Kyle's point sailed right over my mother's head, as did most things worth paying attention to. He stood at my side, remaining composed despite the judgy arrows my mother's eyes aimed at his baseball cap.

I looked toward the open front door and watched my father's figure disappear from the space. He avoided my eyes, forcing my stomach into a shape a lot like shame. My dad was the parent who'd always accepted me as I was, unlike my mother who twisted my persona in a facsimile of my true self. She'd embellish me, cut me up, reassemble me according to her will. My dad, though. He'd never.

I brushed past my mother and waved to Kyle to follow me inside the house. "Mom, Kyle's with the FBI," I said without a backward glance. I didn't add that he'd been the one to arrange her ridiculous gala supplies with the organizational finesse of one of her "Good Housekeeping" articles. "He's investigating some death threats that were made to Mr. Wilkes."

My mother's forehead crumpled into a piece of composition paper lined with mis-directions. "What happened to your eye?" she asked. "It's red."

"The liberal news media."

"That is not funny." My mother didn't like a lot of things, and what she called my "progressive beliefs" was in her top five. She also couldn't let go of the embarrassment she'd felt during the year-and-a-half I was a practicing vegan. "What really happened?" She rounded on Kyle. "Did you do this?"

"Mom!"

Kyle pulled his hands from his pockets, two innocent white flags. "No, Mrs. Scissors, I would never."

133

My mother yanked me close.

"Ouch!"

"Dalmatia," she said in a voice all urgent secrecy but without the whispering, "did he assault you to get you to talk about Walker? Good cop, bad cop?"

"You're holding me tighter than an extra-small wig grip."

My mother yanked her hands back to herself, rubbing her arms over and over again like she'd been the one infringed upon.

"I had a simple corneal abrasion from an accident. I used an antibiotic. It's fine now," I said. Her mouth gaped open once more. "And it had absolutely nothing to do with Kyle."

My mother didn't look so sure, but she jumped on the chance to tackle her favorite topic. "Have you tried Walker's number seven?"

"I'm not taking any of that bullshit."

"Dalmatia!" She clutched the space where her heart should've been. "To insult the name of the dead!"

"Mrs. Scissors, is there a place we could talk?" Kyle asked.

"Yes, she can talk," I replied for my mother. "Let's go into the living room."

My mother followed, pointing out the increasing cloud cover above and her lack of time to sure up things for The Barbara Gala as if the potential for rain impacted sorting through seating arrangements and silent auction prizes. After being inside Wilkes' house, my parents' place was an assault on the senses. Faux floral arrangements, a handmade wreath on every wall, craft show knick-knacks making sure no one would forget the current month and season. Kyle sank onto his second couch of the day, no doubt wondering if Raymour and Flanagan was his true partner.

"Mrs. Scissors, I'm investigating a series of death threats made to Mr. Wilkes in the months before he died. Do you know of anyone who wished him harm?" Kyle's face was a neutral mask of professionalism, but I knew that's not what my mother would notice. She'd see what every member of The Committee had been trained to detect in anyone asking questions.

I helped translate. "Mom, was Walker upset about anything? Had he talked to you about it?"

Walker Wilkes' attention had been my mother's favorite thing, which had always done more harm than good. My father and I reaped the benefit of her long-perfected manicotti, but it was a poor consolation for what she'd resisted giving us. Hopefully what she could give Kyle now would help him get to the bottom of this death threat business.

"Mom? Did he say anything to you?"

"Dalmatia, I *heard* you. Please, this is a very difficult time." She dabbed her eyes with the tip of her index finger. It came away dry, with no tears being shed. "If you're asking about the letters, yes, I knew about them. I was Walker's closest confidant."

"Did he have any idea who would've sent them? Anyone he was having issues with?" Kyle asked. Wrong question. Wilkes needed to be painted in the very best light possible. No one outside of The Committee would understand that, especially someone in law enforcement. Kyle was lucky to have my help. He wasn't kidding about needing to sure up his knowledge of high-control groups.

"When Walker talked to you about how he was feeling, what precipitated it, Mom?" I asked.

"There you go with those big words, Dalmatia, as if I've never been to school. It's all that homeschooling you'd done at the Shears' house." I wouldn't take the bait. As if being pulled from public school was my idea. My mother waved off my highfalutin' vocabulary but answered just the same. "Walker was concerned about the gala. It's our largest fundraiser of the year, and he'd had reason to believe someone was trying to sabotage it."

135

"How?" Kyle and I asked at the same time.

"Well, it could be nothing really," my mother said, backtracking as usual. "Snafus."

I knew she wouldn't appreciate the sarcasm, but I couldn't help it. "Is that the name of some transient gang?"

"Dalmatia, I do not appreciate the sarcasm." My mother arranged her hands in her lap like the victim she obviously was — a victim of us, Kyle and I and all of our misunderstanding questions. I hadn't known damsels in distress could wear Mom jeans and Alfred Dunner. "We'd had some banking issues," she finally admitted. "Little things. Missing funds. Not enough to stop the gala but…concerning."

"Mr. Wilkes' Barbara Foundation is a non-profit for which you're acting treasurer. Is that correct, Mrs. Scissors?"

"That is correct."

"And you keep the books for the organization?"

"For The Committee, no. For the charity, yes. Walker trusted me with it." My mother scraped at a thumbnail. She was upset. Not guilty, but definitely agitated.

"You two had a special relationship," Kyle continued.

"We *do* have a special relationship," my mother answered. "He's with me all the time."

I cringed, unable to help myself. Kyle sat beside me on the couch and glanced at where I worried my own thumbs in my lap. His knee tapped mine.

"Did Walker have any suspicions about why the account was missing money?" Kyle was being careful now. He was getting the idea.

"He had a couple thoughts," my mother said. "We'd set up a new eBay account to buy clip-on bangs, which had required a small amount to be deposited into the bank account. I noticed the first unusual withdrawal shortly after. I assumed it was a service deduction or something of the sort." My mother blushed. "I don't always read the fine print. So tedious."

Unlike her zeal for Walker Wilkes' self-help propaganda. Full-page paragraphs and nine-point font were not tedious at all.

"How large were the withdrawals?" Kyle asked.

"Not large. Ten, twenty dollars. I don't think there was anything over thirty."

"How many times?"

My mother's mouth pinched. She was thinking. She was stalling. "Less than ten."

"Less than ten?" Kyle asked.

My mother nodded. "Less than ten."

"Mrs. Scissors, would it be possible to have a copy of those bank statements? I know that being Mr. Wilkes' treasurer you'd have kept them in a secure place." I waited for my mother's response to Kyle's schmoozy request. There was one thing about her he hadn't planned on.

"I'm sorry, but I'd need a court order for that," my mother answered, a saccharin smile spread across her face. "Professional policy. Being as I am also the secretary of the Barbara Foundation, it's imperative I ask that everything be done according to the letter of the law. The board demands transparency."

Kyle paused, and I could see the wheels turning in his head as he regrouped. My stomach began to churn. My mother was a delusional housewife with far too much minced garlic in her pantry, but she was sharp as a tack when it came to protecting Walker Wilkes.

"But you'd know that, of course," my mother continued. "Nonprofit organizations are required to file Form 990 every year, which lists the names of board members. The Barbara Foundation's attorney is also a member of its board, so why you're here and not at

137

Geoffrey Greenbean's office is quite perplexing."

My insides were a balloon about to pop.

"I appreciate your time, Mrs. Scissors," Kyle replied, surprised or humiliated. Maybe both.

And so the ritual of leaving began, my mother admonishing my eye redness for being uncouth. She gave Kyle her sweetest smile and offered him Walker's favorite homemade cashew butter, which she'd freshly ground that morning. "A nice antidote to all that processed junk in protein bars nowadays," she told him. "You look like the athletic sort."

Buttering up Kyle, by nut or by flattery, served to emphasize even further the divide between my mother's cunning and what he'd assumed. Kyle Alaric had erroneously supposed what everyone else did about a woman of my mother's age — that she was a grandmotherly sort with a weekly Bunco habit to satiate, a church meal train to organize, and maybe an inappropriate political meme to obliviously post on Facebook. But he now realized her for what she was.

My mother was exactly why a dangerous organization like The Committee continued to exist.

"Geoffrey Greenbean," Kyle repeated with a forced grin as we headed back to my Beamer. "I'd almost think you guys were all in Wit Pro or something given these names."

I waited for the joke to continue, but it didn't.

"Wit Pro is—"

"Witness Protection," I said. "I know."

Kyle nodded.

We drove back to Wilkes' place to get Kyle's car, which he had emptied of garbage, as a sheet of rain sliced through a day that sorely needed to wash-up and start over. Kyle was quiet. I should have filled the silence with jovial chatter or an apology for the ego killer that was my mother. But all I could think about as the day turned gray, was that before turning to go, my mother had grabbed me in an uncharacteristic farewell hug. Watching my parents' home disappear in the rearview mirror of my BMW, their maple tree and picket fence and ridiculous pumpkin-themed mailbox cover becoming indistinct, her parting words replayed over and over in my head.

"He is no cop, Dalmatia. Be careful."

17

Banana Pepper

After Kyle and I parted ways, I bought myself three more and called Aashri. I needed her help to make sense of everything that'd happened in the past few days as well as my newfound obsession with artificially fragrancing my whole apartment.

"You're going to burn this place down," Aashri said from where she stood in my kitchen, sipping a cocktail called Crank Juice that she'd learned from Bartender Tom. "Maybe you'll meet one of those hot firemen on the apps." Aashri had taken to swiping Tinder, dating anyone who wasn't Tom since Tom had apparently been friend zoned. I knew better. She was afraid. Who wasn't? I wouldn't push her on it.

"One can only hope," I replied. "Try not to sprain your finger, though."

Aashri took another sip. The glass in her hand was a tie-dye blend of I-Still-Like-Tom-But-Don't-Want-To-Get-Hurt. I'd rarely seen this side of her and wondered if maybe I'd simply missed it.

"Are you okay?" I asked.

Aashri gave me the finger. "Why wouldn't I be okay?" she answered through a mouthful.

"When did Tom tell you how to make that?"

"Two nights ago. Are you trying to figure out why I'm back on Tinder? Spoiler alert, Mom. I never left."

Tunneling deeper into Aashri's psyche wasn't happening, so I changed tack to the real reason I'd asked her over. Inhaling three kinds of alcohol and five grams of sugar through a straw wasn't it. "Something's going on with my mother. All this stuff with Wilkes and Kyle and Jenna. It's weird and doesn't make sense."

"And James," Aashri added.

"Not James. I don't care about James."

She laughed and licked a bit of pink juice off her lip. "Oh, yes, you do."

"Are you going to help me figure out if Jenna Shears murdered Wilkes or not?" I asked, snipping the wicks off my new candles. They burned more evenly that way.

Aashri knew my thoughts on Jenna Shears. "Just because she was a nightmare at age eleven doesn't mean she took a scalpel to Wilkes."

"Do you really believe the story about how he died?"

"Didn't your boy in blue show you the medical examiner's report?" Aashri read my silence for what it was. She nodded to herself. "He's a reporter, isn't he? I knew it."

I stopped snipping long enough to drop the blade of my scissors into my lap. "What?"

"Be careful!" Aashri bounded into the living room, clonking her glass on the counter. "You just got out of that eye patch, and you're already headed for a femoral amputation!"

"What do you mean a 'reporter'?"

New ideas swirled in my head, ones I should've been formulating all along. Never seeing Kyle's FBI badge or hearing him make a phone call to a partner or a team or a someone-official. Not going directly to Geoffrey Greenbean, Esquire. Not at least *threatening* my uncooperative mother with a warrant. Most glaringly, Kyle Alaric played good cop a little *too* well, acting all romantically interested in me as a possible means to get me to talk. Talk about what? Wilkes? I wasn't close to him. I hadn't been a practicing member of The Committee since it became a choice I was legally allowed to make.

"Aashri," I said again. "What do you mean?"

She took the scissors from my hands. "I mean that it's weird how you met is all. He ambushed you outside work, left a business card in your car, and recruited you to be his partner in crime all without giving you something in return. It's like he baited you."

Aashri wasn't wrong. Those things did happen. But they weren't the whole of it.

"The Committee is unique," I said. "How would someone in the FBI know how to handle investigating something like that without insider knowledge?"

"You're not an insider anymore, Dalmatia." Aashri went back to her drink. Her bare feet, neon-green toenails, pulled away like a passing car.

"Just say it," I told her.

Aashri turned my way, positioning herself with the kitchen counter between us. "I think you want to feel important," she said. "I think you haven't felt that way since James left. You don't have to agree. It's just my opinion."

"This isn't about James."

"No?" Aashri asked. "Then why didn't you change your locks before now? Why aren't you worrying about whether or not he still has your number instead of running around with Sir Lies-A-Lot and interrogating your mom?"

I was not mad at her. I did not want to be mad at her. I told myself that I was not going to get mad at her. "Aashri, I'm not saying Kyle's methods aren't weird, but the FBI isn't the Cormoran Police Department. They're much more covert and nuanced. This case is sensitive, discreet."

"Sounds like you're talking about adult diapers," she replied. Her mouth was a hard line. I wanted to pry it open and make her take it all back. "Tell me this, Dal. Why you? Why are *you* so necessary to the FBI, an organization with expertise on Jonestown and the Branch Davidians? You've done the research yourself. You do *all* the research yourself! And why? Why are you so obsessed with cults?"

"It sounds like you're going to tell me."

"It's because of James. It's always been because of James. He left. You had no closure. It's not The Committee you can't leave behind." I opened my mouth to protest, but Aashri snapped her fingers in the air. "And don't give me any lip service about your mother or how hard it is to pull away completely. You work for them, Dalmatia. Your BMW came from James! A preschool teacher who won't even get an annual flu shot because she can't bear to be in the presence of a trained physician after years of being traumatized by a false prophet only to fall in love with his son, waste three years of her life on him, and then wake up one morning to his…what? What would you call it that James left behind?"

"Nothing," I whispered.

"Exactly." Aashri's anger had overtaken my own. I hoped it wasn't meant for me, but her fury didn't sound as if it all stemmed from James Wilkes and The Committee. "He left you with nothing. And now here you are letting some guy take from you without being straight-up about what he's playing at. And you know this, Dal. *You*

143

know this."

I wanted to tell her that Kyle wasn't like that.

I wanted to tell her that I didn't even like him and our date had been a way to pass the time.

But Aashri came back to my side and hugged me close as disappointment spilled down my face.

"Tell him you're done," she said. Her voice was gentle, and her demand made sense. "Tell Kyle no more. He can investigate Walker Wilkes with his agency's resources. And, as a tax-paying citizen, you've provided those anyway."

I nodded. I agreed. It was done.

Kyle was done.

But James?

I wished I could be sure.

I sent a simple text.

Busy with work. Will be in touch. Sorry.

Good enough. Kyle had to be working more cases than just this one, and he had a son. When did the man get a chance to sleep? Not something I wanted — or needed — to think about. A stitch pulled tight in my chest, and, true to my name, I snipped it. I would not attach to Kyle. I *was* not attached to Kyle. I certainly wasn't thinking about what he looked like newly awake from sleep, hair messy and chest without a shirt and maybe all of him without a shirt. Or pants. Or — no. No more. I was obviously in over my head but, thankfully, had regained the wisdom to pull back.

A similarly simple text arrived in return.

Ok.

So that was it, then. I had zero plans to ever contact Kyle Alaric again, and I was sure he wouldn't pursue me any further. Not that he had. Not really. The business card situation was cringey as was his whole aesthetic. I hoped he'd quit wearing those joggers one day. It did nothing for his professional reputation. It also did very little for my mental health to turn the image of Kyle into some sort of paper doll, dressing and undressing him at my will. An idea of him swept through my mind — well-fitting suit, dark leather shoes. The Barbara Gala. Kyle could've been my date. He *would've* been my date.

It didn't matter.

I suppressed the urge to stalk Kyle online. I didn't really believe Aashri's conspiracy theory that the guy was some reporter looking for new details on The Committee, not with actual crime and far more interesting people than Walker Wilkes still living, still doing weird things. But maybe Kyle wasn't as high-ranking an officer in the Federal Bureau of Investigation as I'd believed. I had never really asked. He could've been trying to crack the death threats case, believing it'd be his big break. Promotion or something. It had ceased existing as my business.

Since it was Sunday night, I started to sort through the new children's books I'd bought to read to the kids the following week at the learning center. I rolled my eyes at *Clucky in the Pumpkin Patch*, a watercolor chicken with an exaggerated smile adorning the cover. It was a reminder that autumn in Cormoran meant more than just The Barbara Gala. Contrary to popular belief, The Committee was not the largest high-control group in town. I'd leave that to the professionals.

Chick-Chick-Chicken.

The place was a local legend. Chicken in all its most stunning forms: nugget, sandwich, Caesar salad. That last one was a little soggy and way too light on the dressing, but twenty-five herbs and spices made the grilled chicken quite a chef's kiss experience.

Besides being heavy-handed with paprika, Chick-Chick-Chicken was also famous for its optimistic company culture. Workers came pre-programmed with a high tolerance for toxic positivity, easily conditioned to rattle off the fast-food chain's signature catch-phrase — "pass along a smile!" — with each order. Two dollars over minimum wage made it surprisingly easy to join.

In addition to peppy customer service, Chick-Chick-Chicken employees wore a sunshiny uniform of black pants and honey mustard yellow T-shirt with a beaked smiley face front and center. Residents of Cormoran, as well as two hundred other cities throughout the Eastern Seaboard and Midwest, dressed up in their best imitation of happy-go-lucky on the first Friday of each October to snag a free combo meal, drink not included.

The Committee did not like Chick-Chick-Chicken.

The restaurant chain embraced all that Walker Wilkes despised: joy, service, and the commercial broiler industry.

Members of The Committee did not eat at Chick-Chick-Chicken no matter how much their junior capitalists begged. And beg they did. I saw it firsthand when children born to "outsider" parents invited a Committee kid to a birthday party hosted at the indoor play place in the rear of Chick-Chick-Chicken. Apart from the prevalence of food allergies and occasional outbreak lice, parents' biggest complaint about the learning center was its policy of allowing students to distribute birthday invitations during class hours. Being as the school was run *by* The Committee but *for* the public, like Quaker or Catholic institutions, both of which became synonymous with excellent educations, there wasn't much I could do to curb these parents' qualms about smiley faced invitations that promised an afternoon of lunch and RSV.

Aside from tacking up an advertisement for a local indoor trampoline park onto the bulletin board in the lobby of the learning center, there wasn't much I could do. When it came to the first Friday of each October, members of The Committee were free to wile their children away out-of-town or barricade them in the basement to avoid the rest of the Cormoran population slapping on as much yellow as they could find and skipping into Chick-Chick-Chicken for their free combo meal, drink not included.

As a personal rule, I did not eat at Chick-Chick-Chicken. I'd snuck over there with Aashri either our sophomore or junior year of high school, visiting the bathroom while she waited in line for as many nuggets as we could buy with twenty-five dollars and seventeen cents, which was when I saw that, according to a posting on the back of the ladies' restroom door, the bathroom had last been cleaned April 17.

The date of my covert poultry rebellion was April 5.

And so, I did not eat at Chick-Chick-Chicken. I'd almost caved and ordered a milkshake in the drive-thru once, but I went home and blended a smoothie, slicing open my index finger on a freezer-burnt strawberry, like a woman with strong will power and even stronger convictions.

But I thought about it now, that chicken. Warm, crispy, dusted in enough herbs and spices to blanket a large-scale agricultural operation. I wanted it. In a sandwich. With mayo. Maybe a leaf or two of wilted lettuce and a wet tomato.

I would get myself that chicken.

I dropped the books onto the kitchen counter and rushed to my bedroom. While rifling through my closet, it was no surprise that the happiest thing my wardrobe contained was a plastic shopping bag from the taco place on Bird's-Eye Street. Big red letters on the front hoped I'd HAVE A NICE DAY and held my collection of unmatched socks. I pushed aside tops dangling from hangers and pulled sweaters and pants from their assigned spots, already knowing the truth: everything in my wardrobe was brown, black, gray. A palette of tooth decay.

Amazon! Amazon would get me something. Or Aashri? No, I wouldn't let her know I was dressing up for Chick-Chick-Chicken Day. She wouldn't understand. I didn't even understand. Regardless, Saturday was the day.

I was compelled.

Or tired. Maybe a little upset about Kyle.

Probably all three.

I pressed BUY NOW on a sunny little number, feeling good about this unexpected turn of events. I was doing something new, something common, regular. I finished up selecting books about trees and tannin and tractors for class the next day, registering an uncharacteristic swell of optimism. Golden hour streamed through the panes of my large windows, falling against the kitchen counter in geometric blocks. I didn't know what was happening to me or why I suddenly needed to engage in an act of rebellion against The Committee. I wasn't ignorant: I knew that free chicken wouldn't affirm my autonomy. I reached into my closet for a pair of cute shoes to complete my new outfit anyway.

The week began, delivering me a Monday stamped with busyness. I was asleep by nine o'clock that evening and woke on Tuesday morning to a package in the vestibule that contained a very bright weekend ensemble. It felt almost criminal, pleasantly so, tossing the mailer onto my couch before getting to work.

148

By Thursday, I had hung up more than just the ridiculous outfit I planned to wear on Saturday.

I was finished with Kyle, but now I was through with Jenna Shears, too. Specifically, my unwarranted conjectures about her involvement in the death of Walker Wilkes. He was a lunatic who'd probably micro-dosed himself to expiration with a blend of Roundup and hand-harvested mushrooms. I had to focus on moving past these one-sided obsessions, the ones in which I became too invested in a man or a cult or, maybe, a fast-food chain's blatant attempt to swindle thousands of people into paying for overpriced beverages. But until I developed a codependency on Dr. Pepper, I was safe from the latter.

"You're done with men?" Aashri said when I called her during dinner that night. Pushing lukewarm risotto around a plate as a party of one had stolen a bit of my newfound positivity.

"Not men in general," I told her. "Kyle."

Aashri's smirk was an audible sound through the ether. "And…"

"And Walker Wilkes. I'm done investigating his death."

"Being an armchair detective didn't suit you. Your head's too big for a helmet," Aashri answered.

"You're funny after lifting, did you know that?"

Aashri smacked two kisses into the phone. "For my majestic biceps."

"Of course," I replied.

"For real, though, Dal, I'm glad about Kyle. He was sketchy. Even if he wasn't some undercover reporter bro, FBI agents could get sent anywhere at any time. You never leave Cormoran. How's that supposed to work?"

"It doesn't have to work because I'm no longer passing him the clicker in this — how did you put it — *armchair investigation*."

"Armchair detective."

149

I stabbed at a pea. "Right. Well, this me is no longer speaking to Kyle, so it doesn't matter."

"And James?"

"I threw his flowers in the dumpster around the back. Mr. Hakema pulled them out five minutes later. I smelled them from beneath the door of his apartment."

"Stalking now?" Aashri asked.

I finally succeeded in spearing that pea. "James was the stalker."

"Exactly," my best friend said. "Enough reason to stay away from him, too."

Aashri had a point. I was doing new things, and there was no energy for what'd kept me trapped in my past. I'd even deviated from my schedule and given my students an extra ten minutes of recess in the beautiful weather earlier that day. Rules, desires, and white board agendas did not bind me.

And in two afternoons' time I would be another cog in a conveyor belt headed straight for unrestrained chicken sandwiches, drinks not included.

18

Crisis

The year was 1916. Dr. Otoman Zar-Adusht Hanish relocated from windy Chicago to sunny Los Angeles, bringing his neo-Zoroastrian cult, the Mazdaznan Master-Thought Sect, to the West Coast. Dr. Hanish was not unlike Walker Wilkes, ascribing to a similar philosophy of wellness and dietetics, as well as claiming to be a Persian prince in much the same way Wilkes insisted his ancestors invented the cure for scurvy on the Nina. No, the Pinta. Must've been the Santa Maria.

1916 also happened to be the year White Castle opened in Wichita, Kansas.

All hail the first American fast-food joint, serving up burgers at five cents and laying the groundwork for McDonald's, Carl's Jr., and, of course, Chick-Chick-Chicken.

It was Saturday of this year, not 1916, when I learned there's something worse than wearing a banana-yellow jumpsuit to one of the year's largest events in your not-large town. The jumpsuit itself was a long-sleeved V-neck number made of a comfortable cotton blend with legs wide and loose enough to be both flattering and fashionable. I texted a pic to Aashri, eliciting a reply comparing me to a walking, talking Percocet.

When The Terrible Thing happened, I was dressed far more oddly than usual but not as bizarre as the family of nine who showed up in Minions costumes. Prior to the incident, I parked along Main Street and walked two blocks to a very packed Chick-Chick-Chicken. I remembered the time — 3:45 PM — because of those numbers, their sequence. I'd gotten a text message from my mother asking if I'd do her a very kind favor and serve as an usher for The Barbara Gala, only two weeks away, when I saw the time and thought immediately of Negative 48, the numerology-based Q-Anon cult that claimed a certain former living United States president was in fact *another* former president, who was very thoroughly deceased.

Unhinged conspiracy theories aside, I boldly stepped toward where I'd never gone before, my Rothy's flats moving gingerly over fallen leaves as bright as the fast-food fast fashion I'd adorned myself in. It'd been quarter to four when I began my journey, and five of four when I arrived in the parking lot of Chick-Chick-Chicken to take my place at the back of a line I hadn't known could exist outside a merch booth at a Taylor Swift stadium tour.

"Get me a number seven. No drink. I'll bring wine," Aashri texted as I eyed the shoes of the couple in front of me. Twin pairs of big yellow Tweety Bird slippers.

"Huh?" I texted back.

"I'm three blocks away," she answered before my thumbs could even meet the air.

"You can't line jump."

"It's not line jumping. You're saving me a spot. And I'm bringing you wine."

Dressing like a banana pepper came with enough anxiety. I did not need Aashri complicating things by getting us kicked out for butting ahead of the twenty-or-so people now trailing behind me. "No," I texted in reply. "I'll buy you a meal and bring it to your apartment. ETA is tomorrow at noon."

Her only response was, "I'm parking."

"Shit," I said to no one and everyone.

"Miss, there are children here."

For the benefit of the man ahead of me in line, I twisted my neck left and then right as if the cussing culprit had split. Mr. Voice of the People resumed staring at the entrance to Chick-Chick-Chicken, which was smart because glaring at something long enough usually bends it to your will. The line shuffled forward, kids hanging off their parents' bodies like bits of macaroni and cheese clinging to a serving spoon. I reminded myself that I was, at the most, a half-hour away from a free meal, drink not included. Aashri's Yeti tumbler of wine no longer sounded so preposterous. A few families filed out the exit, kids fisting milkshakes.

Big Terrible Thing began on the heels of a chocolate shake knocked from the hand of a little boy dressed as a yellow M&M. In response, the boy, a younger brother, aimed a partially eaten order of curly fries at the head of the offender: Clumsy Older Brother. The latter, apparently the sole member of his family to pay for food, whipped off a blue hoodie and snapped it toward Yellow M&M. Yellow M&M grabbed onto a sleeve and tugged. Older Brother's milkshake splattered onto the pavement dangerously close to where I waited in line.

Inserting himself into the ruckus, the man in line ahead of me reprimanded Older Brother.

KELLY MACPHERSON

Older Brother's Dad reprimanded the man in line ahead of me.

Yellow M&M tossed a fry at said man.

From out of nowhere, said man's small son tossed a shoe — *a shoe* — toward Yellow M&M.

The shoe missed its target and hit Older Brother's Dad, who also happened to be M&M's Dad, instead.

Chaos reigned for a few long minutes before a pair of bulky Chick-Chick-Chicken employees hustled the whole shoe-pitching, candy-coated mess away from the line. Several others accompanied them, free lunches forgotten in the face of providing the most salacious eyewitness account. I'd committed to finishing what I'd started, so I shuffled ahead to within a few yards of the restaurant's doors. What should've been a neighborly day out had become, for some, a nastily penned email to corporate. For me, it was about to become something that no manager could make right with a BOGO coupon.

Chick-Chick-Chicken's building design included double doors at the front of the building, the left for entering and the right for exiting. The exit had been shut no more than thirty seconds after FryGate when I watched it spit out a tall, thin man with bottlebrush mustache and a boom mic over his shoulder. He was a cartoon runaway, a naughty kid who'd packed nothing but snacks, only to make it two blocks before slinking home.

I texted quickly texted Aashri. "Your favorite podcaster is leaving with honey mustard breath right now."

Tom the Bartender was leaving with something else, too. *Someone* else.

Jenna Shears.

Aashri's retort chimed from within my palm, but I was too fixed on Tom and Jenna, smiling, laughing, small-talking their way out of Chick-Chick-Chicken and toward the parking lot. Would they leave in one car? Had they arrived in one car? Why were they together?

154

And what was the boom mic all about?

"Podcast," I said to myself.

"Forecast?" replied the lady behind me. "Sunny until four with a fifteen percent chance of rain."

"Thanks," I mumbled.

With all this yellow, sunny was a given. But the way Jenna chatted up Tom as he loaded the mic and a duffle bag into the trunk of a dark green VW Bug had a storm surge pushing at the edges of my brain. Tom worked at a podcast studio. Tom was a podcaster. Jenna Shears was an Urgent Care PA. He was obviously here doing a segment on Chick-Chick-Chicken Day, which put an end to any intrigue I'd felt about the guy's media career. Had he meet Jenna on the fly, interviewing her for the segment? Both wore yellow tops, hers a slightly plunging V-neck sweater and his, an oversized neon T-shirt with the name of a landscaping company across the chest. Had they come together as friends? As more than friends? Two bananas in a bunch?

I'd been foolish to think that investigating the death of Walker Wilkes was my responsibility but writing off further inquiry into Jenna Shears' reappearance in town had been my truly foolish move. I'd made an impulsive decision to let it go after feeling good about my equally impulsive decision to attend this cluckin' occasion. It felt more important than anything else to find out why she was all buddy-buddy with Tom. Not to mention where she was staying, who she was staying with, why she'd come back, her college GPA, and any outstanding warrants for her arrest.

The little things.

"Hey, where's my man?" Aashri jogged over, hip bumping me to the side. She was slightly out of breath, her well-lined eyes scouring the scene.

"You just missed him," I said. No need to mention Jenna. "He

155

left with a boom mic, though."

"Cool," Aashri answered. "Mixing business with pleasure."

"And what's all this about him being 'your man'? I thought you were over Tom the Bartender?"

Aashri answered a different question instead.

"I thought you were over Detective Kyle?"

First Tom and Jenna, and now Kyle. Chick-Chick-Chicken was vomiting Cormoran's finest. Kyle had just stepped through the exit when he met my eyes. I cursed myself for being so obvious. And yellow. He waved. I did not.

"Don't be rude, Dal," Aashri said. "Kyle! Hey! No dressy-dressy?" Aashri pointed to a smiley face button she'd pinned to the front of a black Nike sweatsuit.

"They're not going to serve you in that," I said under my breath.

She pushed a fist into the air. "Let them try and deny me!"

"Hey, Aashri, Dalmatia." Kyle approached with a curt nod. His voice was far gentler than I'd suppose for a man whose face was a haunted house. Whatever I'd seen in his eyes as he'd waved had vanished behind dark windows, shuttered and drawn. "I'm guessing neither of you are here for the low-key vibes."

"Oh, I am," Aashri said. "Nothing's more relaxing than watching parents mindlessly scroll their phones while their kids barf half-chewed white meat inside a tunnel slide."

"Aashri!" She was being disgusting for nothing more than the reaction Kyle would give her. I didn't want to stand by while they did this. The line surged ahead. I was almost at the door.

"You're really here for this?" Kyle asked me.

I gestured to my jumpsuit. "I'm not Spongebob, so obviously."

"I was going to guess cute Minion," Kyle said with a bit of a smile. He was trying.

I was not.

156

"It's been done to death," I answered. No eye contact.

Fingers feathered against my arm. "Dal, what's going on?"

"I'm not *Dal*," I said. "And nothing. I told you. I'm—"

"You told me." Kyle's voice was suddenly as foul as my attitude. "See you, *Dalmatia*."

Away he went. From me, from the line, from a hundred yellow eye sores. Kyle wore jeans and a gray hoodie. He'd been at this ridiculous charade for a reason other than free food. A reason other than proving he wasn't a follower. I looked around, refusing to aim my eyes in the path he cut through the parking lot. I hadn't wanted to keep on doing things The Committee's way — changing what I ate, what I thought, what I wanted. Aashri was right: I didn't just work for them. I *was* them. I'd changed myself once again because of The Committee, even if my actions were in direct opposition to theirs. I'd continued making choices that were rooted in the way I was raised, and no amount of fried chicken or impulse fashion would change that.

Standing single file in one line didn't mean I'd left the other.

"I have to go," I said. Aashri lifted a Yeti tumbler toward me, a question in her brows. I shook my head. I wouldn't cry here. Not in this jumpsuit.

My best friend took my place, asking no questions as I stepped out of line. "I love you, Cruella."

I could've smiled at that, a joke from back before I cared that my name would never be on a souvenir keychain. Back when I thought that who I am was determined by me and me alone.

I bid farewell to the dream of a chicken sandwich with no strings attached, or drink included, and made my way through a sea of yellow for an island that did not exist.

He was there when I got home.

Of course, he was.

Hours had passed since I'd fled Chick-Chick-Chicken, pulling before my apartment to parallel park on a street almost empty of cars. Saturday night. I dripped like candle wax out of my BMW, his eyes scooping the sight of me into his hands. I would've burned anyone else, but not this man. He was the flame, and all I'd ever done was melt before him. A wet leaf stuck to the bottom of my shoe. It'd rained in the hours I'd driven aimlessly around Bywood County, wondering if the Chick-Chick-Chicken line had waited in the downpour. I wondered if Aashri had made it inside before it began. I wondered about Tom and Jenna. I wondered about Kyle. But I mostly wondered what'd possessed me to show up there in the first place.

But now I was here.

"What are you doing?" I asked, standing on the slick sidewalk before the front steps up to my place. I could barely feel my legs. They ended in cute, damp shoes, but there was nothing solid in between.

"Where've you been?" James asked.

I laughed. It was not kind. "Where have you?"

The streetlights would wink on at any moment. In the far end of twilight, James' hazel eyes were a sparkle of black and blue in the dark. I wished I'd forgotten how well I remembered them.

"Can I use your bathroom?" he asked.

"You have to use my bathroom?"

"Yes."

I could've sent him to the deli across the street. It didn't close until nine.

"Fine," I said.

James followed me up the stairs to my building and then up the stairs to my apartment, me aware the entire time that he'd made this journey the other night with a key I never should've let him keep.

"I threw your flowers away," I told him, stepping inside my place with his body at my back.

It wasn't clear if James cared or not. His hands were on my hips, his chest against my spine. He was tall. He was so tall. God, he hadn't changed. The streetlight flickered on outside my window. I saw it; I looked at it. And I saw, too, my reflection mirrored back in the shadowed windowpane. James was behind me, only a weak image.

And then he was before me, mouth on mine.

We moved through the hours, together, joined. James using me and me letting him. I did what I wanted. James was what I wanted.

Self-hate makes good girls good lovers.

159

CULT & RUN PODCAST TRANSCRIPT
SEASON 2, EPISODE 5

ALEX PARKER: Before we start the show, a few announcements. Pod Squad, this Friday we'll be—

SHEENA FAVROSIAN: Ew, Alex. Cringe. Pod Squad?

ALEX PARKER: I'm fostering a sense of community.

SHEENA FAVROSIAN: Oh, Alex.

ALEX PARKER: As I was saying, my little Cult-cumbers—

SHEENA FAVROSIAN: No better.

ALEX PARKER: Your favorite podcast hosts will be making an appearance at Chick-Chick-Chicken Day, starting at 2:30 pm and lasting through whenever they run out of spicy nuggets. Do you like the spicy nuggets, Sheena?

SHEENA FAVROSIAN: I love the spicy nuggets, Alex. And the honey mustard sauce? Chef's kiss.

ALEX PARKER: So, dress up in your best abusively optimistic attire and come on out to eat free food and say hi to Sheena and me as Cult & Run interviews Bex Jung, manager of Chick-Chick-Chicken and, apparently, a fan of this pod. It'll be our first ever live interview with a former member of The Committee turned happy poultry cult leader. Bex, if you're listening, I'm joking.

SHEENA FAVROSIAN: Alex and Bex?

160

ALEX PARKER: We're starting a cult of our own. The Exes.

SHEENA FAVROSIAN: Alex, with a dating history like yours, I'd keep brainstorming.

ALEX PARKER: Ouch, Sheena. Ouch.

19

Bruce Banner

He left while the glow outside was still artificial.

It was the real thing by the time I awoke.

I didn't roll into the spot in my bed where James had laid but faced the wall instead. I looked for a text, knowing I wouldn't find one. I checked on the kitchen counter, the overdone coffee table, the itty-bitty dining table. In the bathroom, in my shoes, in my purse, in my fridge, in my fucked-up mind for a goodbye, a farewell, a this-isn't-me-being-a-jerk. Again.

I had let myself fall asleep with his arm around me, while not really believing it'd be there in the morning.

But I'd hoped.

Aashri had texted me one, two, seven times. I didn't answer. I cried in the shower, pulling the mascara from my wet lashes in globs. I wanted to say something to James, words in the shape of questions. All of them ending in swear words. I didn't dry my hair. Water dripped down my bare back. I'd slip on this floor later. I'd hit my head on the side of the bathroom sink. I'd die.

I knew I should call Aashri. I had no other friends. I had no one. I'd slept with a man who couldn't care less about me. His fingerprints were on handle of my bedroom door. I'd unscrew it, remove it, throw it in the dumpster. I'd get a new one. I'd get new friends. I'd get more friends. I'd get a new job. I could move. What ties did I have? My mother hated me. My dad now hated me, too. I'd done something, not realizing it was wrong.

But this, *this* was wrong.

James was James. No different than before.

And neither was I. How easily I'd slipped right back into making it okay for him to treat me however he wanted. James hadn't said a word about how he'd left or about his plans in the present. I had wanted answers for a long time, but instead of demanding them, I'd eaten up every syllable his body had given me. *Yes, yes, more, please.*

When I'd finally texted Aashri back, she'd guessed.

"I saw him at your parents' house," she said. "I drove by, and he was pulling out."

It wasn't twisted logic that Aashri viewed James' visit to my parents' place as a precursor to me sleeping with him, because it was a pattern. It was history, a rewind. The last night I'd seen him, he'd told my father of his plans to head out West. I hadn't known until after.

After he'd told me he loved me.

After I told him I'd felt the same.

I wish he'd left me wondering.

Instead, I had spent three years replaying our relationship, our situationship, our whatever it was, on a loop in my mind, the recordings scratched up and warped by time and feeling, vivid enough for a bit of clarity only in my dreams. Clarity that arrived as regret. The regret that I hadn't been a healthier version of myself when he'd lived here, in Cormoran, able to know me as I would someday be without the worry and the anxiety and the fear. Without the pressure. Had I pressured James? I thought so. And yet throughout all the time we'd spent together before he'd left during the night, I had changed myself to be what I thought would keep him beside me.

It hadn't worked then.

And I was right back to doing it now.

"I have something we can talk about besides James," Aashri texted. "Want to meet at Tom's?"

"I don't want to talk about Jmaes," I answered back, cursing my fumbling fingers for not auto-correcting his name.

"Jmaes doesn't deserve you talking about him." Aashri sent a photo. In it, she sat beside a large, healthy fiddle leaf fig with googly-eyes stuck to the front of its pot. She did not own that pot. She did not own healthy plants.

"Where are you?"

"I already told you."

"Tom's? Like, his house?"

A devil emoji and an address were her reply.

I contemplated changing out of sweats but grabbed my purse and replied to Aashri instead. "If Tom isn't trying to sell me Arbonne, then I'm out."

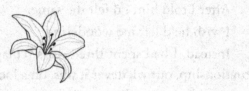

I never failed to be surprised by people's homes.

They're either cleaner than I'd guessed or decorated with less finesse. Sometimes there's a secret wife upstairs. That last one is the plot of *Jane Eyre*, but who would've thought Rochester's digs were hiding that? The first time I'd visited Aashri's home as a kid, her mother's handwoven tapestries, gemstone colors of spun silk, had been the most beautiful thing I'd ever seen. And there they were existing in a simple split-level in Cormoran, down the street from a Dairy Queen that used to be a bank. I enjoyed learning something new when visiting a home for the first time, which isn't an activity I did very often, but still looked forward to all the same.

If Tom the Bartender was harboring a crazy spouse in his attic, I'd have been less astonished than what actually greeted me at the place he called his own.

First things first. When I pulled up to the address that Aashri had texted, I arrived at *a garage*.

Not a particularly bad-looking garage, but a garage. A two car, detached garage.

Since the final leg of directions had taken me down one of Cormoran's tight alleyways where standalone garages and car ports weren't uncommon, I should have guessed. I'd assumed Tom lived in a back apartment or a walk-up whose entrance faced off-street. But Tom lived in an honest-to-goodness garage with a dark green, peeling door — a *garage* door — and a little window on the side with a window box full of the healthiest, prettiest mums I'd ever seen.

I circled the structure, registering the long, narrow strip of green lawn that separated it from a three-story Victorian townhome. Its roof was a cobbled and re-cobbled mess of four decades' worth of shingles, and its exterior ran the gamut from stucco to brick. The garage was in better shape, but it was, as I have made quite a point of saying, a *garage*.

165

Beside the window box was a screened-in storm door. I spied Tom and Aashri through the open main door behind it, a heavy wooden thing that looked as if it'd once been part of the Victorian's former grandeur. The duo sat on a mint green velvet futon, smoking weed. I rolled my eyes and knocked on the storm door's aluminum frame.

"Mom's here," I heard Aashri say with a smile.

"Aashri, why would you invite me over if this is what you're doing?" I asked, stepping into Tom's garage. "Hi, Tom. Where's the Lexus?"

Tom laughed. It was a pleasant sound, the kind that seemed for others instead of himself. "Actually, a Volkswagen, but it's parked out front."

I looked out onto the lawn.

"Of the main house," Tom said. "Along the street."

He passed his blunt to Aashri. "Your directions didn't take you that way, did it?" he asked with an apology in his voice. "There's a walkway that leads back here from the front."

"I'm parked on the grass next to your, um…this."

Tom gestured for me to have a seat in one of the rattan chairs opposite the futon. In the center stood a coffee table put together from a garden gate, which had been painted glossy purple and laid atop four equally as indigo cinderblocks. "I share the place with a few buddies," Tom said. "Not *this* place," he added, catching himself with a laugh. "The property. I like the garage. Good acoustics."

"Sit, weirdo." Aashri pointed the blunt toward a chair. I sunk onto a brilliantly-patterned cushion that reminded me of the textiles in her mom's house. Tom's garage proved not half-bad. It was colorful yet relaxing, and he'd filled it with plants: plants hanging from the ceiling, plants in pots, planters in hydroponic set-ups.

I pointed to one in a corner. "Is that—"

Tom blushed. "Yeah, cannabis. It's a blend called Mean Green Queen."

"I'm fine about that," I said. The surprises kept coming. "I'm not against weed. Whatever you want to do. I like plants. I'm not good with them, but I like them. I've never grown marijuana myself, but I assume it's as easy as a pothos?"

Aashri laughed. Tom grinned and sat back down beside her on the futon. "Can I get you anything?" he asked. "Even some water?"

"You're a very good host, Tom. No thank you," I adjusted the cushion beneath me. "Aashri told me she'd had some interesting news, which I'm now guessing is a marijuana farming opportunity?"

"Actually, yes," Tom said. He pulled a manila packet from the floor beside the futon. "I have an excellent business opportunity I'd like to extend your way. For an investment of only ten thousand dollars—"

"Ten thousand dollars!" Aashri had tricked me into a viper's nest. She'd lost her mind. I may have slept with James, but it turned out I wasn't the most batshit crazy person I knew. "I swear, Aashri, I am not even able to process this right now! I was joking about the Arbonne. Holy shit! What are the two of you thinking? What on earth are—"

"Dalmatia, stop!" Aashri set the blunt down in a small ceramic sombrero on the coffee table. She gripped her stomach, fingers digging into her perfect eight-pack as she laughed.

"So, this was all…a joke?" Of course, it was. Aashri was a gym rat who invested her disposable income into creatine powder and personal training sessions. Funnel money into a cannabis startup? Not unless it guaranteed the ability to squat four hundred. "Okay, you guys are obviously very high, so I'll just leave you to it and come back when things have calmed down. I have a library book to return, so it's no big deal."

KELLY MACPHERSON

"You are so fucking weird," Aashri said, wiping a tear from her eye. "Stay on that alpaca wool butt pillow or I'll kick your ass."

"You get so much nicer when you're stoned," I told her. Tom looked visibly discomfited by our banter. I still wasn't sure why either of us were in his garage.

"Tom, show her the stuff." Aashri motioned to the envelope Tom held in his hands. He wore quite a number of raffia string bracelets on his wrist. One got caught on the prong closure.

"You guys said this wasn't an investment scam."

Aashri was no longer laughing. "It's not."

Surprise number three.

Photographs.

"I do some photography work on the side," Tom said. His front teeth worried at his bottom lip. "I didn't want to show you this, and I shouldn't, but you're Aashri's friend. You're my friend." He passed me the envelope, and I withdrew a thin stack of five-by-seven photos.

What I saw were three very troubling things.

Three photos, all taken at my parents' house.

The first showed Jenna Shears speaking to my father on the front porch. Her face was partially obscured by a hanging mum, but I knew it was her. She wore her Urgent Care doctor's jacket and everything.

The second had been shot through my parents' kitchen window. My mother and James sat opposite each other at the kitchen table where I'd had coffee with Kyle while doing grunt work for my mother's ridiculous gala.

Third, and worst, was the one I stared at long enough to know it'd redevelop itself over and over against the back of my eyelids when I failed to find sleep that night. James. And a woman. A beautiful woman in a lavender hijab who laid her hand on his arm in a way that made me feel as if my brain was splintered glass.

168

"Why do you have these?" My voice wasn't a whisper; it was a mistake. I didn't want to know. I didn't want to see these images.

"He can't say, okay?" Aashri answered with enough bite to prevent me from asking again. I kicked myself for cutting things off with Kyle, because the guy could've run a background check on Tom. If I was in the home of some sort of private investigator or peeping Tom — of course, he was a peeping Tom! — I'd know. "I know Jenna, and I know James," I said. God, how I wished I didn't. "But who's this other one?"

"She works with Tom," Aashri answered. "What did you say she does?"

"Social media manager," he replied. "I do some podcasting stuff on the side."

I already knew that. It was what I didn't that had me in a spin.

"I wonder how she knows James." I glanced up at Tom and Aashri, the two of them wearing twin looks of concern on their faces. "I'm not asking you guys, geez," I said. "I'm just wondering out loud."

"Don't you think the real question is what's Jenna doing with your dad? And James with your mom?" Aashri raised her palms before me. "No swinger jokes, promise."

Below his mustache Tom pursed his lips. I didn't care how cute he found Aashri's sense of humor. Why show me these photos? "How come these aren't these on your phone?" I asked. "If you're a photographer, why are you creeping on the properties of private citizens?"

Tom took a hit of the blunt. "Birds."

"Birds?"

"Birds."

I barely talked myself out of smacking him. "What does that even mean?"

Aashri reached for the photos, and I passed them into her hands.

KELLY MACPHERSON

She turned them this way and that. "Tom was following a hawk migration," she said.

"Hawks migrate?"

She kept twisting the pictures. "Sure."

These two were more evasive than a FedEx tracking number. "Tom, you want me to believe you were following the migration of a hawk over, what, my parents' house? And that's how you got these photos?"

"It's true," he said. "You can tell they're from inside my Bug."

"Were you also smoking a blunt inside your Bug at the time?" I asked.

Aashri pointed to something atop the sycamore in my parents' backyard, visible just over the roofline of their home in the photo of Jenna and my dad on the front porch. "See? Hawk or cryptid, either way this is what Tom was going for."

"I'd have cropped your dad out," he said. "I use a DSLR."

"Okay, but James…"

Tom flushed. "He's good-looking," he said. "And I knew he was sort of famous."

Aashri's expression did a little one-two step. It was hard to read, but I think even she was surprised at Tom's response. "What do you mean 'sort of famous'?" I asked, bypassing Tom's take on James' looks.

"Walker Wilkes' son," Tom said. His eyelashes fluttered. Was it a tell? Did he know more than he was letting on? Did he know about *me*? "He's doing that whole thing over in LA."

I made a face. "Fitness?"

"What?" Tom asked.

Aashri laid a hand on his knee. "Dalmatia thinks you're talking about a gym. In any other conversation, I'd be proud of her."

"A gym? No, Los Angeles," Tom said. Aashri kept her hand

170

where it was. Tom didn't seem to notice.

"Are you saying James Wilkes was doing something in California?" I suddenly had the feeling that Kyle had been keeping a lot more from me than I'd been keeping from him. My suspicions about Jenna Shears were a paper cut, but this news about James had me bleeding out.

Tom glanced between Aashri and I as if we'd missed the obvious. "You guys don't know what I'm talking about? James Wilkes? The guru guy?"

Tom had my attention, and it wasn't because an alarm had started going off near one of his plants.

"Sorry about that!" Tom jumped from the couch. Aashri pretended he hadn't sent her hand flopping into her own chest as he quickly began tending to a convoluted system of tubes and tunnels across the room. Plants were involved, ones that looked like ferns and others adorned with tiny fruit barely visible to the naked eye. The whole conflagration looked like a hamster habitat.

"Stop staring at Tom's ass," Aashri whispered.

I twisted around, craning my neck. "Thought I heard some aloe vera running on a little wheel."

"Had to CalMag the Bruce Banner," Tom said, reappearing. He settled back into his spot beside Aashri, who pretended not to notice that his explanation made no sense.

I couldn't believe so much hinged on these two. "Okay, so, what's the plan?" I asked.

Aashri smiled. "I think you know."

An invisible string lifted Tom's eyebrows straight up the center of his forehead. He looked once more from Aashri to me, me to Aashri. "I'm in," he told us. "Whatever it is. I'm in."

Tom was in. Aashri was in.

I had no idea what any of us were getting *in*to, but circumstance

KELLY MACPHERSON

had thrown us together with quite a bit of new knowledge. What exactly was going on in the Wilkes family? What had James been up to in California?

And why were my parents somehow mixed up in it all?

20

Dal...matia

It was all fun and games until I went home.

Literally.

Tom the Bartending Cannabis King was a board game aficionado, so we rounded out my time at his garage by playing Clue. The electronic version. He kept a vintage edition in his bedroom, which Aashri was trying hard to gain entrance to. I'd never seen her come on so strong. She'd had WikiClue open, rattling off random facts about the game's origins and quizzing Tom on its history. The nearest to this level of investment I'd ever seen Aashri make had been her commitment to Whole30.

Despite the distraction, I couldn't get my night with James off my mind. I'd done okay at Tom's, all things considered, but I'd begun to drown in regret as soon as I was back in my car. Replaying my poor choice with James was the debris; him leaving without saying

173

goodbye had been the wrecking ball.

We hadn't talked much the night before, James and I. It wasn't that sort of thing. Over the years, I'd had the urge to know what he was up to but refused to search him up online. Finding out about a new girlfriend through social media would've sent me into a spiral I couldn't be sure I'd crawl out of. Despite this relatively weak self-restraint, I had still wanted a connection with him again. Badly. But James' face on a screen wouldn't do a thing to make me feel better, because I ached over wanting to touch him again. Hold him. Feel him solidly in my grasp, the skin of his biceps, his tall body bending to meet mine, that soft hair at the back of his neck. The parts of him that'd electrified my entire being. I'd wanted it back, knowing all the while there was nothing I could do to make that so.

Until last night.

I'd touched him, held him. Finally. And in doing so I'd let James into me with more than his body. It hadn't been fast, and it hadn't been once. And now I was plagued with imaginings of him above another woman, making her believe that the pressure of his weight against her, the insistency, his need, were for her alone. James Wilkes did whatever he wanted, and what he wanted changed so fast.

I sat on my couch for thirty minutes after returning from Tom's, because it was the most comfortable place James hadn't touched the night before. Somehow it felt as if sitting there, in the center of the room, meant I had eyes on whatever feelings would creep up and drag me down. I hadn't felt this bad since he'd left the first time. It wasn't remorse, exactly. If he walked in the door that very moment, I would've let him do whatever he wanted. I'd been that addicted to him three years ago, and despite believing otherwise, I still was.

Which is exactly what I hated.

That I'd let it last.

My regret wasn't James Wilkes. It was *me*. It was that I hadn't been born into a life that James would choose to be a part of. As if I could control that. As if he'd ever be satisfied by what I could offer.

I threw up lunch. It was disgusting anyway. I cried in the shower. I put my bed things in the washer. I put the banana pepper outfit I'd been wearing the night before in the trash.

I had to stop before I started dismantling my dining table for reasons I hated to remember.

Leaving the apartment would mean James won, but the logical part of my brain knew that wasn't true. A larger-than-I-wished part was stuck back in my late twenties when James Wilkes took up the entire sky above my head. He'd left, and the storm clouds had cleared for everyone but me. I was still standing outside, waiting for it to pour. The least I could do for myself today was get an umbrella.

I called Kyle before I could change my mind.

It went straight to voicemail.

"Hey, it's Dal...matia. It's Dal. I'm fine with just Dal. I was tired the other day." I paused. "No, I wasn't tired. I was upset." I took a deep breath. Not deep enough.

"I'm—"

I hung up.

What was I doing? I pushed the phone back to my ear as if it'd somehow reveal the answer and flinched when it buzzed against my earring. I hadn't even remembered keeping them on. Those would go in the trash, too.

"Hey, Dal...matia. Want to get a coffee?" Kyle had texted.

I didn't waste a second. "Definitely."

175

We met at the coffee shop where Kyle had been spying on me that first day he'd come to my apartment. Our togetherness wasn't a date, but it didn't feel platonic either. After last night, I couldn't even think about touching the same napkin dispenser as Kyle. Aashri had guessed the despicable thing I'd done with James, but no one else had to know. Kyle probably began to wonder what he'd gotten himself into when, after the barista called for "Daniella" and I picked up my iced latte, I didn't touch the cup again until the whipped cream had melted into a curdled puddle.

"Does that happen a lot?" Kyle asked, lowering his coffee as we sat opposite one another in a booth. He took it black, one sugar.

"Almost every time," I said. "With someone new at least. I don't recognize anyone working today." I removed the lid and finally put the rim of the latte to my lips.

"Do you want a straw?" Kyle asked. He'd gotten me one, of course. And, no, I did not want to touch it.

"I'm good, thanks."

I could tell he didn't believe me. "What other names do you get called?" he asked, changing the subject but not the weather. I felt sick. A tall body, sandy brown hair, caught my eye through the window. Would I spend another three years looking for his face where he never intended for it to be?

"Um, a bunch," I said, forcing my attention to this man, this moment, this reality. "I'm sorry. I'm so tired."

"I get it," Kyle said. "Luke had me up twice last night."

Luke, his son. I'd almost forgotten.

"Why?" I asked, unwrapping the straw a bit more.

Kyle's eyes watched my fingers. I pretended his look of concern was over what another unnecessary piece of plastic would do to the environment. "He was scared. We'd been reading that book *Scary Stories to Tell in the Dark*. Probably not the best thing before bed."

"I loved those books. Especially the big toe story." I abandoned clawing at the partially unwrapped straw and made an okay sign with my thumb and forefinger. "Golden."

Kyle took the straw before I could stop him. He unwrapped it gently and popped it in the top of my latte. "Hold on a sec," he added, rising with my drink in his hands. Before I could tell him not to abscond with my lukewarm property, he was back with fresh whipped cream on the top. "Told them it was for our mutual friend, Donatello." Kyle grinned.

"I'm going to assume you're equating me to the artist, not a sewer-dwelling reptile."

"Amphibian, but of course," he replied.

"Your son probably likes those turtles, huh?" I asked, returning Kyle's smile. I also returned his kindness and pulled a long swig of caramel iced latte through the straw. It was chilled once again. Kyle'd had the barista refresh the ice, too.

"He does." Kyle gripped his own cup with both hands. Big hands, masculine hands. If I let them touch me, if I promised him the rest of the day, just me and those hands and my bed stripped of sheets, would it rid me of the self-hate James had left me with? "He's also into Care Bears, Stumble Guys — that one's an iPhone game — and Bakugan. Eclectic taste."

Kyle was a father. I wouldn't jump from one distracted man to another.

"Luke sounds very cool," I said. "Some of my students are into Bakugan. I lost five to two battling during a show and tell last year."

Kyle laughed. I liked it. I really wished I didn't.

"Luke would love you," he said, catching his tongue on the last word. "Like, as a teacher. He'd love a teacher like you."

I made my mouth into something I hoped passed for a genuine smile. "I knew what you meant."

"It's not always easy, being a dad." Kyle looked uncertain. Maybe he was trying to gauge how personal he could be with me. How personal he *should* be.

Screw it.

"I'm sure it's not," I answered. I pulled my legs up onto the padded seat of the booth, sitting comfortably for once. I was in sweatpants, which, even if they were branded as luxury fleece, weren't much different than joggers. "My students are three and four years old. It's supposed to be about getting them ready for kindergarten, but most of what we do together feels like building safety. Being good friends, honoring our emotions. Sharing, but knowing when and why. That sort of small stuff."

"None of that's small."

Kyle's deep brown eyes fastened on mine. He leaned forward, arms on the table.

"Luke doesn't go to school in Cormoran, right? Because Marissa doesn't live around here," I said. "You can tell me to stop if that's personal. I don't mean it to be intrusive."

"Not intrusive at all." Kyle laced his fingers, body bent toward me. "Actually, no. He doesn't. His mom sends him to a private school in Glenmore."

"I know the one," I answered. "William Yancy Academy?"

Kyle's head dipped in a single, strained nod. "That's it."

178

"Good school."

"Very good school."

"*Rich* school."

Kyle sat back away from the table. "Very rich school."

He wasn't a fan. I could tell as much. I wondered at the salary of an FBI agent. Was it enough to afford a private school like William Yancy? And what about Marissa? She was a shelter director, but did it pay?

As if my mind had broadcast its thoughts on my forehead, Kyle cleared up my questions. "Marissa is remarried," he said. "Her husband Mark is the headmaster at William Yancy. Luke's tuition is comped."

I didn't know what to say.

"It's not that I'm against a good education," Kyle continued, playing with the cardboard wrapper designed to protect his fingers from the hot brew within his cup.

"Of course not."

"It's not even a private school thing. School is school. It's just that William Yancy is…"

I pulled the cup slowly from his hands. "It's snobby."

Kyle took a deep breath. He smiled again, an upward curve of relief. "Yes," he answered. "Very snobby."

"I'm sure Marissa does a good job counteracting that," I said, giving a woman I didn't know the benefit of the doubt. It felt like a slightly noble if not proper thing to do. "The fact that you didn't mention Luke being an equestrian or violin prodigy says a lot."

Kyle's brows pinched together. I'd seen that look when we'd first sat down.

"What?" I asked him. "Did someone just call out a coffee for Dentition?!"

He laughed. "You definitely don't know Marissa," he said.

"Unless she was the lady dressed in a blow-up sumo-wrestling chicken costume at Chick-Chick-Chicken yesterday, then, no, I don't. That lady and I are best friends now, by the way."

Kyle clutched an invisible string of pearls. "Does Aashri know?"

"Oh, yes," I replied. "We're polyplatonic. She plays Clue with her buddy Tom, and I hit up the freebies circuit with, uh, Colette."

Kyle choked on a sip of coffee. "Your other best friend's name is Colette?"

"Yes," I said with rebounding composure. "Her mother was a French percussionist who gave birth to her in the elevator of the Eiffel Tower."

"Wow," Kyle said. "Your friends are very cultured."

"Cultured," I said, lifting a finger. "But not snobby."

"No, never that."

"Except when it comes to board games. Thanks to this crush Aashri has on a bartender, I have now learned that Marvel may or may not have a stake in the marijuana growing business *and* the original patent for the game of Clue included an Irish walking stick as one of the weapons."

"I wish they'd kept that," Kyle said. "I loved that game. Luke has the electronic version. It was the first game he could sit still long enough to finish. I was just happy his favorite birthday gift that year came from one of my friends and not Marissa's husband." Kyle's lips curved into a sheepish half-grin. "I sound like a dick, don't I?"

"You sound normal. Trust me."

Kyle was quiet. I wondered what he was thinking.

When he spoke, his voice was almost a hush. "Do you trust *me*?"

Of course, I didn't. I barely knew him. And I hardly trusted anyone. I hardly trusted myself. After last night, even less so.

I was, therefore, unsure why I answered honestly.

"Yes," I told Kyle. "Even with a shillelagh."

"Irish walking stick." He smiled. "What about the syringe?"

I smiled back. "Not a stranger to Wikipedia yourself, huh?"

"Actually, The History Channel. 'The Games We Played' or something like that. The syringe was another weapon that got the boot when Clue was released. Did you know it was based on Agatha Christie?"

"I did," I replied. I'd forgotten all about my latte and James. "And the creator sold it to finance his career as a concert pianist."

"Did he make it?" Kyle asked. "As a pianist?"

I considered. "You know, I'm not sure. I'll have to look it up."

Kyle leaned toward me once more. "Why did you call me, Dal?"

Honesty. It had brought me this far.

"I'm not sure." My hands crept toward my drink, but I pulled them back and looked Kyle in the eye. "Because I wanted to."

The tension within his body, imperceptible to me before, dissipated. I watched the shift and felt it too, like pins and needles in my chest. Could a heart fall asleep? If so, what did it take to wake it?

"Dalmatia, I have something to tell you," Kyle said.

"Then we're even, because I have something to tell you, too."

"Do you want to go first?" he asked.

I reminded myself that I was being honest here. Not just with Kyle but with myself, so, no, I didn't want to hear whatever he wanted to say. I didn't like how his eyes looked. I didn't like how the rhythm of his breath seemed to echo some internal sense of danger.

So, yes, I would go first.

"I wanted to ask if you'd help me," I said in a rush. "Aashri, too. And our friend, Tom. He has an interesting mustache, but he's a good guy. Not that I have anything against facial hair." Kyle bore a dark shadow himself. I'd barely noticed it before. "My parents are in deep with some weird Walker Wilkes shit, and I have to know what's going on. I want to be back on the case."

KELLY MACPHERSON

Kyle sat back, pulling all my confidence away with him. I'd been ridiculous to invite myself back into his investigation and even more ridiculous to think he'd care about my stupid life.

"I'm in," he answered, laying a hand flat on the table.

I was surprised enough that I almost set mine atop it.

"Good," I said. I should've been more relieved than I was. Instead, I was afraid. "Good. Thank you."

"And Dal," Kyle's fingers moved closer. By the time I had a chance to unstick my anxiety and take them in my own, his hand had rounded back toward his cold cup of coffee. "Just so you know, there's no case for me without you."

182

CULT & RUN PODCAST TRANSCRIPT
SEASON 2, EPISODE 6

ALEX PARKER: Shag, Marry, Kill, The Committee Edition...and go!

SHEENA FAVROSIAN: I'm cringing because you just said shag.

ALEX PARKER: It's the name of the game. Go, Sheena, go!

SHEENA FAVROSIAN: Okay, okay. Let's see. Who do we have? Walker Wilkes, obviously. As we've heard through the magical, mystical grapevine — $19.99 per ounce — Wilkes does in fact wed ladies post-death, so he's a possibility for tying the knot.

ALEX PARKER: So, you're marrying Walker Wilkes?

SHEENA FAVROSIAN: I didn't say that.

ALEX PARKER: Then you're marrying the son, James Wilkes aka Guru Jimmy Sway.

SHEENA FAVROSIAN: I swear, Alex, I'm going to kill you.

ALEX PARKER: I'm not an option. Okay, we've got Walker Wilkes, the dad, head-honcho—

SHEENA FAVROSIAN: Please stop using words that mean other words.

ALEX PARKER: James Wilkes, the son, thirty-two years old and following daddy's footsteps with a YouTube channel and nominal cultish following out in California.

SHEENA FAVROSIAN: Although, unlike Papa Wilkes, Baby Bear Wilkes preaches manifestation. Specifically, manifestation within the context of an acting career. What was that movie he was in?

ALEX PARKER: Coins of Death II. He had a bit part playing a Central Park jogger sliced to pieces by a hoard of mutant pennies.

SHEENA FAVROSIAN: I assume it won Sundance?

ALEX PARKER: Yes, obviously.

SHEENA FAVROSIAN: Okay, I'll commit. Marry Walker Wilkes, shag James Wilkes. He's hot, Alex, even for a lunatic who can't even take me to Sundance.

ALEX PARKER: I'd rather see you kill the guy, but do who you want, Sheena.

SHEENA FAVROSIAN: Not a fan of Jimmy Sway?

ALEX PARKER: Not in the least.

21

Early Bird Special

In eighth grade, Jenna Shears showed up to my birthday in costume.

It was *not* a costume party.

I'd turned thirteen the week before, and my mother had arranged an indoor luau in the middle of a Pennsylvania winter. Convincing teenagers to don leis at the door was an even harder sell than tempting them to sample my mother's take on Polynesian cuisine. The luau theme had been her idea, not mine. My family didn't even own a pool. My mother's attempt at throwing the party of the year promised to be a challenge.

And then Jenna came dressed as Lola Bunny.

A sexy cartoon rabbit drank pink lemonade from a plastic coconut for two-and-a-half hours while nine other girls in faux grass skirts shuffled around uncomfortably as Don Ho played from a speaker in the living room. No one said a word about the get-up. Not the other girls, not my mother. It'd been left to me to let Jenna know that not only was this not a Warner Brothers production nor a follow-up

185

attempt by Michael Jordan to diversify his sports career.

Again, it was also *not* a costume party.

"But you're in that fringy thing," Jenna had said, sucking the last dregs of liquid sugar through a straw.

"It's a grass skirt," I'd answered back. "Because this is a luau."

Jenna made a show of roaming her eyes over my parents' living room. My mother had hung cardboard palm trees on the walls and covered the windows with blue tissue paper and cut-outs of tropical fish. My dad built a working volcano from papier-mâché, but the right side had melted when he'd left it on the kitchen counter too close to a pot of water my mother had been boiling for spaghetti.

"Doesn't look like California," Jenna had said.

"Hawaii," I'd replied through gritted teeth.

"Same diff."

Memories of Jenna Shears and her fake coconut, Jenna Shears shoving my birthday cake into her pinhole of a mouth, Jenna Shears flapping her dumb bunny ears at my mother who'd pretended to be delighted by the whole thing — "How creative she is, Dalmatia!" — all came back as she walked into the coffee shop where Kyle and I sat.

"Fuck," I said.

Kyle looked seriously taken aback. "Are you okay?"

"No."

"Did I do something?"

If I stared too long at the look of concern on his face, I'd end up telling him all of it. My suspicions about Jenna and my past with her, too. I'd end up sounding like a neurotic jerk. What thirty-one-year-old woman gets her hackles up over a neighbor who'd annoyed her eighteen years ago?

"It's not you," I said, wanting to fast pitch a coconut at Jenna Shears' forehead. "Not at all. Someone I can't stand just walked in." I tried for a smile. "Now you probably think *I'm* a dick." I immediately regretted that final word as if Kyle could discern the weight of irritation unfurling in my brain. My neck felt warm, and my head began to throb.

"Want to leave?" he asked in a quiet voice. "I know another—"

"Yes, Caroline. I saw."

Jenna's voice.

Her unmistakable nasality carried through the coffee shop, settling over Kyle and I like a fire alarm. She'd been cornered by a group of Committee Members who lived in a retirement community not far from Cormoran. I couldn't imagine what brought them to a coffee shop. Probably doubling down on espresso so they're make it to the early bird special at the Cormoran Diner later on.

A twin pair of chimes went off, and Kyle's face mirrored the discomfort on my own. "I'm so sorry, Dal, but I actually have to go." He fumbled with his phone, holding it up before me quick enough that I couldn't see the screen but knew it likely held work communication.

"No problem," I said.

"Cool. I'll text you later."

My ears were trained in the direction of Jenna, but my eyes watched Kyle as he slipped out the exit, taking anything good I'd been feeling right along with him.

After Kyle left, I hid in the bathroom for twenty minutes.

Jenna was gone by the time I emerged, my hands raw from washing every time someone entered the three-stall restroom. I'd needed a cover. One of the retirees, a lady with a beaded tropical bird on the front of her sweatshirt eyed me warily. Her gaze switched back and forth from my face to my hands. "Something you know that we don't?" she asked. "Health inspection-wise?"

I couldn't wait to get out of there. It didn't matter where to so long as it wasn't my own apartment. When my mother texted — in all caps — I was more obliging than usual.

"Why did you offer to babysit his plants?" I asked Aashri. She'd met me at my parents' house, waiting while my mom tapped the final touches on what she promised was the final draft of the final email going out to remind attendees of the amazingness of the items slotted to be auctioned off at The Barbara Gala.

Aashri and I waited in the living room, because we'd been told that my mother had broken her Internet and trusted only Aashri to take a look at it. Aashri had helped my mother Ebay a wheel lock for my dad's truck in 2006; therefore, she was an IT tech.

Instead of an insidious virus, all that'd been wrong with my parents' computer was that it needed to update.

Aashri walked my mother through the process, earning herself an everything bagel. She then joined me on the back patio "just in case" my mother needed her again. This was a woman who'd stuck three pieces of duct tape over her PC's webcam and recorded her passwords backwards in a spiral notebook labeled CHRISTMAS RECIPES. As with all of her relationships, the one my mother shared with the World Wide Web was interesting.

"Back to the plant sitting. Doesn't Tom worry you're going to smoke all his Hulk while he's gone?" I dipped my own bagel into a ramekin of melted butter. It was a thing I did, and I liked it. Aashri reached across and did the same.

"I'm not going to do that. But it was weird. Like, one second we were eating Pad Thai and the next he was asking if I knew how to operate an automatic watering system."

"And you said yes?"

She dipped again. "I said 'sure'."

"You like him too much," I told her. "And now you're going to kill his agriculture."

Aashri shrugged. "Then he'll have more time for me."

"And the investigation."

Aashri gave me a thumbs-up. "The investigation."

I'd already briefed her on my coffee meet-up with Kyle, which she'd called a date and which I knew wasn't. Aashri also briefed me on a run-in she'd had with Jenna Shears at Costco earlier in the day, a serendipitous meet-up in which she had learned that Jenna was temping at Urgent Care in between hospital positions. While saying something about an expanded emergency medicine department due to open at one of the larger facilities outside Bywood County, Jenna had checked an incoming text message. Aashri, stealthier than I'd given her credit for, spied the name of the sender while pretending to squint closer at a price tag for a five-piece non-stick cookware set.

"Why was Malorie texting her?" I asked. "Could they work together in some capacity? They're both in medicine."

"Yes, they could," Aashri replied. "Have you thought to ask questions instead of hiding in a bathroom?"

"And say what?" I cleared my throat. "'Hello, Jenna, do you know a woman named Malorie who happened to be your ex-cult leader's home nurse and maybe killed him because you told her how to do it?'" I stuck the last bite of bagel into my mouth. "Would that be rude?"

"You should probably call Malorie a 'home health aide', but, aside from that, it sounded good." Aashri had already finished her food. Now she stuck one finger in the butter and sucked it off.

"You ruined my lunch."

"You ruined mine."

My mother ruined our moment by hurrying into the backyard in an apron, her irrepressible buzz of chaotic energy in tow. "Girls! This is it! This is *it!*"

"What's it?" Aashri whispered my way.

I pushed the butter toward her. "Just wait."

My mother continued her proclamation. "The fourteenth annual Barbara Gala is in three days, and neither of you have RSVP'd! I am absolutely at the end of my string—"

"You mean rope," I offered.

"…trying to get you both to commit to coming *and* bringing dates."

I opened my mouth, but—

"Dalmatia Louise, I know you're going to tell me that Aashri is your date, and that has been fine and good in the past, but this year I would like you to both bring someone who has not had a chance to be entertained and enlightened by the Gala thus far."

"So, you want fresh meat to bleed for cash?" I asked with a grin.

Aashri feigned horror. "Mrs. Scissors! You're going to kill people?"

My mother's impatience was more obvious than the fact that she still hadn't mastered chicken piccata. Her apron was covered in white wine stains. "Who's on the docket, girls?"

"I guess Kyle," I told her.

The bag of bagels my mother had brought outside did not make it to the table. She hugged it right back to her chest. "Uh-uh," she said. "Not that one."

"*That one* is the closest I have to a date," I said, a flush creeping up my neck.

"Actually, I think it'd be lovely if you allowed James to take you to the gala," my mother replied.

Aashri looked as ill as I felt.

"No," I told my mother. "I'm not doing that." I shifted in the plastic patio chair, rocking sideways on its uneven legs. The knowledge of what James and I had done swept through my body like a flame on dry wood. I was going to vomit.

"He's only back in town for a short time, Dalmatia, and it'd be a good way to reconnect. The way you'd left things with him was just terrible."

I jumped to my feet and made it to the bathroom before Kyle's whipped cream rose up and slapped my mother in the face.

A few minutes later, Aashri was a voice beyond the door. "Your mom says she's sorry, which we both know she isn't, but she said she won't pressure you anymore. Also, I just got the weirdest text and think you need to come out and see this."

I wiped my mouth on my mother's hand towel as retribution, realizing too late that I was the one receiving all the germs. My mother touched a lot of shopping carts.

"Look." Aashri handed me her phone after I joined her atop the plush mauve carpet in my parents' upstairs hallway.

Tom had texted Aashri an article about a Brooklyn restaurant that served only hydroponic produce. It was called Stem, which I found unimaginative. Below a photo of a bearded man in a straw-hat hand-harvesting beets in the middle of a historic parlor, was a photo of a woman I'd known my entire life. A woman who'd served The Committee faithfully and unwaveringly in Cormoran until she'd left to become a missionary in the seventeenth wealthiest state in the country.

Mrs. Shears had given an interview.

I glanced down the staircase and locked eyes with the oversized photo of Walker Wilkes my mother had recently hung.

I could've sworn it smirked.

22

Baptism by Fire

The headline at the top read "BEHIND THE BEE POLLEN OLD-FASHIONED", and a subtitle below mentioned something about Cormoran and The Committee and Exposing a Cult's Poisonous Agenda. Mrs. Shears' expression read as scandalizing as the article promised to be. Her once unadorned face wore a slash of dark lipstick and enough concealer that Aashri's phone screen was a grainy facsimile of a woman who'd, at times, been as involved in my life as my own mother.

But unlike my own mother, Mrs. Shears had done the one thing Committee members did not do.

Turned traitor.

I should've been glad. I should've liked her for it. But I didn't. Too many years of pain and confusion laid between the Mrs. Shears of my childhood, a wicked witch riding her broom past my bedroom window, and the hardened version who stared up at me from an article on "The Cut".

193

Aashri and I discussed it as quietly as we could while in the presence of my eavesdropping mother. I decided straight-away that Mrs. Shears' newfound animosity toward Walker Wilkes would be cause enough to involve her daughter in a plot to kill him, but Aashri wasn't as convinced. Jenna Shears had the knowledge to do so, and, with Malorie Kurtz-Hathaway at her disposal, the means. Aashri encouraged me to keep an open mind and agreed to discuss it later. After we parted ways, Aashri to her job at the pharmacy and me to dwell on this new information, I called Kyle.

And he invited me over.

On any other day, at any other time, I may have declined, opting instead to meet up back at the coffee shop. I also could've gone for a McDouble. However, fueled by adrenaline and what felt very much like a ticking time bomb leading up to The Barbara Gala, not to mention a grand chance to expose The Shears Family for the murderers they were, I said okay.

As I followed iMap's directions to his place, I used my Beamer's Bluetooth feature to call Kyle and expound upon the dissonance I was experiencing between the Mrs. Shears of old and this new version. His calm, inquisitive voice and my hyperactive conjecturing served as a good distraction from worrying about what it meant to show up at Kyle's house for the first time.

Kyle had already been inside my own residence twice, but his first visit had been to elicit my help in his investigation and the second had occurred because my apartment appeared to have been in the throes of being burglarized by a professional sporting mascot. It wasn't as if I'd invited him in to spend the night. I pushed the thought away, unwilling to let what I'd done with James take up space in my head. I had to stay clear, focused. James Wilkes remained characteristically mute, but I didn't. I kept talking to Kyle.

Losing myself to nerves, I even told him about the infamous

highlighter incident. I forced myself to pause and take a breath mid-sentence. Kyle lived fifteen minutes from my parents' house by car, but it felt as if I'd been sprinting the distance.

"Listen Dal," he said. "I do have to warn you. I have quite a few pens lying around, and I'd feel really weird if you start, like, chewing on one." If it were anyone else, I would've taken offense, but I could hear the smile on his face.

"Trust me, Detective, you should worry about what else I can do with a ballpoint. You don't strike me as a gel-tip guy."

Kyle's voice threaded like smoke through my BMW's speakers. "What did you have in mind?"

He made me dizzy. This was flirting.

"I didn't know you were into that stuff," I said. "Office supply play and all that."

Kyle seemed to have forgotten his sudden change of heart. "I'm into it all, Dalmatia. You have no idea."

What was happening? I was tired. I was worked up over the Malorie text and the Mrs. Shears article. I was more than worked up — I was devastated — by what I'd done with James. And there I was receiving signals from a man whose attention I clearly wanted. When I showed up at his house, would Kyle be waiting for me with the lights low and a pencil sharpener grinding in the background?

"Of course, I'm only kidding," Kyle said. I'd gone quiet on him. "I'll leave my pens out as a good faith gesture, though," he added.

"Very brave of you," I answered, sliding a vision of his eyes, warm brown and bright, into my pocket.

"Or foolish," Kyle said. "Have you eaten? I could DoorDash Chinese if you think you can't control yourself. I have one or two pencils around this place, too. I'm not sure how you feel about erasers…"

"I'll always choose won-ton soup over synthetic polymers." My Beamer interrupted with instructions to take the next left. "I'm not that bad."

"I'd sort of like to see you bad."

I almost blew my turn.

"Sort of?" I asked, my heart beating in my throat.

"Completely."

"You shouldn't say these things while a lady is driving a dangerous machine. Zero to sixty in 2.5 seconds." I swallowed. "Can you do that?"

Kyle's voice mingled with his breath. He sounded close enough to be right beside me in the car. "Uh-huh."

"Okay, well, I'm almost at your house, so…"

"Oh, shit!"

Kyle's sudden exclamation forced me into a hard pause at a stop sign, the final one before turning right onto his street.

"Dal, I'm so sorry. I'm really sorry. If it's not a problem with you, I'd still love for you to be here. But, if it is, I understand and it's totally fine." Kyle's words fired through my speaker like BB gun pellets.

"It's okay," I told him, not wanting him to feel embarrassed by flirting so unabashedly. It was nothing, just light banter between friends. "I'm not upset. Nothing you said was upsetting."

"It's not us, what we were just…it's Luke," Kyle answered. "And Marissa. I'd forgotten they were picking up Bug and Face for a 4-H thing out Marissa's way. It wasn't supposed to be today, but she had to reschedule, and I hadn't marked it down. I'd usually have talked to Luke this morning and he'd have talked about it enough to remind me, but I didn't have a chance to call because Marissa brought him on a run to—"

"Luke and Marissa are at your house?" I asked.

Yes, they were. I could see them.

A dark-haired woman with thick curls held off her face by a top-knot headband was opening the door of a white Suburban for a little boy with Kyle's brown hair and the woman's thick waves. We hadn't even embarked on a proper second date before fitting in both dirty talk and meeting the family on the same afternoon.

"Well, I hope they're not hungry," I told Kyle. "Because I lay claim to those pens. Pencil erasers, they can have." I wondered if I'd been too snarky. I wondered if he'd follow up on the *lay*.

But Kyle had already hung up and was now standing on the front step of a well-kept, single-story house to greet me as I parked before his front lawn. Cindy the dog bounded through the grass in figure eights. Marissa turned my way and smiled. Luke turned my way and scowled. The automatic sprinklers turned on and sprayed me in the face the second I stepped from my car. Cindy fled back into the house.

Walker Wilkes had taught that all relationships began and ended with one person trying to mind-read the other. While hurrying through a suburban monsoon toward Kyle, who'd flashed me a horrified look and ran inside, I realized that Wilkes hadn't been far off the mark.

A second after the sprinklers went dry, Kyle returned breathless and visibly apologetic.

Luke pulled his father's arm across his shoulders.

Marissa waved.

In the short time between learning what I'd be arriving to and deciding to show up anyway, I'd assumed a far different outcome than what appeared to be transpiring. Marissa, remarried to another man and devoted to animals, may not care about my involvement in Kyle's life. Luke, on the other hand, was ready to flush me down the toilet.

As for Kyle, he simply smiled.

And held up a pencil.

197

Once inside Kyle's place, he offered me a sweatshirt, a bathrobe, and a shopping spree to make up for the baptism on his front lawn. The only thing worse for wear was my pride.

Kyle made several apologies as he also made proper introductions between myself, Marissa, and Luke, the latter of which said I looked tired. Kyle had ducked his head toward mine and quietly apologized again as he led me to a sofa in his living room and took a seat on the cushion beside me. In turn, I made a good-humored quip about the wisdom of children. After all, I was a teacher, and I *was* tired. And I also knew what little pains in the ass children could be.

But what a situation.

"What's your favorite part of being a teacher?" Marissa asked. It was a thoughtful question, a kind one. I hadn't taken her to be the most beautiful woman in all Bywood County when I'd first spied her through the windshield of my BMW, but I now thought that was the product of either low washer fluid or my own stupidity. The more I interacted with Marissa, watching her manage a fidgety Luke and an equally as fidgety Kyle, I wondered why on earth I was even there. She was lovely. She was smart. She was funny. She shouldn't have been the *ex*-wife.

"I like giving kids a place to be creative," I answered in as steady a voice as I was able. "And being told by four-year-olds that their mothers look younger than me." She asked other questions, eliciting a variety of answers such as French onion soup, the Florida

Everglades, illegal fireworks, and Dyson vacuums. I asked about her work at the animal sanctuary and the many pets she had at home. Cindy took up lounging across my mostly dry shoes as I listened. "Animal companions", Marissa called her pets. If it wouldn't have hurt Kyle's feelings, I may have asked for Marissa's hand in marriage.

"Do you think you'll work there forever, at the learning center?" Marissa finally asked. Kyle hadn't spoken much apart from a half-dozen bad dad jokes and some oversharing about pranks he'd pulled in college. If this was Kyle's nervous side, I was concerned about the FBI's decision to grant him security clearance. Good thing we weren't discussing *his* work.

Kyle ended the worst bit of his stand-up routine — "it was a walnut disguised as FDR" — and I answered Marissa.

"I'm not sure," I said. "Honestly, I like the kids but I'm not much for bureaucracy. You wouldn't think we'd have much of that at a small educational center serving newborns up to age five, but you'd be surprised."

Marissa and I sat across from one another, me next to Kyle on a distressed leather couch I thought I'd seen in an Instagram ad, and Marissa and Luke in matching wingback chairs. Kyle's taste was surprisingly nice. He was also a legitimately gracious host and had taken Luke into the kitchen to get Capri Suns while I answered Marissa's many questions.

"That's what I was getting at but didn't want to step on your toes," Marissa said. "You work at that Committee place."

I'd always wanted to see stars. The kind that swirl above your head like a little galaxy, prompting you to beam back down to earth. I knew it meant I'd need to be knocked out, concussed, flummoxed, and yet the stars aspect seemed a mystical, magical experience, an out-of-body one, to which nothing in my life even came close. But hearing Marissa refer to my school as "That Committee Place" had supernovas popping before my eyes. And it was nothing I ever wanted to experience again.

"I'm sorry," Marissa said, drawing back. "I shouldn't have said that." Her mouth looked like she was tasting an old shoe.

"No," I replied. "I don't care at all. The Committee is what it is. I was raised in it, but I'm not a part of it."

"But you work there?" Marissa continued, chancing that a wet shoelace would slip out.

My insides felt like they'd been inside a Vitamix.

"Marissa, it's not important," Kyle said, reentering with a bunch of Pacific Coolers in his hands. Luke held a matching tray of Fruit Punch. "Change of subject. I once knew about this kidnapping at a school, and you'd never believe what happened."

"After fifth period he woke up," I finished.

Kyle smiled. "You've heard that one."

"I know a lot of dads," I replied.

Kyle didn't look too pleased at that, but he rallied. "Do they tell jokes?"

"One gave me a Yeti tumbler as a teacher Christmas gift two years ago but must never have taken it out of the box. It was engraved with the name of a local orthodontist, so, no. Most don't tell jokes. Most are jokes."

"I know that ortho," Marissa said. "Doesn't even do good work." She grinned and toasted me with a Fruit Punch.

Kyle sat beside me once more, his thigh touching mine. I leaned closer. Marissa asked Luke to grab some Twinkies and ushered him into the kitchen to help. I figured it was a make-up for the gaffe she'd made earlier, but it didn't matter. Nothing Marissa said would cause me to turn away from how Kyle was looking at me.

"Your eyes are the color of the Pacific...Cooler," he said.

"And yours," I answered, "are finer than a BOGO sale at Office

Max."

Kyle pulled one of my hands between his. "That place closed." His fingers laced with mine, the rough hands of a man who knew how to use them. "Bankruptcy," he added, enunciating every syllable.

Legal foreclosure had never sounded so sexy.

CULT & RUN PODCAST TRANSCRIPT
SEASON 2, EPISODE 7

ALEX PARKER: Okay, Sheena, move Donna Shears to the top of the pyramid. Go, go, go, there she is! Donna Shears dethrones She Who Must Not Be Named Under Threat of Legal Recourse as the top spot in our whistleblower pyramid! It's a fine day at Carbon Fiber Studios.

SHEENA FAVROSIAN: Don't forget Carbon Fiber also produces Hot Plot Hot Pot, and I don't think Susie Kee would be thrilled that you've deemed the Donna Shears article a bigger deal than her mealtime interviews with best-selling authors.

ALEX PARKER: For the purpose of our pyramid…Susie, my apologies. Go, Donna!

SHEENA FAVROSIAN: Susie, have Hiram Sheldon put a hit on Alex in his next thriller.

ALEX PARKER: Speaking of hits, what's your take on Donna Shears' theory that Walker Wilkes' death involved a member of The Committee?

SHEENA FAVROSIAN: It's highly likely given the four decades he spent prescribing false remedies for everything from indigestion to breast cancer. I'm not sure I could've let him grow old in grace.

ALEX PARKER: Likewise. Donna Shears describes a period of intense unrest within the group shortly after Wilkes' diagnosis with type 2 diabetes six years ago. It's no secret he proclaimed it as a test of the ego and further evidence of his being preordained to

Cult & Run

enter The Realm as Most Enlightened. Apparently not everyone who'd pledged loyalty to The Committee had such unwavering belief in Wilkes' divinity.

SHEENA FAVROSIAN: Because he was a quack.

ALEX PARKER: The boldest among us usually are.

23

Gristle

By the time I left Kyle's house, my bladder was fuller than the Chick-Chick-Chicken parking lot on a Saturday night.

Luke had volun-forced me into a child's version of a drinking contest at which I tried not to best him. I lost of no accord but my own, Luke: five Capri Suns; me: seven. As if that wasn't tenuous enough, Luke *mistakenly* flushed a hotdog down the toilet, which put the guest bathroom in Kyle's place out of commission. Kyle's son then proceeded to occupy the master bathroom for an amount of time that should've produced a ninth grader instead of a smug seven-year-old who told me he'd "let drop a big one".

Kyle had to take a work call shortly after, and Marissa had a commitment at the sanctuary. Luke would be staying the night at Kyle's, so my time there was done. It was just as well. Sitting beside Kyle on that couch, my body had responded with an ease that left me anything but carefree.

I'd texted Kyle goodbye while he was on the phone, adding that

Cult & Run

I'd talk to him later. Marissa encouraged me to wait, but things had gone far enough. She and Cindy walked me to the car after helping Luke set up a Nintendo Switch, for which he said he needed no help whatsoever. His mother kissed him goodbye, and Luke gave me quite a victorious smirk as I walked toward the door. I refrained from tossing him the evil eye. That bit of apotropaic magic was intended some five thousand years ago to ward off wickedness, not repay it. There I was, a thirty-one-year-old woman, abandoning maturity to feud with a minor.

After leaving Kyle's I could have done a great many things. It wasn't the weekend, so I had prep to do for my class — decorations on the Cricut, books to pick up from the library, Pinterest boards of process-oriented children's art projects to peruse. My job wasn't easy, but it also wasn't terribly taxing. Luke Alaric wouldn't have caused me to bat an eyelash if he wasn't connected to Kyle.

But worse than that: Luke reminded me of James. The arrogance, the inability to be responsible for it. I hated that a child could cause me to think of a man so low, so despicable.

I hated that my brain even made the comparison.

It was probably best to spend my evening taking a breather from the whole Walker Wilkes thing, Kyle thing, James thing. From *everything*.

And so I headed for Sephora.

The beauty conglomerate, founded in 1969 in Limoges, France had been named for Zipporah, one of Moses' wives in the Hebrew Bible. I wasn't in love with the fact that Moses had several wives, some of whom had been given to him by their fathers, but I'd done enough cultic studies on the Old Testament to understand that systems of female oppression are sometimes tinted in Easter pastels.

Zipporah, an Ethiopian Midianite known for her good looks, inspired the name of the beauty chain to which I was headed. She

205

meant something different to me, though. Zipporah had been forced to slice off her son's foreskin and wipe it on her husband's feet after an angel of God pulled an attempted murder on Moses. Pissed off that her mate should've been the one to perform the rite of circumcision but had probably been too busy collecting wives with daddy issues, Zipporah and Moses' relationship tanked after the incident. Zip and her two sons returned to her father's land, while Moses went on to part the Red Sea.

It's funny, not ha-ha but ironic, that Moses wouldn't have freed a people and risen to biblical fame if his wife hadn't saved his behind in the first place. I didn't buy my makeup from Sephora because Zipporah was its namesake, but it didn't dissuade me.

I parked in the garage at The Good Mall, which meant it had a food court without a Sbarro, and hurried toward the black and white stripes that'd wipe all my tears away. The pleasant fragrance of two hundred perfume testers greeted me as I entered the warm incandescent lighting of the beauty store. I inhaled strong notes of citrus and musk on my way to the clean moisturizers.

But I didn't make it.

Blocking my path was the last person I'd ever expect to find flanked by hundred-dollar skin creams and dewy eye gels. When it came to surprise reappearances, the Shears family was like mother, like daughter.

"Dalmatia Scissors," Mrs. Shears said. "Long time, no see."

Mrs. Shears had become a trimmer, more stylish version of her old self, never one to care about her own looks but insecure enough on behalf of others to suggest improvements to theirs. I'd struggled through a particularly challenging year in high school when my mother had, under the influence of Mrs. Shears, forced me to jog around the neighborhood for thirty minutes three times a week to "lose those extra five pounds on the thighs". I hadn't owned five

Cult & Run

pounds to lose and hated running. Not to mention the *neighborhood*.

"I'm sure by now you know I've given an interview," Mrs. Shears continued, her mouth a maroon pucker at the center of her face. The skin around her eyes was tight, but her neck betrayed her. Mrs. Shears was my mother's age, even if she wanted to pretend that time had been kinder than it had.

"I've seen it," I told her. "Walker is dead, so I guess anyone can say anything they want now."

Mrs. Shears laughed. Her face was a balloon tied too tight. "Is that what you think? He's dead?"

Sephora suddenly felt far too warm, too stifling, too full of sprays for hair and sprays for skin and sprays for setting foundation that'd cake on thick and heavy. Walker Wilkes was dead, and no amount of Mrs. Shears' ridiculous assertions would change the fact that no product in that store could make his buried corpse look anything less than dead, dead, dead.

Dead.

She stepped closer. "Have you seen the body?"

I tried to tamp down the sass a couple decades in the making. I failed. "Have *you*?"

Mrs. Shears reached for a lipstick off the shelf. I was close enough to read the label, a color called Gristle. "I think you should talk to your mother." She uncapped the top of the tube, which happened to be a tester, and pressed the flattened nub of scarlet-purple to her thin, maroon lips. One color slid slowly over the other, catching a fleck of dry skin here, crossing a lip line there. The result was a macabre mess of artificial red that made my stomach hurt.

"My mother's busy," I told her. The mall had been a bad idea. "The Barbara Gala is in a few days."

Mrs. Shears smiled. The stretch of her mouth was a joker's punch. "Her baby," she replied. "The gala."

KELLY MACPHERSON

"It was good seeing you again," I said, nodding slightly as I turned back the way I came. The reward points in my Sephora account couldn't tempt me to stay in that place one second longer.

"Dalmatia Scissors!" The sound of Mrs. Shears calling out my full name was a cold blade down my spine. "Go to The Garden."

"Okay, thanks. I'll add it to my schedule." I slammed into an endcap full of bath bombs.

Mrs. Shears lifted another lipstick from the shelf and waved goodbye.

24

Same Shit, Different Day

Staples provided the relief Sephora failed to give.

Mrs. Shears certainly would not be lying in wait between clear sheet protectors and laminating machines. I wandered the aisles wondering if I should book a one-way ticket to Bali and be done with it. No, not Bali. I burned too easily. Ireland. An Irish pub with a swoonworthy barkeep who'd inherited a castle and was looking for a full-time shut-in to add a touch of intrigue.

Instead of beginning a new life overseas, I bought a large whiteboard, dry erase markers, and a pack of funny pens for Kyle, inscribed with wit such as GET TO THE POINT and MOM'S ALWAYS WRITE. Kyle's dad humor would appreciate them.

Tom was at Aashri's apartment when I walked in the door.

"Whoa! We could've been naked!" she said, a little too loudly for my taste. Tom was using the bathroom less ten feet away.

"Well, you're not," I replied. "And if you were, I'd hope you'd lock your front door."

"We DoorDash'd Don Pablo's."

"And did you want your delivery driver to find you in the middle of a sex act?"

Aashri shrugged. "Depends." She took the whiteboard from under my arm. "And ew. 'Sex act'. You're a 1940s church organist."

"Maybe, but I'm an amateur sleuth, too. And so are you and Tom. I've decided that we need to commence our investigation ASAP."

Aashri grimaced. "I hate when you use acronyms."

"LYLAS."

"IDGAF."

I began unpacking my supplies, and Aashri helped. She set the whiteboard against the bottom of a wall, and we gathered around it like my students at Show and Tell time. Tom exited the bathroom and joined us with a thumbs-up. He smelled like Aashri's lilac soup.

I listed what we knew so far, filling in Tom and Aashri on what Kyle and I had learned from Marlorie's house and Walker Wilkes's garbage.

MRS. SHEARS HATES THE COMMITTEE
JAMES IS BACK; FOR MORE THAN THE FUNERAL?
SYRINGE AT WILKES'
DOORBELL CAM AT WILKES'; MISSING FROM
    MALORIE HK'S?
JENNA SHEARS KILLED WALKER WILKES

"First of all," Aashri began, "I don't like how familiar you get with semi-colons."

"That was a quote I added to your birthday card. The semi-colon was borrowed."

Aashri pushed a hand through her hair. It stuck up. "And you don't know that Jenna killed Double Dub."

"I do," I answered. "It's obvious."

"You said she's the lady who helped me find my car at that chicken event?" Tom asked. "The chiropractor?"

"Physical assistant," Aashri replied at the same moment I said, "serial killer."

Aashri pulled a face like a flat tire. "Oh, come on, Dal! She's killed, at the most, one man!"

I shrugged. "That we know of."

"How many do you suspect?" Tom asked, eyes stretched in wonder.

Aashri swatted him in the chest. He laughed and grabbed her hands.

"There's one more thing." I told them about my run-in with Mrs. Shears. "I think we need to check Wilkes' grave for ourselves. Mrs. Shears had a reason for telling me to go, and it wasn't to express my grief."

"Maybe you want to leave this one to the professionals," Tom said, readjusting himself into something yogi and Bavarian pretzel-esque. "Grave digging may not be wise in a small town like this. I'm pretty sure Alice next door is onto my horticultural activities."

"Alice is a cat," Aashri said.

Tom shuddered. "She knows things."

"I'm taking Mrs. Shears' suggestion with a grain of salt," I said. "But I'm also going to look into it. I wonder if Kyle could get us access to The Committee's private burial site?"

Tom twirled a dry erase marker in his fingers. "Like a Sphinx?"

211

"Yes," I said. "A Sphinx. In Cormoran. Where the tallest building is a two-story bank."

"I wasn't thinking," Tom answered. He looked a bit stung. Aashri aimed me a sharp look.

I sighed inwardly. "No, you're fine, Tom." I deflected another pointed glance from Aashri. "You're closer to fact than you realize. Walker Wilkes placed a large emphasis on the burial process, like the Ancient Egyptians. But unlike ornate sarcophagi, Wilkes didn't believe in closed caskets, or caskets at all, because they'd constrain one from ascending to the afterlife. He called it The Realm, which I'm pretty sure was an idea repurposed from either Edgar Casey or the Swedenborgians. Wilkes posthumously married my mother to make sure his harem had enough chicken parm to last them for eternity once she kicks the bucket."

"Walker Wilkes is married to your mother?" Tom asked.

"It's complicated."

"So, when do we hit up the burial site and repossess Wilkes' body?" Aashri asked, giving her biceps the slightest flex. She was fired up and ready to go.

"We should see if Kyle can help us," I told her. "I don't want to do something illegal. It'd impede our investigation."

"I can ask him," Tom said.

The guy must've been all up in Bruce Banner that morning. I looked his way. "How would you ask Kyle?"

Tom unwound his legs and slouched to the side. Casual. Not the look of someone being evasive, and yet I had the sense he was holding back. But why? And why would Tom contact Kyle, a man he didn't know? "I just thought that maybe neither of you wanted to ask him yourself," he said. "I'd do it. Sort of a man-to-man thing."

Aashri's eyebrows touched her hairline. "Man to man? About raising the dead?"

"No one is raising the dead." I stood and rubbed my hands together as if the weirdness of this planning sesh could slough away. "We are going to poke around at The Committee's burial site — it's called Bompasero Garden — and check if Walker Wilkes has a grave."

"And what if he doesn't?" Aashri asked, standing too. "What then? You didn't attend the funeral, remember? You can't know for sure what your mom was up to." Aashri pulled Tom up by his hand. She did not let it go.

She was right. I'd made a point of being absent. But my mother hiding a still-living Walker Wilkes in my dad's lawn care shed? Doubtful.

"If Wilkes is still walking, talking, and publishing his BS to Kindle Unlimited, then we'll tackle that when we have proof. Mrs. Shears didn't seem…all there." I recalled the lipstick.

"So, do we call Kyle?" Aashri asked before turning in Tom's direction. "Not you," she said to him. "I'm man enough for the whole group."

Tom held his hands in the air, long fingers and pale palms forming a white flag of acquiescence.

I thought of the pens I'd bought. In particular, a pink one covered in looping silver script that read NOT THRIVING, JUST SURVIVING. If a pen could express my internal state of affairs, that was it.

"I'll text Kyle," I said. "I have a present for him anyway."

Aashri whistled.

"SAME SHIT, DIFFERENT DAY," I messaged his way.

"Pretty much," came Kyle's response not ten seconds later.

And my follow-up: "What do you think about helping us exhume a body?"

213

Aashri Bahtra did not frighten.

    Except when it came to graveyards.

    Especially in the dark.

    "I thought you were a member of the four hundred club? Couldn't you squat press one of these marble stones?" I asked her, sliding my BMW into the parking lot of a beer distributor about a quarter mile from The Committee's private burial site. We'd go the rest of the way on foot to minimize the chance of exposure. Both the beer distributor and the Panera next to it were dark except for a flickering sign for Pabst Blue Ribbon.

    "It's not the grave stuff," Aashri answered. She released a long breath. "It's what this humidity is doing to my hair."

    I stepped out into the evening, a rare autumn balminess squeezing us tight. The LL Bean boots I'd chosen for this covert mission weren't proper of camouflage, but I didn't own a pair of black shoes without heels. These felt like a sensible choice for graverobbing.

    "We're not graverobbing." I wanted to reassure Aashri. I wanted to reassure *myself*. If we did find something evidentiary to prove that Wilkes was less six feet under and more offseason beach house down the Shore, would I be able to remove it from the site? Would I have the stomach for it? Would I have the stealth?

    Once upon a time, Walker Wilkes had kept Bompasero Garden a secret. Formerly known simply as The Garden, it'd been renamed for what Wilkes considered the best whack on "The Sopranos". Over the years, The Committee's burial grounds had been found out and photographed by news reporters and nosey folk intrigued by the cultic practices inside my small town. Occult rituals were one thing, but The Committee was about self-improvement. No virgin sacrifices or hellacious branding. If anything, Walker Wilkes was the Tony Robbins of a mid-sized incorporated municipality. He invited curiosity, not gothic lore.

Criminal complaints, however, were not as few and far between as the man wanted his followers to believe. Most cult gawkers didn't care too much about those when the man in charge was known for claiming to improve orgasms with wild dandelion syrup.

Death threats aside, it was surprising that Wilkes had eluded being charged with financial crimes or criminal conspiracy. The Barbara Foundation may have been a non-profit, but it was a monster of his own making, funding Walker's extravagant lifestyle and allowing him to self-publish all that self-help junk with heinous grammar and way too many expostulations about his own emotional intelligence. There was a reason he'd never made it onto a bestseller list, and it had nothing to do with being an indie author. Some of my favorite reads were by indie authors. Walker Wilkes' writing was simply bad, and his ideas were colorless reformulations of other thinkers' suppositions.

Kyle's Jeep and Tom's Volkswagen slipped into the spots on either side of my Beamer.

"You okay?" Kyle asked. He cut a shadow in the faint glow of a streetlight at the far end of the parking lot. We'd spoken by text only briefly while making the plan for this evening. His replies hadn't come as quickly as they would've if I thought he'd been fully on board. For an FBI agent, Kyle sure did work conservatively.

"I'm good," I lied. "Aashri forgot to bring a hat."

Kyle ignored my attempt to infuse a trepidatious situation with humor. "Desecrating a grave is a second-degree misdemeanor," he said.

"One to five in the clink," Aashri added.

"Or up to a fifty thousand dollar fine," I chimed in. "We're aware."

Kyle looked around the dark parking lot. No one but our party occupied the space. No one but us planned to do what we were planning. Who would? "There are other ways," Kyle said.

"Yeah?" I asked, immediately rueful at coming off as snarky as I felt. "When has the law protected anyone from Walker Wilkes? Why should it protect *him* now?"

Kyle's eyes roamed the empty lot again, filled with an expression less indulgent than I wished.

"We walk, we enter, we look around, we come back." Aashri rattled off the plan we'd practiced.

I patted the top of her head.

"At least you know your way around," Kyle said to me. He came to my side as we began walking, taking off in the direction that'd lead us to Bompasero Garden.

In addition to the burial grounds of The Committee, Bompasero Garden included Wilkes' first home. After his wife had died, over twenty years ago, Walker moved to the compound where I'd recently had a run-in with his son. The fate of the original residence was a mystery to me. Probably used for storage.

Bompasero Garden was sectioned off into a large cemetery as well a gathering place for functions exclusive to The Committee. It was not unlike an old-fashioned church camp, pavilions with wooden picnic benches bolted to concrete beneath, and a large hall for indoor affairs. Potlucks and last rites both took place on the ten-acre parcel of land surrounded by trees and mystique.

Cult & Run

And, thankfully, a broken security system.

"Why leave the place so exposed?" Tom asked. His cell phone was out, and he tapped away at the screen. I almost admonished him for texting, but the flashlight app activated as my mouth opened.

"I don't think anyone cares," I told the group. "Graves are graves. The outbuildings are all locked up. It's just the peripheral fence that doesn't have a working system. At least, it shouldn't. My mother has an appointment for the alarm company to come take a look on the last Friday of this month. Aashri noticed it on a post-it stuck to the side of her PC tower."

"Poor customer service for a product that's supposed to be comforting," Tom replied.

Chatting fell away as we neared the site. The boots I'd worn had been a solid choice, but they weren't broken in enough to prevent a blister from forming on the back of my left heel. My socks kept slipping, balling up against my toes. I could've stopped to fix them, but who wants to pull sweaty fabric off her feet in front of a man she'd bought funny pens for? While on a covert mission?

The socks were also covered in baby seals, and that felt personal.

By the time we arrived at the entrance, sweat poured from the soles of my feet up to the space between my shoulder blades. Tom's flashlight app switched off as I pushed open a pair of large, modern fiberglass privacy doors to slip inside a place I hadn't been to in thirteen years. The tall fence wrapping the property was designed to protect all that was inside from prying eyes. I hoped it'd protect us. We set our feet on the paved path connecting the entrance to either the gathering areas or the cemetery.

"What do we do when we find Wilkes' grave?" Aashri asked as we walked.

Moonlight pulled the overgrown grass at the edge of road into spiky shadows across my feet. "We take a piss on it and leave."

217

"Dalmatia Louise!" Aashri shrieked in a whisper. "Forsooth!"

"Forsooth?" Kyle asked.

"I am positively aghast," Aashri continued. "Urinating in public! Do not Pass Go. Seven-hundred-fifty dollars to the banker."

"I'm kind of worried by how you two know so much about Pennsylvania's vandalism statutes," Kyle said.

Aashri laughed. "We know a lot more than that."

She wasn't wrong. I did know a lot more.

And I should've known *better*.

Because I had led us somewhere I'd once sworn I would never go again.

25

Graverobbing

I decided to tell a story as we walked.

We had a small trek ahead of us, since the cemetery was at the far end of the property. I spied it in the distance through an old iron gate that was missing a door and twined with enough ivy to make it a proper fortress barrier. Purely aesthetic, the gate encircled both the cemetery and the original Wilkes home. It was gothic, eerie, a veritable scene-setter for a tale.

When it was still a way off, I started.

"I want to be upfront," I told the group. "I've been here only once before, to the cemetery. Many times to the Great Hall or the Picnic Area, both proper nouns. There's a welcome center to the left of the entrance. Wilkes liked brochures."

No one interrupted.

219

"I was a junior in high school the first time I was invited to a burial. These aren't funerals like what you'd think a funeral should be. The dead were buried prior to the gathering at their gravesite, so no open casket, no eulogy, no luncheon afterwards. Definitely no consolation casseroles. Flowers, yes. Black mourning attire, no. Feet are bare, which I remember not particularly enjoying because landscaping here is about as reliable as the security system. I wore an Easter dress.

That was the interesting thing about The Committee. It wasn't branded as a religion even though it was meant to be one. We didn't go to church, my family, but we had baskets full of dyed eggs and jellybeans that tasted like Vaseline. Christmas gifts were less abundant than I saw other kids receive since Walker Wilkes demanded firstborn children *and* a sizable financial contribution to The Committee."

We kept walking. I kept talking.

"The year I attended my first and only burial, James got a car for Christmas. A BMW, M-series. He'd done donuts with it in the driveway at Wilkes' house before it'd been paved."

"James Wilkes," Kyle said. It hadn't been a question, but it felt like he was asking one all the same.

The dark made it easier to hide all I was feeling. "The one and only."

Probably not the right words to say. Not the right words to think. I couldn't understand it, but whenever I talked about James Wilkes, whether cursing his name or explaining away his selfishness, my language had the look of suede. Smooth and sleek, yet able to be destroyed by a sudden downpour. It never felt that way at first, but I'd always notice later on how speaking of James left my throat raw.

I pushed on to the next part.

"July seventh was the burial." I scuffed the toe of my boot on a ridge of concrete, forced out of shape by the long roots beneath the pathway. "I was sixteen, so I could attend. Children did not unless they were a nursing baby. Wilkes wasn't a fan of babies, though. He used them enough in his literature to describe the baseness of anyone not actively seeking enlightenment, i.e." — I said the names of the letters, *I* and *E* — "memorizing his work and reciting it back to him in the form of a personal check. Before Venmo, that is."

A wall of midnight green loomed ahead. There'd be a couple hundred graves in the cemetery, probably more since I was no longer privy to the names of those who'd prepaid for their plots. That info was printed in a monthly newsletter, sent out electronically to The Committee members to save costs. It required a log-in password to access it. I knew my mother's. It was *moja_ljubav*.

Croatian for "my love".

It's what she'd called me as a baby, but I wouldn't have a memory of that. My father's parents had died before I'd been born, and my mother's returned to the Adriatic Coast not long after. It was during that time, as new parents barely past being newlyweds, that my parents fell in with The Committee.

My name had come from the Dalmatae, my mother's ancestors, a group of Illyrian tribes whose sovereignty was habitually extinguished by the powers in and around their small European homeland. I hadn't been privy to these particulars of mine and my family's history until James had told me. He'd learned it from his father who had heard it from my mother. It was the first time I'd been angry at her, truly angry. She'd given Wilkes something that she should've given me — a piece of my identity. Most painful was that nickname, *moja ljubav*. A memory that could've been shared between us.

I'd slept with James that night.

We'd been seventeen, a year older than in the story I was currently telling the group. I'd had sex with James in the back of the

BMW he'd received that year to replace the one from the Christmas before. It was quick, and it was fast, but it meant something to me. Not because of James, but because of his father. I'd taken something that'd belonged to Walker Wilkes, and he'd never know it. Walker may have been James' father, but I was a woman. I meant more. What we'd done would be a secret his father would never be on this side of.

I left this part out of my story.

We stopped at the gate. The ivy looping through the iron bars was half-dead, the gate itself shorter than I remembered. The perceptions I'd held as a teenager fought for space amidst the observations I now made as a returning adult. If I hadn't grown so big around it, I'd have almost believed it was possible to inhabit my childhood once again.

"What happened next?" Tom asked.

"Walker made me lie down in a grave."

"Excuse me?" Kyle's eyes were furious. Even in the dark, they filled with fire. "He did *what?*"

The door to the gate surrounding the cemetery had long been removed from its rusted hinges.

"Watch your step," I said as I entered ahead of the group. A broken padlock was looped through one of the iron bars, useless without a door. I wondered who'd bothered to attach such a thing. Ridiculous, unnecessary. Same as when Walker forced James and I, along with Christina Harvois and Remi Lee, to lie in the plots our parents had purchased for us. The senior Wilkes' voice had been bombastic as he'd spoken over us, not once looking at the silent son whose eyes didn't leave mine until both our heads had ducked beneath the edge of the dirt.

"From the earth, I've saved you.
To the earth, I release you.

A place in The Realm has been prepared for you,
My daughters, my son.
Worthy have I made you on this journey.
Worthy are you to obtain the reward."

I'd never told Aashri what had happened that night, instead leading her to believe I'd made out with James behind the Great Hall as Mrs. Corrigan's remains were lowered into the ground. She also hadn't questioned the story that my mother had grounded me for a week after the burial when, in fact, James and I hadn't as much as touched hands that night. The experience of lying in my own grave had wrecked me, and I couldn't do much more than lie in bed spinning out when I wasn't at Mrs. Shears house being homeschooled.

When it came to the actual details of my confusing relationship with James, Aashri was no stranger. She knew I'd slept with him the following year and then hadn't touched him again until after I'd graduated high school, moved three hours away to attend college for my teaching degree, and returned to a town I hated and a family I no longer belonged in. By that time, James Wilkes had also left Cormoran only to sweep back in, as well. Except that he'd been through stuff — travel, other women, experiences he never shared. What James had been before was like a shell to an egg. Cracked, ruined, exposed; his golden insides undeniably alluring.

I'd wanted him more than I'd ever wanted anything in my life.

Even my freedom.

I'd taken the job at the learning center to be with James. I'd taken his car because why not? Why not have what his father could so easily replace? Walker Wilkes owed me. He owed me the BMW I would continue to drive until it dropped its engine onto the asphalt. He owed me the son I'd fallen in love with, making the messiness of our union somehow all the more meaningful for it.

Walker owed me.

223

KELLY MACPHERSON

And he'd had never paid up.

In the graveyard, the sting of James' rejection, both then and now, almost flattened me to the ground with its weight. Anything we found at the site tonight wouldn't make it any better for me. I wanted to know the truth about Walker Wilkes, and I wanted him to pay for tricking so many for so many years. But, more than that, I wanted a man I shouldn't have.

It was becoming harder to breathe. They stared at me — Aashri and Kyle. Even Tom seemed unsure of what was happening, both within me or within the context of this stupid plan.

I tried to catch hold of myself. I wasn't a sixteen-year-old lying frozen with fear in a plot of earth that this group of mine was certain to discover. Aashri's hand was on my arm, attempting to be a comfort. She couldn't know about the memories squeezing my lungs in a vice. No one had known but James and The Committee members who'd been there that night, my parents included. Afterward, I'd learned from my mother that Walker performed the rite on all sixteen-year-olds. Her omission had made me sick. Her confession had made me furious.

"Are you okay? Dalmatia?"

Aashri had been speaking to me. How long had I been locked in my mind? I pulled a deep breath into my lungs, the knowledge of where I was, standing in the middle of Bompasero Garden thanks to Mrs. Shears and her lunatic assertion, whooshed out of me with relief.

"I'm good," I told her. Aashri didn't look convinced. "I am."

She nodded. The fear I'd felt, and the fury, too, fell away like dew drawn up toward the sun. No one asked me to expound on being forced to lay in a grave, and we moved deeper into the cemetery, mist mingling in the air. The place hadn't been spooky when I'd last been there, despite the *company* being terrifying, but tonight it was

224

straight out of a movie. The four of us stepped around granite structures less like traditional gravestones and more the stuff of a museum. Gargoyles meant to ward off evil stood rigid on platforms etched with names. Dates were smaller, sometimes obscure. Time had no currency in The Committee. Walker Wilkes was eternal, enlightened, endless.

What length of life lived could compare?

I found Mrs. Corrigan, Jean. She'd been the only deceased person lowered into the earth on the same night I'd been. I found others, too. Sonya Dalembert, Horatio Kilbury, Evelyn Wilkes, no relation but plenty of confusion. Children were not buried in Bompasero Garden unless their parents had purchased a place for them prior to death. It made me ill, kids laid to rest all alone in public cemeteries where trashcans outnumbered benches. Most were cremated. Families scattered ashes on their properties or in places they'd loved. Beaches, forest trails, locations children go because they are children and not because they have yet lived enough life to decide what they liked. Adults informed them of those things, as adults tended to do.

Even when those children are no longer children.

"Dal, there are a lot of graves here," Aashri said. Her eyes were funny. "Maybe this isn't..."

I was crying. I didn't know when it started. I could've sworn that what I'd felt had been relief.

But I was crying and Aashri was holding me. We stood like that for a few not-long-enough seconds. Tom and Kyle gave us space, weaving among the graves.

"I'm okay," I told Aashri, face planted onto her shoulder.

"You don't seem okay."

"I found something," Tom said in a quiet voice behind us. His flashlight glowed against a granite gargoyle, obtuse in design but friendly in face. It was smiling. "James Wilkes," he read. "No dates

KELLY MACPHERSON

or anything. Isn't that the son?"

I'd barely lifted my head from Aashri's shoulder. "I want to leave," I said, eyes shut before the nausea took me under. My own plot was two spaces away.

"We're going." Aashri pulled me back toward the cemetery's entrance. "Come on, guys. This isn't going anywhere."

Kyle jogged to catch up. Tom lingered behind, confused.

"You okay?" Kyle asked. "Dal?"

"No," I answered. "Not at all."

I sobbed the whole way back to the car, grateful no one asked me why.

26

The Barbara Gala

Kyle called the next day. He'd texted twice, but I hadn't answered. That's how I knew it was a pity call. I told him that the Barbara Gala was in less than a week and my mother needed me. He offered to help sort blondes from brunettes, even sneak a Founding Fathers wig into the bunch, but I declined.

James remained MIA as was his MO. It did nothing to help me forget what we'd done together, although "together" implies a union. What we'd done had not been that.

"Do not ask that man," my mother said over the phone. She'd called me not long after Kyle. I almost wondered if she'd hidden a nanny cam in my apartment, but my mother could barely open her own email. "I have someone for you to take to the gala!"

Her announcement was triumphant. She obviously hadn't heard about Mrs. Shears' interview or else this conversation would've begun on a much more somber note. I wouldn't mention the article, and I wouldn't mention my run-in with the woman herself. I also wouldn't agree to go to The Barbara Gala with whatever mildly pleasant convenience store gas station worker she'd lured in with an old photo of me and the promise of fresh mortadella.

"I'll come to the gala," I told her. "But as an usher. Not a guest."

"No one said you'd be a guest, Dalmatia. But you need to bring a date. I have the loveliest person for you!"

"Did you meet this lovely person at Sheetz?" I asked. Maybe he'd be a dentist. "Don't tell me the Costco parking lot."

"That was one time. And, trust me, dear, I know you're not interested."

"I'm not interested in this either."

My mother sighed. "Dalmatia, when are you going to grow up?"

Her words were a punch to the gut. Who was she to ask me that?

"Please just consider it." My mother's voice sounded regretful, but I knew her better than to assume that.

"Who's your lovely suggestion?"

"Jenna Shears."

"Jenna Shears?!"

My mother laughed. "It's platonic, Dalmatia! My word! Jenna Shears is an adorable girl, but I'd like a grandchild one day. Don't go getting any ideas!"

I was *this* close to explaining both adoption and homophobia to her, but I'd been down this road with my mother before. She believed JFK was alive somewhere in the Galapagos Islands, feeding anti-vaxxers misinformation through a tin can and string he'd managed to rig across oceans. "What am I supposed to do with Jenna Shears? Am I getting her a corsage? Do people still hire limos?"

"You want to help an old friend feel at home, Dalmatia. That's what you say." My mother resumed her normal tone, the one that made it sound as if I couldn't learn to blow my own nose without getting boogers all over my hand. "You'll welcome guests to the silent auction, help them find their seats, and then share a table with Jenna. I'm not asking you to waltz with her."

"Are other people going to be waltzing?" I asked.

"Can you please remember, for one second, that The Barbara Gala raises thousands for a cause that you personally contribute zip to?"

"Am I supposed to contribute? To a hair loss foundation?"

"It is not a hair loss foundation." My mother blew a long breath through what I knew were gritted teeth. "I must end this conversation now. I am building a boundary against you."

"I'm not sure that's how that works."

My mother ignored me. "I've been seeing someone—"

I couldn't resist. "Does Wilkes know?"

My mother carried on as if I hadn't spoken. "This person, my therapist, assures me that your emotions are your responsibility as mine are mine. I expect to see you at the gala, Dalmatia. I will have your father text you Jenna's telephone number. I cannot make you do what I think is best, but I'm hoping you call her and make plans to attend together." She paused, and I wondered if there was a script spread across her kitchen table. "I know you resent me for raising you the way I did, but that's no reason to blame anyone else."

"Mom, where's this coming from?"

The call ended.

Five minutes later a text from my dad came through. A simple phone number. No "hi, kiddo" or "your mother is bonkers, but she loves you." Nothing like that. Nothing like him at all.

And so, I did something I didn't want to do. I ordered a dress from Zara that could arrive in a few days and texted Jenna Shears. At the very least I kept my budget intact and gained myself an easy opportunity to work her into giving over some information about the death of Walker Wilkes. I wasn't sure where my amateur sleuth quartet stood, but Panic at the Cemetery made a better band name than it did the look of a leader.

Before I had a chance to back out, Jenna was in.

Her enthusiastic reply came quick enough that I couldn't backtrack and thumb out, "Sorry, actually fleeing the country on that date." The gala had gained a new reason to be awkward. My interaction with Jenna at Urgent Care didn't leave me feeling on renewed terms with my old acquaintance, but it wasn't that I'd ever felt like more than forced-together allies at times and quietly feuding cousins at others. Whatever we were, it wasn't going to improve over a leg of lamb and ridiculously high bids for a weekend away at the Wilkes family timeshare in Myrtle Beach.

But getting my mother off my back was better than nothing.

The Barbara Gala was lights, camera, action.

That is, if lights, camera, action was a ten percent chance of rain that turned into a sure thing, a professional photographer with a perspiration issue, and me snapping the strap of my LBD in the parking lot of the Bywood County Art Museum.

"What is this?" my mother asked, gesturing at my left shoulder. She'd spied me from across the ballroom, an hour into set-up and a light drizzle, and sashayed her gold-sequined self right over to where a disappointingly low budget had evidently dragged me in.

"A statement piece," I answered.

"A statement piece is an earring, Dalmatia. Why didn't you wear something new?"

"Why did you dress like an Academy Award?"

My mother's unnaturally pink mouth became a jellyfish, all downturned and floppy.

I didn't want to make her feel bad. Not tonight. "Everything looks great," I added. "And it smells good."

My mother waved out the open door to the atrium where the pre-game cocktail hour would be held. "There's Jenna!" She spun me around toward an ambient glow that turned out to be a photographer sweating bullets.

"Warm night," he muttered, wiping his face with a handkerchief.

"Jenna, you look beautiful!" My mother kissed the cheek of a newly appeared Jenna Shears, laying it on as thick as some hard-up European baroness whose wealthy father-in-law had just dropped dead. "And a doctor! Weren't those Covid deniers a funny bunch? I'm sure they made you see red!"

My mother was one of those Covid deniers. When asked to please mask-up in a Wegman's grocery store, she'd held a one-dollar bill over her mouth because, according to the constitutional genius that she was, my mother was exercising her "Bill of Rights".

"The height of the pandemic was a trying time for everyone, Mrs. Scissors," Jenna replied with a smile. She was clad in a chic ivory pantsuit that definitely didn't arrive via UPS the previous morning. "I love those earrings, Dal. How's the eye?"

"Nothing that forcing the entire staff of *The New Yorker* to walk the plank didn't fix."

Jenna laughed. My mother frowned.

I found myself laughing, too, despite both.

Jenna asked what she could do to help. She addressed me, not Mrs. Scissors who hung on her every word like free Xanax. Jenna and I would enjoy cocktail hour and then show guests to their tables for dinner, dancing, and the silent auction. Until then, she could make the rounds. I wondered how The Committee's most loyal would react to the daughter of a traitor. Judging by the way their phony smiles cast sunshine on Jenna's face, tonight wouldn't culminate with her being tarred and feathered.

That was good. Because once alone, I had a chance to breathe.

James still hadn't texted. I'd tapped out and deleted no less than a dozen messages of my own, ranging from cutting demands for answers to flippant false apologies designed to make him doubt I'd ever cared.

And yet James couldn't put my mind at ease. He'd never give me the answers I wanted. I mistakenly believed I'd done the heavy work of letting go, but now I knew I hadn't. Not so much. Not at all. Over the years I'd toggled between believing that I was okay without James in my life and also okay with how he'd left it. But I was not okay with either.

I needed a distraction.

And I got one.

Detective Kyle Alaric, number one on my mother's Do Not Attend List stood by a champagne fountain. It must have been donated by someone whose wealth my mother wanted to court because she hated champagne. She would hate if I drank it. She would hate if I drank it *with* Kyle.

"Hey," I said, sliding between Kyle and the champagne fountain. In a navy fitted suit, skinny black tie, and white dress shirt, he was a Gucci ad come to life.

But those dark eyes were simply Kyle.

"Hey, Dal," Kyle said, his face turning into a giant grin.

The fountain tinkled behind us "I see your invitation didn't get lost in the mail," I said to Kyle, reaching as far as a glass flute. I'd play this exchange calm, cool, and collected.

"I'm a donor," he answered.

I'd recovered enough composure to allow the fountain to begin sloshing bubbles into my glass, but jerked at his response, spilling what I'd gathered all down my side. "Shit."

Kyle leaned in. "Here," he said, wiping my hip with the sleeve of his suit jacket.

I met his eyes and started to laugh.

Kyle laughed, too.

"My mother is going to love us," I told him.

He kept smiling. When it fell from his face, I wanted to tack it back up with my mouth. "Dal, I need to tell you something."

I'd go with humor. "Are you a convert, Kyle? Did my mother win you over to The Committee? Is that patchouli I smell?"

Kyle grinned, his head giving the slightest shake to the side. His eyes didn't leave mine. "That's not it."

"You're a Lizard Person, aren't you? I knew it. I've seen you eat."

"I'm not a Lizard Person…but how would you be able to tell from the way I eat?"

"I'd prefer to keep that information to myself," I replied. It was strange to talk through so much smiling. It was strange to *do* this much smiling, especially at The Barbara Gala.

"I have something I can't keep to myself," he said.

I did not make a joke, because it was then that I realized that Kyle's smile didn't fill his eyes.

"I'm so sorry, Dal."

"About what?"

"About—"

"Your mother's not happy with you," Jenna said, suddenly right

233

KELLY MACPHERSON

next to me. Her timing was as exquisite as when she'd done the Macarena at my birthday party.

"Jenna, could we have a minute?" I asked.

She looked puzzled. "Um, sure."

I turned back toward Kyle. "What did you want to—"

He was gone.

I thought I spied the back of his head wending its way through a throng of waiters pouring through the swinging doors of the kitchen, but he'd vanished before I could know for sure.

Jenna looped her arm through mine, pulling me toward a small alcove off the ballroom. "You didn't tell her about Paolo."

"Who the hell is Paolo?" I asked. I stepped on the back of her shoe. "*What* is Paolo?"

"The photographer. He passed out. His assistant seems to think he'd told you he wasn't well. He has a sodium problem."

"His assistant? Sodium? What are you talking about? I didn't talk to anyone!"

We squeezed into the alcove, which was no more than a very packed coat closet, and stood before the slumped body of what I assumed was Paolo, very much alive and fine except for being relegated to a chair by my mother. He was sipping a can of Diet Mountain Dew through a straw.

"His assistant told you I had something to do with all this?" I angry-whispered into my mother's ear.

"Whose assistant?" she angry-shouted back.

"His!" I pointed to the photographer. "Paolo's!"

"I have no assistant," Paolo replied. "I am a one-man show."

My mother laid a gentle hand on his shoulder. "You finish up that soda, Mr. Suarez. Get your bearings back."

I turned to Jenna. "Why did you say—"

She pushed in close. "You'll thank me later."

234

The evening had been a dream. I'd fallen, hit my head, and would up in a nightmare.

By the time I left the scene of Paolo's recovery, I couldn't see Kyle anywhere. If he'd rushed off to use the restroom, he'd unfortunately flushed himself down the toilet. But I knew what'd really happened. He'd had something important to tell me, and I hadn't shown enough compassion. Kyle's red Jeep was navigating its way into his driveway right that moment as he wondered why he'd ever let Marissa only to take up with a woman who made stupid, insensitive jokes.

I turned our brief interaction over and over in my mind as the cocktail hour wound down and it was time to lead guests into the ballroom for the main show. Jenna helped. We checked off names on the guest list as we showed people to their seats. Kyle's name was a question printed in Arial font. He'd certainly donated or else he wouldn't be on the list. My mother tolerated him for the money, of course. And yet Kyle was a no-show for his three-course catered meal, with zero explanation.

I should've been used to that from men.

After the servers began setting fruit cups before the guests, I gathered Jenna's clipboard, and she took her seat at our table. My mother did her best impression of a happy hostess, but I knew her stomach was in knots making sure the evening went off without a hitch. She was a misguided woman but not a bad one. I watched her schmooze the room, my father helping himself to the melon in her fruit cup, and wished she'd turned her compassion toward a worthier cause.

I witnessed my dad eat a chunk of pineapple off his lap as a voice slid into my ear. "Hey," it said.

If I didn't answer, then he really wouldn't be there.

"This thing started?" James asked.

235

KELLY MACPHERSON

He'd moved to my side. "Cocktail hour started an hour ago," I said, not looking his way.

"Are you eating?"

I hugged the clipboards to my chest, and my pen clattered to the ground. "Do I look like I'm eating?" I snapped.

James bent to retrieve the pen. He held it out to me. I took it without a word. "Are you mad at me?" he asked.

All the texts I hadn't sent. All the phone calls I hadn't made. They scrolled through my mind. I could read them out loud right now. James was here. This is what I'd wanted. Wasn't it? Without a word, I dumped the clipboards behind a potted plant and joined Jenna at our table.

She pushed my fruit cup closer.

"They weren't going to give you one," she said. "Because you weren't here. Cheap bastards. I made sure they did."

"Thank you," I told her.

"It's no problem." She glanced back at where I assumed James remained, standing casual and cool. "I tried, you know," she said. "James was heading straight over to where you were talking to that guy. I'm sorry if it was important and I messed you up. All I could focus on was the look on that smug asshole's face."

Jenna had tried to protect me. I was at a loss for words and said the only ones I could.

"Thank you," I told her. Jenna nodded once. "And no, he was no one important."

236

27

Three Dots

For a silent auction, it wasn't so silent.

In the middle of a bidding contest over a year's membership to the Bywood County Country Club, my phone buzzed with a text message. I wasn't interested in three-hundred and sixty-five days of broken-down golf carts and a tavern that'd made an episode of "Unsolved Mysteries" in 1995. I also wasn't interested in the way my mother's psychic antennae perked up three tables away. As if she knew who'd sent me a text during the enthusiastic gavel pounding of the winning bid, her sharp gaze stung me with something like voodoo or familial guilt.

It was Kyle.

"Can we meet up after this thing is over?" he asked. "I'm sorry I had to run."

"I'm supposed to help tear this shitshow down," was my reply.

"Will everyone be gone?"

"Yes," I texted.

237

"I'll help."

"I don't think my mother likes you."

Three dots. Nothing. Three dots again. Nothing.

"That's actually a compliment toward you," I added while waiting.

"I only came tonight to see you," Kyle said. "And I came to see you so I could tell you the truth about something you deserve to know."

Oh my God. He meant Wilkes. He knew who'd sent the death threats. Even more, my hunch had been right, and he'd been murdered. Kyle knew who'd done it. I glanced over at Jenna. Her eyes were fixed on James as he chatted up some guest at the back of the room.

"Okay," I told Kyle. "Where do you want to meet? I'll skip out on the clean-up."

"Marissa has Luke tonight. My house?"

I remembered that I was in fast fashion evening wear and wondered if Kyle was still in that sexy suit. I caught James' eyes by mistake, not realizing I'd let mine wander. I sent Kyle one final text. "Let's do the diner, Sixth and Moore."

Bidding on the next item began, and my mother formed a grim smile in my direction. One lucky bidder would win six months of free quarter-page advertising in *The Cormoran Daily Chronicle*.

Not even typos and poor punctuation could cramp my mood.

At last, I would find out what happened to Walker Wilkes.

"Please, Dalmatia. What else do you have to do?" My mother's bare feet, high heels tossed beneath a table once the gala had wrapped, proved more distracting than the sound of my father singing Lana Del Rey's "Ride" with the new guy who delivered their mail. Tearing down The Barbara Gala was more eventful than the actual event.

"I have plans," I lied to my mother. "I can't get to the bank that early."

"Then do it now," she said. "I just need you to deposit the money before it gets stolen."

The gala had wrapped for the evening, and she was referring to the bids, of course. My mother did this every year: deposited the winners' cashier's checks and cash payments before the clock could strike twelve and the people of Bywood County realized they did not truly want a five-hundred-dollar gift card to The Puzzle Emporium. What my mother would not mention was the year she'd left the money box in the back of her car while supervising the post-gala clean-up. Before Mrs. Shears had become a vigilante, she'd been my mother's partner-in-crime. Not understanding that my mother's "safe place" for the money had been the backseat of her locked sedan beneath an afghan crocheted into a picture of Diana Ross's face, Mrs. Shears had filled any and all open space in my mother's Ford Taurus with leftover food. By the time they'd found the money box, the cash smelled like baked ziti and the checks retained a faint whiff of marsala.

The money had never been stolen, but we let my mother talk as if it had.

When it came to saving face, at least hers wasn't smeared with a shade of lipstick named for a butcher shop.

"Fine," I told my mother. She gave a little squeal. Depositing the money would be my only task. "But I'm keeping one of the wigs."

"You can't keep a wig. They're going into storage for next year."

"I'm keeping that one." I pointed to the bald cap my mother had shoved into her own purse atop the table where she'd stashed her shoes. Its rubbery top, protruded from the open flap of the side pocket where she kept her travel-size Kleenex. My mother looked at it, pulled a face, and shook her head.

"Whatever you want," she said. "Just don't do anything lewd with it."

"What lewd thing am I going to do?"

My mother's frown deepened. Her face was a suspension bridge held up by nothing but an awareness of all the people surrounding us in the ballroom, those cleaning up tables and chairs and sneaking food into their cars. "Don't do anything torrid with that man," she said.

"Now I'm doing something torrid?" I asked. "I thought it was just lewd! I'm getting worse!"

The gale force winds created by my mother's eye roll almost propelled the leftover antipasti right out of Hannah Ballerini's hands. "I accepted his money, Dalmatia, because it was for a good cause."

"Hair extensions."

"Hair *restoration*." My mother's finger was a spear aimed at my chest. "But I will not accept him for you."

"Maybe he's hoping you figure out a cure for male pattern baldness. Did you ever think of that?" I asked, walking over to her purse and saving the wig cap from certain disposal.

My mother said nothing. She waved a security guard our way. He handed me the money box and gave me a kiss on the cheek. It was my father. "Have a good rest of the night, kiddo," my dad said. They were the warmest words he'd spoken to me in weeks.

"I will," I told him with a smile. I held thousands of dollars' worth of cash and checks in my hands and a bald cap under my arm, but I was going to see Kyle. And he was going to tell me something that would change everything:

The name of Walker Wilkes' killer.

Because the man hadn't died of a heart attack. My intuition had known it this entire time. Not even burnt lamb scented rubber could overrule what Kyle was going to confirm: that, for all my life, what I had felt to be true was not, as everyone around me insisted, wrong.

The reality in which I'd been brought up was a lie, a ruse, a misguided attempt at safety crafted by adults who needed parenting classes and relocation. I hadn't been the crazy one, the difficult one, the doubting one who couldn't commit. I'd been the only one in the whole of Walker Wilkes' world who had seen the light.

And I was about to bask in it.

28

Hi, We're
the Bad Guys

"Aashri, it's me."

"I thought we didn't do phone calls?"

"We don't. I'm just…"

"Dal, are you okay?"

"No."

"Are you home or still sweeping up hairballs?"

"Home."

"I'm coming."

29

Check(mate)

The history of envelopes was less boring than that of looseleaf paper but without the intrigue of the cardboard box.

The first envelopes were developed in ancient China, clay spheres designed to hold royal correspondence and be smashed upon receipt. In the Middle Ages, paper envelopes became sturdy enough to send messages, usually between the Church and aristocracy. Later, Sam Adams, patriot not brewer, sent the first long-distance letter in a proper envelope from Boston to Philadelphia during the American Revolution.

Kyle sent his donation to The Barbara Gala in an envelope, too.

My mother mustn't have realized she'd stuck a few last-minute donations into the silent auction money box. She would have planned to hit the bank — or forced me to do it — after everything had wrapped, so I guessed she'd popped them in there for safekeeping.

"I'll ask him," Aashri told me. "I'll call him right now."

We sat on my couch, me still in the dress I'd worn all evening and Aashri in a gym hoodie. I'd given her the night off from her usual attendance at the gala since I assumed I'd have my hands full with Jenna, and so Aashri had been in the middle of racking her bar when I'd called. Being the very best person in the whole wide world, she'd known it was me. Aashri bid her lifting partner farewell and headed to my apartment. I was chest-deep in misery when she got there.

"No," I said. "Don't call him. Not right now."

Aashri pulled me back into a hug as I cried. All my mascara had already come off in the parking lot of the Bywood County Art Museum. I'd been in the driver's seat of my Beamer, sifting through the money box and organizing the cash and checks into piles to make it easier to stick in the twenty-four-hour deposit box at the bank. Kyle's envelope had not been the last, but it'd been the last I'd touched before my whole world imploded.

"I fucking hate him," Aashri said. I didn't know if she meant Kyle or Tom. Both, probably. The open laptop on my coffee table showed a row of three grinning faces. Kyle, Tom, and the woman in the photo with James that I'd seen at Tom's place. I'd never told Kyle about those. I hadn't wanted to involve my parents too deeply in his investigation, since they'd been featured in the photos.

My concern didn't matter now.

Because Kyle wasn't Kyle.

He was Alex Parker, host of The Cult & Run Podcast and employee of Carbon Fiber Studios.

The woman, Sheena Favrosian, was his co-host and producer.

Tom Daly was his tech guy.

"He used me," I said. My throat was as raw as if I'd been screaming when I'd barely said more than a handful of words since Aashri

244

had arrived. I had handed her the envelope labeled "Kyle", which contained a check signed by an Alex Parker and drawn on Carbon Fiber Studios' account. Upon first opening it, I'd immediately remembered Tom's LinkedIn. Unable to refrain from Googling the connection, finding the company website didn't take long.

"He's a fucking idiot." Aashri had torn the check to pieces after she'd taken a photo of it. "Your mom's toupee coalition doesn't need anything from those assholes. It's blood money."

"Why would he do this?" I asked her, pulling away to scratch my eye. Aashri made a face. "It's sensitive. I've been crying a lot."

"He's a fuckboy, Dalmatia."

"I don't think Kyle is a fuckboy," I said back.

"I don't think he's *Kyle*."

She was right. He wasn't.

"There," Aashri said. "I did it."

My eye burned like crazy. "You did what?"

She turned her phone screen my way. A second ago, Tom Daly — or "TOM fire emoji fire emoji fire emoji" — had received a photo of a check for four thousand dollars signed by Alex Parker.

"Blue dots," Aashri told me.

"I don't want to know what he says."

Aashri pressed closer to me on my couch. It would've reminded me of Kyle at his house if Kyle hadn't been a heartless, soulless bastard named Alex Parker who'd weaseled his way into my life to make a juicier podcast. It didn't take a rocket scientist to know that the whole FBI agent persona was a facade. I should've trusted my gut. Detectives didn't wear joggers.

I laid my head on Aashri's shoulder. "I'm not looking at the phone," I said.

"He's still typing." She pressed a kiss to the top of my hair. "Love you, Cruella."

245

"I love you, too," I said. She was the only one I really did. I couldn't believe how thin I'd spread myself between James and Kyle — actually *Alex* — and my mother. Even Walker Wilkes. I'd given so much to them, whether body, mind, or both. And what had they given me? A shitty childhood, trust issues, and four thousand dollars that wasn't even mine to blow on shoes.

Aashri blew a long breath through her teeth. I raised my face to hers in time to see her run a hand through her spiky hair. "Wow," she said.

"Wow what?" I asked. "No, I don't want to know."

"I think you do."

She passed the phone to me, and I took it against my better judgement. Hot Tom the Liar had responded with a photo of his own: a screenshot of James Wilkes looking like a Jesus Christ wannabe in white linen and a beard in a YouTube video entitled "Flow Manifestation." A new message popped up beneath it along with a link and a third "I'm sorry", which Aashri immediately deleted.

"What is this?" I asked.

"James trying to summon a menstrual cycle?"

"Click it," I told her. Aashri did as I requested, and our behinds fell asleep as we stayed on my couch for the next hour and a half watching video after video of James Wilkes, also known as Jimmy Sway, teaching followers how to speak their wildest Hollywood dreams into existence.

Aashri finally said what we'd both been thinking. "What is this madness?"

"Not an ad for Tampax," I replied, transfixed by the tens of thousands of followers subscribed to Jimmy Sway's channel.

Aashri tapped out a message to Tom. "What the fuck?" was all it said.

Three dots, three dots, three dots.

I hated three dots.

Aashri's response to Tom's text was in the shape of a punchline, but her tone was anything but. "Looks like James is his father's son after all."

Mrs. Shears had given a second interview. This time, it wasn't about Walker. Aashri clicked on the link Tom had sent.

"James Wilkes," the first line began, "stole my son from me. When Justin left home for California, I was devastated he'd turned his back on The Committee. He'd been raised in the group, a part of something bigger than himself. Justin had always been a wild one, but I should've known he'd never escape the Wilkes family. No one does. My boy fell in with a group in Los Angeles who took an acting class led by a man going by the name Jimmy Sway. I'm only grateful that Justin had no desire to become an actor and lose what he'd earned to a con artist.

By the time my son left, he'd seen hundreds of people give their last dime to Jimmy Sway in order to learn his 'secrets' of manifestation. They were all kids. Kids who wanted to be in movies. Why would they question a seemingly kind, confident man who promised to get them there? That's the dangerous thing. We brainwash kids into believing their independence is dangerous when what we should be teaching them to do is think for themselves. I haven't heard from my son in years, but if he happens to see this, I'd want to tell him that I'm sorry.

I'm sorry, Justin.

I'm sorry I chose Walker Wilkes over you."

247

Aashri and I'd had enough.

We were leaving.

For the rest of the weekend. But it counted. Aashri booked an Airbnb at an old farmhouse in Lancaster, Pennsylvania, also known as Amish Country. "Trading wig caps for prayer caps," she told me as I packed a bag and checked my cell for the one-hundredth time in case Kyle had texted.

The answer was no.

Same for Jimmy Sway.

"Do you think Tom told him we know?" I asked from the front seat of Aashri's big black Silverado. We planned to stop at her place so she could throw some clothes and rum in a duffel, and then we'd trade Cormoran for buggies and bonnets. "Of course." Aashri said, taking a hard left. "Sorry. I'm feeling…"

"Angry."

Aashri nodded, throwing up a finger at a bicyclist who'd given her one first. "I was going to say starving, but that, too. And who rides one of those things in the dark? It's almost midnight!"

"Do you think Marissa knew? About what Kyle was doing?"

I'd told Aashri all I knew about Kyle's ex-wife and held my breath as I waited for her reply. Relief flooded through me when she shook her head. "No," Aashri said. "I think she was as clueless as you were. You never called him Kyle around her?"

"We weren't at his house together that long," I said. "But no, I don't think I did. He'd really risked it by inviting me over, didn't he?"

Aashri pulled to a stop at a red light. "He hadn't expected his ex and his son to show up, though, right?"

Right.

"And you were basically already on his doorstep, so how would he look if he'd told you to just forget it?"

"He'd look mean," I said in a small voice. I hated the tiny fizz of hope in my chest. I knew better than to let it grow.

Aashri was tender but firm when she next spoke. "He liked you, Dal. I could tell. But that doesn't mean what he did wasn't bad."

We pulled into the parking garage of Aashri's building, which was a co-op situation in an old warehouse in downtown Cormoran. Cormoran wasn't large enough to have a downtown that drew anyone not already a resident of the town, but the area had seen a revitalization in the past few years. Aashri's building was a coveted address. She slid her truck into a spot, wedging it beside an old pick-up with the mark of the beast on its back.

A Carbon Fiber Studios bumper sticker.

Aashri slammed the driver's door shut. "What are the actual odds in the hell?"

"It's the Baador-Meinhof Phenomenon," I told her. "The Frequency Illusion. Something's on your mind and you see it everywhere."

"Okay, but Carbon Fiber Douchebags only have a thousand followers on Instagram. We're not talking Wondery here."

"The world is weird," I said, pulling my bag from the car. I wanted my phone close. I was dumb.

Aashri and I left the junky truck behind, which, in addition to its disgusting bumper sticker, also included a pair of fuzzy pink dice hanging from the rearview mirror. The sleek lobby of the building was warm and still smelled of new construction renovations. We passed a few late-night partygoers while taking the elevator up to Aashri's place on the fourth floor. Two tipsy guys asked if we were up for an afterparty, but the shorter one changed his tone real quick when he recognized Aashri from the gym.

"Hey, girl," Bud Lite said with a measure of reverence.

"Hey, yourself, Paul Manowitz. Does your girlfriend know you're not at that sales conference?" Aashri blew a kiss to Paul Manowitz's curly-haired friend who made a show of catching it in his hand and rather enthusiastically making out with his palm.

"Aashri, come on!" Paul Manowitz held his arms wide open in a plea. "My bro from college is only in town this weekend!"

"And here I am letting Pandie think you're in Tuscon networking over laser printers while she mans the reception desk at 365 Fitness. All those flexers paying her all that attention." Aashri let out a low whistle. "Sure hope she can handle it."

It took Paul Manowitz half a second to move his cell from pocket to hand. His friend gave Aashri a wide smile and attempted to slide his arm around her shoulders, but she gave him an expression that had him hurrying down the hall after his buddy real quick. The last we heard of them, Paul Manowitz was shoving some story into his girlfriend's ear about his flight being canceled. His friend, the self-love wonder, followed behind, singing Rihanna. If I could've said one good thing about that night, it was that all the tone-deaf men who'd decided it was the right time for a public performance had chosen their music well.

On the keypad above the doorknob, Aashri quickly tapped out the code to unlock her apartment.

"We fell in love in a hopeless place," I told her.

"That we did," she said, turning the handle.

"Hey, are you Aashri Bahtra?"

Cult & Run

At the sound of a feminine voice coming from the apartment behind us, the formerly vacant one across the hall, Aashri turned so quickly that I tumbled back into the eggshell ochre cinderblock hallway wall as she did. My purse slammed into my thigh, and the bald cap fell onto the parquet floor.

"Is that a scalp?" the woman asked.

I righted myself in time to see Aashri's expression go all Tell Me Again Why Women Shouldn't Lift. "I don't know, Sheena Favrosian. Is that what it looks like?"

Sheenva Favrosian, one-half of the Cult & Run Podcast and Alex Parker's righthand woman, stood in the open doorway of the apartment across from Aashri's place. Smooth Mama M's reward poster had been taken down, replaced by an autumn wreath. A pug dog in a plaid puffer vest poked its head from between Sheena's legs.

"I got your mail," Sheena said, eyeing Aashri and I as if we were one lose screw away from crazy. She pulled a few envelopes from a table off to the side and handed them over. I cringed, remembering an envelope like one of those, and, inside, a check that'd upended everything.

I couldn't stop myself. I pointed to her dog. "Carbon Fiber's really keeping a certain animal sanctuary in business, huh?"

Sheena's bemused expression turned wary. "I think animal sanctuaries wish they wouldn't have to be in business." She backed up a step. "Do I know you?"

"You tell me," I answered with as much menace as I could muster. It sounded a lot like a head cold.

However, Aashri's menace sounded like menace. "Why don't you ask Kyle who we are?"

Sheena looked even more confused. "Who's Kyle? Am I missing something here? Is this about the co-op association? I read the bylaws. Seasonal wreaths are allowed."

"Why don't you tell Alex Parker that his show's shit, and so is he," Aashri spat out. "And next time he even thinks about coming near Dalmatia, I'll shove his balls up the exhaust pipe of that stupid piece of crap."

"Wow!" Sheena's eyes had gone wide. "I still don't know who Kyle is, but I'll let Alex know you won't be leaving a five-star review. It's okay. Cults aren't everybody's thing." She shoo'd her little dog back inside and shut the door.

No, they weren't.

And neither were podcasters who made a buck off them.

Aashri stamped into her apartment. I set Sheena's fancy wreath askew and followed right behind.

30

Blitzed

"You're Blitzed!" Aashri laughed and smacked her final card down on the farmhouse dining table. "Drink!"

"Do the Amish know this game has a double meaning?" I asked, lifting Aashri's Lancaster County version of a Bloody Mary to my lips. She called it a Bludich Ida, and it tasted delicious. Aashri beat me three times in a row at Dutch Blitz, a simple yet highly competitive card game, before I called a truce and asked her walk with me to the outlets.

"Uh-uh," she said. "I don't do outlets."

"You do outlets," I answered. "We've gone together."

"I was drunk then, too," Aashri replied. "You coerced me."

I stood and stretched. A late arrival last night had become a late awakening that morning, which had then become an early lunch and an earlier than usual sense of restlessness. I needed to move my body,

253

and a two-hour car ride to Lancaster County, Pennsylvania didn't count.

"I want to text Kyle," I said. It'd been less than twenty-four hours since I had learned of Kyle's duplicity. I set the dregs of my Bludich Ida on the hand-made farmhouse table and stood to attention. "I want to tell him I hate him."

"Tom's already told him that, I'm sure." Aashri did a round of quad stretches.

"I hope so," I said. I chugged the final sip of my drink and lifted it in the air. "Because I'm going to report him to the FAA and Sheena Favrosian to the HOA!"

Aashri took the glass from my hand. "First of all," she said. "I think you mean the FCC. The FAA regulates air travel. Secondly…no, forget it. Yes. Please report Sheena Favrosian to my HOA because that's definitely what it's called."

"Her wreath was fugly!" I cried with a fist toward the ceiling.

Aashri sighed. "Now you're using slang from the early two-thousands. No way am I going to an outlet mall with you. It can only end with me leaving with something from the Gap clearance rack."

"Everything is technically on clearance," I said.

Aashri raised her eyebrows. I'd made her point.

"So, you don't want knock-off Ariana Grande perfume from Scent-stravaganza?"

Aashri's middle finger traced an invisible tear down her cheek. "I'll try to live without it."

I gathered my phone and AirPods from my purse. Our Airbnb was within walking distance of the outdoor outlet mall, so the trek wouldn't be tedious, even with Aashri's bartending working its way through my system. I checked myself out in a rustic full-length mirror beside a basket of quilts. The woman frowning back was a mascara-less disaster in sweats and a pair of Allbirds a size too big because taking returns to the post office was apparently something she did not do. Fresh air would help. A little.

"Hey," I said before heading out the door. "I'm sorry about Tom."

Aashri couldn't betray her hurt. "Me, too. And about Kyle." She leaned back in the rocking chair she'd been hogging all morning. "Mostly about Kyle."

"Don't worry about him," I said, knowing I was in-part using my anger at Kyle to distract myself from my anger at James. All this adrenaline would lead to a crash soon enough, but I didn't want to think about how I'd feel when it did. "I'll see you later."

"Don't buy something two sizes off just because it's a good deal," Aashri answered, flicking her eyes at my shoes with a smile.

I smiled back, stepping into a day clear of both clouds and men I hated.

The outlet deals weren't as good as I'd expected, and I didn't possess the motivation to pay twenty bucks for a pair of boots that'd end up in my trunk. It was for the best, because I'd found myself attracted to a pair that was impossibly uncomfortable, thigh-high, and studded with spikes. On a typical day, I would not be interested. But while in emotional turmoil? I carried those boots around in a shopping basket for thirty-five minutes.

KELLY MACPHERSON

"Excuse me, but are you going to buy those?" asked a man in a Pittsburgh Pirates ball cap. He was pushing sixty and carrying a diaper bag. Even if I could wrap my head around him, I wouldn't have the energy.

"All yours." I handed him the box and was out of that place before he could say Trophy Wife Gone Wrong. "I hate this," I said to no one but the overcast sky and my own sense of failure. "I. Hate. This."

My cell phone buzzed, and my nerves almost had me pitching it into the path of the nearest moving car. The caller was listed as unknown, which screamed scammer but also provided a momentary reprieve from thinking of Kyle, James, and a pair of boots I'd never wear but somehow believed would lead me into a grand adventure.

I answered on the third ring. "Hello?"

A pause.

"Hello? Is anyone—"

"Dalmatia? Dalmatia Scissors?"

"This is her."

Mrs. Shears gathered her breath. I'd realized who was on the end of the call the second she'd paused. "I need to apologize, dear. And I'd like to do it in person."

How do you tell a woman you'd grown up loathing that you were in Amish Country and could meet at a Panera beside the Tanger Outlets at her earliest convenience because you have nothing left to lose and nowhere else to go?

You say that. But just the first part.

As it turned out, Mrs. Shears could be there in an hour. I wandered a bit more, not buying several things and checking for texts on the cell phone I continually wanted to destroy. I seated myself at Panera to wait out the final fifteen minutes of Mrs. Shears' drive-time, but when the woman herself approached my table, my French

256

onion soup spilling over a bread bowl, I found myself lost for words.

"Hello, Dalmatia," Mrs. Shears said. "Could I sit?"

"Of course," I replied. I swiped my hand through the air like a ringmaster on the verge of bankruptcy. "The elephants have gone feral," I told her.

"What?"

"Nothing. Bad joke. Bad week. Did you want to go order something?"

"Would that make you more comfortable?" Mrs. Shears asked. "I've already left you to wait on me. I appreciate this."

Her earnestness was visible past the lacquer on her face. I couldn't bring myself to respond with snark.

"It's fine," I said.

Mrs. Shears lowered herself opposite me in the booth. An art print depicting an abstract loaf of sourdough hung on the wall above her head. "Dalmatia, I owe you some answers. And an apology."

I shook my head. "You don't," I told her. "We were both a part of the same thing."

Mrs. Shears gave me a pointed look. The woman's eyeliner was not something to mess with. "You were a child," she answered. "I was not. All of us adults should've known what we were doing. *I* should've known what I was doing."

"And what was that?"

A pause. "Doing whatever a psychopath told us and pretending it wasn't our choice. I'm sorry, Dalmatia, because children don't get to choose their parents, and they certainly do not get to choose what madness their parents pull them into."

I almost couldn't breathe. I certainly couldn't eat. My stomach was a mess of memories, as if the past lived somewhere behind my navel. A physical reminder of all the times I'd felt alone, misunderstood, unacceptable.

Ashamed.

And here was Mrs. Shears saying all the things that'd been fogging up my head since I was a kid. The highlighter incident had been the first time I'd felt the wrongness of it all. The confusion. Mrs. Shears had been there then, and she was here now, a windshield wiper of injectables and regret, clearing the way for me to admit how damaging my childhood had been.

"You don't have to say anything," Mrs. Shears tried to make eye contact as I stirred my soup. Onion flopped beneath the sinking layer of cheese.

"It was hard," I told her, unable to drag my eyes from the laminate tabletop. "Leaving school."

"Dalmatia, I am so, so sorry." Her hand was suddenly on mine, and I was holding it. They were warm, Mrs. Shears' fingers, and they held my own as if it wasn't something she should do but something she wanted to do.

"I saw Jenna," I said, looking up. Mrs. Shears didn't pull away. If I was testing, she was passing. "I cut my eye and had to go to Urgent Care."

Mrs. Shears' well-blended foundation paled with concern. "Oh, my goodness! When did this happen?"

"A couple weeks ago. I had an eye patch and everything."

"You're the same Dalmatia I knew way back when." She smiled. "And I am so glad."

"I'm not the same," I said back. "Not at all."

But I was a liar.

I'd been spending my autonomous, free adulthood acting like it was my personal responsibility to prove to myself that The Committee hadn't ruined me. I researched cults and boycotted fads, held absolutely zero political beliefs, and couldn't go to the doctor without my best friend kidnapping me into it. I'd more likely bleed out on my kitchen floor after a mishap with an apple peeler than put on a Band-Aid.

Even if that wasn't true, there was one fact I couldn't ignore. The perfect yardstick to measure how little I'd grown in the past many years.

I'd given myself right back to James.

As if the past had been nothing.

And what did I think? That he'd stay this time?

That I'd be enough to make him?

"I'm leaving my job," I told Mrs. Shears. I took back my hand and rolled it into a fist in my lap. A little boy, no more than two or three, ran past our table with his mom at his heels.

Mrs. Shears laid her palm flat against the table, close enough to a drop of spilled broth to make me uncomfortable. "You don't have to do that if you like it."

I did like it. Why was I saying this to her?

"Dalmatia, can I tell you something?"

I didn't answer.

"Jenna didn't come back to Cormoran to work at Urgent Care with a bad-tempered woman named Kim." Mrs. Shears laced her fingers like a congressman in confessional. "She went to medical school, yes. But Jenna works for the FBI."

She absolutely did not. "She gave me a prescription for azithromycin," I said.

"Jenna is a special agent, Dalmatia. She was a trained medic in the Navy and then recruited into the FBI."

"Jenna?"

"Jenna."

"But why?"

Mrs. Shears grinned. The dark lipstick no longer made her mouth look so sinister. "Why do you think she's in Cormoran?" she asked me. The skin between her eyebrows puckered. "Why do you think I gave those interviews?"

"To expose Wilkes."

Mrs. Shears nodded.

"Who else knows about this? Wilkes is dead. I don't think there's anything left to expose," I answered.

"Have you talked to your mother lately?"

"Is she being investigated?!"

"No," Mrs. Shears replied. "She's assisting with it."

"My mother?"

"Your mother."

I tried to push all these pieces together into a picture I could understand. I had a few edges right, but the middle was a murky mess of wet cardboard. "How?" I asked.

"Six months ago, Walker Wilkes began receiving anonymous death threats. But they weren't anonymous. They'd been from James."

Jimmy Sway.

"He'd been living in Los Angeles and run out of money. Walker refused to give him any. When Walker got sick — he was diabetic — James proposed returning to Cormoran and taking on a leadership role in The Committee. What he really wanted was access to the group's bank account. Walker said no."

"I always thought Wilkes wanted that," I said. "For James to be in charge."

"He had," Mrs. Shears answered. "But that was before James left."

It turned out I hadn't been the only one spurned by James Wilkes.

"Dalmatia, The Committee barely exists anymore. The elder group is thinking of dissolving it altogether. No more 501C, a phasing-out of all activities."

"The school?"

"The school would stay. The Committee has planned to bequeath it a significant amount to cover costs."

I leaned into the cushioned back of the booth, its synthetic cover squeaking against my body. Judging by its give, the space where I sat had been heavily trafficked by people experiencing similar bouts of shock and awe.

The Committee was dying. My *mother* was helping to kill it.

James had attempted to extort money from his father.

And an FBI agent was indeed mixed up in all of this…but that agent was Jenna, not Kyle.

Although Kyle hadn't been Kyle to begin with.

"About Wilkes…does this mean he died from, what, diabetes?" I asked.

Mrs. Shears nodded sadly. "Walker Wilkes was just a man, Dalmatia. Nothing more."

But that wasn't true. He'd been an icon, a master, a dictator.

Hadn't he?

I leaned forward quickly as if it would've been possible to leap across the table and rip the answers that I needed directly from Mrs. Shears' head. "But at Sephora you said — you *made me believe* — there was something weird going on with Walker's death," I told her. "Why would you do that?"

And that's when it switched, Mrs. Shears' expression.

Up to that point, Mrs. Shears had maintained her composure. Nothing she'd told me seemed difficult to say, I realized. She'd intended for it to be a relief to me. To provide a sense of safety. But I could tell that her next words would not bring the same.

"Why?" I asked again.

Mrs. Shears folded her hands in her lap. "Because of the house."

31

Love Island

"What house?"

"Think, Dalmatia. Remember that night. In the cemetery." Her haunted expression left no room to pretend I was clueless as to the incident she referred to.

Mrs. Shears was asking me to remember the night Walker Wilkes made me lie in my own grave.

"Do you remember what happened after?" she asked.

I wanted to tell her that, no, I did not. But she was obviously no longer lying to herself, and so I wouldn't lie either. "We ate, shared a meal," I answered. "In that house in the back. James' old house. The one he'd lived in before his mom died."

"James wasn't staying with Walker when he came back to Cormoran," Mrs. Shears told me, eyes fastened on my face. As much as I knew she was being honest, empathetic even, I was less than receptive to the desperation radiating from her whole being. I owed this woman nothing. I owed Walker nothing. I should leave. "He was staying in that house. The one in Bompasero Garden." She finally looked away, and I could swallow. "Idiotic name."

James had been at the house.

On the night I'd taken Aashri, Kyle, and Tom to the cemetery, he'd been there.

I needed a minute. I needed a lot of minutes.

It all made a sort of twisted sense, what Mrs. Shears had shared about my mother and Jenna, James, and the house. But the syringe and the doorbell cam, how about those? I was glad of this new information — and a legitimate FBI investigation — but the parts of this story felt miles apart from one another and even further from a place where, together, they'd all make sense.

"You know," Mrs. Shears said. "I wouldn't have known any of this without Justin."

"Justin?"

She smiled. "Edward Scissorhands."

I saw myself once again, seven years old on my lavender Huffy bicycle with the streamers in the spokes. "Your son was an asshole to me," I told her since we were being honest.

"He could be that, yes," Mrs. Shears replied. "And you'll know that we sent him to Utah after a few concerning incidents at school. He was acting out because our home was unstable. I didn't see it at the time, but Justin did. The way I acted, the way I raised him and Jenna. The way I raised you."

She had, Mrs. Shears. She'd been my homeschool teacher. Who I was today was, in part, a reaction to who she'd been back then.

"Did Justin tell you about James?" I asked, apparently into recapping every ounce of childhood trauma over cold soup.

"Justin ended up in California, because he's, well, *Justin*." She

263

laughed. "Sending him to Utah just made the trip shorter. He fell in with a group who took acting classes from a man calling himself Jimmy Sway."

"I heard about that," I said.

"James Wilkes never had the brightest mind," Mrs. Shears frowned. "You know he couldn't properly tie his shoes until he was eleven? Never did learn to write in cursive either."

The failings of James Wilkes were a topic I could listen to all day.

"Justin ran into James in LA," Mrs. Shears continued. "James was running a group acting class, but he also taught manifestation. As if he even knows how to spell it." Mrs. Shears pulled a tube of lipstick from her purse, receipts and car keys rustling from within it. She reapplied some gloss and smacked her lips. "He was stealing money, Dalmatia. James was swindling people out of all they had. He promised them Hollywood success, said it was all about speaking what they wanted into existence. He called it 'rebooting' or something like that. Justin immediately saw Walker's own brand of conspirituality in what James was preaching."

"Did James know who Justin was?" I asked. "Did he recognize him?"

"No," Mrs. Shears said. "They hadn't spent much time together growing up. Justin wasn't homeschooled, and James wasn't socialized outside The Committee." Mrs. Shears clicked her plum purple acrylics on the table. "I'm not even sure I'd recognize Justin now. He and I...he blames me. Rightfully so. It's been years since I've had more than a phone call from him. He never forgets my birthday, though. Never." Her right hand clenched into a fist, releasing just as quickly. I could hear the emotion on her tongue.

Mrs. Shears continued. "James began sending letters to Committee members after his father's health took a downturn, asking for financial support to cover Walker's medical costs. Your parents thought it was odd. Your mother and I have kept in touch all these years, and she mentioned it to me. I mentioned it to Jenna, and Jenna opened an investigation into James. That's what brought her back to Cormoran: James' homecoming. What reason would he have to leave an income stream in California unless he thought he'd somehow come into a windfall here?"

"So, Jenna's just posing at the Urgent Care?" I asked.

Mrs. Shears nodded. "And your mother saved the whole thing," she said, smiling at my bemused expression. "James would've forged Walker's signature to become the beneficiary of The Committee's bank account except for her. Your mother agreed to become Walker's — I don't even know what it's called — corpse bride? He put her in his will." Mrs. Shears laughed. "I asked if they were registered at Bed, Bath and *Beyond*."

That got a slight grin out of me.

"Listen, Dalmatia, I didn't come here to lay this all on you like a burden. Obviously, I'm not supposed to reveal any of this, but I can't just...I can't let you think you were wrong."

"Wrong?"

Mrs. Shears took my hand once more. "To stay," she said. "It wasn't wrong to stay."

The will to argue was a flash flood in my brain.

But it evaporated as quickly as Mrs. Shears' hand had clasped mine. "You could've left like Jenna," she said. "Or like Justin. And Jimmy Sway or whatever bullshit name he wants to go by." She laughed at James. "You stayed, and it's not because you're scared. It's because you're not."

"Mrs. Shears, I am scared, though. I always have been."

Mrs. Shears squeezed my hand. "Scared people run, Dalmatia Scissors. And that's exactly what you didn't do." She smiled. I no longer noticed all the ways that the years had changed her. "And no more of that 'Mrs. Shears' stuff. We're both adults here."

This time she didn't try to hide the tears in her voice.

"It's Donna."

Sarah Edmondson escaped NXIVM, the Keith Raniere sex cult, with the help of her husband, Nippy. Together they freed several women, including actress Catherine Oxenburg's daughter, India. I didn't have a former college quarterback or "Dynasty" star on my side, but also absent was a brand on my ass marking my allegiance to a sexual abuse ring posing as an MLM. I did, however, have the Shears family, as well as a member of the FBI, at the ready to take down James Wilkes.

I still couldn't reconcile Kyle Alaric with the name Alex Parker, so Kyle he'd remain. As it turned out, Kyle may have inserted himself into my life with a fake name and phony persona, but he was right about one thing: the FBI was interested in Walker Wilkes.

Only not just Walker.

James, too.

"Are you sure Jenna will want your help with this?" Aashri asked. She sat opposite me in a booth in the same Cormoran coffee shop where just the previous week I'd hidden in the bathroom to avoid Jenna. Kyle had been my companion that day, and remembering his face across from mine was like rubbing a slice of fresh lemon over a blistered hand.

"Donna said so," I answered, tapping my foot and watching the door. The only person who entered was a lady with a high ponytail that inspired envy. Jenna was ten minutes late.

"You're on a first name basis," Aashri replied. "This is getting serious."

I swiveled at the sound of a knock on the window beside us.

"Oh my gosh," I murmured into my flat white.

Sheena Favrosian pulled her jacket tight against the wind. She pointed toward the door and then our booth.

"I think she wants us to adopt her," Aashri said. "She'll need to get her shots first."

I nodded Sheena's way. Aashri's face tumbled into disbelief.

When Sheena blew in with the autumn wind, I made space for her to sit beside me, but she rushed to the table with anything but aplomb and squeezed next to Aashri with a similar sense of obliviousness. "Thanks," Sheena told us. "I know I'm the last person either of you want to talk to."

Aashri toasted her with a cappuccino. "I can think of a few others."

Sheena pressed her lips together. Whether she swallowed down an apology or an excuse, it didn't matter to me. I wanted nothing from her, not a justification as to why her podcast felt entitled to take advantage of me and especially not a "he's sorry" on behalf of Kyle.

"What's up, Sheba?" Aashri asked, leaning back with a nonchalance she didn't feel. Aashri was very much chalant. We both were.

Sheena wore an unsteady grin. "I don't blame either of you for being pissed. What we did — what *I* did — was wrong. So wrong."

"Pretending to be a federal employee is illegal. But you know what's *wrong*?" I pressed the soles of my shoes to the sticky coffee shop floor beneath our booth. "What's wrong is pretending to" —

267

care for someone — "be friendly to get a story."

Aashri leaned both elbows on the table. "Out with it, Favrosian."

Jenna still hadn't arrived. My stomach hurt. I couldn't even pretend it was my appendix.

"Carbon Fiber has information on James Wilkes that I think would be valuable to both you and the FBI. I'm aware he's being investigated." Sheena met my eyes. "For real."

"You're not telling me anything I don't already know," I replied. Jenna walked into the coffee shop on the tail-end of my words. "Get my number from your colleague and we can talk. I'm meeting someone." Jenna caught my eye, and I waved her toward where we sat.

"Just so you know," Sheena continued, rising, "those photos Tom showed you guys? He did it because he cared. I met with James Wilkes to get information about the scam he's running in California by posing as a new member The Committee who was interested in helping him take—"

"Hey, Dalmatia, Aashri." Jenna rubbed her hands together. "It's frigid as a—Sheena?"

"Got that right," Aashri mumbled under her breath.

Sheena avoided Jenna's stare. Jenna, on the other hand, seemed to see straight into Sheena's soul. Her head did a little double-take thing between the front door of the coffee shop and a woman she obviously knew. What was I witnessing?

"We're not meeting for another hour. What are you doing here?" Jenna asked. Her eyes ran over my face, Aashri's face, Sheena's face like some sort of federally investigative headcount. "What's going on?"

Sheena bit her lip. She released it just as quick. "I was picking up your suit from the dry cleaner and saw them in here. I thought…"

Jenna sighed. "I know what you thought."

I shook my head. "Wait a minute. Why would you have Jenna's

suit?" Burgeoning awareness prickled at the edges of my mind. "The one from the gala?"

The pink flush covering Sheena's neck told me all I needed to know.

"Is this 'Love Island'?" Aashri muttered into her mug. "Can no one couple up outside the DoorDash delivery radius?"

"Why do you two know each other?" I asked. Sheena looked at Jenna. Jenna looked at Sheena. "And how?"

"Jenna is the one good thing James Wilkes did," said Sheena. "But not like that! He didn't *do* anyone. Well, I'm sure he's *done* someone. It just wasn't Jenna. At least, no, I don't think so? Jenna, you two…"

"Not a chance in hell." Jenna picked a crisp bit of maple leaf off Sheena's shoulder. Sheena leaned into her touch. "Obviously."

"A man who calls himself Jimmy Sway." Sheena pretended to fan herself. "How could anyone resist?"

The milk in my flat white was a curdled mess of nausea in my abdomen.

"Sheena, join us since you're here already." Jenna addressed Aashri and me. "Sheena is a podcaster. She contacted me a few months ago after a listener tip came in about James Wilkes' con scheme in Los Angeles. Except it wasn't only about acting or manifesting or whatever woo-woo guarantee he made to every Z-lister ready to throw away whatever they had to snag an Oscar," Jenna told us. "Sheena's show is doing a series on The Committee, and she's providing me with anything she comes across that could help bring down James."

I should ask about Kyle. Had it all been a ruse? A ploy for information that I actually didn't have?

Staring into my now defunct beverage, I realize that it wouldn't matter. Kyle didn't matter. This was about James. Making him pay.

KELLY MACPHERSON

Once and for all.

"How can I help?" I asked.

Aashri looked straight at Jenna. "How can *we*?"

270

32

People Falling Downstairs

It'd been only a few weeks since I'd not been robbed by an NBA mascot or harbored the erroneous belief that Jenna Shears had killed Walker Wilkes. In reality, Benny the Bull had been a mega-load of lilies and Jenna Shears was an FBI agent. Sometimes life throws a person a surprise. And other times…

It throws them Paul Manowitz.

That Paul Manowitz.

"Aashri, you know I've got this," Paul said, tapping away at his laptop while Jenna, Sheena, Aashri, and I stood behind his luxury desk chair. It was a Timko Genuine Leather Executive by a company that sounded like a beautiful nail polish shade. I grabbed Paul

Manowitz's shoulder.

"Ow!" he cried.

I needed a manicure.

"Are you finished yet?" I asked, more growl than question.

"Yes, hold on. Yes!" Paul whipped around, knocking me into Aashri who fell against Sheena who grabbed onto Jenna. Jenna grabbed onto Paul's affectionate friend from the other night.

"Hey," PDA Guy said.

"Hey yourself," Jenna answered, dusting toxic masculinity off her sleeves.

"All you need to do is stay within these sight lines, and I'll get it all." Paul gestured toward his open laptop.

"Pennsylvania is a two-party state," Jenna said. "I don't have enough for a warrant to search the Wilkes place, which is why we're...here."

"Doorbell cam recordings are considered public," Paul replied. "You're good."

We rehashed the plan, and Aashri promised to spot Paul on Tuesday. Project Cult was a go.

"After this is all over, we're going on a real vacation," Aashri said as we got into my car. "Somewhere at least three states away." Our girls' weekend had ended on a strained note thanks to what Mrs. Shears had shared about James and Jenna — and my mother — but I'd promised a redo. "You're bringing the bonnets this time around," Aashri told me.

"Maybe we could go somewhere that doesn't involve headwear."

"Where's the fun in that?"

I headed for home, while Aashri left for my parents' place. She and my dad would have a good time watching YouTube clips of "America's Funniest Home Videos" as she helped him address envelopes destined to hold thank you cards for those who had attended

The Barbara Gala along with an official letter from the elder board of The Committee, informing them that it'd be the final one. Once they'd completed their task, Aashri would show my dad how to find YouTube videos of people falling downstairs. He was in for a treat while they ran through a package of ballpoint pens. Plus, Aashri's handwriting was exquisite.

My mother would be out for the day. I'd spoken to her only briefly since my meeting with Mrs. Shears, but she hadn't found the same enjoyment I did in my new awareness of the actual state of The Committee. I didn't blame her, even if I held it against her. Walker Wilkes had been a part of my mother's life for so long that her identity could no longer be parsed from the man himself. She'd done what she had to protect him, not anyone else. And now Walker's name would be dragged through the mud thanks to his son.

I got why she couldn't send out those cards. I got why she didn't want to speak to me.

I'd deal with it later.

I was on my way to James.

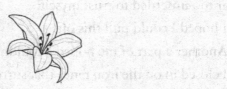

The drive to Bompasero Garden was both quicker and longer than I would've liked.

The truth was I did want to see James. But the reason for texting him and asking if I could come over? Not quite full transparency.

KELLY MACPHERSON

He'd responded almost immediately, which made me feel even worse. And more confused.

My clean laundry was relegated to a few pairs of sweatpants and jeans that'd begun to slip out of style, so I pushed a warm flannel dress over my head and knee-high leather boots up my legs before I left. I washed my face. Took off mascara, brushed my teeth. A makeover was a luxury I had both too little time and money to afford, but it was fine. I'd meet James in the dark as Dalmatia, pure and simple. Not who I'd been with him before. Not a woman colored in shades she'd only guessed he liked.

I'd taken one last look at myself in my bathroom mirror before I left. A bulb had blown out above the vanity, and the harsh edges of the gathering dusk showed themselves on my face. I resisted the urge to dab bronzer on my cheeks and show up late, but I didn't own any bronzer and I didn't want to be late. I needed to stay focused and keep my wits about me. I needed that most of all.

I parked in the dirt lot of Bompasero Garden when I arrived, directly before the front gate. The trek up the paved road to the cemetery didn't feel eerie this time. It didn't feel like anything. I was too expectant, too nervous, spiraling in a tornado of emotions that'd left me far too unsettled to trust myself.

I hoped I could pull this off.

Another a part of me hoped I couldn't.

I closed in on the iron fence that surrounded the burial grounds and spied him before I even reached the hollow space where the entrance grate once stood. James moved within, a ghost among marble. He stood tall and still, watching my approach. The night was cool against my bare neck. I should've worn a jacket, gloves. But I didn't. I hadn't thought to. My mind had been caught on other things.

"Hey," I said. James remained several feet away, an invisible boundary drawn between us. "Thanks for seeing me," I added.

274

Geniality was a sword in my throat.

"Sure," James answered. His eyes were locked on the dark behind me. It wasn't possible James knew what we'd planned. He was a six-foot-two idiot. He was Jimmy Sway.

James pushed his hands into his pockets and met my eyes. The weather had turned legitimately cold. Autumn's breath was a gathering breeze, a long sigh blowing past us. The strings of James' hoodie fluttered against his chest, and I thought of Kyle. I had a type. Liars in loungewear.

I shivered. "Can we talk?" I asked. "I don't need much time."

James looked once more past my head into the dark. "Yeah, okay. In the house."

Perfect.

We began walking side by side. I didn't know what I'd expected, but it wasn't James' hands in his pockets and his willful distance making me second guess every single last thing in my life. For my own part, it wasn't like I was giving more than that myself.

"How long have you been in town?" I asked. The house grew closer in the distance.

"Not long," James said.

"I'm sorry about your dad."

"I'm not."

The original Wilkes house stood beyond the final two rows of resting places, glowing spectral white in the dark. I needed to get James to the porch, and I had to keep him there.

And yet before my feet had even crossed the space where the last row of graves had been dug into the earth, James' mouth took mine. If I'd had gloves on, the North Face ones I wore because they were thin but warm, I wouldn't have felt his five o'clock shadow against my palms. I moved the tips of my fingers over his jaw, marking him with the stain of a mind he'd destroyed. Two major arteries, one-hundred milliliters of blood, ran through the brain. I wanted to smear every inch of his skin with what he'd tainted. I'd never unbuckled a man's belt by the light of the moon but found it wasn't too hard.

"You're beautiful." James breathed the words into my ear as the inky sky melted down toward the earth, onto all the other idiots who'd come before us.

The porch was close, a rustic slab and four wooden steps. James pulled me toward them. I kissed him harder than I could help myself. His lust was a route I knew well, and my need to walk it, run it, lose myself in its familiar tracks, consumed me. I would drag myself over James' body until it swallowed me whole. I could lie in this cemetery, beneath this man, and be done with it all. I'd worn a dress on purpose. I hadn't realized it until then, but of course I'd done it for James. To make it easier for him to say yes. It's what I'd always done: wiped away the risk. For him.

And, in doing so, I'd only ever increased it for myself.

James chuckled in my ear, pulling me down to the second stair. "I'm going to ruin your dress," he said.

Why was I doing this?

"Here, get on top." He sank onto the edge, pulling me over his lap.

Why was I doing this?

"Now I can see you." James' smile was a slice in the dark, the pith of an orange. I wanted to peel it from his face. I wanted to squeeze him until he cried. For me to stop. For me to continue. For me.

Why, goddammit, why was I doing this?

As I rose above him, pressing myself down toward the only part of James he had ever fully given me, I stopped. James lifted toward me, but I froze. He brought me down for a kiss, his body curving to

Cult & Run

get where it needed to be.

I was not doing this.

"Are you Jimmy Sway?" I asked against his lips.

"What the fuck?!" James shoved me off him. He bucked up from the steps and righted himself as if he'd just realized we were in, while not a public place, an exposed one. "What the fuck!?"

"You said that already," I told him. I smoothed my dress and pulled my jacket shut. "Why are you still in Cormoran?"

James held my eyes. "Why are *you*?"

I shivered again. Almost getting screwed in a cemetery didn't make the best foreplay for an inquisition, nor did the weather's colder turn. But I had to keep James in front of the house. "I'm going," I said, not meaning a word of it. "This is too much."

"Dalmatia, wait." James had my arm in his hand and my will in his palm. I took a step but in the wrong direction, moving closer to James, not my BMW. *His* BMW. It'd been a ruse, saying I was leaving. James could see it, couldn't he? "I like being with you," he said, seeming to see nothing at all.

"Don't say things you don't mean."

"I don't," he answered.

We kissed.

And yet even as James led me up the stairs and across the porch, I knew I'd end this night alone.

James Wilkes wouldn't stay, and I wouldn't try and keep him.

More than that, he wouldn't want to. Not after I did what I needed to do.

I followed James through the weathered door of the saltbox house that'd belonged to his father. As if reading my mind, he said, "The last time I'd been here was when my mother was sick."

The door clicked lightly shut behind us, and my eyes focused on glow of the waxing moon as it filtered into the darkened room

277

KELLY MACPHERSON

through thin curtains. The place was lived-in, but like a memory. Something not quite right, something changed. James laid a hand on the mantle of the forgotten fireplace. His eyes were far away.

"Did your dad talk about her at all?" I asked. "Before he passed?"

"Do you want me to bring some wood in?" James met my gaze as if I hadn't spoken.

"It doesn't look clean," I told him, gesturing to the fireplace. "I'm not sure it's safe."

"It's safe," James said. He stepped through an open doorway into a kitchen, all yellowed linoleum and nineteen-seventies tile. The bang of a door, the hiss of the wind. I had to get him back out onto the porch. The doorbell cam wouldn't record inside the house. I considered pushing open the window beside the front door, but would our voices record from within the living room? Not with the gusts whipping up outside. I couldn't risk it. A second bang brought my attention back to the living room. James appeared with an armful of firewood.

"Where'd you get that?" I asked.

"Back porch."

James went to work stacking wood in the hearth. I knew nothing about building a fire. A collection of instruments for doing so leaned against the wall, old and severe in the shadows. James took an iron poker in his hand, the ashes of a former fire clinging to its shaft. He pushed it against the logs before turning my way with a smile. "It'll warm up in a minute."

"Have you been staying here since you got back?" I asked. Was it possible to be colder inside than out? The bulb in the table lamp flickered and died. I tried a wall switch. Nothing.

"Yes."

"Is the electric out?"

James lifted a bottle of lighter fluid from between his crouching

278

form and the fireplace. He aimed it toward the hearth and squeezed. A single match flick later, the pile ignited in a violent haze.

I jumped backward and smacked right into the front door. "James!"

"Calm down," James said, laughing.

"Why are you acting like this?" I'd had my hand on the knob before the words had slipped from my mouth. I shouldn't have come here. I shouldn't have attempted to trick him. When had I gotten so stupid?

James approached me. "Come here," he said, voice soft and low. He smelled of lighter fluid and cologne. Both worked their way into my insides, numbing the part of me that wanted to flee. James drew me into a slow dance, his face in my neck. "Isn't it good like this?"

We moved together, James humming the melody of a song I did not know. I was bound to him, to what he was doing, to the vibration of his throat above my head. James brushed his thumb over my lower lip and moved closer.

"You're going to leave again," I whispered into his mouth.

James said nothing.

"You're going to—"

"I might stay," he said, sounding like he almost meant it.

I wanted to die.

We made love in the dust of a plaid couch that smelled like mold. Not naked, not quick. And not love as much as I'd once wanted it to be. I couldn't define them, the things I felt for James. I couldn't define him, either. But I could hold him, which is what I did. I kept him against me as the night became a colorless dome, too dark to know if the light flickering against the window beside the door were the embers of a dying fire or the coming of a pink-gold dawn.

James had fallen asleep beneath me, one leg hanging off the

KELLY MACPHERSON

couch. I laid awake long enough to make sure the hearth was nothing but a faded dream.

And then, while wishing I didn't have to, I left.

33

PSOAC

Aashri and I finally got our weekend.

After a week of low student attendance thanks to a seasonal cold, we headed down the Jersey Shore. Walker Wilkes had loved Ocean City. Something to do with the pizza. Aashri and I chose Cape May, finding the longer drive plenty worth it. We also added a couple new faces. Sheena and Jenna would arrive the day after we did, joining Aashri and me at a charming Victorian Airbnb replete with modern amenities and beach walkability.

I spent the first night exploring the downtown. Aashri was due a squat challenge accountability check-in with Pandie over Zoom, so she stayed behind while I ate fish and chips at an Irish pub set along a red-brick road complete with glowing streetlights and little foot traffic. The tang of wet leaves mixed with the scent of salt in the air, and I decided that visiting the beach in autumn was not going to be

281

a one-and-done thing.

By the time Sheena and Jenna arrived the next morning, I was ready to relocate.

"You could winter here but not summer," Aashri said. "You'd see one boardwalk evangelist and go hole up in your bedroom. Plus, you're the type to get septic poisoning from cutting your foot on a shell."

"I'm at least going to do more than I have been," I told her. "And I may get a new job."

I thought about what Mrs. Shears — *Donna* — had said. I'd stayed in Cormoran despite it all, through it all, and that was brave. I wasn't sure I believed her, but it didn't feel as bad as thinking I'd chosen to stay stuck.

"What'll you do?" Sheena asked, testing one of Aashri's beach-front versions of a Bludich Ida. The Dalmatia Stepped on a Conch was an homage to both hemoglobin loss and sand.

"I don't really know," I answered through a sip of water.

I'd had enough alcohol for a while. It was surprising how little I cared to numb away the intrusive memory of what James and I had done together. The biggest twist was how much time I'd spent regretting him only to have a sense of satisfaction now that the relationship was finally over. After three years spent alternating between rage and despair, I knew now why sleeping with him this final time hadn't pitched me into my usual quicksand pit of self-loathing.

I was here at a beach house with friends, a glass of lukewarm tap water, and a weekend of cold sunshine on my skin, instead of lying on my bedroom floor feeling used and left. I was myself; Dalmatia at her rawest, unsure of what comes next but not wanting to pretend myself away.

I was okay because I was okay with myself.

Maybe the real reason victims join up with cults, high control groups, or toxic partners is that being with yourself is hard. The quickest advice given to someone in an unhealthy relationship is to leave it. But what about when that toxic partner is you? When the toxic voice in your life is within your own mind? I didn't have the answer, but I was beginning to have the compassion.

Aashri tucked her phone beneath a vintage TV guide on the coffee table.

"If you think Carl Winslow is going to protect you from Pandie, then you're TGIFing out of your mind," I told her.

"It's Tom," she said, a mix of emotions wiped across her face. "He's been texting me."

Sheena shifted uncomfortably where she stood at the quartz-topped island in the large white kitchen.

I curled my legs beneath me. "Are you going to talk to him?"

"Why would I?" Aashri answered. "He could text me an explanation or at the very least voice note one. He's all 'can I call you?' like a mother-in-law who makes you think someone's dying but really just wants your cheeseball recipe."

"Do you have a cheeseball recipe?"

"No."

"Then maybe you should call him."

Sheena watched us. The rental was an open floor plan.

"Are you kidding me right now?" Aashri almost choked on her DSOAC. Its celery garnish sloshed side to side as she set it back on the coffee table. "Why don't you call Kyle, then?"

"Do you want to weigh in here, Sheena?" I called across the room.

"I don't know if you guys want my opinion," Sheena mumbled into her mug.

Aashri squished into me and patted a space for Sheena to take a seat on the couch. "Try us," she said.

283

Sheena padded across the room as if nervous we'd bite her. Her hijab was as blue as her eyes, and, for a second, I was mesmerized by the play of sunlight on her face through the windows overlooking the ocean.

"You know something," I said.

Sheena bit her lip and sat. Her gaze turned down the hallway where Jenna was currently showering in the bathroom. She looked back at me without a word.

"Tell us," I told her.

"Alex — Kyle — isn't—"

A noise like a bird crashing into a window interrupted whatever he was or wasn't.

"Holy shit!" Aashri jumped off the couch, her drink creating a crime scene all over the carpet. Very apropos of its name. "What was that?!"

That was a bird.

Crashing into the window.

Sheena looked around wildly as if searching for a baseball bat, animal control, the rest of the flock. I walked to a window seat where a moment before a large white something had smashed into the glass above it. A smudge and a single feather were evidence that none of us had hallucinated the experience.

"Did it see a French fry?!" Aashri shrieked.

I'd forgotten a very important fact about her.

"Aashri doesn't like birds," I told Sheena, who stood in the middle of the room, ready for someone to toss her a gas mask. "She once got shit on by a hawk and hasn't forgotten it."

"Have you ever been shit on by a hawk?" Aashri asked, peering out the window beside me. "It's traumatic."

"You were hiking with that loser Kevin. That's the real trauma." I grabbed a roll of paper towels from beneath the kitchen sink and began soaking up the tomatoey mess.

Aashri glanced once more out the window. "You're not wrong," she said, coming over to take the soiled towels from my hand. "Thanks. I'll get this. There's a steam vac in the closet. And the bird's gone. Flew the coop. Definitely a Kevin."

I waved Sheena back to the couch as Aashri finished mopping up the drink and headed into the kitchen to clean her hands. Sheena reluctantly settled in the middle, peering at me as if a kamikaze bird was some sort of dark magic Aashri and I had enacted upon her. The two of us squished beside Sheena, bookending her. For safety. For interrogation. "Now tell us what you know."

Sheena smiled. I could tell it was a nervous habit. "Jenna doesn't know this, and it's not my place to tell her."

"Okay, okay," Aashri said. "No one's telling Jenna anything. Got it. Now what do you know?"

Sheena looked my way before addressing Aashri. I was obviously Good Cop in this situation. "Alex and Jenna know each other."

Beyond the house, the surf smacked against the shore. The ocean crashed, wave upon wave, mirroring my life. As one thing settled, another rose to take its place. Connections overlapped so quickly that sense washed out to sea before I had a chance to make heads or tails of it.

Kyle — no, *Alex* — and Tom knew each other.

And now so did Kyle and Jenna.

Marissa was his ex-wife, sure, but that didn't mean Kyle hadn't dated after their split.

"We won't mention anything about Kyle to Jenna," I said too quickly to be natural. The thought of Kyle and Jenna, the absurdity of it, should've made me laugh. Where would they have met? What would they have in common? More than that, though, was the disappointment that Kyle hadn't liked me at all. He'd used me. But not

285

KELLY MACPHERSON

Jenna. I focused on the orange stain setting into the carpet, knowing I should pull out the steam vac quick. My head began to pound, and Aashri gave me a look. "How does Jenna not know you work with him?" I asked Sheena, ignoring Aashri.

"She knows I work with *Alex*," Sheena said, "but they've never met, so she doesn't know he also calls himself Kyle. I met Jenna after Alex started gathering information on James Wilkes. He'd felt bad about leaving all those people behind in LA, all the people James scammed."

"So, Kyle-Alex has sort of been investigating James for real?" Aashri asked.

Sheena nodded. "Something like that."

"But for a podcast," I added. "Which is why he lied and used me."

"He didn't use you, Dalmatia," Sheena said. I was struck again by how blue her eyes were. I could almost believe she was in earnest.

"Did I hear someone scream?" Jenna asked, coming into the room while towel drying her hair from the shower.

Aashri looked her up and down. "Is your entire wardrobe business suits?"

"I have to head out," Jenna said. "But I'll be back tonight." She smiled at Sheena. "You okay?"

Sheena nodded. She didn't look sure.

Jenna seemed to gather as much. "I'll be back," she said, eyes on Sheena. "I heard the Audubon Society is putting on an Autumn Festival downtown. It's mostly eco education. Nature and birds and things like that. But there's supposed to be food trucks."

"I don't think the birds are happy about it," Aashri said, cocking her head toward the window. I nodded in agreement. Sheena looked sick.

Jenna's face scrunched in confusion. "Try not to be too weird in public if you do go out."

"Us? Weird?" Aashri made a face and stuck a finger in her nose. Jenna threw the damp towel at her and left.

New Jersey is home to over four-hundred-eighty species of birds. Among these, the wandering albatross is the largest, boasting a wingspan of eleven feet.

"How big is their shit?" Aashri asked the teen working the booth where we'd encountered the trifold board that'd imparted this knowledge to us. "Like, a cup? Cup and a half?"

"You're disgusting," I told her.

"Hold on," the boy said. "Bryan! This lady wants to know about bird defecation!"

"Is this really how you two spend your freetime?" Sheena whispered beside me.

"About eighty percent," I answered.

After Bryan took a selfie with Aashri, who made duck lips with her mouth and a winged shadow puppet with her hands, we strolled past a booth on mitigating the damage caused by the migration of Canadian geese. Apparently Aashri's concerns about bird feces wasn't as niche as Sheena believed.

We moved past other displays on local flora and fauna along with a multi-booth setup courtesy of New Jersey's Fish and Wildlife

Department. The three of us became honorary deputies for the day with the stickers to prove it. A particularly handsome game warden asked Sheena for her number. She blushed profusely upon refusing, but it only served to make him ask again.

"You should go for him, Dal," Aashri said. "Rebound."

If either of them knew I'd slept with James, they didn't say. Jenna must have, though. After all, she'd have watched the doorbell camera recording. She would've seen us on the steps. She would've watched us enter the house. What happened next would have been anybody's guess from there, but I know what I would have assumed if I'd been on the viewer's end.

By the time we made it to the food trucks in the back parking lot, Aashri, Sheena, and I had learned that New Jersey was one of three states that'd named the American Goldfinch its official state bird. We all considered it wildly uncreative.

"Chicken tacos feel wrong after this," Sheena whispered to me.

Aashri took a bite of hers and flipped Sheena the finger.

We ate at one of many picnic tables set up in the strip of beach behind the parking lot of the Convention Center. Five food trucks offered everything from funnel cake to craft beer. The day was warmer than had been predicted, but I regretted not wearing a jacket. The high of my newfound autonomy began to plummet.

"I'm going to walk over to a beach store and get a sweatshirt or something," I told Aashri and Sheena.

"Are you really that cold?" Aashri asked, mid-bite. A chunk of cilantro-dusted meat dropped from its yellow corn wrapping onto a paper plate.

"Not everything about old Dalmatia was bad," I said. "She planned better for the weather."

Aashri licked sauce from the corner of her mouth. "Nothing about old Dalmatia was bad. I quite like old Dalmatia."

Cult & Run

"I'll take that into consideration when letting her visit."

I waved goodbye and hurried back through the Convention Center, past displays and through the crowd, arriving out front on the sidewalk where a few touristy shops and a place full of beach house furnishings faced me from across the street. I chose the store with the earthiest tones in the window and went inside. The door jingled with my entrance, and a kid stepped on my foot.

"I'm sorry," I said, although I was not. People needed to keep an eye on their children.

"Dal?"

It was Marissa.

Foot-stomper turned around and smiled.

Luke.

"Hey...guys," I said. In no way could I orient myself. Cape May, New Jersey. Audubon Bird Nature Festival Type Thing. A beach house with Aashri, Sheena, and Jenna. James back in Cormoran. And Marissa and Luke...here? CMNJ sweatshirts filled the space behind their heads. My eyes jumped from wall rack to wall rack, unable to land on the faces of the mother and son who watched me, one with concern and the other with disdain.

"This is so funny!" Marissa said. "We're here for a festival but don't set up for another hour. What are you doing here?"

"For the bird thing?" I asked. Luke's feet inched closer to mine. I backed into a rack of sarongs.

Marissa nodded. "We've brought some of our cats for an adoption event," she said. "We do it every year."

"Cats and birds? Don't cats eat birds?"

Marissa laughed as if I was more charming than a large cash donation. "Yes, but actually just as many die each year from flying into windows."

"You don't say," I answered back.

289

"Almost a billion." Luke's first words to me. I kept my feet safely tucked away.

"I'm here with some friends," I said. "And just looking for a sweatshirt. It's cold. I didn't dress right." I rambled on, touching the sarongs as if they'd turn into parkas. I had to get out of there.

"The weather is weird this year. Justin used to complain about it constantly. It was 'California-this' and 'California-that.'" Marissa smiled.

"Wait, Justin who?" I asked. The last Justin I'd heard of belonged to Mrs. Shears. As in Justin, her son. Was some other flagrantly rude Justin running amuck along the Eastern Seaboard?

Marissa's face looked strange.

"Are you stupid?" Luke asked me.

"Luke!" Marissa bent close to his ear. "Stop that now. We've talked about this." She straightened up with a deep sigh. I hadn't before noticed the line between her eyes. "Sorry," she said. "It's been a rough year. Not an excuse, though."

I glanced down at Luke who had the decency to appear chastened. "No, it's fine," I said. "I get it. And, yes, sometimes I am stupid," I told Luke. He looked up at me. "But not when it comes to birds. Did you know that the poop from the wandering albatross provides land fertilizer, unlike Canadian geese who are just disgusting?"

I could tell Luke was impressed. "My dad stepped in goose poop once. In his AirMax University Reds."

"I'd love to make fun of your dad's sneakerhead addiction, believe me, but we need to get going." Marissa laid a hand on Luke's shoulder. In her other she raised a shopping bag. "Saltwater taffy. I'm not above bribery."

"It's a worthy strategy," I replied.

"I'll see you later, Dalmatia. Stop by the Sanctuary's booth if you get a chance. We'll be all set up with a bunch of cute kitties at three.

Justin should be around sometime after that."

"I can't believe you know a Justin, too," I said.

Marissa's grin couldn't mask her uneasy concern. Luke, on the other hand, appeared nothing short of bewildered. Never had I felt so judged for being frazzled by the weather. It wasn't like I'd been in the best state of mind to coherently pack my suitcase.

"We'll see you later, Dal," Marissa said. "Come on, bud." She ushered Luke past me and my cocoon of sarongs and out into the chilly afternoon.

Luke met my eyes as he left.

But my toes, he avoided with intention.

34

Air Max

University Reds

An hour after leaving the beach shop with a zip-up hoodie the color of wet sand, Aashri and I were holding kittens in our laps, talking each other into, out of, into, and out of adopting one. I couldn't do it. Those claws would be the end of me. My eye stung at the thought.

During the time I'd been denying the ease with which I could've become a cat lady if not for the sharp instruments of death embedded within those cute little feline paws, my father had left a voicemail. I decided to wait to check it until after Aashri and I had walked back from the Convention Center with several brochures, zero game warden phone numbers, and my growing concern over what I'd find in my messages when I finally checked.

Sheena arrived back at the Airbnb a few minutes after we did, her arms loaded with bags full of groceries from an overpriced food store in town. She and Aashri began to push around ingredients in a pan, cooking up something they saw on TikTok. Jenna still hadn't returned.

I closed the front door behind me and stepped through the wind-scattered leaves on the porch. My cell was a cold weapon in my hand. I could use it to call my dad back. It's what he'd asked me to do. It's what I knew I needed to do. I could also use it to call Kyle, Alex, whoever he was. There were no messages to compulsively check and recheck since James was no longer a leaking wound in my gut. I'd given up wasting time trying to staunch it with all my strength, which led to the realization that he'd never been the problem. Part, yes, but not the whole.

So, I made the call.

To my dad.

And he told me about James.

The FBI had arrested James August Wilkes the morning I'd left him in the old house in the graveyard. Rumor had it he'd been halfway to the airport when he was picked up. If it was true, I wouldn't be surprised. I'd blocked him from my phone. I wouldn't have known if he'd called or texted. I also wouldn't have known if he hadn't. That'd been the whole point. I also didn't know how the authorities gotten him, since all the doorbell cam would've shown was me humiliating myself with a man I'd claimed to hate.

James had been charged with fraud and conspiracy after swindling just shy of a million dollars from his followers in California while also attempting to recruit members of The Committee for a new group, The Branch, in Los Angeles. Together they would develop a community without the oversight of Walker Wilkes and the moody weather of Pennsylvania. Self-help literature would give way to online video courses, and monthly checks would become auto-debits. James had it all figured out.

Except he didn't.

As my father told me over the phone, leaves whipping into a violent tendril around my ankles, Mrs. Shears and my mother had joined up against James Wilkes in the final days of Walker's life. They'd hired Malorie Hathaway-Kurtz to keep an eye on things. They'd also installed a doorbell cam at her home after James had shown up one day, attempting to convince her to run away to Los Angeles with him. Malorie was no idiot, and neither were the Poms. They'd yip-yapped James all the way back to his Jeep, allegedly taking a chunk from his left shin on the way.

When I told my father how it was all almost too unbelievable to be true, he asked if I wanted to talk to my mother. I couldn't do it but also couldn't give a reason why.

"Give her some grace, kiddo," my dad said. Mrs. Shears' apology played in my head. My mother should've been the one to give me that. I wasn't ready to hear her version of saving the world from James Wilkes when mine had been imploding for years because of her choices. Doing one thing right didn't make all the wrong okay.

And so I said goodbye to my father and sat on the wicker loveseat on the porch, listening to the noises of a beach town in the fall. I hadn't expected quiet, but I also hadn't thought I'd see so many people. Families rode rented bicycles down the sidewalk like rows of ducks in bucket hats and fleeces. Joggers loped and power walkers tore it up, speed not the most important thing when the ocean was within eyesight. I imagined Cape May in the summer. Ceiling fans hung from the covered porch roof, and the window boxes boasted orange-gold mums. In warmer weather there'd be zinnias. Maybe daisies, geraniums. I liked those. I'd freshen up my place when I got back. Not that I had a balcony to stick potted plants on, but I could do one of those windowsill gardens.

Jenna pulled before the house, parallel parking like a champ in a cherry-red Audi. Who was I to think I'd be able to house flowers on the two-inch deep windowsills in my apartment? Let alone keep them alive on the ride home from the nursery? Jenna clomped up the porch stairs with wooden legs. Her hair had dried frizzy, and she pushed it behind her ear when she saw me. It sprang right back.

"Are you okay?" I asked her.

"No. Yes. I don't know." Jenna slumped beside me on the loveseat. I was reminded of my luau birthday party when she'd accidentally smacked me with her Macarena hands. Not to mention the many times she had invited herself to my house when the last thing I'd wanted was Jenna Shears making comments about how I could improve the realism of the horses I'd like to draw or the eyeliner I later experimented with. She'd also asked a lot of questions about Aashri and my parents. I remembered her wanting to know if Aashri watched "Glee" and what she thought of it. Jenna had been a Rachel Berry fan. I should've ridiculed her for it but had just let her talk, because, with Jenna, that's what she was going to do anyway.

But sitting beside me, worn out from a job and a life I couldn't even begin to understand, Jenna said nothing.

"What's going on?" I asked. "Is it about the case? I heard about James."

"There is no case," Jenna told me. "James was released this morning." She looked at me with nothing but despair in her eyes. "I tried. Damn it, I really fucking tried."

I didn't know what to say. Nothing felt right.

Even worse, what I felt didn't feel right either.

"Jenna," I said, turning to her. "It doesn't matter."

She hadn't been crying. Her eyes were red, but not from tears. From exhaustion. I realized then that I'd never seen Jenna Shears cry.

Not when falling off her bike as a kid. Not when her brother called her Humpty-Dumpty when she'd tumbled from the top of a shed while trying to cartwheel onto it from the edge of her home's sun-porch roof. Not when I told my mom there was no way in hell I would attend Jenna's fifteenth birthday party, the last one I ever did. I hadn't seen Jenna cry when hurt. I hadn't seen her as much as frown when disappointed.

Had she been disappointed?

Looking at her now, I thought I'd misunderstood a whole lot more than the criminal justice system.

"We made it out of The Committee, Jenna. It doesn't matter what happens to James. It really doesn't." She opened her mouth to protest, but I continued on. "There will always be people who scam and swindle and cheat and steal. People who need to control others because everything within *them* feels out of control. But, Jenna, that's not us."

She let out a breath, a ragged little thing that sounded as if she'd been holding it all day. "My nerves are frayed, Dalmatia, and then you go and say something all emotional like that."

"Is that a good thing?" I asked.

Jenna smiled. "It's a very good thing. You really don't get why, though, do you?"

I was beginning to realize that what I didn't understand was a lot more than I'd guessed. "You can tell me," I replied.

"Before my brother left Cormoran, The Committee didn't matter, Dalmatia. It really didn't."

"Your brother," I said. "Justin."

"He'd never been into it," Jenna continued. "Justin made my mom's life so much harder than it had to be. She'd say it was because our dad had left when we'd been so young and that it affected boys more than girls. Bullshit, of course. But she excused Justin's behavior.

Do you remember he even got to go to school?"

I did remember. I remembered him yelling "Edward Scissorhands" at the top of his lungs as Justin and his friends rode their skateboards down the center of our street.

"Do you remember how stupid he was with that skateboard? Doing ollies or whatever they were called? The tricks?"

"Sort of," I lied.

"And the shoes. When he scuffed those Jordans, I will never forget the sound that came out of his mouth. I'd asked if he wanted me to ride my bike over to the Walgreen's and get him some diapers. Big baby about shoes. Probably still is." Jenna smiled. Her eyes looked a little brighter.

"Men and their shoes is a whole thing," I said. I was talking about Kyle before I could stop myself. "I was kind of seeing a guy," I told her, remembering uneasily that Jenna and Kyle had some sort of connection, too. "It wasn't anything real." I couldn't be sure that was entirely correct, but Kyle was nothing to me but an anecdote about men's footwear, so it wasn't totally wrong. "The first time I saw him he was in joggers and Nikes and then he was in *another* pair of Nikes when we had a date."

"Are you sure that wasn't Justin?" Jenna said with a laugh. "Sounds like something he'd do. When he'd called Mom and told her he had come across James Wilkes in California, she said she'd asked if Justin was wearing flip-flops yet. 'No, Air Max University Reds,' he'd told her."

I grabbed Jenna by both arms.

She screamed.

"Jenna, where does Justin live now?"

Jenna did not pull her arms from my grip. I think she was afraid her skin wouldn't make the trip. "Here," she said. "In Pennsylvania."

"Where?"

297

"I don't know. I don't want to know. We don't talk. He only talks to Mom."

"Jenna, you work for the FBI. You should find out," I said. I looked like a madwoman. I *was* a madwoman.

"Dal, you're making me nervous."

I was making myself nervous.

"Aashri! Aashri and Sheena! I'm…you guys…we need to…go! We need to go!" I was through the front door, inside the house, and smack-dab in the center of the kitchen with Jenna on my heels.

"Dal's on drugs," Jenna said, rubbing the spots on her arms where there'd be Dalmatia Scissors-shaped bruises tomorrow.

"I have a theory!" I shouted. Aashri maneuvered me away from the hot pans on the stovetop.

"Could we hear it over dinner?" Sheena asked.

"No! Pack it up! Pack it all up!" I announced. "Cormoran is calling!"

"Dalmatia, you are way too energetic right now to be anything other than high. What were you doing on the porch? How much catnip did you sniff at the bird show today?" Aashri held me at arm's length with a spatula.

"Wait! The show! Never mind, never mind. We need to go right now! Before Marissa leaves!" I tapped my cell phone, not to make a call but to prove a point. "Does Justin have social media?" I asked Jenna. Sheena had brought her an egg roll.

Jenna took a bite and answered through an approving nod toward Sheena. "Again, I don't know. It wasn't me he'd contacted. It was Mom. What's going on?"

I opened Safari and arrived at the truth with a single finger. "This."

Justin Shears' Instagram profile filled the screen of my phone. There he was with a goofy grin on his face and rich brown eyes looking right into the camera. The account was private, but it didn't matter. I'd seen all I needed to.

"This is Kyle," I said. "Kyle Alaric."

"Wait." Jenna's expression was a pole vault frozen mid-air. "That's Justin, my brother."

Sheena, in an uncharacteristic display of boldness, grabbed the phone from my hands.

"No," she said. "It's Alex Parker."

35

Al

When four women show up at your ex-wife's feline adoption event, it can be overwhelming.

But when the one you'd taken on a date while lying about your identity shows up to pet cats, it's earth-shattering.

The world of Justin Shears was due some shaking up.

Locating Marissa's contact info wasn't tough. The animal sanctuary had a website, Facebook page, and even a TikTok. A bunch of videos of Luke and Marissa doing complicated dances together while playing with a brood of cute dogs was both perplexing and heartwarming. I'd never really seen Luke smile. But he did, in the videos.

It took Marissa almost no time at all to respond to my text.

"She's still there," I told the group. "So, I'm going, right? This isn't an all-for-one, one-for-all thing?"

"It's that, for sure," Sheena said. "But us backing you up from our phones. I know Alex. He's not going to like being ambushed by all four of us."

Alex, right.

I considered the guy. Did *I* know Alex? I sort of knew Kyle. I also sort of knew Justin. I couldn't believe the boy who'd teased me as a kid was the owner of the brown eyes I couldn't get out of my damn head. He was also, as Sheena's words reminded me, her podcasting co-host who'd been informing the world about the muddled legacy of Walker Wilkes.

Jenna laid her hand on my arm as I packed my purse. I didn't need anything, but my brain found solace in bringing along three tampons, deodorant, and twelve band-aids just in case. "Dal, are you going to tell him about me? That we're friends?"

I thought for a moment. "Do you want me to?" I asked Jenna.

It was clear from her face she wasn't sure.

"You're my friend, Jenna. Whatever you want comes first."

Her hand fell from my arm. She pushed her hair behind her ear once more. It was still messy. She was still tired. Jenna nodded with a sigh and a smile. "Whatever you need to say today, you should say." She looked at the sofa, at Sheena, at a terrible watercolor hanging on the wall across the room. "Justin left, Dalmatia. He may have gotten in touch with my mom, but he didn't get in touch with me. He left, and, as far as I'm concerned, he stayed gone. But you…you stayed. You've been in Cormoran my whole life."

My chest rose and fell, heart beating fast. I didn't know what to say, but I knew what she was trying to.

"You've been the steadiest person I've ever known," Jenna said. "And I am grateful."

When I hugged her, she didn't pull away. "I promise not to leave a bruise."

Jenna laughed into my hair.

The three of them wished me God Speed and May the Force Be with Me — Aashri was a closet "Star Wars" fan — and I was on my

301

way. I'd walk to the Convention Center where Marissa would be waiting with Luke and hopefully Justin Shears. She'd be harboring the impression I wanted to adopt a cat. Any guilt I felt at the ruse was squashed flat by the pounding rhythm of louder, heavier emotions: anger, anxiety, excitement. What on earth was I excited for? Justin Shears was my childhood arch-nemesis. I'd spent years believing it to be Jenna when the greatest foe of my youth was her older brother, a boy who'd made me feel like some sort of weirdo on a ten-speed bike who should've just stayed home on the couch.

The Convention Center loomed large in the distance. The gravity of what I was about to do, the surprise I was about to inflict on three people, did, too. I needed a minute. I'd take a minute. Maybe a few. Maybe a lot. I sunk onto one of the wrought iron benches lining the street. A plaque on the back read "Walter and Marge, That First Summer to Forever, 1998". I brushed my fingers over the brass.

"Who were you?" I asked it. Talking to a metal rectangle seemed like the least crazy thing I'd done lately. "Did you trick her, Walter? Or was it you, Marge? What did you have to go through before that forever?"

"If I'm not mistaken, Walter robbed the Cape May County Bank and Marge was the teller he'd fallen in love with during the stick-up."

When I turned around, the man I'd known as Kyle Alaric was behind me.

No, not Kyle. Not Alex either.

Justin Shears.

"You're here to see me, aren't you?" Justin asked. "I deserve it. Whatever you have to say, I deserve it."

I slowly pulled myself away from the bench, keeping it as a buffer between us. "How'd you know?" I asked.

"Marissa said you were down here for the weekend and were coming back to adopt a cat. You wouldn't adopt a cat, Dal." Justin made paw motions with his hands. "Claws."

I'd been ready to unleash hell on this man, but all the words I'd been counting on were lost in the look on his face. Some would say it was contrition. I wanted to agree but couldn't.

"Are you Alex Parker?" I asked.

"I am," Justin said.

"And you're not Kyle."

There was pain in his eyes. "I'm not."

"Do you remember me?" I asked. "From Campbell Street?"

Beneath the cold blue of the coastline sky, Justin's face was flush with the past. "Purple Huffy."

"Do you know what I was going to say when I saw you today?" I moved around the bench, coming to stand before him. Justin's hands were in the pockets of his jacket, and he wore stubble on his face. I would've found it compelling if my heart wasn't being squeezed from the outside-in.

"What?" Justin asked.

I leaned in close and looked right up into his eyes. "Edward Scissorhands."

"Huh?"

"Edward Scissorhands," I said again, with force this time. "You used to call me that. I hated it. I hated you."

Justin did the one thing that made it all so much worse. He laughed.

"You're laughing at me now?" I took a step back.

"I'm not laughing at you, Dal," Justin said. "I don't remember that, and I'm just...this is..."

"I'm something to laugh at," I said. "I'm ridiculous, right? I'm that kooky girl from the kooky cult who does school in that kooky house who—"

"Dalmatia, stop." Justin grabbed onto me, fingers flexing against

303

my arms. He closed the gap between us, and I turned away to face the street. "You are not any of those things," he said, low and gentle. "You aren't."

"You wouldn't know," I answered back. "You weren't there."

Justin didn't let me go, but I felt the change in his body. The shame. I turned my head his way, eyes hovering at his chest. "Jenna missed you," I said. "And I've..."

"You've what?"

My will power was breaking. I lifted my face to his. "I missed you. This past week, I missed you. I didn't want to, but I did. And then I learned who you were — you're Justin, the boy who made me feel like an outcast. How could Kyle, that sweet, handsome, funny man, be *Justin Shears?*"

"Handsome?"

My expression shut him up instantly.

But not for long.

"I'm still Kyle." Justin said, shaking his head as if shedding his boyhood could be done so easily. "You know what I mean. I hope you do. I shouldn't ask you for anything, Dal. I'm just sorry. But I wasn't pretending when I was with you. I was, but I wasn't." A couple on bikes swerved around us. "I'm really sorry."

I stepped closer. Justin smelled like a warm day, a sunny dream.

But dreams don't keep. And it was time to wake up.

"You'll always be Kyle to me," I said. Justin opened his mouth to speak, looking so much like his sister. And, just like Jenna, he closed it when I shook my head. "Because that's how I want to remember you. I'm leaving Cormoran. Justin Shears lives there, and I can't. I can't be back on that street." It didn't matter if he had no clue what I meant. I laughed once, short and harsh. "Hell, you were *married.*" The weight of that last part, uttered in a half-whisper, sank down deep in my chest. "You kept your child from knowing your family. From your mother, your sister. The Committee wasn't the only thing you ran from."

Justin said nothing. Maybe I'd gone too far. I wasn't at all sure what I was doing. I just knew what I could handle, and it wasn't a man who'd always cause me to wonder what he wasn't saying.

"I never mentioned you on the podcast," Justin said as I started for the Convention Center. I had no intention of leaving Marissa and Luke high and dry, but nothing Justin could say would change how I felt about him. I knew why he'd settled in Bywood County. His mother had left. His sister had left. Zero risk. I didn't need to know the specifics of when he'd returned from California or why. I didn't need to know anything. Did I want to know? Yes. Although, in time that'd fade. I was betting on it.

"Bye, Justin."

By the time I said it, I was too far away for him to hear me.

The doors of the Convention Center opened automatically, the tile beneath my feet a red carpet fit for someone with nothing to her name but her proximity to a fringe group of lunatics. Marissa was holding a Bengal cat when I walked up to her booth. The other stations were all broken down, but she and Luke had waited. "His name's Leonard," Marissa said. "I'm shocked he's still available because Bengals are rare. But he's old. I think that's why no one's scooped this fella up."

"A senior guy, huh?" The name Leonard wouldn't do. I had another in mind for him. "Al," I said, glancing at Luke who stood not far from Marissa. He'd been messing around on a tablet but looked my way. "After the bird who makes the biggest poop."

Luke's laughter was full and round, a shape I hadn't known I could draw on my own.

"Normally we'd need to do a home visit," Marissa said, "but if your apartment allows cats, then I think I can get around that for

305

you." She grinned.

"How do you know I have an apartment?" I asked. "I've been trying so hard to give off homeowner vibes. Did you see the WD-40 I carry in my purse?"

"Justin told me," Marissa said, frowning. "He told me a few other things, too. I can't believe him. I really can't."

My new cat-son peered at me with milk saucer eyes. I wondered where Justin had gone after I'd left.

"I'm sorry, Dal. I thought you knew. He gave me the impression you did. That day I met you at the house and made that stupid comment about The Committee." I almost told her she had nothing to be sorry for, but Marissa silenced me with the hand not cradling Al. "It was dumb. I was nervous. Justin hasn't really dated. It was easier when we were in California."

Al purred against Marissa's chest. I hoped he'd like me. I'd never been an animal person, and I was pretty sure animals could tell. "You met in California?" I asked.

"Luke was born there. We divorced there, too. When Mark and I relocated to Pennsylvania for his job, Justin came. Mark only took it because we all agreed to do this together — to move. I know what they say about co-parenting, and it's definitely not the easiest thing. Losing a marriage, losing someone you'd loved…that's hard. But co-parenting with Justin never has been. He's the best in that way."

Al watched me with a curious expression as if trying to ascertain what sort of socioeconomic situation he was about to enter. The idea of a Gucci cat carrier was semi-appealing if out of my price range. I still had one question. "You knew he" — I didn't want Luke to hear me mention that his father was a liar — "used a pseudonym?" I banked on a seven-year-old not knowing that word.

Luke perked up. "Like a spy?"

I was continually surprised by this child.

306

Marissa sighed. "It's not uncommon to have a professional alias," she said. "But the other stuff, turning into whatever he needs to be in order to get a story. Let's just say there's a renegade part of Justin that didn't lend itself to marriage, but which does make him a pretty prolific podcaster."

I had no plans to listen to Justin's podcast, so I wouldn't know.

Marissa lifted Al toward me. "Ready to hold him?"

Not really.

"Sure." I took the cat in my hands. No, not *the* cat. My cat. My son, Al the Cat. He sure was beautiful. "Hey, Al," I said. "Go gentle on me, okay? Believe it or not but you're my first pet."

"You've never had a pet before?" Luke asked, suddenly at my side. He slid his fingers gently over Al's back. "Not even a betta fish?"

"A rock once. But it'd been more of a paperweight, and I'd almost broken a toe."

Luke shrugged. My lack of pet care experience didn't seem to worry him.

"You can come visit him, you know. Maybe give me some cat tips," I said. "I don't live very far from you."

"My dad can bring me," Luke replied. "Next time he comes to your house. Or you could bring Al to my house if you ever want. If he's good in the car. Some cats aren't."

"Luke, do you want to help me get Al all packed up? I'm sure Dalmatia will know soon enough whether her new friend finds cars seaworthy." She smiled hopefully, which I knew was about more than just Al.

"What do you think, Al the Cat? Are you going to ride out your golden years with me?" I asked him.

My new cat didn't as much as purr, but he didn't claw my eyes out either.

It was a good sign.

307

36

Live From Dal's Apartment, It's Chaos

Rehoming animals is one thing. Rehoming synthetic hair is another.

The Barbara Foundation was no more. Its infamous gala would go down in history as the most ridiculous fundraiser that ever was funded. James Wilkes may have been released due to lack of prosecutory evidence, but that didn't mean the FBI was through with The Committee. The whole time I'd been unpacking wigs and arranging place cards, helping my mother create spreadsheets of silent auction donations and addressing thank you card envelopes, Walker Wilkes had been laundering money through the 501C's account.

Surprising to most, but not surprising to me was that he'd been working with the Porta family.

As in Frank Porta, mob boss.

The first time I saw a photo of Nancy Sinatra was when Jenna showed me pictures of what the FBI had recovered from the old white house in The Committee's burial compound. Walker Wilkes owned heaps of Nancy Sinatra paraphernalia. It seemed my mother wasn't the only one hot and heavy with eBay. Mrs. Wilkes, James' late mother, looked an awful like Nancy with her beehive hairdo and sultry eyes. She was nothing more than a fading shadow in the few memories I had of Committee summer picnics with The Committee when I was a young child. Back when summertime didn't feel so different for me than it did for other kids. Before things turned dark. Jenna had told me they'd recovered a single photo of Mrs. Wilkes in all of Walker's many possessions.

One.

Hundreds of Nancy Sinatra. Plenty of Committee members. More of my mother than made me comfortable.

Only one of his wife.

I wasn't surprised. I'd gone from the scandal of a former cult to finding myself shocked by how little Al the Bengal Cat left in the litter box I'd set up in my bathroom. I wondered daily if I'd stumble upon a hidden gem somewhere in my apartment. Al the Cat wasn't living up to his namesake, but that was in no way a disappointment. I'd planned a little shindig to celebrate our first two months of being roommates. Time had never moved so fast.

"I'm bringing my new dog," Aashri texted an hour before she was due to arrive. She'd insisted on making a cocktail in Al's honor and needed to stop at Wine and Spirits for brandy and Cointreau. The Bengal Tiger was a recipe she'd found online, but I'm sure it'd

309

be rebranded as was Aashri's trademark.

"You don't have a dog," I texted back.

"Yes, I do," she replied. "Named Tom. After the biggest shit I know."

I sent her an LOL.

Aashri's reply came quick. "See you soon, Millennial Karen."

"With a C," I typed back.

I received a devil emoji in return.

"What do you think, Al?" I asked, flopping down on the couch and crashing his nap time. He wasn't offended. After tossing out all those ridiculous candles and knickknacks from HomeGoods, Al had appropriated my coffee table as his favorite siesta spot. I didn't mind. Al was good company. He kept his opinions to himself and was mindful of my side of the bed. The litter box was a compromise I'd learned to live with. "I've never seen Aashri like this. You think she's going to pick things back up with Tom?"

My firstborn smiled. It was a nose thing he did, but I took it for what I wanted it to be. Aashri said I'd been doing a lot of that. Jenna, on the other hand, refrained from commentary and just sent me funny, borderline inappropriate memes from D.C. She'd gotten back in town that afternoon, and Sheena and I had stuck a giant welcome home poster to her front door.

"She's going to tell us how she could've been robbed," Sheena had said that morning as we'd used up two rolls of tape to keep it from falling. "The welcome home part."

"Small window of opportunity," I'd told her.

I wasn't the best at decorating, former coffee table aside, but the Jenna poster must have twisted a spigot of creativity that'd long been rusted. Two months ago in Cape May, I had told Justin I'd be leaving Cormoran, but the longer it took me to find a new place to live, the more I wondered if I really wanted to.

310

By the time Aashri shuffled through the door, I'd crashed right into a bad mood.

When Aashri tickled Al's nose with a cat toy she'd pulled from a bag, I wasn't sure if she'd made it better or worse.

"What is that?" I tried to grab it from her hand, but she was quicker. "Is this what I think it is?"

"A sex toy? Yeah." Aashri made little cooing sounds as she traumatized my son.

"Get that away from him! He's a baby!"

"I thought he was an old man?" she answered. "Can't an old guy have a little fun? Whaddya say, Al?"

"Unless you have some hot young thing hidden in that bag, you're just a tease."

Aashri unpacked a box of fancy cat treats instead. "That's very derogatory, Dal. You can't assume that Al's interested in younger women. He lives with you, doesn't he?"

"We have a similar sensibility," I replied. "And good luck, because he's in a bad mood today, too."

"No, he's not," Aashri said. She tickled his head. "Look how happy he is! We're the A Team!"

"This is getting weird." I crossed to the kitchen and began laying out cheese and chopping meats for a charcuterie tray.

"Don't get hurt," Aashri ordered. "Jenna doesn't work at the Urgent Care anymore, remember? And my truck's already got a full tank of gas."

"It was a good cover, though." I sliced some pepperoni dangerously close to my thumb. "Good way to gather information."

"Did Jenna tell you about Malorie? That home health nurse?"

"A little. She recovered the doorbell cam video of James Wilkes threatening her and posted it on TikTok."

Aashri popped something in her mouth, talking as she chewed.

"She's an influencer now. Guess what for?"

"Are you eating a cat treat?"

"Baby carrot."

I narrowly avoided another miss with the sharp edge of my blade. "What kind of influencing is Miss Hathaway-Kurtz doing?"

Aashri smiled. She had carrot in her teeth. "Female hair restoration."

"What a world this is."

"What a world, indeed."

As Al's guests arrived, I passed around Aashri's latest cocktail, which had turned out quite pretty with a fresh tiger lily popped into each. Drinks in hand, we all settled in my living room surrounded by snacks and copious amounts of cat hair.

"You look happy," Sheena said.

"She's in a bad mood," Aashri interjected, pointing a piece of crostini bread my way.

"I thought that was the cat?" Jenna asked.

"Both of them, apparently," Aashri replied.

I'd expected Jenna to storm in steaming mad about the poster, but she'd liked it enough to put it above her mantle. At least for the time being. "Is it anything to do with James Wilkes?" she asked now. "The mood?"

"I'm not really in a mood," I said with a long sigh. I'd planned this little party as a way to put a cap on the past few months of upheaval, but my mind and body both felt like a decade's worth of uninterrupted naps. "I'm tired. I love Al. He's great. It's everything else."

No one asked. We'd shared a beach house and a criminal investigation. Each of the three women in my apartment knew my face well enough to realize when sharing wasn't going to happen.

"I brought games," Sheena said after a few quiet beats. It was the broadcaster in her. She needed conversation. "Oh, this one is so funny!" Sheena pulled something from her purse, and I was worried it'd be another sex toy. "Clue!"

"Like the movie?" Aashri asked. "Don't you like that one, Dal?"

She evidently did not remember our day at Tom's garage as well as I did.

"Look," Sheena continued. "I have the Murder Mystery version. We all get a character. I have props and cue cards." She began taking items from inside her purse and laying them beside where she sat on my living room floor. Sheena's interpretation of a party was proving to be fascinating. Al had been watching from the kitchen counter but came closer once Sheena pulled out a feather duster.

When the next object appeared in Sheena's hands, I sidled up even closer than my cat. "What is that?" I asked, digging my hands into my carpet to make sure the floor hadn't given out. It sure felt like it had.

"A syringe?" Sheena gave her answer like a question. She shook the Ziplock bag encasing it, the syringe bouncing against thin plastic walls. Sheena laughed to herself. "It was in the original game. Before the creator guy got a patent. I'd pranked Justin with it at the studio but thought it'd fallen out of my purse the day I met up with James Wilkes at his dad's house. But I guess not because later on I found it back at the studio with Justin's stuff." Sheena set it on her lap. "I think it was one of a few weapons that didn't make the final game."

"Shillelagh," I said.

"God bless you," Sheena answered with a smile. When I didn't respond, her confused eyes scanned the faces of Jenna and Aashri. Their concern became her own. "Am I missing something?"

"An Irish walking stick," I whispered.

I was going to be sick.

Aashri had me off the couch in an instant. "Okay, you. Come

313

on." She propelled me into my kitchen and turned on the tap. I'd remember the incident as waterboarding, but Aashri would always insist she'd been trying to prevent me from passing out.

"We could've done this in the bathroom!" I said, sputtering water out of my mouth.

"Didn't think you'd make it. You're pale as death."

I felt even worse.

"What's wrong?" Aashri asked. "You haven't been right since the Shore. What happened? And don't tell me you're allergic to cats or anything cute like that."

"I'm cute?"

"Dal, so help me or I will rack your ass like a Swiss bar."

"I don't like that," I told her. "Doesn't sound fun."

"Know what else isn't fun? Being kept in the dark by my best friend."

The party in my living room had the good manners to pretend they hadn't heard this entire exchange. Al did not, however. He sat on the counter behind my kitchen sink, swishing his tail with smug satisfaction.

"You never asked," I said to Al. "I took it that you didn't like emotional women."

"He doesn't like his mom slowly sinking into depression," Aashri answered for him. "What's going on?"

"I'm not depressed."

"You're not yourself."

"I am myself!" I yelled at Aashri. "That's the problem!" My chest hurt like a bruise, and I pushed past her through the kitchen. It wasn't easy. Aashri was rooted like a brick. "I'm sad, okay? *I'm* tired!"

She followed me with eyes too kind for the tirade I was having. "We're all tired, Dal. It's okay."

"You're not all tired! I'm tired!" I made eye contact with Al. He

Cult & Run

turned away and jumped down beside my toaster. "Nothing's different for me! Can't you see that? I have a cat, and he's great. He's so great, but I'm…I'm still…I'm just here."

Sheena moved to my side. She and Aashri had me cornered. One hugged me. The other made a face, a sad one.

"You have no idea what to do with me, do you?" I asked Aashri over Sheena's shoulder. Sheena's hijab got in my mouth, but she only laughed. I let her keep her arms around me until I was holding on just as tightly.

"You're too hard on yourself, Dalmatia," Sheena said.

Across my apartment, Jenna swirled her drink. The ice cubes inside clinked against the glass. "Oh, I don't know. I think she's feeling exactly how she's supposed to."

Sheena covered my ears. "Jenna!"

Jenna stood, not making eye contact with anyone but me. "There was no justice," she said.

It wasn't hard to read her mind. Jenna's face wore it all — the loneliness of growing up in The Committee and the betrayal that it had taken this long, *so* long, for our families to realize how fucked up it all was. More than that, though, was a fury undergirding her despair. Rage born of the robbery we'd both experienced when James Wilkes had snatched away the dream of making someone pay — for his sins, for his father's. It was that last one I couldn't turn away from. I saw myself in Jenna's eyes. We were the same, she and I. Sheena and Aashri could try, but they'd never understand.

"Then how can we get it?" I asked.

"I don't think that's a good idea," Aashri said.

Jenna ignored her. "He's at the Cormoran Inn. Ticket booked for Sacramento tomorrow morning, layover in Dallas. If he's smart, he'll get to Philly International by six."

Sheena was between us, one hand laid on my arm. "You two

315

KELLY MACPHERSON

need to stop."

The door to my apartment opened and shut. Aashri had left.

"Sheena, no offense," Jenna said, "but this doesn't concern you."

Sheena crossed to the living room. Al jumped off the counter to follow. "Doesn't concern me? You wouldn't have known half what you do about James Wilkes without me!"

"Or without my brother? Isn't that what you mean?" The gentleness Jenna usually showed toward Sheena had fled the building. "You should've told me he was Alex Parker."

"I didn't know, okay?" Sheena's heartbeat was visible through her thin blouse. I didn't want to see her cry, but I didn't want to stop Jenna either. Some things had to be said. "He lied to me, too! I figured it out later. After you'd told me about Justin, I realized it sounded so much like what Alex told me about himself…about his sister, his mom. I've only been part of Carbon Fiber for a year and a half, Jenna. I've only known him that long. He lived in Cali before that. How could I have known who he really was?"

Jenna's eyelids slid shut. "You couldn't."

Sheena went to her. They embraced, and I turned toward my refrigerator. Al swished his tail against my ankles. I opened my arms wide to him, but he loped toward my bedroom instead.

The loud sound of my front door swinging open stopped me from curling up beneath my blankets right along with him.

It was Aashri. She waved her cell phone in the air. I grimaced. I'd had enough of phones for all time. "Tom's on his way. We're going live. For the podcast."

Sheena whipped around, leaving Jenna hugging air. "Here?! We're not set up for that!"

"Here," Aashri answered. She looked at me. "Justin, too."

"No," I told her. "No way."

"With a special guest," Aashri added.

316

"Absolutely not!" Jenna said before I had a chance.

"Buck up, gang, It's a special night!" Aashri checked her Apple Watch. "Thirty minutes till Jimmy Sway is in the house!"

My mouth opened and closed, but nothing came out. Maybe a squeak, maybe a futile attempt at some final words. I backed up into the doorway of my bedroom while the three women in my apartment watched me with expectant concern. Aashri turned her phone my way. Tom had been with us on FaceTime for the duration of her announcement. He waved from beside a plant topped by a tiny, crocheted hat.

I passed out. Or I got dizzy. Either way, I slumped to the floor.

I also found out how correct I'd been that my son Al had been avoiding the litter box.

37

And We're On

Once upon a time, there'd been a boy named James Wilkes.

Tall, lean. Prone to wearing board shorts year-round. Not one for many words.

We'd never properly dated, James and me. Not as teens, and not later after reconnecting in our twenties. It'd always been complicated. A hustle, really, James taking what he could from me and me thinking I'd convince him of something I wasn't even sure of myself.

I wouldn't admit it, but I wasn't surprised James had become a YouTube con artist. He was magnetic, even though, as children, his influence seemed to settle over me alone.

We hadn't been close as kids, for as much time as we'd spent together, and the few conversations we'd shared had been about his music. James was a pianist. Long, elegant, and quick, were his fingers. I'd fallen in love with those hands, or at least what they could do with a set of keys. He'd caught me watching him once, practicing a piece I'd later learn was his own composition. I would hear many more over the years. Beautiful, slow melodies full of sorrow. Melancholy, sure, but that'd been James. I'd loved it about him. How he expressed himself. How he expressed the things going on within me that I had no way to voice.

But neither of us were those kids anymore.

I was in the bathroom when James arrived at my apartment. Not on the toilet, nothing that mortifying, although a good round of stress diarrhea was in order. I'd been taking a breather from the group assembled at my place while they set up an impromptu sound studio in my living room at the same time Al tried to rub his scent glands all over the microphones. He was one more lewd act away from being arrested by Jenna for disorderly conduct.

The timber of a voice I'd wanted so badly to forget slid against me as I pulled open the bathroom door. I thought about closing it right back up, but Aashri made eyes at me from across the room. She stood next to a speaker, holding a pair of headphones in one hand. Tom was beside her, talking to a brick wall. That brick wall, of course, was Aashri. Whatever goodwill she'd shown him during the phone call that set this whole plan in motion had vanished in the space of the fifteen minutes since he'd walked through my front door.

Aashri handed me the headphones. "Try not to slice your ear off on these," she said.

"We're going to talk about this later," I whispered.

"Let's, uh, test the mics." Justin was a few feet away, standing behind a folding table that looked better equipped to host a Labor Day barbecue than a podcast. "Here," he said. I took a bottled water from his hands. Justin looked anywhere but directly at me.

James, on the other hand, looked nowhere else. I could feel him, standing in my kitchen beside Jenna, eyes boring into the back of my head. I hated that I wondered what he thought of me. I hated that he could show up here after all that'd happened. I should've cared more about the arrest, the criminal behavior in California, the death threats sent to his own father. I should've cared so much more about all of that, but my mind and body were suddenly back in a shadowed house at the far end of a graveyard. I had thought I was leaving James, but he'd been leaving me. Again. His silence was a closed book, a turned back. James didn't care. He never had. And I'd cared too much.

But I wasn't the only one with a shit ton of emotional baggage.

Jenna said something to James about his Miranda rights. He laughed. It was a joke. James said something back. Jenna responded, but her eyes were trained firmly on the brother who had just taken his place at the table.

"Okay, everybody, let's get started," said Justin. He was seated second from the left beside Sheena. That left James as their guest.

And one other seat.

"Go get 'em, Tiger." Aashri pushed me toward an empty chair. James took it before I had a chance. One other remained, right next to Justin.

James on my left; Justin on my right.

Some women would've considered it a dream.

They'd be psychopaths.

I tried to catch Jenna's eye, but Sheena had laid a hand on her arm. The coolness she'd directed toward Justin became a warm glance at Sheena's smiling face. Who would glance warmly at me? Aashri helped Tom hold some weird fuzzy tech contraptions a few feet before the table. Al had been shut in my bedroom after an unceasing amount of PDA with a microphone I hoped hadn't been assigned to me. I'd rather slice my eye open again than be on a podcast. I didn't know what we'd be discussing or even why Aashri'd had this idea. It'd do nothing but force listeners to hope I was at least photogenic.

Justin looked at me. I looked back. James cleared his throat at my side.

Tom gave a thumbs-up in our direction. "And we're on."

CULT & RUN PODCAST TRANSCRIPT
SEASON 2, EPISODE 9

ALEX PARKER: Today is a special day at Carbon Fiber.

SHEENA FAVROSIAN: Sounds like you're toasting a five-year-old's birthday, Alex.

ALEX PARKER: Wait, is that not what we're doing? I brought a cake!

SHEENA FAVROSIAN: And you're wearing the pointy little birthday hat to match. Cute.

ALEX PARKER: Today is both a special day and an unprecedented one. Joining us in studio...er, in apartment...is James Wilkes. You may know him as Walker Wilkes' only son. Most recently, James—

SHEENA FAVROSIAN: Jimmy Sway.

JAMES WILKES: Hey, there.

ALEX PARKER: —has been the subject of an FBI investigation into his role as a self-styled Hollywood manifestation guru. Wilkes escaped charges, which include criminal racketeering and impersonation. James, you look amused. Would you add something different to this introduction?

JAMES WILKES: No, man. You're doing great.

SHEENA FAVROSIAN: Also with us is a former member of The

322

Cult & Run

Committee, which, as you'll know from this series, is the Pennsylvania self-help cult founded by James' Wilkes' late father, Walker.

ALEX PARKER: We'll be keeping the identity of this mystery guest private.

JAMES WILKES: Is that what she wants?

SHEENA FAVROSIAN: You and James grew up together as part of Walker Wilkes' community here southeastern Pennsylvania. Was James the same as a child?

GUEST: We weren't really friends.

SHEENA FAVROSIAN: What was he like?

GUEST: I don't know. I don't really remember.

ALEX PARKER: That's okay. No worries. Sheena, why don't we—

GUEST: He was quiet. James was quiet.

JAMES WILKES: You're making this sound like the origin story of a serial killer.

ALEX PARKER: We'll wait for that conviction to land.

JAMES WILKES: Excuse me?

SHEENA FAVROSIAN: What were you like as a child, Miss S?

GUEST: Is that what we're calling me?

323

KELLY MACPHERSON

SHEENA FAVROSIAN: Are you okay with it?

GUEST: It's fine. I just...it's fine. I was quiet, too, I guess. But in a different way. James wasn't shy. He was more...reserved. Watching, listening. Walker was his father. It was hard to get a word in around him. James was a gifted musician.

JAMES WILKES: I wouldn't say that but thank you.

GUEST: He wrote his own music, played piano, violin. I'd forgotten that, about the violin. I remember him at the piano mostly.

JAMES WILKES: My father bought me the piano. The violin had come before when my mother had been alive. She'd taught me to play. She was the musician, not me.

SHEENA FAVROSIAN: Did you study music, James?

ALEX PARKER: His father was a cult leader, Sheena. He did not study music. Why did you eventually leave Cormoran?

JAMES WILKES: Whoa, easy man.

GUEST: James had an offer he couldn't refuse.

SHEENA FAVROSIAN: In California?

JAMES WILKES: No. And why would you say that, D—

SHEENA FAVROSIAN: How old were you then?

JAMES WILKES: I was nineteen years old.

SHEENA FAVROSIAN: Nineteen is young. Did your father bless your decision to leave The Committee?

JAMES WILKES: I didn't leave The Committee.

ALEX PARKER: You ran off to Florida, not California like our guest believes. Isn't that true?

JAMES WILKES: Yes.

ALEX PARKER: You left everyone and everything behind. Your family, your friends.

JAMES WILKES: It wasn't a choice, but yes.

SHEENA FAVROSIAN: What made you decide to relocate to California instead? Florida's a beautiful enough state. Plenty of beaches. More bugs, but there's spray and all that.

JAMES WILKES: It wasn't my decision.

SHEENA FAVROSIAN: Your father's? It's surprising you'd have his blessing to leave the community everyone had assumed you'd lead once he was no longer fit to do so. When did you find out he was sick?

GUEST: Walker got sick after James left. They hadn't been in contact. He wouldn't have known.

ALEX PARKER: Is that true, James? You didn't know about your father's failing health?

JAMES WILKES: No, I didn't know.

325

KELLY MACPHERSON

ALEX PARKER: Because you didn't care.

JAMES WILKES: What are you getting at?

ALEX PARKER: You swindled people out of close to a million dollars in California. But you'd been pulling cons for a long time, isn't that right, Jimmy Sway?

SHEENA FAVROSIAN: We'll be back after a word from our—no? I'm being told we're staying live.

JAMES WILKES: This is live?

ALEX PARKER: Of course. Isn't that what you'd agreed to?

JAMES WILKES: Yes, no. I guess so. I'd like to ask your other guest a question.

ALEX PARKER: What were you doing in Florida, James? And then California? Before Hollywood. Before YouTube. Before white collar crime and the hint of a receding hairline.

SHEENA: Alex.

JAMES WILKES: What were you doing at nineteen, Alex Parker?

GUEST: Let's all agree that it was a less than memorable year all around, okay?

ALEX PARKER: I was in Utah. I worked a ranch for two years after earning my way into the Troubled Team Industry for not wanting to do things the way a douchebag cult leader told my parents they should be done.

326

SHEENA FAVROSIAN: Tom, let's cut to some ads.

JAMES WILKES: One lazy turn from becoming Justy Sway yourself, isn't that right?

ALEX PARKER: Sounds like a stripper.

JAMES WILKES: Hey, I'm not saying what your gimmick would've been.

GUEST: Tom?

JAMES WILKES: I left Cormoran when I was nineteen to go to rehab in Florida. The place is called Coastal Causes Recovery. Made me think I was going to clean up an oil spill, not kick a heroin addiction. I wasn't a musician. I was a junkie shooting up because I hated my dad, and my mom was dead, and I had only one friend in the entire fuckshow that was my dad's group of idiot assholes. I went to rehab because I would've died if I didn't.

SHEENA FAVROSIAN: I'm really sorry, James. Addiction is brutal.

JAMES WILKES: Thank you, Sheena. It's a bitch. And Florida's full of crackheads. Turned out that wasn't the best look for me.

ALEX PARKER: Oh, I don't know about that.

GUEST: Why don't we talk about The Barbara Gala? I'm sure your listeners would find it interesting to know that the priciest item ever won at silent auction was a four-pack of tickets to—

JAMES WILKES: You, of all people, should be glad I made it to

327

LA. I had sort of a reunion there. Reconnected with someone I'd known when we were kids. I was a few years younger, but that never stopped him from hating my guts. Right, Justin?

GUEST: —MuPaul's Drag Race on Ice. It was a cheap knock-off, but you wouldn't believe how my mother's friends threw their cash into the air for those tickets!

ALEX PARKER: You're right. I hated you then, and I hate you now, James.

SHEENA FAVROSIAN: Obviously, this episode is taking an unexpected turn, but Carbon Fiber has always been known for our cutting-edge coverage of—

ALEX PARKER: You're a sack of shit.

JAMES WILKES: I'm a sack of shit? You pretended to be someone else to, what, host a podcast about me? It's you who should be the subject of whatever this is you want to call reporting. Sheena, you seem great. I'm sorry you got mixed up with Justin. How would I describe him? Oh, what about this. A sack of shit?

ALEX PARKER: And what about you, James? Swayze Jim? Jimmy Sway? Whatever stupid name you gave yourself. Your dad courted mobsters, and you, what, thought you'd become the next Scorsese with your phony acting classes and zero experience?

JAMES WILKES: I was doing my thing. That's no one's business.
SHEENA FAVROSIAN: What made you choose to go into acting, James?

JAMES WILKES: I'm not really sure, Sheena. A gut feeling. Justin here would be the expert on playing make-believe.

ALEX PARKER: This interview is done.

JAMES WILKES: Running away. Nice, Justin. Same old you.

ALEX PARKER: I wouldn't say I'm the one being evasive.

JAMES WILKES: Really? Producing a podcast as another—

GUEST: He didn't run away, James. You did.

ALEX PARKER: Tom, let's wrap up. Sheena, you okay with that?

JAMES WILKES: Wait, what? Dalmatia, why are you saying that?

GUEST: Because it's true. You left.

JAMES WILKES: I went to rehab!

GUEST: How would I know that? You made it seem…you know how you made it seem. Then you were gone. I didn't see or hear from you for three years.

JAMES WILKES: It wasn't three.

GUEST: It was three, James.

JAMES WILKES: I'm sorry. But I came back. You know that. We were…together. You were okay then.

GUEST: I was never okay. I just didn't know how to say it.

KELLY MACPHERSON

JAMES WILKES: Can we be done? Sheena? Is that okay?

SHEENA: Tom, go to commercial. Now.

330

38

Triscuits

"Will you talk to me? Without them?"

James stared into my face, headphones off and body electric with tension. I kept mine on, an anchor against the way my mind was tossing the past before my eyes. I blinked away the James of ten years ago, the James of three. I answered the one in front of me now.

"There's nothing left to say."

"You left *me*," he said. "So why are you the mad one?"

I slammed the bottled water on the table. I hadn't known I'd reached for it. "I am not having this conversation!"

James' eyes flared with anger. "I don't think you get to make that choice, Dalmatia!"

"You're done here." Before James could brace himself, Justin shoved him right into a wicker basket of Al's cat toys.

"Get the fuck off me!" James pushed him back.

331

The folding table went down first.

By the time Tom scrambled forward for the mics, Aashri had James by both arms. "Hold up, Cypress Hill."

To James' credit, he obeyed. His chest rose and fell, the vein in his neck pulsing like hell. I'd laid my lips against it years ago, a couple months ago. God, he'd been everything to me. It'd be so easy to tell my best friend to get her hands off the only man I'd ever loved.

And I wouldn't be lying.

But that didn't make him worth it.

What had Donna Shears told me? None of the pain I'd experienced because of The Committee had been my fault. Why then did it feel like everyone gathered in my living room, amid the carnage of a dumpster fire of a podcast episode, have something to lay at my feet in blame?

Al stalked across the carpet toward me. Jenna's hand was on the knob of my open bedroom door, and her lips mouthed an apology. I slipped off the headphones and laid them on the coffee table that'd been pushed up against the wall.

"Let him go," I said to Aashri, who hadn't eased one bit in restraining James Wilkes. I bent to the ground and scooped my cat up in my arms. My head was a pounding mess of frayed nerves and tired reasoning. I knew nothing about accepting apologies and even less about making them. Jenna owed me nothing. I had no one to be angry with except myself.

"Dal, please, can we talk?" asked James.

James, James, James.

My temples ached to the tune of his name.

"Fuck off, Justin!" he said, interrupting the melody.

Justin had stepped between me and James, brow low and teeth clenched tight. I turned, my shoulder brushing Justin's arm. Before I knew what I was doing, I'd taken hold of him, fingers winding around his bicep. Justin pulled me close, and I let him. I hung on, my nose pressed into the crook of his neck. I cried. I cried hard.

"What's wrong?" James asked. "Dal, what's wrong?"

The tenderness in his voice made it worse.

Justin swept me from the center of my living room back into the corner where the door of my bedroom met the one that opened to my full bath. It wasn't a far distance, but he gently positioned me up against the shut door, his back hiding me from view. I sobbed as Tom and Sheena, Jenna and Aashri packed up supplies. James lingered. His gaze was on me. I felt it. I heard his nervous small talk, too. Stalling. Waiting for me.

"You're safe," Justin said in a hush. The cotton of his flannel was in my fists, and his body fit against me safe as life. It was a phrase from a book I'd read once, and I hadn't understood it then. One of the only things I'd read for fun in all the years I'd been an adult. All that non-fiction, all that research. The websites and the interviews. The articles, journals, Reddit threads. It'd gotten me…

…here.

"Ask them to leave," I told Justin.

He searched my face. I wasn't sure he'd heard me.

"Please, Justin," I whispered, unable to keep from pressing my body against his. "Ask them."

Sheena broke the spell. Tentative at first, and then oddly enthusiastic, she called Justin's name once, twice, again and again. Noise from the others tugged at him, sounds of a celebration. Incongruent with what'd just happened on air. Incongruent with what was happening between the two of us.

"I'll get them out," he breathed against me.

"Justin! Get off Dalmatia and look at this!" Sheena grabbed his arm this time, and Justin couldn't avoid the cell phone being thrust in his face. "Look!" Justin took the phone but held onto me tighter all the same. I inched my face toward the screen to see what'd been so important.

It was us.

On YouTube.

"You'd video'd us." Justin stated it like a fact. A fact that was causing a large amount of anger to form like a sunburn up his neck. "That wasn't cool, Sheena."

"It wasn't Sheena," James said from the center of my living room. It had been returned to its regular non-broadcast state. "You guys thought you'd pulled one over on me, huh? With your little cam thing? I'm sure you figured out what Dal and I did that night besides her attempt to get me to incriminate myself." James' dark stare carved straight into Justin's face.

"Shut up." Jenna stomped James' foot. She'd worn heels.

He wailed like a chihuahua getting a bikini wax. "What the fuck!"

"And watch your language," she added.

"He hid his phone on the kitchen counter. Propped it up between that supporting column and the box of Triscuits that Dal pretends she likes," Aashri said. "And he's an asshole for doing it."

"If you would've just had a conversation, Dalmatia, I wouldn't have had to post it." James straightened up, all six feet and two inches of him trying to look like the bigger person. "All you had to do was talk."

Sheena pressed the phone toward us again. "Dal, Justin, *look*."

I looked. Wow, I looked.

And what I was seeing didn't seem real.

Hundreds of comments. They just kept coming.

Jimmy Sway stole five thousand dollars from me...
...and kick him in the nuts, Alex!

James Wilkes conned my mom into signing over her Pontiac Grand Am. It was a 1989 but still...

I paid for three months' worth of acting classes and then he blocked my number...

Does Sheena have a man?

James sold my sister cocaine in LA this past July. How can I report this?

And others, so many others.

James hadn't realized that his congregation of YouTube followers included more than only those who'd subscribed to Jimmy Sway for career advancement. Others, like the authors of the comments piling in, wanted to see a star fall. He'd become one after all. Dream accomplished.

By the time I looked up at him, James had deflated. But ever the performer, he pulled up his big boy pants, setting that haughty gaze on me one last time. "I'll be ready to talk when you stop acting like a child," he said. My front door slammed. James was gone.

Al jumped onto the coffee table.

I motioned to pet his fuzzy little head, but my hand was in Justin's. When had that happened?

Justin looked down at me. "Are you okay?" he asked.

"Not at all," I answered.

"Well, I tackled someone on camera. That shit never gets erased from the Internet," he said with a sheepish grin.

"Not sure Jimmy Sway counts as anyone anymore."

"Yeah?" Justin asked.

My throat was thick with an explanation I had to give. "Listen," I began, "what James said about the night we'd hacked the cam. About what happened. I hadn't planned on—"

"Shh, Dal. Don't." Justin's hands hovered over my face, unsure,

335

wanting. They came against my skin, and I exhaled. "You don't owe me anything. You don't owe anyone anything." His throat bobbed up and down. A beat passed. "I wish I'd stayed in Cormoran. The way I acted as a kid was stupid. It was selfish. I wrecked so much."

I pulled his hands from my face and held them between us. "I thought that me staying wrecked everything, too, but it didn't. Everything happened how it was supposed to."

I dropped Justin's fingers and raked my hands through my hair.

"Besides, if you'd stayed? This—" I gestured between us. There was barely space to point. "—it wouldn't have happened. You called me Edward Scissorhands, remember?" I said with a smirk. "Oh wait, you *don't* remember, right?"

Justin pursed his lips. His eyes were bright.

"You remember," I replied, wanting to do so much more than take his hands. None of it involved a bottle of Tonic No. Seven, as had been my revenge fantasy as a kid.

"Dal, I never could have forgotten you."

"Then it's mutual," I said.

Justin reached for me, and our fingers tangled. I thought about all we could do and all we shouldn't. I leaned in close, the scent of my hair conditioner all over his neck.

"Are you thinking what I'm thinking?" he asked, his voice barely more than a hush.

Somewhere behind us Al did a number on my macrame curtains. "Is it fries? And ranch?"

Justin's face dipped slowly toward me. His kiss was not a surprise, and yet what I felt as his mouth held mine was unlike anything I'd ever thought possible.

Absurd. And uncertain.

Elsewhere in my apartment, an eighty-six-inch curtain rod came down upon two ceramic owl bookends and several works by

336

prominent authors well-versed in high-control groups.

Whatever was happening between me and Justin was bound to be unpredictable. Probably very messy.

An adventure.

I broke the kiss. For a moment at least. I had to.

I was smiling.

Epilogue

"Could this be something we do, I don't know, *never?*"

"You told me you don't want to buy things you can't own," Aashri answered.

We walked through downtown Cormoran, a shopping bag and caramel frappe in my hand and a lone iced coffee cup in hers. I'd dropped my first frappe half a block from our destination, forced Aashri to go back with me to get another, and then popped into an old stationer's shop that sold socks covered in cat faces uncannily similar to Al's.

"What does that even mean?" I asked Aashri. We'd made it to our stop. My stop, actually. Aashri was there to make sure I didn't turn tail at the last minute. I'd tried by dropping that frappe on the curb, and I'd tried by having a millennial temper tantrum over needing another one. I was trying now via an attitude as foul as the weather had turned. Autumn didn't last. Winter was inevitable.

And good therapists were hard to find.

"I'm saying you're wasting time wasting time, Dal. There's a hot man cat-sitting at your apartment right now, and you're going to head home to him and say you couldn't make therapy because the dopamine hit from a third lukewarm frappe was time better spent?"

My voice was small but insistent. "It was caramel."

Aashri threw her hands in the air. I was glad her drink had a lid. "Okay then! Caramel! Does Pfizer know about this? Eli Lilly?"

She'd made her point. "I'm going in," I said. I clutched both my purse and my bag of socks to my stomach. "I just...don't want to."

I hadn't wanted to see the first therapist, a week after James had posted his now infamous video on YouTube. It wasn't that I'd had a breakdown exactly. But what was it that Justin and Aashri had said to me that night while making me tea and ordering in nachos and playing videos of cats overcoming humans on TikTok? It was a breakthrough. I was having a breakthrough.

Jenna wasn't some criminal lunatic.

Justin wasn't a man-child who spent all his money on skateboards.

My mother wasn't a lifelong space cadet.

My father wasn't emotionally absent.

And I was not Walker Wilkes.

Because that was it, wasn't it? From the outside, I seemed careful, circumspect. Responsible, perhaps a bit more heavily-boundaried than most, but with on-time bill pay and a properly warm winter coat. But the unseen side of me remained unseen not because it was no one's business — which it wasn't — but because I knew what it evidenced.

Control issues.

I wore gloves and a scarf and barely had sugar from Halloween through Valentine's Day because I absolutely didn't want to see a doctor for an illness that I should've been able to prevent. I paid my rent on time, early even, because living independently meant no financial ties to a community. I didn't want to grow up and step away from The Committee only to find myself recreating its toxic control through the bonds of romantic relationships and borrowing my parents' second car when my Beamer needed new brakes. My insurance covered a rental. I paid enough in premium to be sure.

And so it'd be easy to say that the day I'd hosted an episode of what ended up as one of the highest charting podcasts on Apple that month had also cracked something open within me, something that needed to be split apart so the real Dalmatia could burst forth wild, free, and all dripping yoke. I was no fully formed baby bird. I could barely make it through the string of trauma counseling appointments I'd collected over the many weeks since my apartment had become a podcasting studio. Seven appointments, four therapists.

I'd hated every single one.

"Not the guy with the sweaters," Aashri liked to remind me. "You liked him!"

"He was twelve years old and wore shirts with his dog's face on them."

Aashri gestured wildly at my arm. "You literally have a bag full of AI knee-highs in your hand!"

We stood at the entrance to the office of therapist number five, soon to be the regretful facilitator of appointment number eight. Aashri urged, and I lingered. I knew the place, an old Presbyterian church on the corner of two streets both named Button. "Almost as weird as the clumsiest person in the world marrying a man named Shears," Aashri added.

"I am not marrying Justin," I told her. The old church wasn't as imposing as an office suite, which is all I'd visited so far. I found that at least a bit comforting. "And I'm not going to trade one blade for another."

"Sure," Aashri replied. She did that thing with her face that let me know she believed zero of what I'd said. "Just promise me this.

You're not naming your firstborn child Swiss Army."

I smacked her with the sock bag and put one palm against the heavy wooden door. "I'm going in."

I entered, letting the door gently shut. "Not Ginsu either!" Aashri called after me.

The vestibule smelled like vanilla, and a dog's water bowl rested beside an umbrella stand. The stand was empty; the dog bowl was not. "Who brings their pets to therapy?"

"Separation anxiety is a real and pertinent concern for many pet parents," said a woman's voice. A figure stood before a door at the very end of the hallway. "As are phobias about visiting the veterinarian," continued the woman, stepping out onto the plush carpet runner. "And, of course, loneliness. All those Covid pups who thought life would forevermore be owners working remotely and their cute antics interrupting Zoom calls. I'm guessing you're Dalmatia Scissors?"

Had this random animal lover noticed all the cat hair on my jacket and mistaken me for a kindred spirit? She couldn't be my therapist. The woman was around my mother's age, lower half in a denim pencil skirt and upper in a matching blazer with a high bun, brown with streaks of gray, held atop her head by a pencil.

"I'm Belinda Nails," she continued.

The name on the confirmation email for today's appointment, the latest to take a shot at sorting out my jumbled-up psyche.

I slowly edged toward her, the office door, the appointment. "Your last name is Nails?"

"Yes," Belinda said, lifting one bandaged hand chest high. "Doesn't mean I should use anything but command strips, though."

Now that was interesting.

"So, the animal thing." I followed her into the office, noticing a basket of dog and cat toys in one corner and a mint velvet couch

KELLY MACPHERSON

flanked by two leather armchairs along the far wall. "You do pet therapy, don't you? Like with kids?" I thought of Norman Hathaway. He'd be at Marissa's animal sanctuary in a few hours, ready for his weekly shift as a new volunteer.

Belinda smiled. "For kids, but with pets. Yes."

"I have a cat," I told her. I wasn't sure why. "Al."

"Short for Albert, Alfred, or Aloysius?" she asked.

She'd certainly caught me off guard. I was lowering myself down onto the couch before I knew it. "I don't think any."

"Allison?"

"My cat?"

Belinda Nails nodded.

"Albatross, technically. But he just looked like an Al."

"Al's a good name," she said. "But, yes, he may like being asked what he thinks about his name. Kids usually do favor having input into decisions of identity, fur or no fur. Children deserve to have a voice, too."

Her clipboard was out, paper was secured to it.

I was on the sofa, my purse at my feet. Five quick jumps to my left stood the door. I could make it.

Belinda Nails pulled a cup of pens from a table between the chairs. "Dalmatia," she said, "I'd like to tell you about myself as a therapist before we begin. And then you can tell me about yourself — what you're looking for from me, how I can help you. Is that all right?"

I nodded once, and then I watched as Belinda Nails, this animal-affirming therapist clad in denim on denim, lifted a neon yellow highlighter from the cup. She pulled off the cap with her teeth.

Belinda Nails laughed. "Sorry," she said. "Bad habit. We all have them, you know?"

"Oh, I do," I told her. "I definitely know." I adjusted myself on

342

Cult & Run

the couch. It really was very comfortable. "I think I know where I should start," I said. "I have a story."

"Stories are good," Belinda answered, nodding. She laid the highlighter on the clipboard in her lap. The office smelled of vanilla and baked ziti. I noticed a filing cabinet tucked into a corner with a small microwave on top.

I sat back. I took a deep breath.

And I began.

Acknowledgements

This story exists because of the encouragement of many. Writing a book isn't a single task; it's a lot more than sitting down at the keyboard with an idea and a bit of hope. *Cult & Run* is a story of friendship, and it's the product of friendship, too. I want to thank my Thursday Co-Writing Gang: Laura McCorry, Eden Wilder, Rain Sullivan, Stacey Fabion, Geeta Shrayter, and Lindsey Schmitz. I wanted to quit so many times. I wanted to be anything other than a writer. And yet, where you guys were is where I wanted to be. Creativity is birth, and I guess what I'm saying is that you are the midwives of this book baby. Laura, you were the first to hold it. I am grateful. Our friendships are some of the best things to come from my writing career. I love you all so much.

To Grace Buddenhagen, thank you. For so much more than I can share in this space.

Thank you to everyone who has shared my hope for this story.

And to my dog, Beast. You are, of course, Al the Cat.

Kelly MacPherson is a native of Clifton Heights, Pennsylvania and now lives with her husband, five children, and two dogs in a small town where no one claims street parking with lawn chairs.

She kind of misses that.

Connect with Kelly on Instagram at @kellywritesabook

Printed in the USA
CPSIA information can be obtained
at www.ICGtesting.com
LVHW031149261023
762201LV00016B/2061